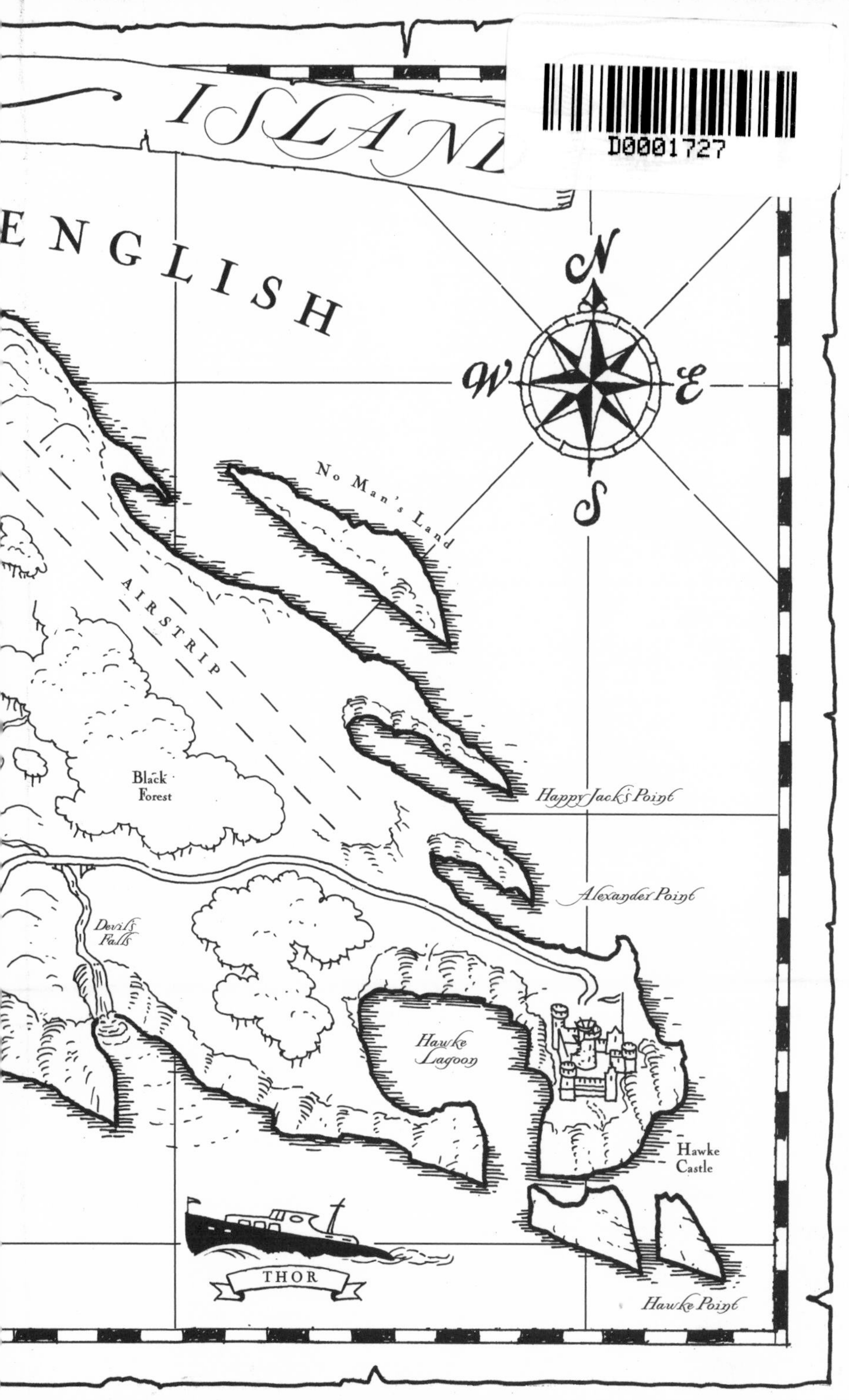
ISLAN
ENGLISH
N
W
E
S
No Man's Land
AIRSTRIP
Black Forest
Happy Jack's Point
Alexander Point
Devil's Falls
Hawke Lagoon
Hawke Castle
THOR
Hawke Point

TAYLOR

NICK
· OF ·
TIME

ALSO BY TED BELL

Tsar

Spy

Pirate

Assassin

Hawke

NICK
· OF ·
TIME

Ted Bell

ST. MARTIN'S GRIFFIN
NEW YORK

 For information, address St. Martin's Press, 175 Fifth Avenue, New York, N.Y. 10010.

www.stmartins.com

Illustrations and endpaper map by Russ Kramer

ISBN-13: 978-0-312-38068-7
ISBN-10: 0-312-38068-2

Original edition published in somewhat different form in the United States by Xlibris Corporation.

First St. Martin's Griffin Edition: May 2008

10 9 8 7 6 5 4 3 2 1

For my daughter, Byrdie

And for Mike, Pendleton, and Sally

Also for Benji and Alex,
and all the other kids in the neighborhood

ACKNOWLEDGMENTS

I should like to thank, first and foremost, my wife, Page Lee Hufty, who always believed in this book and would never let it die. Her abiding love and support are, and have been, indispensable.

Also, my undying thanks to Matthew Shear and Charles Spicer at St. Martin's Press for believing in my story.

And my thanks to Russ Kramer, whose artwork adorns these pages and adds immeasurably to the reader's adventure.

And, finally, to my daughter, Byrdie, who inspired me to write this book, my first.

CONTENTS

I. THE JAWS OF GRAVESTONE ROCK 1
II. THE SECRET DRAWER 10
III. NAZIS IN THE STRAWBERRY PATCH 24
IV. THE SEA CHEST 36
V. THE DARK CAVE 44
VI. BILLY BLOOD 50
VII. TWO TERRIBLE LETTERS 62
VIII. A COUNCIL OF WAR 72
IX. THE LEVIATHAN 82
X. THE NANTUCKET SLEIGH RIDE 92
XI. THE ELECTRIFIED LAGOON 102
XII. THE CHINESE BUTLER 111
XIII. CAPTAIN THOR'S SURPRISE 122
XIV. LORD HAWKE'S TEA PARTY 130
XV. THE MYSTERY OF TIME 141

• CONTENTS •

XVI. THE TEMPUS MACHINA 147

XVII. CAPTAIN MCIVER'S LETTER 159

XVIII. *DAS KAPITÄN*'S CABBAGES 168

XIX. *TEMPUS ET LOCUS* 177

XX. PIGS AND STOWAWAYS 184

XXI. A BUMP IN THE NIGHT 197

XXII. IN THE PIGSTY 208

XXIII. A SKIRMISH IN THE DARK 216

XXIV. CAPTAIN MCIVER'S CANNONBALL 232

XXV. THE WINDOWLESS SUBMARINE 245

XXVI. IN THE NICK OF TIME 257

XXVII. KATE SAVES THE DAY 265

XXVIII. A LANDLUBBER ALOFT 272

XXIX. SPIES FOR SALE 291

XXX. IN THE SICK BAY 300

XXXI. THE FULLY HATCHED SCHEME 307

XXXII. THE SPANISH MASQUERADE 314

XXXIII. NAZIS IN HAWKE LAGOON 341

XXXIV. SNAKE EYE AND THE KINGDOM OF LOST CHILDREN 366

XXXV. *MERLIN* VICTORIOUS 383

XXXVI. A GLORIOUS FAREWELL 397

XXXVII. LANDING AT HAWKE FIELD 405

XXXVIII. CHURCHILL AFTER DINNER 420

EPILOGUE 427

POSTSCRIPT 434

A hero is no braver than an ordinary man,
but he is braver five minutes longer.
–Ralph Waldo Emerson

A good ship is never tested in calm waters.
–Richard Trench

NICK · OF · TIME

CHAPTER I

The Jaws of Gravestone Rock

· 3 June 1939 ·

OFF GREYBEARD ISLAND

Hard a'lee, me boys!" shouted Nick McIver over the wind, "or be smashed to smithereens in the jaws of Gravestone Rock!"

The dog Jip barked his loud agreement.

Nick, at the helm of his small sloop, *Stormy Petrel,* that afternoon, was almost at the end of his first day-long voyage around Greybeard Island. He was hard on the wind, making a good seven knots as he tacked homeward. Just now, he was approaching the treacherous reefs that guarded the entrance to Lighthouse Harbor. Jip, on the bow, was howling into the strong headwind, enjoying the pounding sprays of seawater every bit as much as his skipper.

But now Nick was watching the western sky and the rapidly rising seas uneasily. Maybe he should have nipped inside the huge Gravestone Rock, in the lee of this wind. Probably should have known better than to sail the long way home in weather like this. Should have done this, should have done that, he silently cursed himself. He *did* know better, in fact.

But he and Jip had been having such a splendid time, bounding through the waves, he'd simply ignored the storm warnings. A little cold spot in the pit of his stomach was growing. He hated that cold feeling. He'd not even spoken its name.

But it was fear.

The glorious empty bowl of blue that had been the morning sky now featured stacks of boiling cumulus clouds, all gone to darkening greys and blacks. Billowing towers of purple clouds loomed on the western horizon, swiftly turning the colors of an ugly bruise. In the last hour, clouds of spume came scudding across his bow and through the rigging of *Stormy Petrel.* Above the howl of the elements was the high keening whistle of wind in the sloop's rigging. Salt spray stung Nick's eyes. But he could still see the sky overhead, boiling and black.

Nick leaned hard into the *Petrel*'s tiller, putting the weight of his lean body against it, fighting to keep his bow to windward of Gravestone Rock. He had both hands on the tiller, and they'd gone clammy and cold. Looking up in awe at the giant rock now looming before him, he wiped first one hand, then the other, on his soaking trousers. The Gravestone. A terrible thought shuddered unpleasantly through Nick's mind. Would that famous stone tower today mark still another watery grave? His own, and his beloved Jip's? He cursed himself for his stupidity and leaned into his tiller with all his might. Hopeless. The bow refused to answer the helm, to come up into the wind.

However could he keep his small sloop to the safe, windward side of the massive stone looming ever larger before him? And to the leeward side lay the Seven Devils. On a calm day, Nick might pick his way through these treacherous reefs. But now, in a blow, they were deadly.

He was fresh out of options.

"And you call yourself a sailor, Nick McIver!" he cried aloud. But not even his dog heard his bitter cry of frustration above the roar of wind and water. He should have known better. There was a terrible price to pay for carelessness at sea. Especially when you were anywhere near the Gravestone.

It was a towering monument of glistening black granite that now rose before him. Thrusting from the sea like some angry tombstone, it had claimed the lives of skippers and sailors a good deal saltier than Nick and Jip. As Nick had known from earliest childhood, countless ships and men had gone to the bottom courtesy of the Gravestone Rock. Or the seven deadly spines of rock spreading like tentacles in all directions from its base. The Seven Devils, the reefs were called, and not for nothing either. Here was as fiendish a bit of coastline as ever there was.

This perilous coast had finally led to the building of Nick's home. Even now, the great Greybeard Light sent yellow stabs streaking overhead through the darkening sky. This flashing tower atop the cliffs off his port bow held special meaning for Nick McIver. It was both a warning to stay away and a summons to come home.

For Nick lived atop that lighthouse, he was a lighthouse keeper's son. And now it looked as if the famous rock below it might claim the boy, if the boy didn't think of something, and quickly. IF THE GRAVESTONE DOESN'T GET YOU, THE SEVEN DEVILS WILL! read the legend carved into the mantel at the Greybeard Inn. And the long-dead British tar who had carved it there knew well whereof he spoke. At that moment, Nick wished he himself had carved those ancient words of warning into the pitching deck he now stood upon.

"We're not going to make it, boy!" shouted an anguished Nick. "I can't keep her pointed high enough!" Indeed he could not steer, nor will, the bow of his small boat to windward of the ever larger Gravestone. For every foot of forward motion *Petrel* gained, she was losing two feet to side-slipping. Adrenaline poured into Nick's veins as he realized the potential for total disaster in what he was about to do.

A whispered prayer to his long-dead hero escaped his lips.

Nelson the Strong, Nelson the Brave, Nelson the Lord of the Sea.

Nick faced a terrible decision. The most brutal maneuver any sailor could make in such a dreadful blow was a jibe. Jibing meant turning the boat away from the wind, instead of into it, so that its brutal force passed directly behind the mainsail. The huge mainsail and heavy boom would then come whipping across the cockpit with a violence that could easily rip the mast from the boat. But what choice did he have? The terrible decision was already made.

"Jibe HO!" he shouted to his shaggy crew. He pulled sharply back on his tiller instead of pushing against it. The bow swung instantly off the wind. "Mind yer heads!" Nick bellowed. The stout wooden boom and violently snapping mainsail came roaring across the small open cockpit like the furies of hell. "Down, boy!" Nick cried, and ducked under the heavy wooden boom at the last second, narrowly avoiding a blow to the head which would have sent him, unconscious, overboard. The lines, the sails, the rigging, every plank of his boat was screaming, at their breaking point. She'd been built of stout timber, but he could feel *Petrel* straining desperately at her seams. If a plank should spring open now, this close to a rocky lee shore, they were surely done for!

But she held. Looking aloft, he saw his mast and rigging mostly intact. By jibing the boat, he'd gained precious time to think.

Nick feverishly eyed his options, now rapidly dwindling to nil. There had to be a way out of this! Nicholas McIver was not a boy destined to die such a stupid, unseamanlike death. Not if he could help it. He had a healthy fear of dying, all right, but now, staring death square in the face, he was far more afraid of letting them all down. His mother. His father. His little sister, Katie. His best friend, Gunner.

Wasn't that a fate even *worse* than death, he wondered? For a boy to slip beneath the cold waves without even the chance to prove to those he loved that he was a brave boy, a boy destined to do great things in this world? A boy who might one day be–a hero?

The already fresh wind had now built into something truly appalling. *Petrel* was rapidly running out of sea room. The sickly green-yellow sky cast its unhealthy glow over the frothing sea. Nick heard an ominous roar building on his port side. Just as he looked up, a wave like an onrushing locomotive crashed over the windward side of the little boat, staggering the tiny vessel, knocking her instantly and violently on her side. Nick was buried under a torrent of cold seawater. He clung desperately to the tiller to avoid being washed overboard. He was thinking only of Jip, again standing watch up on the bow. As the weight of her heavy lead keel quickly righted the boat once more, Nick, sputtering, strained forward, rubbing the stinging saltwater from his eyes. His dog was still there. Heaven only knew how the creature had managed it. In fact, Jip was barking loudly, surely in anger at the wave that had almost done them in.

"All that lead we hung off her bottom is good for something, eh, Jipper? Hang on, boy!" Nick cried. "I'll think of something!" But what, his mind answered, whatever *could* he do? He knew that the next wave they took broadside would be their last. He fought the tiller, determined to get the towering waves on *Petrel*'s stern. It was his only chance.

Just at that moment *Petrel* was lifted high above a cavernous trough by the hand of another huge wave. For a brief moment, Nick could see most of the northern tip of his island. And he knew in that instant what he had to do. There was no escaping to windward of the Gravestone Rock. Since *Petrel* could never make headway back into the teeth of the storm, he now had no choice. He must fall off to the leeward side of the rock, sailing a dead run before the wind, directly into the waiting jaws of the Seven Devils! Nothing else for it, he thought, more grimly determined than ever.

From the crest of the wave, Nick had seen a small flash of white on the rocky shore dead ahead. It could only mean a sandy cove, one of many along this coast where he and Kate played on sunny days.

If he could somehow time the waves precisely, so that *Petrel*'s keel might just brush the Devil's deadly tops, he just might have a chance at beaching the boat on the sandy shore of that little cove. Yes, he just might.

Now that he had a plan, the boy's spirits soared. It wasn't much of a plan, but it was the only chance he had. If it failed, why, he–

"Shorten sail, lads!" Nick cried to his imaginary crew, clenching the damp and salty mainsheet in his teeth as he loosed the main halyard with his free hand. In a blow like this, reducing sail area by reefing the main wouldn't decrease his boat speed by much, but it might just be enough to control his timing of the waves over the reefs. It was clear that Nick would need all the seamanship, and luck, he could muster to get captain and crew safely ashore.

Jip, as if recognizing the desperate seriousness of their situation, came aft to stand watch beside his master. Nick was glad of his company.

"Steady now, steady," cried Nick, bracing his knees against the thwart seat and winding the mainsheet round his fist to secure it. The force of the wind on the shortened sail made Nick's arm feel as if it might be pulled from its socket. "Steady as she goes, lads!" Wind and water were tossing the sloop about like a pond boat, throwing his timing off dangerously. Entering the procession of towering rollers, Nick felt his sloop surge forward. "Look alive, Jip, we're in for a bit of a sleigh ride!" he cried. Jip growled and stood his ground.

The trick, and it was a good one, was keeping *Petrel* out of the sequence of huge waves rushing toward the treacherous shore. To wait until the timing was precisely right. "Right" meant that *Petrel* was lifted at the precise moment her keel was passing over each one of the jagged Devils. It was going to take luck all right, bags of the stuff; luck and no small measure of skill.

"Easy . . . easy . . . and . . . NOW!" cried Nick, heaving the tiller to starboard to swing his bow around. If there was a tinge of fear remaining in his voice you couldn't hear it for the wind or the spray or the sheer exhilaration of the moment as he steered the little boat down the broad steep face of the wave toward the deep trough below. *Petrel*'s moment of truth had finally arrived.

"We need to come up, now, boy," Nick said, holding on to his tiller for dear life. The Gravestone Rock loomed dangerously close to his left as *Petrel* plunged deeper into the trough. "We. Need. To. Come. UP!" Nick held his breath. He'd seen the ugly spine of the first reef from the top of his wave and knew that *Petrel*'s keel could clear it if only he had timed his descent into the trough perfectly. He clenched his jaw, unaware how painfully tight it was. Jip, too, was rigid, staring at the wall of water before them, sensing the moment.

Petrel's bow suddenly lifted. She was rising high on the majestic swell and Nick waited for the tearing sound of her keel on the deadly jagged rock. It occurred to him in that moment that it would probably be one of the last sounds he would ever hear.

It didn't come.

At the wave's crest, Nick could see that he'd timed it perfectly. The waves would now lift him over the two razor-sharp reefs that remained between *Petrel* and the safety of the sandy cove. Jip scrambled forward once more to his station at the bow. He barked loudly in triumph, daring the forces of nature to do battle once more with the mighty *Petrel* and her daring crew.

"Hooray!" Nick cried in both relief and exultation. "We did it, boy, we perfectly well did it, didn't we?"

In the deep bottle-green safety of the cove, it was simply a matter of running *Petrel* toward shore until her keel beached on the soft sand. That done, Nick quickly freed the main and jib halyards and all the wet canvas fell to the deck. As the boat swung round and listed to her starboard side, a happy Nick and Jip leapt over the gunwale and waded ashore. Nick made fast a line from *Petrel*'s bow to a large rock on the shore. Then he and Jip ducked into the mouth of the nearest cave to escape the fury of the storm.

And they had been safe, perched on a deep ledge inside the cave, waiting for the storm to blow itself out before sailing home for supper.

This cave, it occurred to Nick as he and Jip climbed back into the boat, might make an excellent hiding place someday. Either as a place to hide from bloodthirsty pirates, or a place to secret any treasure he and his crew might find during their future navigations.

"All right, boy," Nick said, hauling down on the halyard that raised his mainsail once more. "Time to fly away home!" Now that the storm had subsided, he was confident he could pick his way through the reefs with little trouble. After all, he knew their locations by heart.

Yes, you could always rely upon young Nicholas McIver to get his crew home safely. After all, was there a more reliable boy in all of England?

CHAPTER II

The Secret Drawer

· 3 June 1939 ·

AT THE GREYBEARD LIGHT

"That boy," Emily McIver said to herself, "is the most unreliable boy in all of England!

"Where *is* that child?" she added, half aloud, for at least the tenth time since he'd missed his supper. "Honestly!"

Worriedly brushing a stray wisp of honey-colored hair back from her brow, she pressed her nose once more against the steamy kitchen window. Masses of purple clouds had been gathering in the west for the last hour and now heavy drops of rain were spattering hard against the glass. First real storm of the summer, she thought, plunging her hands into the hot soapy water, pulling out another supper plate. It looked a blow and of course her son was right out there in the thick of it, as usual. Missed his supper again. Soaked to the skin. Chilled to the bone in the bargain.

Emily tried to push her rising worries over her only son down to a place where she could control them. Only a little wind, wasn't it? He'd certainly come through worse, hadn't he? Had his oilskins on, hadn't he? Oh my, look at that lightning! Heat lightning. Summer lightning.

Summer had come at last to this smallest of four little islands stuck out in the English Channel. Although they were English isles, fiercely held for many centuries, they lay very close to the coast of France. The names of many streets and villages were still French, but the islanders were loyal only to England. Greybeard Island, the smallest, was famous for having more cows than people. And the fact that there was not a single car. The few people who lived here were hardy seagoing folk, now mostly farmers and fishermen. True, nothing much ever happened here. Still Emily thought it the loveliest place; the rocky coasts, the rolling pastures, and now, of course, the glorious roses. Emily had joyously announced summer's arrival in her journal that very morning:

> *After an icy winter and a cold, wet spring, the sun has suddenly rained warmth down on our little green island. The summer of 1939 is here at last! Every lane has a leafy green roof vaulting overhead, every field is carpeted with buttercups and periwinkles, and in every orchard clouds of white petals float to earth, then swirl in eddies beneath the boughs, and drift up against the gnarled and twisted trunks of the trees like snowdrifts. Roses, too, climb once more to the rooftops of the little stone cottages scattered hither and thither across our tiny island, as if some giant has just flung out handfuls of them and then, overnight, picket fences and flowerbushes spring up just to bind them to the earth!*

Even this old lighthouse, she realized with a shudder of pleasure, home to the McIver family for generations, was once more wreathed with great spirals of heavy roses. The "Tower Roses" they were called, and featured on the cover on the island guidebook, weren't they? Emily cracked the kitchen window a bit to inhale the blossoms' sweet perfume, the scent of rain and roses wafting in on the wet air.

Emily leaned forward again, peering intently through the darkened kitchen window. She saw only veils of rain along the empty path leading down to the harbor. Where is that boy? she wondered for the hundredth time. But she knew well enough where her boy was.

Well, at least little Kate isn't out there with him, Emily thought with some relief. No, her daughter was snug and safe up in her warm bed, recovering from a nasty bout of measles. Otherwise, sure as daylight, she would have been out there tossing about on that boat. Her husband, Angus, however, *was* out in this dreadful storm tonight on a silly errand to– A sudden noise behind Emily almost made her jump out of her slippers, and she dropped a supper dish with a terrific splash into the soapy water.

"Goodness!" she cried, spinning to see her kitchen door fly open. Two dervishes, whirling in on a gust of wet wind, one a twelve-year-old boy, one a loudly barking black retriever hard on the boy's heels. "Two demons out of the night and what a start you've given me!" she cried, vainly trying to brush the soapy water from her apron.

"Close that door! Can't you see there's rain blowing in!" Inside, she breathed an enormous sigh of relief at the sight of her boy safely home.

"Only me and Jipper, Mum!" said Nick, leaning all of his weight against the heavy oak door. "Not late, are we? See, we got caught in this bit of a blow and we–Jip! No, boy, don't!" Nick cried, but it was too late.

Nick, who knew he had trouble enough already, watched his big black dog walk over to where his mother stood and violently shake every drop of water from his body in her direction, a shaggy, four-legged rainstorm.

"Why, thank you, Jip!" Emily said, brushing this fresh deluge from her apron. "Lovely! I'm glad to see you haven't forgotten your manners, either! They're just as terrible as they've always been! Just look at this mess, will you, Nick!"

"Just being friendly, Mum, isn't he? Happy to be home?" He tried a smile but couldn't quite get it right. "That means he's glad to see you. He's sort of waving at you, see, in dog language?"

Emily McIver put both hands on her hips and bent from the waist, scowling at her son, now standing in the puddle of rainwater he had created in her kitchen.

"Nicholas McIver! Don't think you can charm your way out of this one, boy! Third night this week you've missed supper! And look at you!" she said, shaking her finger in his direction. "And look at my sorry floor as well, will you?"

Nick dutifully looked at himself, his mother's apron, and the puddle, and had to nod in mute agreement. His shoes were squishing water, and his normally curly blond hair was plastered to his skull. He was late again, he'd made a sopping mess of the kitchen, and the chances of a nice hot meal were decidedly slim. He was ravenous. He was *entirely* ravenous after a hard day on the water.

The remains of a beautiful roast joint of beef caught his eye.

"Sorry I'm late, Mum," he said, picking up the heavy pewter platter that held the roast. "Why don't you turn in, and I'll just stow all these messy supper dishes for you? Least I can do, really, isn't it?"

Emily took the platter right out of his hands. "Good effort, Nicky. Shameless, but good all the same. Supper in this house is exactly half past two hours ago, I'll remind you! This roast is bound straight for the stew pot. Take a turnip and a carrot or two if you like and then to bed with you."

She held out a bowl of freshly peeled vegetables and Nick stuffed his pockets to dispose of them later. He hated carrots only slightly less than turnips. Maybe Jip would eat the stuff. At least they wouldn't both go hungry.

"This time it wasn't my fault, Mother," he said, unable to take his eyes off the pungent roast beef. "There was a terrible blow, you see, and Jip and I–I apologize. We both do."

"Truly. Well, you and Jip can do all of your apologizing to each other. Up in your room and it's lights out for the both of you," Emily said, spinning him around by his shoulders and sending him marching toward the stairway. "Along with you! Jip, you as well!"

Nick paused at the foot of the stairs. "May I ask you one serious question first, Mum?" he asked, his heart suddenly catching in his throat. "Would you say I'm a boy who frightens easily?"

"A boy too clever and too brave for his own good, I might agree with," Emily said. She turned to look at her son over her shoulder. "But then, I'm only your mother. What does a mother know? Do her feet hurt from standing? Do her roses have aphids? Does her heart ache with worry every time her little boy is out in a terrible storm?"

"I am sorry, Mother. Really I am," Nick said. "It was scary, though, out in that blow."

"Tell your mother, Nicholas. Why you're always so afraid of being frightened? It is the most natural feeling a boy can have."

Nick cast his eyes at the rain-streaked kitchen window, struggling to keep his emotions in check.

"Because I think a boy is not *supposed* to be afraid! The boys I read about in books are never afraid of anything! But I *was* afraid, out there today, twice! Twice in one day! Why, I guess I'm nothing more than a measly, sniveling old c-coward!" He sat on the bottom step and swiped away a tear.

"You're not a boy in a book, son, you're just a normal boy. And, being afraid, that's only normal for–"

"I tried, you know! Oh, I tried all right. But I just couldn't get *Petrel* to windward of the Gravestone, and I–" Nick paused, as the memory of that terrible moment came flooding back. "I–I knew our only chance was to try and ride the storm surge in over the reefs, you see, and just then a huge wave hit us broadside, knocked us right over on our beam ends and I thought that Jipper, I thought poor Jip had been–" Nick felt hot salty tears welling up and quickly looked down at his dog. If he ever truly wanted to be a hero, it clearly wouldn't do to have his own dog and his mother see him going all leaky over a few big waves.

"Come here, Nicky," Emily said. Nick rose unsteadily and went to her, grateful to feel his cheek against her starchy, sweet-smelling blouse, a safe place where no one could see the tears of utter relief at still being alive flowing down his cheeks. How he'd longed for the safety of these same arms when the giant rock was looming.

"And, what was the second frightening thing, son?" she asked, gently patting the top of his sodden head. She felt the boy finally stop trembling and held him to her. "Besides the terrible storm?"

"Oh. W-well, that one wasn't so bad, Mother," he said, finally calming down. "It was about noon, I guess. Jipper and I were tacking north around Hawke Point. And then the sky suddenly got all black and thundery, you see, and we thought it was a storm coming. But it wasn't, not yet anyway. No, it was masses and masses of heavy aeroplanes! Bombers! They flew directly over the *Petrel*'s masthead! They were quite low, Mother, it was deafening, really, and Jip and I ran up on the bow to shout hurrah and wave to our boys, but, you see, they *weren't* our boys, Mother. They all had big swastikas painted on their fuselages and wings–they were German!"

"German! They didn't drop any bombs on you and Jip, did they, darling?" Emily asked with a smile. "That *would* be frightening."

"No, they didn't drop any bombs," Nick said, smiling back at her. "And we waved at them anyway, see, and a few even waggled their wings back at us, as if we were friends. That scared me the most."

"I think you're a very brave boy, Nicholas McIver," Emily said, giving him a brief peck on the top of his head. "But brave boys don't get to be brave men unless they're a bit clever, too. Be clever enough to be afraid when you need to be, won't you, Nick? Now, along with you. To bed."

"Is there really going to be a war, Mum?" Nick asked, reluctant to leave her side. "With the Nazis? The Germans, I mean?"

"We've all had quite enough of war for one century, thank you. There shan't be another."

"But, Father says–"

"Nick, listen to me," she said, holding him away from her and looking into his eyes. "Some people, your father for one, believe what Mr. Churchill says. That war with Germany is unavoidable. I choose to believe what our Prime Minister, Mr. Chamberlain, says. My brother, Godfrey, as you well know, spends his every waking hour by the Prime Minister's side at Number Ten Downing. He sees all but the most top secret documents and he's convinced the Nazis have no interest in war with England. I've always believed your uncle, and I believe him now. Isn't that simple? Now. To bed, and no delay!"

Nick looked at his mother. He prayed that it was as simple, as black and white as she portrayed it. His uncle Godfrey, as secretary to the PM, would certainly know, wouldn't he? "Mother, I'm sure you're right. But may I at least tell Father about–"

"Your father's not here, dear," Emily said, putting the last dried dish on the shelf. "He had an emergency meeting of his beloved Birdwatcher's Society." She chuckled at the notion of an emergency of any kind here on peaceful little Greybeard Island. What possible emergency could drive a flock of birdwatchers out on a night like this? Birdwatchers, indeed, Emily thought.

"Oh, Nicky, before you tuck in, bring Mummy's spectacles down, won't you? I left them up in your father's study, on his desk, I believe. And stop poking your great-grandfather's belly, Nicholas, you'll just make him worse!"

At the foot of the curving staircase, that led to the very top of the lighthouse, hung a portrait of a McIver ancestor that

Nick greatly admired. The long-dead admiral hanging over the hearth mantel had a jagged hole in the center of his great belly and Nick loved to stand on tiptoe and jab his fist through the old man's stomach. No one was quite sure how the gaping hole had come to be there, but everyone had their own story about the admiral with the hole in his belly. Surely there was some grand adventure behind the painting and Nick loved to stick his fist through his ancestor's perforated paunch every time he bounded upstairs.

"Sorry, Mum," he said, giving the old admiral one last jab to the midsection. "Dad's birdwatching again? Imagine watching birds on a night like this anyway!" Nick said over his shoulder, and bounded up the stairs, now much comforted by his mother.

Yes, just imagine, Emily chuckled to herself. "Birdwatchers, ha!" she said half aloud and collapsed into the well-worn overstuffed chair that sat next to the kitchen hearth. It had been a long, tiring day. She looked forward to falling asleep by the softly crackling kitchen fire with her needlepoint on her lap. Angus would wake her upon returning from his "birdwatching."

It was, after all, the silliest thing. It was a good thing she loved her husband so dearly, or she'd never have been able to forgive his newest passion. The "Birdwatcher's Society!" Climbing all over the island with their little telescopes and their fat black binoculars. Mud smeared on their faces and bits of leaves and branches stuck in their headgear. And always staring out to sea, they were. Waiting for the Nazis to come. As if the Nazis cared one whit for three or four little English islands stuck in the Channel! Closer to France than

England and inhabited mainly by cows! Imagine, she thought, chuckling to herself. All hail Adolf Hitler, King of the Channel Isles, Chancellor of Cows!

"Nicholas?" Emily cried, still chuckling to herself and kicking an errant little ember back onto the hearthstone. She turned and shouted up the empty stairwell. "Will you please bring me those glasses? You know I can't do a stitch without them!" There was no answer. Where *is* that boy? she wondered, for what seemed the thousandth time that day.

Upon entering his father's study at the very top of the stairs, just below the ladder up to the great light itself, the first thing Nick had noticed was his father's old leather flying jacket. It was hanging on the back of his chair. Slipping into the timeworn garment, which he greatly coveted, he collapsed into his father's desk chair, running his hands over the silver wings pinned to the jacket breast.

A hero's jacket, Nick thought, looking down at the bright wings. His father had been wearing it the day his Sopwith had been shot down, crashing in flames in the Ardennes Forest. Angus McIver had escaped from the burning plane, but had lost the use of his right leg doing it. He'd never flown again after that terrible day and even now, twenty years later, he could only walk with the use of a stout cane.

But he'd returned from the Great War to a hero's welcome on little Greybeard Island, hadn't he, Nick thought. Oh, yes. No doubt about it. A true hero, whatever that was. All Nick knew was that he wanted to be one in the worst way possible, he thought, picking up his father's old briar pipe and clenching it between his teeth just the way his father did. Did he have the stuff it took to be a hero, he wondered, chomping on the pipe stem? Was he brave enough? Strong enough? Smart enough? Well, why trouble yourself, he guessed. He'd probably never get the chance to find out, living on a little island stuck smack in the middle of nowhere. His own father had taken to watching birds, for goodness sake! That's how starved *he* was for excitement.

Now, what was his mission? Oh, yes! Mother's reading glasses. Where were they? He felt around, pushing the little piles of books and paper to and fro. He plunged his hand into a little alcove in the center of the desk, full of old pens and pencils. Perhaps she'd put them–Hold on!–his fingertips had brushed something cold and round protruding from the very back of the alcove. It felt like, it was, a button, and not just any old button, either. A secret button!

Naturally, he had to push it.

With a mechanical click and a soft whirring noise, a drawer abruptly appeared just above the little alcove. Just slid straight out, it did, like an unexpected invitation! It was quite the most amazing thing, and no mistaking it, to be suddenly confronted with what was plainly a secret drawer. His natural curiosity immediately got the better of him and he stood up and peered inside.

Lying at the bottom of the drawer was an old logbook that someone obviously wasn't meant to see. It was a faded red leather binder with the words MIGRATORY BIRDS OF THE CHANNEL ISLANDS stamped in gold on its cover. Well, mystery solved, Nick said to himself. It had something to do with his father's Birdwatcher's Society. He carefully lifted the heavy binder from the drawer and examined it closely. It was curious, he thought, because although his father had loved flying, he had never given a fig for birds, at least until recently.

Feeling the slightest twinge of guilt, Nick opened the thick volume and began thumbing through its yellowed pages. And it was immediately apparent that, indeed, his father was no secret bird fancier. As he rapidly skimmed the book he saw that every day his father was carefully noting the daily comings and goings, the "migrations," of every single German vessel moving through the Channel!

The "migratory birds" were nothing less than the great German liners, merchant vessels and warships steaming out of Hamburg and the Rhine and *migrating* across the Channel! His eye falling to the bottom of the page, he saw this startling notation in his father's hand:

> *Documentation delivered: First March 39, 0800 hrs, believed Alpha-Class U-boat sighting vicinity Greybeard Island bearing 230 degrees, west, increased activity all sectors day and night. Thor acknowledge and forward W.S.C.*

Thor? The beautiful power launch he'd seen slipping in and out of the harbor these last few weeks? And who, or what, was W.S.C.? Or, for that matter, an Alpha-Class U-boat?

Adding to the deepening mystery, Nick saw that there was another secret or two hidden in the drawer as well. Although he could scarcely credit it, at the back of the drawer there was a nickel-plated Webley & Scott revolver, .45 caliber. Picking it up carefully, Nick noticed that it was loaded. His father owned a gun, a loaded gun? Setting the heavy revolver down gently atop a stack of papers, he took a deep breath and reached into the drawer again. The gun had been lying atop a packet of letters, bound with red ribbon. Nick removed the letters, thinking, "in for a penny, in for a pound." Each envelope had the word "Chartwell" engraved in the upper left-hand corner. Each was addressed to his father, Greybeard Light, Greybeard Island. He dared not open a single one, though he was powerfully tempted.

Chartwell, Nick knew from the newspapers, was the name of the country house in Kent that belonged to Winston Spencer Churchill! Yes, yes, grand old W.S.C. himself!

Nick, struggling to contain his excitement, carefully returned everything to the drawer just as he'd found it. First the packet of letters from Churchill. On top of the letters, the loaded pistol. And finally the heavy leather binder. Hold on, had the title been facing him, or away? Away, as he remembered. At the slightest pressure of his fingertips, the secret drawer slid silently shut, locking with a soft click. Staring fixedly at the spot where the drawer had simply disappeared into the desk, he saw his mother's little gold-framed eyeglasses on the shelf just above. He picked them up and placed them absently in his shirtfront pocket.

Breathing hard and feeling slightly dazed, he walked over to stand at one of the many large curved windows that overlooked the channel in every direction. There was a flash of pure white brilliance as the great lighthouse beacon swept around just above him. The storm had by now moved off to the east, over the coastal fields of France. It was still lighting up the sky with crackling electricity, but it was nothing compared to the currents flowing through young Nicholas McIver at that very moment. Maybe he'd been wrong, he thought. Just moments ago he'd been feeling sorry for himself, stuck out here on a rock where nothing ever happened. Well, something *was* happening, that much was sure.

He looked down at the vast black top of the Channel, stretching away now under a moonlit sky. As usual, there was no shortage of the thin white trails, scribbled across the Channel's surface in an eastward direction. But now they seemed to have acquired vast importance. Now he knew what they were. They were German submarines. They were the dreaded U-boats, slipping out of Germany and beneath the waves of his peaceful Channel, perhaps toward England. If his father and W.S.C. were correct, of course.

He shuddered at the little chill of fear, and the sudden sour taste of tobacco in his mouth reminding him that his father's pipe remained clenched between his jaws.

His own father, who built sturdy little sailboats that never leaked, and who laughed and told funny stories when he tucked him into his bed every night, was a spy! This man who tended roses on summer days and recited Wordsworth on wintry nights was a spy! One who kept a revolver–a *loaded* revolver–in a secret drawer and who was by all accounts engaged in this secret espionage on behalf of the great Winston Churchill himself. His own father! It was the most wonderful thing imaginable. Maybe he could scare up a little adventure on this old island after all!

"Mother!" he cried at the top of his lungs and racing down the stairs three at a time. "Mother, I've found your eyeglasses! Isn't that wonderful?"

CHAPTER III

Nazis in the Strawberry Patch

· 4 June 1939 ·

AT THE GREYBEARD LIGHT

A cold, wet nose prying under his chin brought Nick McIver straight up in bed next morning. It was his reliable alarm clock, Jip, who lathered his cheeks with kisses, then bounded off the bed and down to breakfast as was his custom. Through sleepy eyes, Nick saw the dappled sunlight already at play upon his bedcovers. As was his own habit, he swallowed a deep gulp of the briny sea air pouring through the open window. The taste of the tangy air and the sight of the blue channel far below was like having life itself for breakfast. And life, for Nick, was now full of promise.

He had to believe that the view from his room high atop the lighthouse was probably the most splendid in all of England. How many other boys had complete command of the English Channel in all directions from their bedroom windows? From his towering crow's nest, he could monitor seagoing traffic to all points of the compass. Wiping the sleep from his eyes, he was pleased to see the white-hulled French frigate *Belle Poule* out of Calais, steaming once more for her home port. He leaned farther out the window.

Glorious.

The morning sky had been scrubbed clean of all but a few puffy cottonballs and the sea stretched away far below, a rolling carpet of royal blue littered with whitecaps. In the air, great whirlwinds of terns and phalaropes and storm petrels wheeled about, barking at each other and diving straight and true at each flash of silver in the ocean below.

Nick craned his head out farther still, looking in all directions for anything unusual in the morning's seagoing traffic. He saw the *Maracaya*, a rusty tub out of Cartagena, making her sluggish run up to Portsmouth or Devon, smoke drifting lazily from her stacks. Business as usual, he thought, oddly comforted.

Nick smiled, lay back against his pillow, clasped his hands behind his head, and considered the exciting turn his life had suddenly taken. Overnight, it seemed, he'd outgrown this little whitewashed room full of childish, boyish things. He now lived in a grown-up world of spies and secrets and submarines. He was pretty sure that spies didn't get in trouble for being late for supper.

His eyes drifted up to the shelf on the wall beyond the foot of his bed. It was sagging with books and boyhood treasures. Nick's ancient brass spyglass, bequeathed to him by his great-great-grandfather, the most prized of all.

In those days, Nick thought with a sigh, the McIvers had been sea captains. The old telescope was especially beloved because of the faint initials NM on the eyepiece focus ring. Running his fingers over the worn letters, he liked to imagine his salty old namesake heading into battle against the French, manning the helm of an English man-of-war. His ancestors had been men of the sea, real heroes, just like the great Admiral Lord Nelson himself! The sea, that's where heroes were born and bred, and Nick longed for the salty life with all his heart.

Last night's book was still splayed upon his bedcovers. It was an eyewitness account of Admiral Lord Nelson's tragic death, standing on the quarterdeck of his flagship *Victory* at Trafalgar. Nelson, just forty-seven years old, had cruelly been brought down by a French sharpshooter, hanging in the top-gallant crosstrees of a French man-of-war.

The four brightly polished stars on the English Sea Lord's chest had made him an easy target. England's greatest hero had fallen, his blood mingling with the tears of his comrades as he lay upon the deck, dying.

Reading and rereading the passage, Nick always felt his hero's death keenly, with a sadness usually reserved for family.

There was a fleet of little wooden ships beneath his bed. Nick had fought and refought all of Nelson's great sea battles. All except Nelson's last, of course. Nick had decided Trafalgar would be the last battle fought with his wooden fleet, a final tribute to his boyhood hero before he put the toys of childhood away forever.

Nelson the Strong, Nelson the Brave, Nelson the Lord of the Sea.

Suddenly, Nick's bedroom door swung inward with a bang, causing him to sit bolt upright in bed for the second time that morning. There stood his almost seven-year-old sister, Kate. She had one of her many raggedy dolls under her arm and Nick noticed this one had the same big blue eyes and bouncy red curls as his sister did. The little half smile on her face meant he was in some kind of trouble. He'd only had about six years of peace in his life, the ones before his sister had been born, and most of his waking hours were spent trying to keep just a half step ahead of her.

"Oh. Hullo, Nicky," she said, leaning against the doorway. "Are you still sleeping?"

"Tell me something, Kate," he said through a yawn. "Seriously. Have you ever, *ever,* known anyone to sleep sitting straight upright? Think about it."

"Um, well, yes, actually," she said, "I have."

"Oh, don't be such a vexation," Nick said, quoting Mother's favorite word. "Who on earth sleeps sitting straight upright?"

"Father, that's who. In church. Every single Sunday morning!" Kate said, eyes blue as cornflowers crinkling in total victory.

"Oh," Nick said, frowning. "Right." Christmas! Hardly awake for five minutes and already she'd gotten the better of him! It was going to be a long day. He shook his head to clear the cobwebs. "Well, for your information I am not still sleeping."

"That's good because Father wants to know something," Kate said, swinging her doll lazily by the hair.

"What's that?" Nick asked, covering another yawn with the back of his hand.

"Well, he'd like to know if you plan to sleep all day or if you're coming down to–"

"Oh. Breakfast," Nick said, and swung his legs over the side of the bed. Somehow, having gone to sleep without any supper, he'd managed to forget all about breakfast. "Right.

Coming down, straightaway. I'm starving." Pushing his hair out of his eyes, he tried to recall where he'd thrown his trousers.

"By the way, Nicky?" she asked, twirling the doll in a tight little arc. "Do you believe in Nazis?"

"Why, I guess I do," Nick said, pulling his well-worn summer trousers on, two legs at a time. "Much as anything."

"Do you know what Nazis look like?"

"I suppose I'd know a Nazi sure enough if I saw one up close, Kate," Nick replied. "Why do you ask?"

"Well, we're supposed to keep a watch out for them, that's all," she said with great seriousness. "We're going to be birdwatchers, just like Papa. All of us. You, me, even Mummy. That's what Father wants to talk to you about. He already talked to us about them. Mummy doesn't believe in Nazis, I don't think. And Father says Mummy shouldn't go snooping about in his secret drawers looking at his big birdwatcher's book if she–oh, race you to the bottom of the stairs, Nicky!"

She'd seen the stormy look on her brother's face and decided to beat a hasty retreat down to the kitchen.

"Hold on," Nick said. The birdwatcher's book? "He, he thinks it was Mummy found the secret drawer and, what–hold on a tick will you!" But his sister was already halfway back down the twisting stairway. Nick charged out after her, pulling his shoes on as he ran. "Kate! Come back here! Wait! Don't–" But she had too much of a head start on him and was already at the kitchen table when Nick burst into the sunfilled room.

And there, on the kitchen table, just where he'd feared it might be, was the faded red leather logbook from the secret drawer upstairs. On the table right between his parents, who sat staring at each other in stony silence above it. And look at little Katie with the big smile on her face.

"It was me," Nick said simply. They all turned to stare at him.

"What do you mean, Nick?" his father asked, a puzzled expression on his face.

"I opened the drawer. I took out the book. I didn't mean to look inside it, Father, I just, I couldn't help it. I was looking for Mother's spectacles and I pushed the little button and then the drawer just popped out. I didn't mean to look, but–I'm sorry, Father, really I am."

"Thank you, Nicholas," his mother said smiling at him. "I've been trying to tell the old boy I wasn't his culprit, but you know your father." She delicately patted a spot of jam from the corner of her mouth and added, "Well, the cat's out of the bag at any rate, isn't it? At least we don't all have to go on pretending to believe in this silly 'birdwatching' business! Isn't that right, dear husband?"

Nick's father gave his mother one of his looks and said, "Well, I certainly knew *somebody* had been looking at it because the log was put back in the drawer upside down and–well–" He stopped himself and looked at his wife with an embarrassed smile. "Sorry, old thing. I should have known it was young Mr. Curiosity Shop here and not–"

"No harm done, my darling," Emily interrupted. She rose from the table and stood behind her husband, nuzzling his head with playful kisses. "In fact, quite the opposite!" Motioning to Katie, she added, "Come along, Katherine, and bring your berry basket. I'm going to need your help if I'm to get that strawberry pie into the oven in time for supper."

His sister slid by him, obviously a bit disappointed there

hadn't been more of a row and that Nicholas hadn't gotten into more serious trouble. Kate didn't necessarily try to *cause* trouble herself, but she was always quite happy to see it come along. Provided, of course, that it was her brother, and not Kate herself, who was the focus of it. Luckily, that was usually the case.

Nick McIver never looked for trouble, it seemed to look for him.

"Sit up straight and eat your porridge, Nicholas," his father said sternly. "I want a word with you, young man." Nick saw his sister's expression brighten instantly. She imagined he was really in for it now, and she was probably right. She gave him a knowing smile as she rose from the table and was shocked to see the pink tip of her brother's tongue dart from his mouth.

"Mother! Nicky stuck his tongue out at me and–"

"I did not! I was only getting a bit of porridge that–"

"Nicholas, behave yourself! Oh, Angus, by the way," Emily called to his father, as she waited by the kitchen door for Kate to collect her basket.

"Yes, dear?"

"Don't worry. We'll sound the alarm if we discover any Nazis hiding in the strawberry patch! Won't we, Katie?" She laughed and sailed out the door, her big straw basket dangling gaily from her arm. Nick could hear her laughter all the way down the garden path.

Nick's father looked at him. For a second, Nick feared the worst. But then Kate flew out the door, basket on arm, singing about Nazis in the strawberry patch and Angus's face broke into a broad grin. But his father's grin soon faded and he pushed the red logbook across the table toward his son.

"You've read what's in here, I suppose," Angus said.

"Yes, Father," Nick admitted. "Some of it. Enough to know what it is."

"As amusing as your dear mother seems to find all of this, I assure you it is no laughing matter." Angus paused to relight his pipe and sat puffing it, regarding Nick thoughtfully. "I may need your help, son," he said finally.

"Anything, Father," Nick replied, his eyes shining. "Anything at all!" A trill of excitement was flowing through him, unlike anything he'd ever experienced. His life, he knew, was changing before his very eyes.

"There is a war coming, Nick," Angus said. "A terrible war. Your mother doesn't believe it because her brother's in government and the government believes there'll be no war. Most people feel that way and I understand Mother's feelings. But I think war is imminent, Nick. The Germans have fooled us all. Mr. Churchill alone seems to understand England's desperate situation. He has no power, no authority at all, but he is single-handedly trying to sound the alarm throughout England before it's too late."

"Not quite single-handed though, is he, Father?" Nick asked, placing his hand on the Birdwatcher's logbook.

"No, I guess he's not quite single-handed, Nick," Angus said, with an appreciative nod to his son. "Since he's not in government, he must rely on a group of private citizens like me for any little scrap of news about the German naval and air buildup. We're not all one-legged lighthouse keepers tracking the sea lanes, either. There are scores of British businessmen traveling inside Germany who watch the rail lines. I know a group of schoolteachers in Dorset who watch the coastal skies every night. We're a loose confederation of lookouts, Nicky. We work in total secrecy and report our findings directly to Churchill at his home in Kent."

"Why won't the government listen to Mr. Churchill, Father?" Nick asked, his eyes wide as he imagined himself part of a vast network of spies.

"Oh, it's politics, son, of the worst kind," he said, leaning back in his chair and letting a thin stream of smoke escape his lips. "Like most politicians, the Prime Minister is telling the people only what they want to hear. You see, most people are like your mother. They hate war, and rightfully so. As you know, we lost an entire generation of boys not much older than yourself in the last war. And that memory is very strong and very painful. Everyone is afraid of it happening again. Everyone wants peace so desperately that the Prime Minister and His Majesty's government are burying their heads in the sand, pretending that if they give Hitler what he wants, he'll go away and leave us alone."

"I want peace, too, Father," Nick said softly. "Don't you?"

"Of course I do, Nick," Angus said. "But peace at any price is the most dangerous course of action we could take. England is weak, with little stomach for a fight. But fight we will, and sooner rather than later. Right now, today, Germany's Luftwaffe fighters and bombers outnumber our own ten-to-one. Germany's got millions of men in uniform, all highly trained. And they're building the mightiest warships and submarines the world has ever seen. Including some kind of 'super U-boat' that we've only heard rumors about. Highly experimental. I've promised Churchill I'd find out everything I could about her."

"Why are U-boats so important?" Nick asked, making a mental note to tell his father about the bomber squadrons he'd seen off Hawke Point.

"Food, Nick," Angus said. "England is a small island. She can never raise enough food to feed herself. In the first war, German submarines almost succeeded in cutting off our food supply by sinking all the convoys bound for England. That's why, after the Great War, the Germans were forbidden from building submarines by the Versailles Peace Treaty. Hitler is ignoring that treaty, and my weekly reports to Chartwell prove it. We can't let the U-boats gain control of the Channel or the North Atlantic again. If they do, this time we will starve. Understand all of this, Nick?"

"Y-yes, Father, I think I do," Nick replied. He was thinking of his mother's brother, his uncle Godfrey, and his wee children who lived in Cadogan Square in the very center of London. He was thinking, too, of skies over the capital black with thundering bombers like those he'd seen off Hawke Point. And the idea of all England and Europe ablaze. Was it a blaze, he wondered, that could spread all the way to little Greybeard Island? "But what can I do, Father?"

"I've only got two eyes, Nick, neither of them as strong as they used to be," Angus said. "I could use a good pair of eyes alongside mine up at the top of the lighthouse every night. Watching for submarine tracks in the moonlight. And, when you're out sailing on *Petrel*, you could keep an eye out for anything that might be important. Periscopes. Any large convoys of German shipping. Any unusual naval activity you might see. Anything at all, son, just jot it down and I'll include it in my weekly report to Chartwell."

"How do our reports get to Mr. Churchill, Father?" Nick asked, enjoying the chill he got imagining the great man himself reading one of Nick's own reports.

"Ah. I have a contact called 'Captain Thor.' Not his real name, probably, but a code. A former naval man, I believe, and highly experienced at this sort of thing. He's rather the ringleader of our little group of 'birdwatchers,' as we call ourselves. Captain Thor crosses to Portsmouth each week on his sixty-foot motor launch. Delivers the reports to an old fisherman who waits just outside the harbor. Gets them over there in fairly short order, he does, too. Twin V-twelve Allisons below, aircraft engines. She's called *Thor,* in fact. Perhaps you've seen her about?"

"*Thor*! How could I miss her? She's a real beauty," Nick said. "And I've seen this Captain Thor, too, I guess, at her helm." Nick looked at his father in dead earnest. "I'll do anything I can to help the birdwatchers, Father. You can count on me."

"I knew I could count on you, Nick. One final thing. This effort of Churchill's is a matter of the utmost confidentiality. Even King George doesn't know about it! I must swear you to absolute secrecy. What I'm doing is completely against the government's wishes. I'd lose my job if the Ministry ever found out I was helping Churchill. And another thing. When war does break out, the fate of anyone who falls into enemy hands while spying is death. And you're a spy now, son, just like me. Remember that. Can you keep such a big secret?"

"Yes, Father. I swear it," Nick said, but he wasn't really

thinking about Father losing his job or anybody dying before a Nazi firing squad. He was trying to make himself believe that a mere twelve-year-old boy was in on a secret so great that even the Prime Minister and the King of England didn't know about it!

That night, as he drifted off to sleep, an amazing notion occurred to Nicholas McIver. Maybe he was only twelve years old, a boy who'd probably never amount to any kind of real hero, but how many other boys did he know who could claim to be living, breathing *spies*, for goodness' sake?

None, that's how many!

CHAPTER IV

The Sea Chest

· 5 June 1939 ·

AT LIGHTHOUSE POINT

"We've been sitting on this stupid old rock all day and we haven't seen a single periwinkle!" Kate said.

"Periscope," Nick corrected, though he would have gladly settled for a periwinkle at this point.

"Periscope, periwinkle, how can I keep an eye out for Nazis when I don't even get to look through the binoculars?" his sister asked, heaving one of her patented end-of-the-world sighs.

"In a minute, all right?" Nick replied. "Just let me complete this sweep. This isn't supposed to be fun, you know. Spying is very serious business."

It was true. It wasn't fun. Nick wouldn't admit it to Kate, but this entire spy business was not nearly so glamorous or exciting as he'd first imagined it to be. Besides, maybe his mother was right, after all. Maybe the Nazis were going to just leave their country and their little island alone. He hoped that was so, even if it meant he was out of the spy business.

He and Kate had made their way out along the broad-faced rocks of Lighthouse Point right after breakfast. The jetties curved out and around, forming a little harbor where the *Stormy Petrel* was moored. They gave him a perfect vantage point for scanning the seas around the northern tip of the island. They'd brought a picnic lunch out to the jetties and, for a while, with the gulls whirling about and the blue sea splashing upon the rocks, it had been fun. Now, as the afternoon shadow of the great lighthouse on the cliff loomed ever larger across the rocky promontory, and the hours dragged on without even a single periscope or steamship in sight, both children had wearied of spying.

"Here, then," Nick said, handing the binoculars to Kate. "You take another look, while I find Jip. Then we'll go home. Tomorrow's another day. Nazis must take Sundays off like everybody else, I guess."

Nick made his way gingerly back along the curving breakwater for quite some way before he heard Jip barking in the distance. When last seen, the dog had been chasing seagulls and had run off some way along the rocky shore. Nick climbed to a high vantage point and called to the dog, but Jip had run well out of hearing range. He cupped his hands and called back to his sister.

"Come on, Katie! Quickly! We've got to catch Jipper! He's run off!"

As it turned out, they didn't catch up with Jip quickly at all. Not for almost an hour, anyway. Every time Nick and Kate scampered to the top of some rock, they'd see the black dog rounding another cove, out of sight and sound. It was so unlike Jip, Nick thought. He'd never seen the fellow behave in this fashion. Why had gulls suddenly acquired such an attraction? It had to be something else, Nick decided. But what?

Nick finally caught up with Jip circling some prey in a small cove just below. And the sight was startling indeed. His dog was barking, not at a seagull, it seemed, but at a big strangely colored bird perched upon a bit of refuse washed from the sea. Nick climbed down to get a closer look, scarcely able to believe his eyes.

It was, in fact, a huge red bird, perched atop a carcass of old wood, perhaps even a tropical parrot although that wasn't possible! Here was a bird such as had never been seen on this island. One that must have been blown off course thousands of miles to be here! Nick knew such creatures existed in the steaming jungles of Africa and South America, but he'd never dreamed he'd encounter such a specimen right here on Greybeard Island!

He crept down slowly, afraid of scaring the rare bird away.

Edging closer, he saw the bird was not the least bit afraid. Indeed, it seemed to be guarding its perch, an old sea chest, which was lying half buried in the sand at the water's edge. Just sea garbage that had come ashore with the last big storm, or simply with the tide. He certainly hadn't seen the chest the week before, and he was always on the lookout for treasures from the sea.

Sea debris was not at all unusual, but always interesting. The mantel above the fireplace in the lighthouse held proof enough of that.

But, look here. An old sea chest that appeared to have washed ashore almost intact? With an exotic parrotlike bird perched atop it? Well, that was more than just interesting.

And, besides, Nick wondered, cautiously bending down to peer more closely, what about that big, barnacle-encrusted padlock? You didn't put a lock like that on some old empty chest! No, you didn't! Of course his mind went instantly to pirate's gold, emeralds and rubies. But it could always be nothing more than the empty piece of sea junk it seemed to be.

Breathing hard, Kate clambered down from the rocks. "What a pretty bird, Nicky!"

Kate, who happened to have a few crumbs of lunchtime muffin in the pocket of her skirt, and a wonderful way with birds, cheerfully held out this bit to the fantastic creature. The bird cast a quick eye at the offer and immediately removed himself to Kate's shoulder. Kate's eyes went wide with fright, for the bird was nearly as big as she was and its claws were hurting her shoulder.

"Nicky, the bird is hurting my–"

SQUAWK! SQUAWK! the big bird cried.

Suddenly, its sharp beak darted toward her outstretched hand. Greedily, it plucked the treat from her fingers, and darted away, resuming its position atop the little chest. Nick heard a small cry from his sister and ran to her to see what was the matter.

"Oh, Nicky, look!" Kate sobbed, holding up her finger. Nick saw a bright red stream of blood running down Kate's hand. "He bit me, Nicky, the naughty bird! He bit my finger!" Nick took his sister's hand and examined the wound. It was nothing serious, and Kate was barely even crying; still the anger rose in him like a sudden bloom of heat lightning.

"Get away!" Nick cried, waving his arms in anger at the bird. "You want to bite someone, try biting me, parrot! Go! Go! Get away!" Nick picked up a stone to hurl at the now menacing creature and Jip, too, lunged at the bird, barking loudly and baring his considerable fangs. The bird eyed Nick calmly for a moment and then the most astounding thing happened.

The bird laughed at him.

It threw back its huge red head and made a terrible cackling noise that sounded to Nick almost like human laughter. Then it was gone, flapping its giant wings and soaring away with extraordinary speed. Nick stood blinking in the sun, watching as the bird disappeared out beyond Gravestone Rock, already unsure of what he'd just seen and heard.

But he had the strangest feeling that, for the first time in his young life, he might have encountered something truly evil.

Kate bravely wrapped her injured finger in her handkerchief. She seemed to have already forgotten about the silly parrot and stooped to pull the small chest free of the sand. She couldn't move it, which was surprising. It didn't look at all heavy. It was salt-white from the ocean and as sea-polished as any old piece of driftwood. She dropped to her knees in the sand to examine the chest more carefully.

"Nicky, look!" Kate said excitedly. "There's a name carved into the top!"

Nick bent down and brushed some wet sand from the lid of the chest. The letters, somewhat worn, were still legible.

CAPT. NICHOLAS MCIVER
H.M.S. *MERLIN*
EDINBURGH

"OH!" Kate exclaimed. "Oh, Nicky! Do you see what I see?"

"You bet I do," said Nick, rubbing his fingers slowly across the carved letters. "This old sea captain and I have something in common, don't we?"

"Yes, you do, Nick, you both have the very same name!"

And they both stared at the old captain's chest with growing wonder. First the strange bird, and now this.

"Well, Kate, McIver's a fairly common name," said Nick, brushing a shock of unruly sandy-colored hair away from his eyes. "And, Nicholas is, too. But finding a chest with your own name on it is not your typical day in June, is it?" Nick bent to inspect the chest more closely. "Katie, look here!" he said, using his hand to wipe some of the sea salt from the lid. "The thing looks to be in awfully good condition, doesn't it? Why, the wood looks almost brand-new! See how shiny it is?"

He ran his fingers over the name, his own, engraved upon the lid, and felt a sharp tingle of excitement. It was, he realized, the same little chill he got when he ran his fingers over the 'NM' on the old spyglass above his bed.

"Help me, Katie," Nick said. "I've got a strange feeling about this chest! Let's get it off the beach quickly. The tide is on its way back in. Another hour and we'd never even have seen this prize, full of pirate's gold most likely! Or, big emeralds from Brazil or someplace! Good boy, Jip! Looks like you've found us a real treasure this time!" Jip barked his approval and gave the lock a good sniffing about.

Nick and Kate were able to lift the chest, but just barely, because it was surprisingly heavy for its size. It seemed to weigh at least twice what its size would indicate, Nick thought, worrying about his sister holding up her end, especially with her hurt finger.

"Into that cave," said Nick, recognizing the same little cavern where he and Jip had waited out the storm a few days earlier. "There's a ledge in there where we can hide the chest. At least until we decide what to do with it. That way, it'll be safely out of sight."

Using all their strength, they managed to carry the chest into the cave and lift it onto an inner ledge. Nick formed a step with his hands and Kate scrambled onto the ledge, followed immediately by Jip. Nick, his arms strong from rowing his little sloop home on countless windless days, was able to hoist himself up easily.

Golden light penetrated deep into the cave, and Nick examined the chest closely for the first time. It was indeed a Royal Navy officer's chest, the kind used for personal effects. And it was in remarkable condition. Now, in the intense rays of sunlight, the finish of the wood seemed to bear scant trace of who knew how many years drifting in salty seas! And the brass lock, although encrusted with barnacles, was gleaming in many places. A trick of the light?

Nick, who knew about such things, believed this particular chest, despite its newish appearance, had to be quite ancient. This type of chest was from the time of Nelson. It must be nearly a hundred and fifty years old! But how could the wood and brass remain in such condition?

Nick thought about the possibilities. Obviously the chest could have been stored on dry land for all these years and only recently thrown into the sea. But why? And even then the chest should have had some age to it, shouldn't it? Certainly more than it did have.

The sun had dropped to within a palm's width when held on the horizon, and was just opposite the cave's mouth. Brilliant rays now flooded Nick and Kate's new hideout with red-gold light. Nick was using his marlinespike to gently pry the few remaining barnacles from the padlock. It was slow going and Kate was torn between boredom and excitement over opening the mysterious sea chest. It took so long, in fact, that she entered into an imaginary conversation with Jip, planning an elaborate tea party for all her dolls while Nick feverishly worked the lock.

After a time, she dozed off.

Two things happened almost at once, neither of them good. Kate, whose feet were dangling over the edge of the ledge, suddenly awoke to the sensation of cold seawater lapping at her ankles. Realizing immediately what was happening, a scream was forming in her throat when something even more frightening occurred.

The interior of the cave was plunged into darkness. And the scream that burst from Katie's throat filled the darkness with her terror.

CHAPTER V

The Dark Cave

· 5 June 1939 ·

ALONG THE NORTH COAST

Kate, don't worry," Nick said. "Some old 'greybeard' has probably rolled in and blocked the sun from the mouth of the cave." He was summoning up a great deal more calmness than he actually felt. Kate knew as well as he did that their little island was named for the sudden, unpredictable fogs that could turn midday to midnight in minutes. "At any rate, I think that's why not much sun can get this far back into the cave."

"Not much sun? Not *any* sun!" Katie said, and even her voice was shaking. "I can't even see my fingers when I hold my hand up, Nicky! And the cave is filling up with water!"

"It's not filling up with water, it's just the tide coming in. Every cave along here gets about a foot of water inside when the tide comes in. That's why I wanted to get the chest on the ledge, remember? Why, Gunner and I spent a whole night in a cave just like this last summer. Slept out a rainstorm up on one of these ledges, we did, dry as bones, like a couple of babies, even at high tide." He laughed, but it was a hollow laugh, and he was cursing himself for putting his little sister in a frightening situation.

"I'm still scared, Nicky."

Nick reached out in the darkness of the cramped ledge and placed his hand on his sister's shoulder. "Don't worry, Katie, we'll get out of here, I promise. Even if we can't see too well because of the fog outside, we can smell the sea air, right? Take a deep breath and follow your nose, that's the ticket."

"I don't smell anything in this stinky old cave but Jip's breath," Kate said. "And I don't much like that smell, either."

"Right, then, let's get out of here, Kate."

A sharp scratching noise and a sudden flare of burning magnesium pierced the black gloom. "Lucky we've got these matches to help us see where we're going, aren't we? Are you ready? On 'three,' I want you to jump down from the ledge. Jump straight out and bend your knees. Mind your head!"

"Oh, all right, if I have to, but I'll never set foot in this rotten old cave again!" Kate said. On "three" she bravely jumped down into the narrow stream of black water that was flowing into the cave. He heard her take a deep breath.

"Come on, Nicky!" Kate cried. "The water's cold. But I can smell the sea! It's that way! Let's go!"

As Nick prepared to jump, his match went out. He lit another, perhaps his last, he guessed, and with his foot shoved the sea chest as far back on the ledge as he could, wondering if he'd ever see it again, much less solve its mystery. He jumped from the ledge, cupping his hand around the match to keep it lit.

The cold seawater was lapping about his ankles. He'd

been right, the evening tide was on its way in. Hearing a heavy panting noise above him, he lifted the burning match to see. It was only Jip, still up on the ledge. "Come on, boy, jump!" Nick cried, but the dog stayed put. And that's when his match went out. The tunnel was plunged again into total darkness. He'd used his last match.

"It's all right, Kate," Nick said. "We just have to follow our noses."

"Nicky!" Kate said. "What's that noise?"

"It's only Jip, breathing. He's a little scared, too, I guess. Come on, boy, jump!"

"No. Not that noise, Nicky," she said in a low whisper. "Another noise. Behind us. Far back in the cave."

"Another noise? I don't hear anything, Katie," Nick said, listening. But, wait, he *did* hear something! A low, gurgling sound from deep in the cave. It sounded familiar, Nick thought.

Laughter.

"Do you hear it now, Nicky?" Kate asked in a trembling voice. "There's somebody back there, behind us! It sounds like they're laughing!"

"Don't be silly, Kate, that's not possible," Nick whispered. "It's just a trick of the water sloshing around back there inside the–what's that?"

Another sound now, from deep in the cave. It sounded, Nick thought, like heavily beating wings. And it was coming closer. Bats, he said to himself. The whole cave must be full of them.

"Oh Nicky oh Nicky oh Nicky oh Nicky," Kate whispered feverishly and she clung to her brother in the pitch-black darkness.

"It's all right, Katie, it's all right," Nick said. "We're getting out of here right now!" He picked his sister up in his arms and had just started slogging through the black water when there was a huge splash just in front of them!

"Nicky!" she screamed. "What's that? What's that?"

And Nick, too, was terrified at the loud splash until he heard loud barking fill the cave. "It's Jip! He jumped off the ledge and now he's caught the scent of fresh air and is leading us out! We'll just follow him to the opening of the cave! Hold on, Kate, I'm going to run as fast as I can, so put your arms around my neck and don't let go no matter what happens!"

And Nick, with Katie held tightly in his arms, ran as hard and fast as he could, lifting his feet high above the icy water, following the sound of Jip's loud exclamations up ahead in the darkness, until finally they burst from the mouth of the cave into the open air. He took a deep breath, panting with exhaustion, sucking the cool air into his lungs. It was almost like breathing water. Fog, and a thick one, blanketed the little cove.

"Christmas!" Nick exclaimed, staggering up out of the tidal flow at the cave mouth and onto some dry scree. "This fog is a real 'greybeard,' isn't it? That's what blocked most of the sun, see! May I put you down? It's all right, you can open your eyes now. We're safely out of it!"

"Isn't it too early to be this dark, Nicky?" Kate asked, opening her eyes. "What's Jip barking at?" Jip was still looking back into the mouth of the cave, barking fiercely.

"Jip! Come! We're getting out of here, boy!" Nick said to his dog.

"What's in t-t-there, Nicky?" Kate asked, shivering from both fright and her soaked clothing.

"Bats," Nick said, hugging her tightly. "That's what we heard. Whole cave must be full of them." But it wasn't bats they'd heard inside the cave. Someone, or *something* more likely, had been laughing back there. And a bat, as far as he knew, didn't have a sense of humor.

"Can we go home now?" Kate asked, tugging on his sleeve. "I'm v-very cold."

Cold and frightened, Nick knew, with leagues to go before sleep and a warm bed. And his poor mum wondering where they were once more. He took his sister's hand in his own. "This way," he said, mounting a nearby ledge that seemed to lead upward.

And so the little band made its way, cold and wet, up the slippery steps of the rocky cliffside. As they neared the top of the cliff, the greybeard fog became more and more patchy, and, to their increasing discomfort, mixed with a hard slanting rain.

Gaining the top at last, they made their way across the rocky headland. Nick tried to ignore the stinging rain and concentrate on the mystery they'd discovered in the sandy cove. The fact that the chest looked so new and happened to bear his own name was curious enough. But the big red bird, he was a mystery, too. Whatever was such a creature doing on this little island? It was passing strange. And now, slogging across the rainswept fields, tired and bone cold, he came to grips with what had been troubling him since they'd run out of the cave.

The laughter in the cave. He'd heard it before. It had come from the mouth of the red parrot sitting on the sea chest!

They reached the coast road and Nick made a decision.

"We'll stop at Gunner's, Kate," he said. "He's sure to have a fire going on a night like this and I think we could use some warm blankets and a pot of tea."

And so where the road forked, the little trio, led by Jip running up ahead, took the turning east for the Greybeard Inn instead of bearing north along the coast road to the lighthouse and home. Although they were late, and he had surely missed supper once again, Nick decided his shivering sister needed some warm clothes and hot tea.

It would prove to be an unfortunate decision.

CHAPTER VI

Billy Blood

· 5 June 1939 ·

AT THE GREYBEARD INN

A brilliant parade of lightning strokes flashed across the rocky headland, marking the old inn in the near distance and the Greybeard Light in the far. Nick longed for the comforts of hearth and home, but his sister was chilled to the bone and shivering badly. An enormous thunderclap rumbled through the low black clouds and across the plain.

He could just make out the warm glow of oil lamps in the upstairs windows of the inn and, placing his arm round his sister's shoulders, they hurried up the last rise. The inn wasn't home, but it was hearth.

Nick pushed open the heavy wooden door and, sure enough, saw a room lit only by fire. A real corker, too, blazing away in the massive open hearth of the old inn's public room, the flames licking every corner of the ancient space. Rain beat steadily against the windowpanes and jagged flashes of lightning lit the panes from without.

Nick saw two strange figures before the fire. One of them,

a tall fellow wearing a dark cloak, stood with one boot up on the hearth regarding the new arrivals in brooding silence. He was smoking a long bony pipe and held a rum bottle in one hand. His companion sat hunched in the shadows, a brooding presence just beyond the firelight's reach. Strangers, on Greybeard Island? It was a day for strange occurrences, Nick thought, there was no getting around it.

"Master Nicholas!" Gunner exclaimed, coming out from behind the bar to embrace Kate, then Nick, then Jip. "God love you, children! Why you're soaked to the skin, for all love! Which you surely should not be out on such a night as this! Nor in this bar full of alcoholic spirits, either! Into the sitting room with you, now, afore I lose me livelihood! Blankets!" he exclaimed, and rushed up the narrow wooden stairwell, assuredly in search of blankets, because Nick could hear him shouting the word from the upstairs hall, as if he could call a woolen blanket to come running like a woolly dog.

"Children!" he now shouted from the top of the stairs. "Could you come up and help an old blind man locate the warm and cozies?"

"Coming right up!" Nick shouted back. He took Kate's hand and started up the staircase, a puzzled frown on his face. Surely Gunner knew where the blankets were, the same place they always were, stowed on the top shelf of the linen closet at the end of the hallway. Or on the beds in one of the guest rooms.

When they gained the top step, Nick saw Gunner standing in the darkened hallway, a lantern in one hand. He had his index finger pressed to his lips, signaling them to be quiet.

"Shh," he said, "I'll have a private word with you, Master Nick."

"What is it, Gunner? What's going on?"

Gunner ignored his question and said, "Katie, dear lass, would you be a wee angel and hurry down there to the Blue Room? I think I've left me spare blankets in there."

Nick looked carefully at his old friend. This secretive behavior was not like him at all. He watched his sister skip down the hall and enter the last room on the right, the Blue Room.

"Something's wrong, Gunner," he said. "Tell me."

Gunner, the proprietor of the inn, was easily the most beloved figure in Nick's life beyond his own family. Gunner had much to recommend himself to Nick, but foremost was his brisk manner of speech when excited, which Nick found quite jolly, and his general appearance and demeanor, which always put Nick in mind of a Father Christmas who'd spent a lifetime on shipboard. His face was worn and leathered by the years at sea, but his bright blue eyes still held a sparkling clarity, as if the wind and sea had never been quite able to get to them.

Gunner wore a full, snow-white beard that framed his often rosy cheeks, and little gold wire spectacles that were always sliding down to the tip of his nose. To look at him, you'd never guess he'd spent most of his life behind a twelve-inch naval gun. Or that he'd sent not a few German submarines to the bottom with that gun during the Great War. To Nick, who loved the sea, Gunner's stirring tales of naval adventure were only icing on an already favorite pudding.

Now Gunner bent from his waist and put his lips near Nick's ear.

"Be wary of them two down there, lad, and keep your wits about ye."

Billy Blood and Snake Eye

"Who are they? What are they doing here?" Nick asked.

"Very strange visitors indeed. I don't want to alarm your sister. But I'll tell you they've come looking for something on this island. Something they say rightfully belongs to them. Here to reclaim missing property, that's all I know, lad. Just be wary, that's all. And, one more thing. They–"

At that moment Kate returned, dragging two woolen blankets behind her.

"Some tea would be nice," she said, smiling up at Gunner and bouncing down the steps, trailing blankets in her wake.

"Don't be a-feared, Nick, we'll sort these two devils out in short order," Gunner said, following Nick down the steps.

Gunner wrapped them up like two wee Indians and sat them side-by-side on the bench nearest the hearth. "Oh. Blood," he said, tucking in their blankets and nodding to the dark-cloaked man. "Beg pardon, Blood, ha-ha!"

"Blood?" asked Nick, who was accustomed to Gunner's vocal peculiarities. Still he found this mention of "blood" incomprehensible, and found himself looking down at his blanket to see if he'd cut himself. "What blood, Gunner?" He saw a spot of red on the floor and reached down for it, but it was only a singularly large feather.

A red feather.

"Here's yer Blood, boy," came a chilling voice from inside the cloak.

The stranger grinned a toothsome smile at Nick. His appearance was strange indeed, almost like an apparition one could say, especially here in the warm familiar glow of the old inn. Clenched between his yellowed bony teeth was a long thin yellowish white pipe carved out of some kind of bone. He wore his full black cloak over a scarlet blouse and odd-looking black pantaloons stuffed into beautiful Hessian boots. Nick supposed that many might consider the fellow handsome, with his finely chiseled features, his long dark red hair tied at the back with a black satin bow–but to Nick he didn't look handsome. To Nick he looked–and he had to search for the word–*wrong*.

"Yes, yes, here's yer old Blood," said the stranger in that musical voice. It would have been bone-chilling were it not so hauntingly melodious. "And, here be my companion Snake Eye. Leave him be, if I was you," Blood said, with a warning glance at Kate.

But Katie couldn't take her eyes off this other brooding figure. Occasionally, when flames would lick up in the fireplace, she could see his strange face before he turned it away. She shuddered at the sight of him, deciding he'd either been horribly scarred or that his face was covered with the most hideous tattoos.

Blood pulled his chair forward in Nick's direction. He half rose up out of it, locking his jet black eyes on Nick's so strongly that Nick sensed he could almost feel their pull, like moon on tide. There was, too, a strange tinkling noise as the man rose from his chair, and Nick was astounded to see that his full red beard was plaited with braids, and that each long plait was secured with a tiny silver skull! Hollow silver skulls that clinked together musically whenever the stranger moved his head or shook his beard!

"William Blood be my name," the man said, with a tinkling of bells. "But suchlike as you may call me Billy." He drew his thin lips back in something like a smile and regarded Nick and Kate with heavily lidded black eyes. "Won't you join our little party?" He sucked on his bone and blew a foul yellow cloud of smoke in Nick's direction. Then the stranger hooked his boot under the bench where the children sat and drew it near to him. A shiver went through Nick's body as he looked closely at the man's pipe. It was a bone all right, and looked like one he'd seen in one of his mother's anatomy books.

Human anatomy!

"You look chilled, swabbies. A little rum, perhaps? An ancient old grog, mateys, over two hundred years old."

Blood's voice was indeed oddly musical, but it was not a pretty song, Nick thought. Perhaps his voice was the *opposite* of music. He held out his open bottle of rum to Nick, black eyes glittering.

Eyes that narrowed instantly to slits when Nick put his hand over the mouth of his offered bottle.

"Kind of you, sir," Nick said, looking evenly at the stranger. "Truly. But our friend Gunner has a pot of hot tea brewing for us. Besides, 'swabbies' like my sister and I are not allowed to drink spirits. But we do thank you kindly for the offer."

Feeling distinctly uneasy in the man's presence, Nick turned to Gunner who was busily toweling Jip's coat dry before the fire. "Gunner, may we borrow some oilskins for the trip home to the lighthouse? I'm sure our parents are worried. We really should be getting home, shouldn't we, Katie?"

"Lighthouse?" Blood smiled, his voice dripping with mock kindness.

"We live in the lighthouse, Mr. Blood," Kate said. "It's two thousand years old!"

"Lovely, a ruin no doubt," Blood oozed. "My friend Snake

Eye here is a connoisseur of antiquity, he is, seein' as how he's over two hundred year old himself. The two of us must pay you a visit someday, my child," he said, and Kate's eyes went even wider.

"My parents are probably quite worried, Gunner," Nick interjected quickly. "Late again for supper and this time I've got wee Kate with me in the bargain," Nick said, looking at Kate nervously. But his sister paid no heed.

"Can I tell Mr. Blood about the sea chest we found, Nicky?" Kate said. "Down by Gravestone Rock?"

Nick tried to hold the words back for her, even as they came tumbling out. He threw his sister a stern look but wasn't sure she had interpreted it correctly. She was incredibly clever, but she was only six and a half years old. She was still learning about "looks" and how they stood for words unsaid.

"Found a sea chest, did you, dear girl?" grinned Billy Blood. "Fancy that! Me old parrot Bones was tellin' me such a tale, just afore you swabbies arrived. He seen a chest, too! Would it be the same one as yours, I wonder?"

He was leaning right into Kate's face, his lips pulled back into what was meant to be a smile and his black eyes locked on hers. A thin stream of smoke escaped his thin lips, and Katie saw that his yellowed teeth were very large. She drew back instinctively. She had never in her life met a bad man. There simply were none on Greybeard and she had never left the island.

But she had heard her mother describe bad men in stories and this Mr. Blood here and his scary friend certainly fit the description. Even the air around them felt wrong, even the light. Wrong. Bad.

"Just what kind of chest might it be, dear?" said Billy Blood.

"Oh, my, it–" started Kate, and stopped, realizing what she'd done. She looked at Nick for help.

"Did she say sea chest?" Nick said quickly. "My sister has a keen imagination, I'm afraid. Wasn't a chest, sir. No, not a chest, just a pile of driftwood and a rusty old lock." He gave Blood his very best Sunday smile and saw the black eyes go cold.

"By the way, you mentioned your parrot, sir?" Nick asked, eyeing the large red feather in his hand and desperate to get off the subject of his chest. "A red parrot? If so, sir, I'd ask you to keep that nasty bird away from my little sister because–"

"Quiet!" Blood roared. "You dare speak to the likes of me in suchlike ways! Why, I'll have your damned eyes for supper! And Snake Eye your tongue. He likes tongues."

Blood suddenly sat back and regarded the boy in silence, peering intently at Nick through narrowed eyes. And Nick could see him trying to decide whether or not this wisp of a lad could be easily frightened. Nick returned Blood's cold stare, though in truth the man was terribly frightening and Nick's heart was pounding in his chest. Sheer menace seemed to pour off the man in waves, and he said not a word.

The silence remained, hanging heavy over their heads. Katie, Nick noticed, was content to stare at her shoes, while Jip was regarding the Snake Eye fellow with a low growl.

Well, if Blood did mean to frighten them, it wouldn't do to let him succeed, thought Nick; for although this was the first truly suspicious character that he had personally encountered, he'd met their like many times over in the pages of the books that filled the lighthouse library. So this is what they're like in real life, he thought, the bad men, the bogeymen who haunted his dreams.

"Not a chest at all," said Blood at last, in a wicked mimicry of Nick's twelve-year-old speaking voice. "Not a chest at all, you say?" He leaned his face into Nick's just the way he had done to Kate and Nick could smell the scent of sour rum or tobacco or worse on his breath. "If not a chest then what, my dear boy? Do tell, laddie, as you'll warrant Billy Blood's little tolerable of secrets indeed. And old Bones never lies. Never."

"Tea!" exclaimed Gunner, bustling in and placing the tray on the hearth. Nick was much comforted by both the warmth of the liquid and the reappearance of his friend. Gunner was immensely strong, having spent many years mastering the strange game of flinging huge logs–trees, really–end-over-end in the Scottish manner. He was completely devoted to Nick and his sister, and Nick knew he would die himself before he ever let them be harmed or even ill-used by a stranger.

"I believe, sir," said Nick, eyeing the stranger evenly over the rim of his teacup, "that it might have been a chest at one time, but all we found were a few rough boards of the frame." Nick did his best to smile. "Bit of sea trash is all we found. Nothing more, sir."

At that moment, a long, low hissing noise issued from the lips of the one called Snake Eye, but he said no more. In Nick's view, it was clearly time to go. He stood up and took Kate's hand.

"Our parents are probably worried about us, Mr. Blood, so I guess we'll be making our way home. Storm has let up some, too, hasn't it? That's Greybeard weather for you! So, I guess we'll be off now and, Gunner, if we could have those oilskins we won't bother you kind gentlemen any longer, will we, Kate?"

Nick had lifted Kate by the arm and given Jip a rousing nudge with his boot. "And we'll wish you gentlemen a very pleasant evening, too, I'm sure." They made their way to the door, Nick encouraging the growling Jip along with the toe of his boot.

Billy Blood turned in his chair and regarded them coldly. "To the lighthouse, are ye then?"

Gunner helped them into the oilskins. "See you home, Master Nick?" he whispered, with a glance over his shoulder at Billy Blood. "A strange pair, ain't they?"

"Who are they?" Nick whispered, looking beyond Gunner to Billy Blood. "Where'd they come from?"

"They come from out of thin air, is where they come from!" Gunner said in a sharp whisper. "I stepped out into the kitchen for less than two shakes of a goat's tail, and when I steps back, there them two demons are, cozy by the fire! Didn't hear the door, nor the wind, nor nothing at all. They just 'popped' in, guv'nor, right out of thin air! Never seen the likes of it. I think I should see you home, Nick, really, I do."

"We'll be all right, Gunner," Nick said, reducing his voice to an even lower whisper. "But perhaps we could meet tomorrow? We found something on the coast. Something I need your help with as quickly as possible."

He turned to bid farewell to the stranger but Blood had turned his back to them and was once again staring into the fire, puffing on his long bony pipe, the wreaths of wispy smoke hanging about his head like sickly yellow clouds. It was somehow more disturbing than if Nick could have seen his face.

"Aye, tomorrow, lad. And, with these two about, I'll sleep with the heavy artillery tonight. Might even put Old Thunder under me pillow!" Gunner added, whispering in his ear.

"Old Thunder?" Nick thought he heard Billy Blood ask as he pulled the heavy door shut behind them. The boy felt a chill shoot straight to the marrow. There was no earthly way the man could have heard what Gunner had whispered. No earthly way. Nick paused at the rain-streaked window, stood on tiptoes, and peered back inside. Blood and his silent companion were gone. The chairs by the fire were empty, the strangers vanished like smoke up the chimney!

"Do you believe in pirates, Nicky?" Kate asked, putting her small hand into her brother's much larger one as they turned into the road. "Because I do."

"Pirates? No, course I don't. Everyone knows there's no such thing as pirates anymore, Katie," Nick said, patting her wee head. He was glad his sister couldn't see his face, for his eyes surely lacked the conviction of his lips.

"No such thing at all."

So the two children made their way homeward, the Greybeard Light sending great stabs of light into the now lifting fog and Jip running up ahead, leading the way, and all of them anxious to be home and abed.

CHAPTER VII

Two Terrible Letters

· 6 June 1939 ·

AT THE GREYBEARD LIGHT

"Hit the deck, Katie!" Nick cried.

He poked his head inside his favorite room in the old lighthouse. It had been his room once, now the paneled marvel of varnished mahogany wood, rounded to follow the lighthouse walls like the hull of a ship, belonged to his sister. It even had brass portholes that opened to the sky. A master ship's carpenter had fashioned it a century earlier, duplicating a McIver ancestor's quarters aboard a frigate in the Royal Navy.

To this day, there were no electric lights in the room, only candles and oil lanterns hung from the walls. Even the bed was a ship's bunk, enclosed with heavy velvet drapery. Only Kate's obvious joy in the magical room made Nick glad he'd relinquished it to her. He climbed the three steps of the little ladder up to the bed and pulled back the dark green velvet.

"Ahoy, there, matey!" Nick laughed, and bent to whisper in his sister's ear. "Today's a day for secrets, secret plans, and secret secrets!"

He saw Kate's eyes pop open wide from sleep, and a big smile start to form on her sleepy little face. If there was anything she liked more than raggedy dolls and sugary crumpets, it was any plan chockablock with secrets!

"Secrets?" she asked, sitting up and rubbing the sleep from her eyes. "What kind of secrets? The chest? You mean we can't even tell Mummy about the sea chest and those mean old pirates, Nicky?"

"Never!" Nick said, plopping down on his old bed, testing to see if the goosedown filling still had its old bounce. "Don't you see? This is *our* adventure, Kate! And if we tell them, it will become *their* adventure! Or, even worse, it won't even *be* an adventure anymore. It'll be just one more thing we let grown-ups figure out for us!"

"Well," Kate whispered, "can we tell Gunner, then?"

"Of course, we can!" Nick said, laughing as he jumped down from the bed. "We can tell Gunner anything. Just because he's old doesn't mean he's a grown-up! Now, come along!"

Down and down, around and around, they flew, from the top to the bottom of the winding narrow staircase, fairly tumbling into the big sunlit kitchen at the bottom of the stairs. A large bay window to one side of the kitchen hearth overlooked the headland and the sea far below. Nick and Kate found seats on the cozy cushioned banquette that curved inside the window. It was strewn with needlepoint pillows Mrs. McIver had made during the long winter nights. Each pillow had a saying, but Nick's favorite was the one that carried Nelson's dying words: *Thank God that I have done my duty.*

Nick saw his father out on the headland, staring out to sea, leaning on his favorite walking stick, his ancient briar pipe stuck fast in the corner of his mouth, puffing thoughtfully. Nick had seen him strike such a pose countless times and yet it was certainly odd to see him there at this time of morning.

Pure morning sunlight, slanting through the kitchen window, struck fire in Nick's mother's golden yellow hair. Nick was thinking how beautiful she looked, cutting her roses at the sink, when it occurred to him that something was wrong, terribly wrong.

Although no sound came from her, just the set of her head and the trembling of her shoulders told him she might be weeping. It occurred to the boy that he had never seen his mother crying before except for the night Kate's fever was so high she'd almost died.

Nick went instantly to her side and saw the crushed and broken roses at her feet.

"Mother? What is it, Mother?" Nick asked, his hand on her shoulder. She was staring out at her husband, her eyes flooded with tears she wouldn't let fall.

"Your poor father got a letter this morning, Nick," she said, her eyes on the window. "I think you're old enough to read it." She reached into her apron pocket and withdrew a thick cream vellum envelope embossed with a gold ministerial seal and a London Whitehall address. Nick took it, and a nameless dread rolled into his mind like a fog.

Whatever was inside, it wasn't good.

"Oh, and this, too, Nick," she said, pulling still another envelope from her pocket. "It's addressed to you. I don't know who on earth it's from, a friend from school, I suppose, some kind of prank. It didn't come in the mail."

She reached into her apron and pulled something bright and

shiny from the pocket. "I found the letter stuck to our kitchen door with this charming implement." With a sigh of disgust, she flung a wicked-looking knife clattering to the countertop.

It was a dagger, the boy saw to his amazement. A large, bone-handled dagger! Two words went off in Nick's mind like a pair of bombs.

Billy.

Blood.

"Get rid of that horrid weapon, Nick! I'll not have it in my house!"

Nick shoved the dagger deep in his jacket pocket, out of her sight. He then examined this second envelope addressed to him, which was made of thin blue paper, and turned it over in his hands. It was addressed on the front in a very ornate hand to "Master Nicholas McIver, Greybeard Light, Greybeard Island," and on the back sure enough the initials *W.B.* were stamped in a red wax seal.

His heart tripped a beat. *William Blood,* he knew, and he quickly stuffed Blood's letter inside his trouser pocket.

"Read the Ministry letter to your father, Nick," his mother said. "And then go to him. I've done all I can. He knows that I love him with all my heart and that we'll all get through this dreadful time together. He's most worried about you and Katie. Show him what a strong boy you are, Nicky. He needs you."

Nick tore into the letter from the Ministry of Coastal Navigation. It was the department in government that maintained and controlled all the lighthouses of Great Britain, on her coasts and her many islands. It was from the Minister himself, Nick saw, and he scanned the letter quickly, his eye going to the very bottom.

It has come to the attention of the Ministry that certain service personnel, manning both coastal and Channel Island stations, have been engaging in certain activities outside the scope of their duties. Such activities, which could be construed as hostile acts toward friendly nations, are in direct violation of His Majesty's statutes of international diplomacy and are expressly forbidden by Ministry charter. Therefore, we regret to inform you that you are, upon receipt of this document, relieved of your duties. Service personnel who have been found in violation, and their families, will be relocated to the mainland at the expense of the Ministry. However, their obligations to the Ministry will formally cease at midnight, 31 December. Stations in this directive include:

THE SPIRES.
HOGSHEAD LIGHT.
GREYBEARD LIGHT.

How could anyone write such a cold and terrible letter? Especially to someone like his father, who'd dedicated his entire life to the Ministry? It was too horrible, and not just for Nick's family, either. Didn't they realize how important every lighthouse in the country was going to be and, because of its location, especially Greybeard Light? Did Uncle Godfrey know about this? Did Mr. Churchill? They couldn't, Nick realized, because neither would have allowed this letter to be sent.

Service personnel and their families will be relocated to the mainland.

Nick looked up, his eyes finally finding those of his mother. "Relocated? Mother, does this mean that–"

"Go to your father, Nicky," she said, the sadness gone from her eyes, replaced by a look of angry resolve. "Tell him Mother's gone down to the Greybeard Inn to make the necessary arrangements with Gunner. Tell him how much we all love him, no matter what. He needs you, Nicholas."

His mother kissed his forehead, then cupped his face and turned it up toward hers. "Now is the time for my brave boy," she said, and rushed through the kitchen door, her eyes clouded once more with angry, bitter tears.

Nick's life, only moments before so full of blood-stirring excitement, came crashing down around him. He felt his own hot tears rising and choked them back, as all that he was losing appeared as a horrible rush of rapidly fading photographs. His home, the glorious rose-covered Greybeard Light, his room, his window on the sea. His sailing boat, and Gunner and the inn, and the end of the day when the sky in the west was shot with red–he stopped himself. He could feel his eyes brimming and so, crumpling the horrid letter in his hand, he raced from the table to the door and out to his father.

He stumbled once on the rocky ground but somehow kept his feet beneath him until his reached his father, and clutched at his worn khaki shirt, the only one he ever wore, with the tiny holes in the collar where his silver RAF wings had been.

"We're to be relocated? What about our secret work for Mr. Churchill, Father?" Nick cried. "Surely Mr. Churchill won't let them do this to us, will he? Who's going to keep an eye on all the Nazi ships for him?" But Nick knew as soon as he said it that this was a stupid thing to say. Their work was *secret.* His father could never involve Churchill or ask for his help. This was the government's doing, and Mr. Churchill was at war with the government! What were they going to do? What ever *could* they do?

His father said nothing, nor did he look away from the sea. Nick took his father's hand, and pressed it to his face. And still his father took no notice of him, or was so absorbed in his thoughts that he simply was unaware of his son's presence.

"What shall we do, Father? Are they going to take the Light from us? Are we going to have to leave the island?" He fought to keep the sobs from his voice. "We've nowhere to go, Father. This is our home, our only home. I was born in this house. So was Katie. We don't know anything else, do we?" He wanted to be strong, as Mother had asked, but he just wasn't brave enough for this.

He was sobbing quietly now, he just couldn't hold it back. "They can't take our home from us, Dad, they can't! I won't let them! I'll fight them, you'll see! I'll never leave this house no matter what they do to me, they'll have to kill me first, they'll have to–"

Now is the time for my brave boy.

His father squeezed him tight, his strong hands helping Nick to find his own strength.

"Nick, this is going to be hard for all of us," he said quietly. "You have to take care of Kate for a few days. Mother and I are leaving for London on the noon packet boat. We're going to stay for a while with Uncle Godfrey in Cadogan Square. We're going to ask Gunner to take care of you while we're away. He'll board the two of you at the inn until we're home, and you'll have a jolly time. You'll be fine, boy."

"Mother's gone to see Gunner now, Father. She said to tell you she'd gone to make the arrangements. I–I didn't know what she meant."

"Good. She wanted to stay here with you but I need her in London, Nick. I'm going to pay a personal visit to Mr. Churchill down at Chartwell. Your mother is going to see if there isn't some way Uncle Godfrey can help us. Bring some kind of pressure to bear at Number Ten Downing. With war coming, these closures are a dreadful mistake. Our secret work here for Mr. Churchill is vitally important to the country. We'll find a way. But it may take some time. Maybe a week, maybe two."

His father turned and put both his hands on Nick's shoulders, looking directly into his eyes, ignoring the tears streaming down his son's face.

"I've known all along I might get a letter like this one day. But I've always done what I've had to do. You're a brave boy, Nick. I'm counting on you, son." His father pulled Nick to him for a brief embrace. Then he smiled and said, "And so is Mr. Churchill. He needs to know everything we can tell him about those U-boats, Nick. Everything."

"Yes, Father. Of course."

"And I need those two strong eyes out on the water, don't I, Nick? Today and every day, until I can straighten out this terrible business and come back home. No matter what happens, we must always do what is best for the country."

Then his father left his side and went back into the house. Nick remained there, his mind desperately searching for a way, any way, to help his family avert this disaster, but his mind was little help to him now because this was real trouble and his ideas, he knew, were only the ideas of a small boy.

How could his own country do this to his father? Especially someone working so hard to protect it in the coming war? He felt the threat of more hot tears and wiped them away with a furious swipe of his sleeve.

It was then that he remembered the other letter residing in his trouser pocket. When he had first seen the dagger and Billy Blood's seal, he'd been filled with terror, but how could this other letter contain anything like the frightful contents of his father's letter? He pulled the blue envelope quickly from his pocket and ripped it open with an anger and violence he hardly recognized as his own. Billy Blood was fortunate that the letter and not he himself was the object of Nick's fury.

Unseen by Nick, a solitary red feather slipped from the torn envelope and seesawed to the ground at his feet.

He read the letter quickly, fiercely crumpled it into his fist, and ran into the house. He was screaming, then, for his dog.

This is what the letter said:

Dear Master Nicholas,

You are in possession of an object of extreme value to me. I will do anything to get it. Anything. You know what it is, and you cannot hide it from me. I will have it.

I am also in possession of an object, one of extreme value to yourself.

That would be your flea-ridden dog, who will not eat or drink until we meet and you give me what I want.

Would it be possible for us to discuss this matter? I suggest we meet at the deserted shanty down by Old North Wharf at six o'clock this evening.

Until then, I bid you

Fond Adieu,

WILLIAM BLOOD, ESQ.

P.S. DO NOT WORRY ABOUT YOUR DOG. I LIKE DOGS. ESPECIALLY THE HEARTS AND GIZZARDS. DELICIOUS!

Blood

Nick took the stairs up to his room three at a time. When he looked under his bed, Jip was gone, just as Nick knew he would be. From the instant he'd locked eyes with Blood he'd known the man to be a fiend. Capable of anything. Anything.

Nick collapsed on his bed, sobbing.

His dog was gone and there was no use looking for him, not in the cellar or chasing seagulls out on the headlands or anywhere, for that matter. Jip was gone and Billy Blood had him. What was it Gunner had said last night? Was the man a wizard or even a ghost? Did he possess some kind of magical powers? Nick didn't much credit such stuff and nonsense, but seeing, or rather *not seeing* was believing. What had Gunner said?

They come from out of thin air, is where they come from!

Six o'clock at Old North Wharf.

He had just nine hours to find a way to get his dog back from Billy Blood. He sat up and wiped his eyes, done with tears for good.

It was no time for good men to be lying about, after all. Not with black retrievers to retrieve and black-hearted Nazis and evil pirates lurking about!

CHAPTER VIII

A Council of War

· 6 June 1939 ·

AT GREYBEARD INN

"War council!" Nick had said, and after seeing their parents off for the mainland on the midday packet boat, the children had gathered upstairs at the Greybeard Inn. Katie, her brother, and Gunner all sat round a heavy oaken table in a small room at the top of the inn. It was called the "Armoury," because it was chockablock with antique weaponry of every description. Colorful battle flags of many nations hung from the ceiling in a great circle of tattered glory, and among them were suspended many swords, lances, and battle pikes of great antiquity.

It was Kate's view that her brother would use any excuse to have a "War Council." He'd even called one when Gunner's cat had gone missing for less than twenty minutes! But now that pirates had stolen Jip, she supposed that war was actually called for.

Seated below this somewhat frightening display, the little band had an old map of Greybeard Island spread before them, and Gunner and Nick were poring over it inch by inch.

Kate tried to pay attention, but it was hardly her idea of fun, sitting there looking at some old maps with a lot of swords hanging over her head. War, like spying, wasn't nearly so much fun as it sounded.

She was whiling away the drowsy morning watching the cat Horatio, her favorite animal on earth. Gunner's cat was a wily predator with an uncommonly insatiable appetite for any creature smaller than himself that flew or swam. Sitting in the small open window just opposite her, the cat was eyeing a fat red robin perched amid the gently swaying clouds of white blossoms on a crabapple tree.

It was a long jump, from window to treetop to robin, but Kate had no doubt that Horatio would steel himself and make the leap. It was only a matter of time.

It had already been a busy morning. Her mother in tears after reading and rereading a mean letter her father had gotten. Then her parents packing for a trip to London to stay with her uncle, and then Nicky telling her that Billy Blood had stolen Jip because he wanted that old sea chest they'd found, maybe.

And now, she and Nicky were staying with Gunner right here at the inn! She had her own tiny little room, the Blue Room, and it would be most thrilling to sleep somewhere besides your own bed, she thought. She was already missing her mum, but now, with all this talk about "escape routes" and "flanking actions" and "declarations of war," she was simply feeling bored. She took a ball and jacks from her apron pocket and practiced her "threesies" on the Armoury floor.

Nick was describing the sea chest and its location to Gunner.

"It's the chest Billy Blood's after," Nick was saying. "See

that strange look that came over him when Katie mentioned it by the fire last night? He knew about it, but how, Gunner? And how could he steal my dog from under my own bed with only one stairway up to my room and my mum standing at the sink not ten feet away, snipping roses? And where's he got poor Jip now, Gunner? Why, everyone on this island knows Jip's my dog–" Nick broke off, his eyes threatening to go all leaky on him for the second or third time that morning. *No more tears,* he told himself. Never again, no matter what!

"Which he is indeed a strange one, Blood is, Master Nick. Strange bloke indeed," said Gunner, drawing his fingers through his full white beard and squinting at the map through his little gold spectacles.

When Gunner found himself in comfortable, homey surroundings, like sitting here beneath all this sharpened steel, he tended to talk in complete sentences rather than the sharp bits and pieces he used when his nerves were a little scratchy.

"Methinks that cursed pirate'll find himself at the wrong end a'this afore we're done," Gunner said, polishing the walnut stock of a prize blunderbuss he called "Old Thunder." Nick nodded silently in agreement. Sooner or later they'd go to war with Billy Blood and he was mighty grateful Gunner would be on his side.

"The chest is located inside a cave here at Sandy Cove," Nick said, marking the location on the map with a heavy black cross, the kind he'd seen on pirate maps in his books. Odd to be using the pirate's cross, Nick thought, to indicate what might really be a chest laden with pirate's treasure, just like something out of a real adventure story.

"The first thing we have to do is move the chest where the enemy won't be looking. A place where we can get that lock open and find out why that old box has Mr. Blood's blood in such an uproar."

"Blood's blood?" said Gunner, cupping his good ear. "Uproar?"

"Right," said Nick. "And then we've got to find a way to get Jip back unharmed without giving up that chest. Something fairly valuable inside, I'd guess. Gold, I reckon–doubloons or napoleons, maybe, or pieces of eight. It's heavy enough."

"Bring the chest here, Master Nick?" asked Gunner, pointing to the inn on the map. "She'd be safe enough up here in the Armoury–ha!"

"We could," Nick said, rubbing his chin, "but she'd be awfully heavy coming up the side of that cliff, wouldn't she? And I wouldn't want to spend a lot of time lugging it across open ground while that nasty bird of his is flying around out there spying on us."

"Why don't you just go get the chest with your sailboat, Nicky?" Katie asked quietly over her shoulder.

She'd been half listening to them and it was pretty obvious to her what they should do.

"Do what?" Nick asked, frowning. "Sailboat?" But he knew instantly that his sister had hit upon it. "You know, that's not a completely terrible idea, Katie!" he said excitedly. "We could use *Petrel* to go get the chest! Gunner, do you have a pair of dividers handy?"

Nick took the navigator's dividers and put one point on the black cross marking the treasure, spreading the instrument to describe an arc around the center.

"Based on what Blood heard last night, when Kate said we'd found it by the sea near Gravestone Rock, this is most likely the area where Blood and Snake Eye will be looking for the chest. Searching the coast from about here to here. We need to find a way to get the chest out of this circle in a hurry, without bumping into that old pirate, and hide it somewhere where he can't get at it. See this! Kate's right! You could run a boat up on the sand fifteen yards from the mouth of the cave and then–"

A big smile spread across Gunner's face. "You be thinkin' of a *naval* operation, Master Nick? Come in and snatch yer treasure chest from the *sea*? But consider, lad. You'll never get yer boat safely in this cove, never in your life."

"Why not?"

"Use your orbs, boy!" Gunner exclaimed, pointing his finger at the map. "You know what these little squiggidy lines round the cove mean well as I do. Those are the Devil's. Teeth, and they'll rip yer bottom out, of that I'm sure!"

Nick looked at Gunner with his own broadening smile. "Your ordinary seaman might not be up to it, Mr. Gunner, but Nick McIver can get you safely inside that cove! And don't worry about the *Petrel*'s bottom on the way in, sir. I know every square inch of those reefs!"

"It ain't yer boat's bottom I'm worried about, boy. Still, a snatch from the sea is not without its particular merits and feasibilities."

"Exactly my thinking, Mr. Gunner, sir. Exactly!" Nick cried, and he leaned over to give Kate a big kiss on the cheek which she wiped away with a grimace as soon as he wasn't looking.

Excited, Nick ran his finger over the map. "We slip out in

the *Petrel,* tack in carefully through the Seven Devils, ghost up into the cove here and I'll lay her up easy by the shore. Then we'll just hop over the side, go ashore, and we can quickly haul that old sea chest out of the cave and into the hold of the good ship *Petrel*! Right out from under that old pirate's nose!"

"And where we be makin' for then, Master Nick? To stow it, I mean."

"Let me take a look at that tide table, Gunner."

Nick checked the high and the ebb against the naval chronometer weighing down a corner of the map. "If we shove off in the next half hour, and make good time sailing south to the cove, we might just snatch the chest and beat the ebb before it makes getting through the Devils impossible."

Nick picked up the dividers again and swung the silver point along the coast.

"From there, with a good sou'westerly on our beam, the closest safe harborage would be right . . . here!"

The silver point moved south and east and pricked the map at the southernmost tip of Greybeard Island. There, a cavernous lagoon nestled at the foot of a craggy, mountainous headland that jutted boldly into the sea. It was off this very headland, Nick knew, that a good deal of recent U-boat activity had taken place.

And upon that headland there happened to stand one of the most famous and formidable pieces of stonework on Greybeard or any other island in this part of the world. A dark, gothic masterpiece of soaring stone towers, turrets, and battlements where no flag had flown for many a year.

Castle Hawke.

Gunner bent down and peered at where the point of the

divider had stuck, his gold-rimmed glasses sliding down on his nose. He took a sharp breath.

"Why, we can't drop anchor there, never in your life, sir."

"There's a good eighty feet of water in that lagoon, Gunner," said Nick. "*Petrel* only draws four."

"Likely so, likely so. But this be Hawke Castle, Master Nick. That lagoon belongs to Hawke Castle! To Lord Hawke himself! You ain't scared?"

"Why on earth should I be scared, Gunner?" Nick asked, smiling. "Don't tell me you believe your own tales about the castle being haunted?"

"No one's sailed into that lagoon nor set foot on that point o'land since Lord Hawke's two children, little Alexander and Annabel, was mysteriously kidnapped there, nigh on five years now. Lord Hawke has said he'd kill any man that'd dare trespass his castle, said he'd kill 'em himself, he did, and legend has it there's not a man in England more handy with pistol or sword than Lord Hawke himself, him or his ghost!"

"Gunner, you know as well as I do that all this talk about Hawke Castle is nothing but stupid pub gossip, fueled by pints of popskull and rum."

"Some of it, maybe," Gunner allowed.

Gunner looked at Nick and smiled sheepishly. He knew he was the person chiefly responsible for all the gossip surrounding the castle. When it came to weaving tales and embroidering the rich Hawke legend, Gunner had no equal on the island. And, to be honest, he couldn't really remember anymore what was true and what he'd made up after a pint or two.

For years, Nick had heard stories circulated around Greybeard Island about mysterious kidnappings at Hawke Castle and evil goings-on there. Most of them had originated, Nick thought, with Gunner entertaining his patrons around the blazing hearth of the Greybeard Inn. On a small island, he'd learned, gossip spread like a case of poison oak and was usually just as unpleasant.

The strange legend of Lord Hawke and Hawke Castle were well known on this tiny island. Although no one talked much about the great castle or its eccentric owner anymore, stories abounded about why Hawke had gone into voluntary seclusion. The tragic disappearance of his two small children was by far the island's most accepted theory. But no one had any proof, nor had there ever been a police investigation, nor a single word in *The Island Gazette.*

Hawke had been a brilliant scientist and world-class detective. Before dropping out of sight, he had single-handedly solved two or three of Scotland Yard's most difficult murder cases after the famous Yard inspectors had come up empty.

One theory held that a famous criminal mastermind had murdered Hawke out of revenge. He was hiding out from his old gang and the coppers in the heavily fortified castle. Stuff and nonsense, Nick thought–he wasn't buying any of it.

Hawke was simply a modern-day Sherlock Holmes, who'd grown weary of the criminal world, come home to his castle, and pulled up his drawbridge. A drawbridge young Nick had never dared cross, and about which he'd always been intensely curious.

"Gunner, look at it this way. You're Lord Hawke, a brilliant scientist and even more brilliant detective. You've locked yourself up in that moldy old castle all these years. One fine day there's a lad on your doorstep with a mysterious sea chest. A lad who's being chased all over creation by evil pirates. Would you shoot that boy? No, sir, you wouldn't! You'd be glad of a chance to dust off your scientific detective skills and get back in business! Why, you'd be tickled pink to help solve the mystery of that chest!"

"Pink or no, I might be just as tickled to shoot, too," Gunner said, rolling it over in his mind. "Of course, poor ailin' Davies says his lordship flung himself from the top o' that tower and broke his bones on them rocks down below. Like his heart was broken after his wife died of consumption and them two wee children was snatched off the face of this earth that terrible night nigh on five long years ago. Only his ghost livin' there now, is what Davies says."

Gunner sat back and regarded his friend carefully. Nick refused to reply.

"Course, all of it could be, as you say, nothin' but idle pub talk, Nick."

"Of course it is, Gunner! Of course it is! Pirates, maybe. But ghosts? Never."

Gunner looked at the two children with a smile at this new potential for adventure. "Well, ghosts or no, I likes the idea of a naval maneuver! And, we'll have Old Thunder here, won't we? In case those pirates get in our way!"

Nick stood up, a look of rapturous excitement on his face.

"That's it, then! We're bound for Hawke Lagoon, Gunner," he said, rolling up the large map. "It's the only way we can keep that chest out of Billy's hands long enough to find out what's inside it! With or without the help of Lord Hawke or his ghost! All in favor signify saying 'Aye!' "

"Aye," Gunner said, his eyes alight.

"Aye," Kate said simply out of habit, since she'd been paying scant attention all morning. Her focus now was the cat Horatio.

Nick looked at Gunner with fierce determination in his eyes. "We're off, lads! First the chest, and then the little matter of rescuing my poor dog from that cursed buccaneer by six o'clock!"

"Look, Nicky!" Kate shouted excitedly, pointing out the open window. "Horatio's jumped all the way to the top of that tree and is having robin for his breakfast!"

Nick looked out the window. There was only a big white cat among the crabapple blossoms where the fat little robin had been singing.

"Who dares, wins, Kate," Nick said.

"True enough, Nick," Gunner said, slinging his big shiny blunderbuss over his broad shoulder. "With a bit o' luck, true enough."

CHAPTER IX

The Leviathan

· 6 June 1939 ·

AT SANDY COVE

"Prepare to shove off, Mr. Gunner, sir!" Nick said, smiling broadly as Gunner emerged from the cave into the misty sunlight.

He was, Nick was delighted to see, carrying the gleaming sea chest. "And we'll set her hard for Hawke Lagoon, south by southwest, sir!" It had taken Gunner only a few moments to fetch the chest from the cave, while Nick stood guard with the blunderbuss at the cave's mouth, on the lookout for pirates or parrots or both. Luckily, he'd seen neither while Gunner was inside the cave, though he would have happily blown the red parrot from the sky had he seen it.

The mysterious chest now loaded safely aboard, the *Stormy Petrel* set sail once more, having picked her way through the Devils, and leaving the Gravestone Rock growing ever smaller in the wake behind her. They sailed southwest and then in a more easterly direction along the rocky coast, along the southern shore of Greybeard Island, bound for Hawke Lagoon. It was just after two o'clock and the little sloop was well heeled over, slicing through the blue water like a long white knife.

Kate sat happily in the cockpit, chatting with her red-headed doll Rosie, the cat Horatio cradled in her lap, keeping her brother company by the helm. "And what might you be up to now, silly cat?" Kate wondered, as Horatio suddenly leapt from her lap and up onto the roof of *Petrel*'s cabin house, and from there, up onto the boom.

Petrel's snowy white mainsail was sheeted all the way out to the starboard side of the boat to take advantage of the wind coming aft over the stern. The sail, which was stretched at its foot all along the beautifully varnished boom, formed a comfortable pocket when they were running before the wind, and it was not uncommon for Horatio to tred gingerly out along the boom and curl up in the soft pocket formed by the billowing sail, and sleep.

Which is precisely what Kate thought the cat had in mind now, until she noticed that a foolish seagull had taken up residence out over the passing waves at the very end of the boom, thereby shortening its life expectancy by a very considerable margin, given the cat's fondness for seagulls and robins.

As Kate watched spellbound, the little drama seemed to unfold in slow motion.

The cocky bird, perched out over the sparkling sea at the end of the boom, facing into the breeze, unaware of the silently approaching cat.

The dangerous cat, creeping slowly out along the boom, low and deadly, barely moving, an inch at a time.

About three feet to go now, and still the bird remains, incredibly bold . . . or incredibly stupid.

And Horatio lunges with lightning speed. The bird sees him, *feels* him coming and darts into the air with a fierce shriek, and Horatio has finally met his match, his paws grabbing at nothing but air, and this time it's not a reliable crabapple branch with some soft garden grass waiting below but the yawing boom of a moving sailboat over the cold blue sea, and in an instant the cat has landed, on its feet to be sure, but only for an instant before disappearing beneath the waves.

"Cat overboard!" Katie screams, just as Nick taught her, and she jumps to the gunwale, her finger pointed to the spot where Horatio hit the water, watching the tiny area of foam as it quickly disappeared astern. The seagull was hovering over the spot, cawing in victory. Nick had also heaved a floating cushion to mark the spot.

"Take the helm, Kate!" Nick shouts, thrusting the tiller into his sister's hand. "Come about immediately and douse the sails, main and jib, these two halyards here, d'ye hear? Gunner! Please don't take your eyes off me! Stand by with a line!" Luckily, the crew has practiced exactly this man-overboard maneuver dozens of times over. There is no reason it shouldn't work for cats.

But Katie has never seen Nick move this fast. In the blink of an eye, he is on the stern, stripped to his canvas britches, eyes on the spot where the cushion floats, and then a blur, arching out over the water and entering a large blue wave, clear as blue glass, with barely a splash to mark his entry.

It was a lovely dive, Kate thought.

Air, then water.

It was shockingly cold, and Nick felt that his heart would stop or explode from his chest as he dove deep and opened his eyes, half expecting to find the cat right in front of him. He was amazed at how clear the water was, this many feet below the surface. He could see the sun, a dancing, misshapen yellow ball hanging above him. And below, brilliant blue going darker and darker. Nick knew the sun could penetrate to a depth of fifty feet, and he could see down to where daylight ceased.

But no Horatio.

He spun himself through three-hundred-sixty degrees, looking above and below, left and right, until he thought his lungs would surely burst.

Still no Horatio.

Sheer instinct told him he had mere seconds to search, then swim for the surface and grab some air. If he didn't find Horatio on the next dive, they'd be having a cat funeral tomorrow. And a dog one as well? He had scant few hours before his appointment with Billy Blood, and he had begun to wonder if Blood had harmed Jip just for spite.

He shook the thought out of his head as he clawed for the surface.

Air. And brilliant sunshine. No cat, anywhere. Just the slender mahogany bowsprit and mast of his boat bobbing in the distance. Amazing how far it had traveled in such a short time. But Kate now had her headed up into the wind and lying dead in the water. Good old Katie. Quite properly hove to, the little sailor!

The icy cold again and he dove down, eyes open. This was it. Time's up, Horatio, ready or not...

There! Below and to the left! A small shadow, maybe another ten or fifteen feet below him. He didn't have enough air to get down that far. Too deep. But he pulled his way down anyway, down toward the shadow, kicking hard, too. His heart was on fire. And his lungs.

Five more feet. It was Horatio. He reached down, straining for the cat, feeling his brain starting to swim inside his head. He felt himself blacking out. Edges of blackness creeping in around his watery blue circle of his vision. And then he had the lifeless cat in his hands and was turning for the surface and that is when he saw the other shadow, the much, much bigger shadow.

It was moving.

Whale? Maybe . . . maybe too big for a whale. Huge, and black and menacing. What on earth could it be?

He burst into the sunlit air and felt the fire in his lungs as he gulped fresh sweet air by the gallon. He held Horatio aloft, no idea whether the cat was dead or alive, and screamed in the direction of the *Petrel*.

He was dizzy, gasping, and still stunned by the vision of the huge dark shadow moving slowly down there below his bare feet.

He hung there forever in the icy cold, waiting. And, dimly, he saw a sail hoisted, and then *Petrel* gradually getting larger, and then Gunner's expert toss of the line, a loop at the end, three feet away. He grabbed it, and heard his sister's "hooray" as if in a dream, and then he was beside his boat, handing the limp Horatio up to Gunner, who was leaning out over the starboard gunwale.

"Well done! Well done, Master Nicholas!" cried Gunner, who reached down and roughly patted his head. "And as fine a cat-overboard rescue as ever I've seen, little Kate!" Katie gave him a huge smile, and tenderly took Horatio from Gunner, cradling him in her arms and whispering to the limp wet form.

"I need more line, Gunner," Nick gasped, tying the line in the water around his waist with a bowline knot. "Another fifty feet, please!"

"Lord in heaven, Nick, what for?" Gunner said. "Stay in that water much longer and yer blood'll freeze! Here, grab hold and I'll hoist you up. Stick yer foot in the loop!"

"Can't right now," Nick said between breaths. "Have to go back down." He concentrated on his breathing.

"Back down? Thankee kindly, Master Nick, for saving my old tom, but now you've got to get aboard and make for Castle Hawke. That's the plan, lad, remember?" Gunner started to pull on the line, worried about the boy's state of mind. "We be running out o' time and there's pirates likely about, remember? Here, get yerself aboard."

"Can't now, Gunner. Going back down for another look. Something down there. Something big."

"Down there? What's that? What's down there?"

"Not sure, Gunner. Something big. Sperm whale maybe, or a blue whale. Maybe something else, but big. Biggest thing I've ever seen! A leviathan!"

Nick took a deep breath and dove back down into the cold blue. And he was gone, Kate saw, again.

"What's Nicky doing?" asked Kate, cradling the slowly reviving Horatio in her arms. "Why has he gone back down?"

"Your brother's seen somethin' down there under the briny, little miss, and apparently it's somethin' as merits his full attention," Gunner said, peering over the gunwale and watching Nick's shadowy form descend.

"Is it pirates?" Kate asked, looking a bit nervous.

"A big fish is more like it, down where he's headed, Miss," Gunner said, patting her bouncy red curls and then rubbing Horatio's soggy head with his own huge paw.

Nick swam down to the depth where he'd found Horatio, his eyes closed against the burn of salt water until the last instant. When he finally opened his eyes, he felt his heart leap in his chest.

It had risen.

The long black shadow was enormous now, and it had moved much closer to the surface. Nick closed his eyes and with a few powerful kicks, swam down to within twenty feet of the menacing black vision.

It *was* a leviathan of sorts.

It was a monster.

Nick kicked along its black length. He now knew what it was, of course, he could have recognized that black profile in his sleep. He knew packs of these monsters were stalking his home waters, but he could scarcely accept the terrible sight of one hovering just beneath the warm teak decks of his tiny sloop. Just beneath the tiny bare feet of his little sister and his old friend Gunner.

The thing was enormous. It had to be at least three times longer than any sub Nick had ever seen, English or German, and probably half again as wide! Although its black skin was dull and lifeless, Nick could hear faint creakings of steel, and small pings of noise coming from somewhere inside the monstrous dark hull. There were, too, beautiful jets of tiny bubbles streaming upward from various points along the broad sweep of black steel.

"I have met the enemy!"

Nick willed himself to stay down until he had confirmed with his eyes what his mind knew to be true. His lungs were on fire, but he forced himself to ignore them and kicked along the monster's side, taking it all in.

A second later, he found what he'd been looking for.

A German swastika, emblazoned in blood red, high on the beast's broad black flank.

And then, on the huge conning tower rising above the deadly black hull, he saw the legend U-33.

Contact, Nick McIver thought. *I have met the enemy.*

A gargantuan Nazi U-boat, hovering beneath the keel of his tiny sloop *Stormy Petrel*! Could this be the experimental Alpha-Class sub? Yes, he thought, it *had* to be!

Nick hung in the water, willing himself to stay down another minute and make observations.

It hung motionless in the sea, about twenty feet below the surface, streams of bubbles rising from its hull like underwater fountains. Its great flat deck was bathed in dappled sunlight and the massive conning tower loomed high above the midships deck. Nick saw giant fore and aft diving planes and, beneath them, the torpedo tubes. On the bow was the huge deck gun, a five-inch rapid-fire cannon that would be used, Nick knew, against aerial attacks or surface enemies. It was altogether the most awesome sight Nick had seen in his young years. He shuddered at the sheer power and majesty of it.

Nick tried to examine his feelings and certainly there was excitement at seeing such an amazing and potentially unfriendly vessel at such close range. But there was something else, too, something he could only guess at.

Was this the beginning of something too terrible to imagine? Or the beginning of a boyhood vastly more exciting than he'd ever dared dream of on his peaceful little island?

He kicked for the surface, lungs afire, his air exhausted and his mind racing.

One thing was certain, he thought, reaching at last the sundappled surface above. It was going to be quite a summer.

Pirates on top of the water, Nazis below.

CHAPTER X

The Nantucket Sleigh Ride

· 6 June 1939 ·

OFF THE SOUTHWEST COAST

Nick sat on *Petrel*'s bow beside Gunner, dangling his feet in the glassy water. There wasn't even the smallest breath of breeze to move his boat.

"We're going to sit here twiddling our toes while that big U-boat slips away and we miss that rotten Billy Blood's deadline, too," Nick said glumly, looking at the sun's diminishing distance from the horizon. "I'll likely never see old Jip again, Gunner. The best dog a boy ever had."

"We've still got some hours left, Master Nick, we'll make it. Besides, we couldn't give that submarine much of a chase even in a tooth-rattlin' blow, d'ye think? And what's the point of that old pirate harmin' yer doggie? Besides, you know well as I do there's that westerly breeze that kicks up every afternoon."

Nick was a staunch boy, Gunner allowed, but like all boys, he needed a little bucking up every so often.

"That westerly never fills in until just before sunset, Gunner, you know that," Nick said, kicking at the mirrorlike water in frustration.

"So I'll whistle her up early," Gunner said, and began whistling his favorite sailor's ditty. The two friends just sat side by side on either side of the bow, wiggling their toes in the water, as the hot sun dipped ever lower in the western sky. And nary a breeze to ripple the surface despite Gunner's attempt to whistle up a wind.

Suddenly, Gunner grabbed Nick's arm with his massive paw and squeezed, hard. "Don't look now, Master Nick, but yer new Nazi pals have popped up from the briny to eyeball us personally." Gunner nodded silently to his right and then Nick saw it.

The U-boat periscope, water still streaming from its jet black–hooded top!

Glistening in the sun, it had emerged from the water not ten feet from where Nick and Gunner were sitting on the sailboat's bow. Gunner stared in open-mouthed wonder at the nearness of it. Why, he could spit and hit this one!

"An evil eye, all right. German," was all Gunner said. And then he did spit into the water, narrowly missing the scope itself.

"Can he see us now, do you think?" Nick asked, still in a whisper. The periscope was facing almost completely away from them, but Nick could still see a little bit of the lens.

Gunner adjusted his little gold spectacles and peered closely at the top of the motionless periscope. "Not likely. I think we're just outside his field of peripheral vision. Five degrees to port, though, and he's sighted us all right. That might give the young Herr *Kapitän* down there a start, right?" Gunner laughed softly. "An old navy man with a half-drowned cat and a young lad sittin' right on top of his bleedin' head!"

"What's he up to, d'you suppose?"

"Spying, what else?" Gunner said.

"He's looking at our shoreline all right," Nick whispered. "And he's in awfully close. As close as he's going to chance going in, if he's seen the Seven Devils on his chart, I mean."

"Aye. He gets any closer he's going to end up as the island's number-one tourist attraction," Gunner said, getting a laugh from Nick.

"Right, and now he's got himself in here, how's he going to get himself out?" Nick asked, as a crazy notion popped into his head.

"Well, assuming he can get his bow around in here, he'll have to take her out dead slow to the southeast, inside of them shoals over there, lyin' in the general direction of Hawke Point. And then a hard turn southeasterly to open sea."

"Just what I was thinkin', Gunner, just what I was thinkin'."

And at that moment, the periscope began to move through the water.

It was moving slowly, barely causing a ripple, distancing itself from the *Petrel,* and it was moving southeast, precisely the direction Nick and Gunner had anticipated. For Nick's purposes, he calculated, it was precisely the *right* direction.

"Hand me that bowline, Mr. Gunner, if you please," Nick said under his breath. "Easy does it, sir, but very quickly, thank you very much. Thank you."

Nick took the line Gunner handed him and, with eye-blinding speed, tied an expert slip-knot into one end, made the other end fast to the bronze cleat on the bow. He then coiled the line, stood in the bow, swung the loop twice round his head to get the feel of the line, and let the loop fly.

"Slip-knot, Gunner, just in case."

"Case o' what?" Gunner asked, but he knew soon enough. The boy had had another one of his patented ideas.

Nick's artfully thrown loop flew out straight and high and it caught the periscope perfectly. The line to the periscope went quickly taut, snapping loudly where it was cleated on the bow and suddenly the *Stormy Petrel* leapt forward in the water. She was soon steaming along at a good five knots, right in the wake of the German periscope! And they were headed south-southeast and right for Hawke Point, their original destination!

"Hooray!" cried Gunner, a huge smile on his jolly face. "A free ride, courtesy of Herr Hitler himself!"

He was glowing with pride over his young friend's ingenuity and indeed it was suddenly glorious to be surging along over the glassy water under a bright blue sky, all owing to the unwitting German submarine up ahead, moving through the water at periscope depth!

Some twenty years earlier, Gunner had been in the business of sinking these things and he now took special joy in Nick's ruse.

"I'd give three cheers for old Adolf himself right now, if he weren't such a black-hearted dog!" Nick cried, hanging out over the bow from the forestay. "So I'll cheer my old dog Jip instead! Hip, hip, huzzah, Jipper, wherever you are, we're on our way!"

"And here's to us our noble selves!" Gunner cried, joining Nick and leaning out over the pulpit. "None finer . . . and many a damn sight worse!"

"Hooray!" cried Nick, when suddenly the deck was yanked from beneath his feet and he felt himself hurtling backward through the air at an amazing speed. He had about one second to wonder about it and then he struck something hard and solid with the back of his head and all the lights went out at once, even the nightlight.

He was down a deep dark tunnel, lying on the bottom, and up at the top he could hear Gunner calling his name and he must have been in a very deep tunnel indeed, because the sound seemed to be coming from very far away.

"Nick . . . Nick, are you all right? Wake up, Master Nick! Can you hear me?"

Gunner swam into focus inches above his face. It occurred to him that he was lying flat on his back on the foredeck of his sailboat and his head hurt like the dickens. Gunner was asking him a lot of questions about something. It was all very confusing. His sister! Where was his sister? Did Blood have her?

"Katie!" Nick cried. "Is she all right?"

"She's fine, Master Nick. She and her dolly are back in the cockpit, snugged up with a good lifeline round her middle. Enjoyin' the sleigh ride, I'm sure. It's you I'm wonderin' about, lad. That mast you took a shine to is solid spruce, a hard, unforgivin' wood. Let me feel your head, laddie."

Gunner lifted Nick's head gently and felt the emerging bump, already about as big as a hen's egg, but no blood. The boy would be all right in a few minutes' time.

"What happened?" Nick asked, rubbing his head and sitting up on the deck. "Christmas!" he exclaimed, getting a drenching faceful of salty spray over the *Petrel*'s bow. "What's going on, Gunner? A sudden squall?"

His boat seemed to be moving incredibly fast, pounding through the swells, more like a tiny hand-built sailboat, and he wondered if he were still dreaming at the bottom of a tunnel. The flying wind and water were like you'd expect in a gale, yet it was still a fine sunny afternoon.

"Herr *Kapitän* decided to lean on his throttle a bit, now that we've safely cleared the Devils!" Gunner shouted above the spray and the roaring water.

"A bit! I'll say a bit," Nick cried, climbing to his feet. "There's not a sub on earth can go this fast, much less one as big as this! And I never even saw him surface! Let's take a look at him!"

He lunged forward to the pulpit, where he was immediately engulfed in a wall of water as the boat was pulled through a breaking wave by the racing submarine. Nick clung to the forestay and peered through the driven spray, the *Petrel*'s bow bucking beneath his bare feet like one of those broncos the cowboys in his books were always riding.

"Where's the sub, Gunner, I can't even see it!" The waves and the spray were such that he could barely see ten feet in front of his own boat.

"You can't see him, but he be right out there at the end o' that bowline, Nick, just where you left him," Gunner said, pulling himself carefully forward along the lifeline. "Runnin' along at periscope depth, givin' us a Nantucket sleigh ride, just like those whaling sods you're always talkin' about. Ain't it grand? Now, hand me that sharp knife of yours and I'll slice that line. Few more minutes of this, and that U-boat will tear this boat to timbers!"

"Periscope depth! You don't mean he's still *submerged*!" Nick shouted. "But that's impossible! No sub can travel at this speed on top of the water, much less underneath it!"

Unless she really was an Alpha Class, he thought. She had to be an Alpha!

"Which yer soon going to be under water yourself if I don't cut that line! Here, I'll just use me own blade and just–"

"Wait! Please! Don't cut it just yet!" Nick screamed above the roaring water. The *Petrel* lurched violently and Nick lost his footing on the spray-slick deck. He was sliding quickly aft on his back and only at the last moment could he grab a stanchion and save himself from going over the stern.

"What are you doing?" Gunner screamed, cupping one hand around his mouth. "I'm afraid he'll dive! And even if he don't, he's going to pull the bow right off of this little brig! I'm cuttin' her loose!"

"Hold on, Gunner, please!" Nick yelled, struggling forward, slipping and sliding along the careening deck, his arms pinwheeling, wildly grabbing at anything he could find to hold on to. "I've got to clock his boat speed first!"

"Boat speed! Who cares about boat–"

Then the deck went out from under both their feet. Nick was airborne for a moment and then the sloop's cockpit came up and caught him and he slammed his shoulder on the teak deck, safe for the moment, down in the cockpit. He raised his head, spitting saltwater from his mouth, his shoulder on fire. Seeing Gunner still on the bow, safely clinging to the forestay, he feverishly clawed through the sundry items stowed in the lazerette. No log there.

Petrel didn't have any modern instruments, just the old-fashioned log to tell the speed. You had to heave it out over the stern and gauge the boat's velocity by how much and how rapidly the line played out. He finally located the instrument in the sail-locker and staggered aft, leaping to avoid the tiller which was now whipping wildly from side to side. He thought of tying it off amidships to keep from losing his rudder but there wasn't time. Gunner was afraid the *Petrel* could be ripped apart or dragged under at any moment, but Nick wasn't afraid. Heroes didn't have to be braver than normal boys, Nick thought. Sometimes they just had to be brave for a few minutes longer.

"Nick, I'm cuttin' the line now!" Gunner shouted aft angrily. "Screws on the bow cleat is startin' to work, and yer pulpit's ready to give way any second and–"

"No!" Nick cried. "I beg you!" The boat heaved violently again and Nick grabbed for a stanchion to keep from being pitched into the boiling sea. He could hear and feel *Petrel*'s seams strained to the breaking point and he willed her to stay together long enough for him to do what he had to do. He owed it to his father. He owed it to himself. And maybe even his country.

Nelson the Strong, Nelson the Brave, Nelson the Lord of the Sea.

It was then that he saw his little sister out of the corner of his eye. Kate had curled herself up into a tiny ball, huddled against the cabin house bulkhead, with her doll and the cat Horatio both held tightly in her arms. Her eyes were squeezed shut tight, tight as could be, and she was shivering with the cold spray or something worse.

"What's wrong, Katie?" Nick called, but he knew.

"I'm afraid, Nicky," she cried in a tiny voice. "I've never been so afraid."

Nick looked in desperation from the racing submarine up ahead down to his little sister for a long moment and then at the log in his hand. He was deeply disappointed but angry with himself for forgetting how frightening the violent ride must be for his little sister. Hadn't he learned anything? What had his mother said? *I hope you're always clever enough to be afraid sometimes.* You didn't have to be too clever to know this was real danger, did you? He threw the unused speed log to the cockpit floor and bent to kiss his sister's tear-streaked cheek.

"Nothing wrong with being afraid, Kate. I'm afraid, too! I'm going to cut the line!" he said, and then he was leaping up to the cabin top and racing forward.

"Cut us loose, please, Mr. Gunner! Cut her loose, now!"

But Gunner's blade had already sawed through the taut line and it suddenly parted with a loud pop and the *Petrel* almost instantly lost her way, meaning her forward motion, quickly settling down into the sudden serenity of the deep blue sea. She seemed intact and still seaworthy for the moment. Nick joined Gunner on the bow and began pulling their severed line back aboard. He smiled weakly up at his friend.

"Sorry about that," Nick said, breathing heavily and unable to look Gunner in the eye. "Quite a ride, eh?"

"Not that it's any of my business, understand," Gunner said, coiling what was left of the bowline, "but would you mind tellin' me why you suddenly came to your bleedin' senses back there? Another minute and the whole boat was coming apart!"

Nick looked at Gunner. He'd never seen his friend truly angry before and it was not a sight to be recommended to the faint of heart. Nick found he still couldn't even look him in the eye.

"I–I really needed to clock that fish, Gunner. Still, I was stupid not to let you cut the line, when you wanted, wasn't I? I'm sorry."

"I cut that rope regardless of you, boy. Your boat or no, I wasn't waiting for you to sink her." Gunner looked at him, hard, and Nick turned away.

"Sorry," Nick said, and he really was. He'd been terribly stupid, but he was learning, he guessed. Sometimes you really did have to run away in order to fight another day.

"Useless word, sorry," Gunner added. "Ain't it, Nick?"

"It is," the boy agreed. "But still, I am."

"And what's so bleedin' important about Sergeant Sauerkraut's speed, anyway?"

"War, I guess."

"War, Nick?"

"Any day now. My father says it's going to be just like your war, Gunner. U-boats'll cut us off, starve us! That U-boat down there is just what Mr. Churchill is trying to warn everyone about! They're building them again, don't you see? We've got to tell everybody, warn them, Gunner. About these new German war machines! That's why I needed so to log her speed, Gunner! I'd never put anyone in danger and you know it! But the Nazis, they're putting us all in danger and–"

"Oh, look!" Kate said, as a huge black shadow fell across the drifting sloop. She was standing on the cabin top, the lifeline still securing her to the mast. Arm outstretched, her finger was pointing up at an ancient stone edifice towering on the rocky cliff high above them. "A giant's house!" Kate said.

Gunner and Nick looked up, dumbfounded. But Kate was right. The U-boat had unknowingly deposited the little vessel in the very shadow of her destination.

Hawke Castle.

CHAPTER XI

The Electrified Lagoon

· 6 June 1939 ·

IN HAWKE LAGOON

Stormy Petrel ghosted smoothly between the high rocky walls on either side of the inlet and into the shadowy confines of Hawke Lagoon. The afternoon breeze had filled in and Nick had judged his approach to the inlet perfectly. He realized that, if you didn't know exactly what to look for, as he himself did, you could sail by the hidden entrance of this lagoon a hundred times and never see it. He had never taken *Petrel* through the inlet, simply out of respect for Lord Hawke's well-known desire for privacy. And his reputation for accuracy with a pistol, although that, too, was probably only one of Gunner's fireside tales.

Hawke Lagoon was another world. Here inside the rocky cathedral, the air was still and peaceful. The water was a dark quiet pool of glassy green and all around them sheer walls of granite rose to a small patch of darkening sky, high above the little flag hanging limply at his masthead. Nick felt as if he were at the bottom of a huge natural well, and if it weren't for the opening in the cliff that had led from the open sea, it

Ghosting into Hawke Lagoon

would have been a frightening place to be. As it was, he knew they could get out in a hurry, if they had to, and that a quick escape might be a distinct possiblity.

"There's a dock just there, Master Nick!" Gunner said from the bow, and his words echoed around and up the walls of the lagoon.

They had doused both sails slipping into the lagoon and Nick let the *Petrel* glide slowly up alongside the dock. Gunner leapt off the bow at the nearest ladder with a mooring line and cleated it off, while Nick did the same with the stern line. The dock itself was steel, recently painted to a shiny dark green and very well maintained. Nick saw that there was a fuel pump farther along and coils of good manila line hung on the pylons for mooring. Mooring what? Nick wondered. Surely they didn't get many visitors in here. And yet, this was a dock that obviously saw a good deal of traffic. It was odd. But then, so was everything else lately.

While Gunner secured the boat, Nick and Kate walked the length of the dock, searching for a switch box to illuminate the lamps that hung out over the water from each dockpole. The lagoon was a shadowy little world and, now, with the black clouds rolling over up above, it was getting hard to see anything at all.

"There's no doorways and no steps leading up from this dock, Nick, so what's the point of having a dock?" asked Gunner, confirming Nick's puzzling and completely unsuccessful search for a stairway. "Unless yer a ghost, of course."

"Has to be a way up," said Nick. "Otherwise, right, the dock makes no sense."

"Which wouldn't be the first thing has made no sense today," said Gunner. "But then–"

Suddenly, the lagoon was flooded with light. Huge blinding floodlights, mounted in the rock above, and atop all the lampposts along the dock, and even a ring of underwater floodlamps circling the entire perimeter of the lagoon, were illuminated. The enormous underwater lights turned all of the water in the lagoon to a luminous shade of emerald green, like a mammoth fishbowl, and Nick could even see *Petrel*'s keel, hanging below her hull in the bright water. He saw a school of silver fish swim under the keel and dart away with incredible speed.

The world inside the lagoon, now lit from above and below, had become a place of eerie, shimmering beauty.

"You must leave at once!" boomed a voice from an unseen loudspeaker, mounted somewhere among the floodlights above in the rock.

"This is a restricted area. This is a military facility, restricted to government and military personnel. If you have not reboarded your vessel and left the lagoon within five minutes, severe measures will be taken. Extreme measures."

"I told you so, Nick," said Gunner, already uncleating the bowline from the dock so they could beat a hasty retreat. "Lord Hawke is one who likes his privacy. And now he means to blow us to kingdom come! Let's get out of here! Out! Out!"

"You now have four minutes," the voice boomed again, echoing around and around the stone walls. *"The dock you are standing on is electrified to ten thousand volts. Now the power is off. In four minutes it will be switched on. Anyone standing on or*

touching the dock at that time risks serious injury or death. Reboard your vessel immediately. This is your last warning!"

"What does 'lectrified' mean?" asked Katie.

"It means I'm getting your little footsies off this dock just in case," Nick said, lifting Kate up to a foot-wide ledge that ran some distance along the cliff face about shoulder high. Lifting her up, he thought he spied a way inside the sheer wall of rock.

"Gunner, come here! Look at this!" Nick cried, excited. He'd seen some kind of hidden door in the rock face. "There's a small door here! Right here in the rock! Someone's left it cracked open by mistake! I can't pull it open, but you could!"

A large depression just beside Kate's ledge revealed a thick steel door disguised to look like rock. It was open perhaps an inch. A strange red light was escaping around the edges of the stone-clad door. It didn't look very inviting, but it was worth a try.

Nick had somehow convinced himself that Lord Hawke could help them, though he had no real reason to believe this. He reassured himself that his instincts had served him well enough this day and it was no time to just give up and go home. Besides, he had three whole minutes before he'd be electrocuted.

"Three minutes. Repeat, three minutes. Electrification of the dock area will commence in three minutes. Leave the area at once!" the voice resounded.

"Hurry, Gunner!" cried Nick. "The chest!"

"I'm coming as fast as I bloody can, ain't I?" grumbled Gunner under his breath, and banging his head on the cabin top as he lurched below. "Damn that boy," he exclaimed, seeing that there were two leather straps securing the chest to the cabin floor and they wouldn't give an inch. Nick had buckled them too tightly. Gunner tried to work his fingers under the buckles but it was impossible. *Did Nick think someone was going to materialize out of thin air and steal the bloody thing?* Maybe, Gunner thought, remembering the strange ways of Captain William Blood, maybe he did think just that!

He grabbed the two metal buckles in both hands and pulled.

"Two minutes. Two minutes. Warning. Warning. Leave at once."

A loud klaxon horn started wailing, deafening in the confines of the rocky lagoon. Flashing red lights, mounted atop each of the dockposts, threw a whirling glare across the rocks, the water, his boat. Nick could see Gunner below through the portlight windows, straining against the straps that held the chest. Well, that was it then. He'd just grab Kate and jump to safety back aboard his boat. It was obvious they weren't very welcome here at Hawke Castle.

And then Gunner had exploded out of the companionway and was running down the dock toward him, the chest under his arm and a look of crazed determination on his face. "We're-going-to-get-*cooked*!" he cried as he pounded toward Nick and Katie.

"I got the door open another inch, Gunner!" Gunner put the chest down at his feet. "Can you do it?" Nick cried, the wailing horn ratcheting their adrenaline levels up a notch.

The crack in the door was open just wide enough for Gunner to insert his beefy fingers. He pulled mightily.

"One minute. One minute. Final warning. This is your final

warning. Remaining on the deck surface or touching any structure will be fatal to any living thing, human or animal. Repeat. One minute."

The door wouldn't budge.

Gunner looked at Nick.

"Give me a hand here, would you, mate? Maybe two," he said through clenched teeth. "Only if you're not busy, of course."

Nick slid both hands into the crack and braced his feet against the rock wall. "On two!" he said. He smiled up at Kate. He'd learned his lesson. His sister was safe up there and, if they had to, he and Gunner could jump up there as well.

There was a grilled bulb in the alcove above their heads that now began flashing red. Another siren joined the klaxon horn. It was bedlam in the little lagoon.

"Thirty seconds. Repeat thirty seconds. Leave at once!"

"One . . . TWO!" Nick cried and he put every ounce of strength he had against the door. Gunner grunted with superhuman effort, pulling as hard as ever he'd pulled in this life.

The door started to give, slowly at first, and then they had it; it had swung open a good three feet. They were in!

"Fifteen seconds!"

Gunner lifted Katie down from the ledge and placed her just inside the door on the rubber-lined floor. Nick slipped through the narrow opening, picked up Katie and moved a few feet further inside the strange red glow of the tunnel. Gunner lifted the chest, silently praying that it would fit through the three-foot opening. It was tight, but he got it through and placed it inside the tunnel door.

Nick gave a brief look over his shoulder and saw that the tunnel, which was lined with shiny white ceramic tiles, appeared to be about fifty yards long. He saw that it soon began sloping sharply downward, and the strange red light made them all look pink. There was another steel door at the far end.

Gunner turned sideways to squeeze through, and was instantly stuck. "Can't make it, guv'nor," he said, but then he seized up his great belly, drew up his full white beard and massive shoulders, and, looking just like Father Christmas trying to insert himself into a wee chimney, tried again.

Nick and Katie held their breaths.

"Five seconds!"

Gunner popped inside. They were all safe.

"Horatio!" Katie cried out in panic.

The big white cat was standing on the dock just outside the door, looking quizzically at the three of them. They'd forgotten all about him. He was peering curiously into the doorway, about to use another of his nine lives for the second time that day.

"Fish," Gunner said, and Horatio instantly leaped inside as the door swung shut with a loud hiss and then a solid thud, missing Horatio's tail by a fraction. All sirens and horns ceased in an instant. They looked at each other, bathed in the red light and the sudden silence, each taking a deep breath and trying to avoid thinking about what could have happened on the dock outside. The sudden silence was complete and a relief to their still ringing ears.

"Fish?" Nick asked Gunner, finally breaking the silence. "D'you say fish?"

"D'you think the puss would've jumped in here if I'd said, 'lectric dock, little kitty, step lively'?"

Nick smiled. "Right then. Everyone ready? There's another door at the end of this tunnel. It must lead to the castle proper somehow. Let's go find out if Lord Hawke is more neighborly in person than he seems at first glance," Nick said, grinning from ear to ear, and giving his sister a quick hug. He'd taken a calculated risk, but they were safely inside Hawke Castle and his instincts were not abandoning him. Not yet, at least.

"Oh sure, laddie, Lord Hawke's probably saving the real friendly bit for when we ring his front doorbell. Keeps a little bit o' dynamite under the doormat, he does, just to be neighborly, when sociable folks such as us comes callin'," Gunner muttered under his breath, lifting the chest and trailing his two friends into the hazy light of a tunnel that, as far as he knew, led straight down to Hades.

Which, at this point, would have hardly surprised him. "Probably offer us a nice pot o' poisoned tea, too," Gunner added, just loud enough for Nick to hear.

Gunner decided then and there that, after this day, *nothing* on this island would ever surprise him again.

He couldn't have been more wrong.

The greatest surprises of his life were waiting just beyond the next door.

CHAPTER XII

The Chinese Butler

· 6 June 1939 ·

HAWKE CASTLE

There was no handle on this second door, either, and it appeared to be made of steel as thick as Nick's old family Bible. And, of course, who knew what lay on the other side of it? The highly machined and polished steel reflected their three red-tinged images back at them like a mirror. It was not an inviting door, nor was it meant to be. As far as Gunner was concerned, this was probably the way the door to Hades *would* look, and therefore, no surprise to him.

"Why don't we just leave 'em a little note?" Gunner said, stroking his full white beard. "And just say, blimey, sorry we missed you, m'lord, we'll ring you on the telephone first thing in the mornin'."

Nick gave him a look and Gunner shrugged it off as a joke. He saw that look in Nick's eye once more and it crossed Gunner's mind that Nick might one day make a fine officer in His Majesty's Royal Navy. The good ones he'd known possessed exactly this kind of unbending determination. And he also realized that he'd always known this about the boy, ever since he'd been a wee one. He was a boy born with a heart for any fate.

"Maybe there's a hidden control panel that opens the door," Nick said, "but we probably need the code."

"Or maybe you just push it open," Katie said, and put her little hand against the steel. A kind of warning lamp above the steel door illuminated and began flashing. The door opened an inch or so, and Kate said, "See?"

SEA LEVEL. Blink. SEA LEVEL. Blink. SEA LEVEL, the warning sign read.

Nick was just about to wonder what that meant when the door swung fully open with a whoosh and a rush of misty ice-cold air. Gunner smelled something he recognized instantly. Marine-grade motor oil and high octane gasoline. It smelled like a shipyard in there. *Motor oil?* That meant motors, and what kind of motors could there be down here? They were inside a solid mountain of rock unless he was mistaken.

The white mist cleared.

"Well, I'll be blowed sideways to Rangoon," Gunner said, and they all stared in openmouthed wonder at the sight before them.

Another *lagoon*, except this one was entirely *inside* the mountainous rocky cliff!

A cavernous underground lake that was at least twice the size of the one they'd left above. There was a complex system of docks, all painted bright yellow, and boat slips, and connecting bridges. There was even a small crane, mounted on a set of small-gauge railroad tracks that ran the length of the main dock. To Nick's delight, there were several highly experimental watercraft, the likes of which he'd never seen before.

A hazy blue electric light filled the cavern and, here, too, there were underwater floodlights that turned the water a luminous yellow-green. There was a continuous hum in the background that Nick decided was the sound of generators or some other power source. The whole place was utterly astounding and the fact that it even *existed* on a place as remote and desolate as tiny Greybeard Island served only to make it that much more thrilling.

"Nick, look!" Kate said, pointing at one very strange craft. "A big floating cigar!" Nick followed her down the dock.

"Katie, do you know what this is?" Nick asked in breathless excitement. "Only the S-1 two-man aluminum submarine, that's all! The press reports said she went down with two crew off the Azores! And, that the top-secret project had been canceled because of the disaster! Well, then, what is this? The S-1 herself I'll tell you, and–"

Nick stopped dead in his tracks. She was far more beautiful close up than he'd ever dreamed she could be. A low whistle escaped his lips as he read the name painted in gold on the varnished transom.

THOR

What on earth was *Thor* doing in Lord Hawke's secret underground marina? Was this the secret base of "Captain Thor" himself?

She was indeed a boat a boy could only dream of, Nick thought, whistling silently as he gazed longingly at her. Sixty feet of gleaming mahogany, polished to such a luster you could see your face in her topsides! And, in the slip right next to the beautiful cruiser, a triple-engined seaplane, of all things! Nick, feeling like a child in the world's most wonderful candy shop, didn't know where to turn his attention first. The most beautiful boat in the world? Or a sleek, black seaplane deep inside an underground lake?

"Nicky!" Kate cried out from across the smoky blue lagoon. "Nicky, come look what I've found!" But her brother made no reply as he was so busy looking at a funny-looking black aeroplane that floated on the water. He and Gunner were so excited about all the silly boats and aeroplanes that Kate had decided to have a look all by herself.

She had found two strange little illuminated buttons next to another steel door in the cavern wall. There were indeed the two funniest buttons she had ever seen.

One read UP.

One read DOWN.

What on earth could they be?

That's all they said. What went up? What went down? She couldn't even imagine, but she thought they were very funny. She stood up on her tiptoes and jabbed her index finger at the DOWN button.

Nothing happened.

She punched the other one and it started blinking but that was all. Boring. She pushed DOWN again, but UP kept blinking. Really boring.

She turned around to see what her brother and Gunner were doing with the little floating aeroplane. She cupped her hands around her mouth and called out to him across the underground harbor.

"Nicky, come on! We've got to find Jipper and you're going

to be late for supper again!" she said. Not that she was all that worried about Nicky getting into trouble, mind you, but she was getting very hungry herself. She wanted to get home to her book, too–*Black Beauty*. Her most favorite.

"One minute, Katie!" her brother said. He had climbed out on one of the aeroplane's floating pontoons and was talking to Gunner. He was so silly about some things lately that it was starting to make her cranky. All these old boats and aeroplanes. Really. Why weren't they having any fun anymore? Were they ever going to have another picnic? She stuck her tongue out at Nicky and Gunner, even though she knew they couldn't see her, and it made her feel a little bit better.

Now, if she had a horse just like Beauty here on Greybeard, why she could ride all– What was that? She'd heard a funny noise directly behind her. Pirates? She turned around very slowly with her eyes squinched shut just in case.

No pirates, thank goodness, she saw, cracking one eye open the teeniest bit.

Just a silly little room where the big steel door with the buttons had been. A tiny room, actually, with no furniture at all except a pretty wooden bench with a green velvet cushion.

She stepped forward and peered inside.

It was a very nice room even if it was a wee bit small. The walls were paneled with gleaming wood. In addition to the settee, there was a pretty gold mirror with an eagle on top. She wanted to sit on that little velvet cushion, it looked so comfortable. And, after all, she was very tired.

She stepped inside and sat down and it was quite comfortable, indeed. And on either side of the open door were two pretty lamps with an "H" and a crown over it on the lampshades. It was all very fancy, she thought. La-dee-dah, as Mother would say.

Then the big steel door slid shut with a whoosh of air.

Oh my goodness. She seemed to be locked in the tiny room.

Then the room began to shake and rumble and her head fell back against the wall. She felt like the room was moving although that plainly could not be. Rooms didn't move except maybe in China when they had those terrible earthquakes she'd heard about. Was this an earthquake? Inside a mountain? She didn't think so, but you couldn't help but wonder. At least she didn't live in China where you had to worry about such things all the time.

She decided to just sit there and not be afraid and make the best of it. Sooner or later her brother would come over and knock on the door and let her out. He was quite accustomed to rescuing her, after all. She'd just have to wait.

Suddenly, the pretty room stopped moving. It jerked once, then stopped for good. The door whooshed back inside the wall, where it must have disappeared before. She sat on the settee and swung her legs back and forth, waiting to wake up from the funny dream. She blinked her eyes. She blinked them again. It was too impossible.

The room *had moved!*

Instead of all the silly boats and aeroplanes that had been outside the room before, now there was daylight coming through windows and a tall man standing just outside the door looking in at her. He looked just as surprised to see her as she was to see him. Maybe more so because his eyes were staring so hard they were almost coming out of his head and his mouth hung open and he had forgotten to close it. He was very nice-looking, but he did have the most peculiar expression.

"Hullo," Kate said. "Are you Chinese?"

"I beg your pardon, miss?"

"I know they only have earthquakes in China and I've just been in one that made this funny little room move, so I thought you might be Chinese," Katie said, trying to be friendly. She had noticed that the man had a sword in his hand and, although he didn't look the type to be cutting a little girl's head off, one couldn't be too careful.

"I assure you, I am not Chinese. I am, as it happens, from Cornwall."

Katie thought he spoke beautiful English. Deciding he was most definitely not Chinese, she smiled at him.

"Are you going to cut my head off?" she asked.

"Certainly not!" said the handsome man.

"Then why do you have a sword?"

The man looked at the sword as if he'd completely forgotten he was carrying it. Then he looked back at Katie. He kept forgetting to close his mouth when he stared at her. He was funny.

"Well, because I have just been–that is, I mean to say, I have just been giving my employer a fencing lesson. Besides, this is not a sword, as you so incorrectly put it; it is called a foil." He put the foil behind his back. "I say, this is most remarkable! How on earth did you get–"

"So this isn't China?" Katie said, hopping off the settee.

"Hardly. This is Hawke Castle. Look here, I must say–"

Katie offered him her hand. He took it.

"Well! Are you Lord Hawke?" Katie asked. "That's who we came to visit."

"Certainly not. I am in Lord Hawke's employ. Although I very much doubt that you came to visit him. We do not receive visitors here, we generally shoot them. You are quite fortunate to be alive, my child. There is clearly a grievous flaw in the security system. I am in charge of any number of things here, including keeping people off the premises. I seem to be failing miserably. If someone such as yourself, I mean to say, if a mere five-year-old–"

"I'm six and three-quarters, actually," Katie said, "practically seven."

"I beg your pardon, six. If a six-year-old *child* can penetrate–sorry, six and three-quarters–can penetrate our security defenses, then heaven knows who–tell me, how on God's green earth did you come to be in this castle? It's quite impossible, you know!"

"Nicky says nothing is impossible. We came here on my brother's sailboat. It's called *Stormy Petrel*, after the bird that always flies ahead of the storm. Nicky says that's what we do. Fly before the storm, I mean. Have you ever heard of that bird?"

"I have a passing acquaintance with ornithology, yes. You sailed in from the sea, did you? Well, of course, that is quite impossible."

"Why's that?"

"Because, my dear child," the handsome man puffed himself up and said, "there is a thirty-foot chain-mesh curtain called a Seagate that prohibits any boat–or submarine, for that matter–from either entering or leaving Hawke Lagoon unless I open it. It's made of titanium and steel and is virtually indestuctible. When raised, it spans the opening to the lagoon, lying just below the water level so as to be completely invisible. I designed it myself and it's the only one of its kind on earth." The man smiled down at her. "Completely impenetrable," he said, rocking back on his heels in a funny way, as if he was very happy with himself. "Completely."

"So then you must have left your gate open," Katie said with a bright smile. "Or somebody else opened it for you, I suppose."

"Aha! Well, that is quite impossible! You see, the only possible way the Seagate can be opened or closed is with this device here, which is always on my person."

He reached inside the tweed coat he was wearing over his funny white suit. "It's the world's first radio-wave, handheld, remote controller! Just a minute, where is the blasted thing–" He patted all his pockets, finally pulling a small, silvery object from one of them. "Ah, here it is! See, the red button is–I say! That's quite impossible!"

"You really are quite funny. My brother thinks *nothing* is impossible and you think *everything* is impossible!"

"Hold on! Why, the green button is lit! The Seagate *is*, as you say, open! Impossible! How could that–ah, yes. Lord Hawke's thrust to the heart must have struck my breast pocket. Marvelous swordsman, he is. Hit me right in the green button! By jove, that's quite remarkable. Well, well, I suppose I do jolly well owe you an apology. The Seagate is open."

"You see, nothing's impossible. That's what my brother always says. And he's my hero. He saved Horatio."

"Your brother. You mean there are more of you? I must sound the alarm and–"

"Are you going to kidnap me? You can if you want to. My brother will only rescue me again. He always does, you see.

Some people have an angel sitting on their shoulder. I have a brother!"

"Why on earth would I want to *kidnap* you?" the man said, taking a step backward. "Frankly, I am so shocked by your appearance that I hardly know what to even make of you! You say you have a brother? I say! Is he lurking about the premises as well?"

"Well, he is around here somewhere," Kate said. "Since the room I was in moved, I'm not sure where he is exactly. The last time I saw him, he was on an aeroplane. He said it was experimental. He's very interested in anything experimental. Anything at all. He's very smart, actually."

"My word! *On an aeroplane,* you say? You don't mean to say he– How old is this brother of yours?"

"He's twelve. Gunner's probably fifty at least. I'm staying with him now. Right next to the room with all the guns."

"I say!" the man said, looking shocked. "Did you say *guns*?"

"Right, guns. Gunner wanted to put a cannon on our boat but we never got to do it. I don't think we could hit anybody anyway. A very small little cannon. Just in case we ran into any pirates, although you probably think that's impossible, too. Since pirates don't exist anymore, I mean."

"Gunner? Who on earth is he?"

"He's our friend. The one with all the guns."

"*All the guns?* I think perhaps you'd better step inside. What is your name, child?"

"Katie McIver," she said with a curtsy and a smile. "What's yours?"

"Hobbes. Miss," the man said, shaking her hand. "I hold the title of Commander in the British Royal Navy, but that won't be necessary. You may call me simply Hobbes. Everyone else does. You're not Angus McIver's child by any chance?"

"Sure! He's my father! So's that your old 'luminium cigar we saw, Hobbes?" she asked, referring to the small two-man sub Nick had pointed out to her.

"I'm frightfully sorry, I'm afraid my hearing's not quite up to par anymore. Did you ask if I smoked aluminum cigars?" Hobbes replied.

"You can't smoke them, silly, they'd be too wet!" Katie giggled.

"Yes, quite right. Who'd wish to smoke a wet cigar? Ahem. Well, there you are then. Where did you say this brother of yours was? And the chappie with all the guns?"

"I told you! On an aeroplane."

"Ah, yes, you said that, didn't you? Well, there you have it. I say, would you like a cup of tea?"

CHAPTER XIII

Captain Thor's Surprise

· 6 June 1939 ·
HAWKE CASTLE

"You're not a Nazi, are you, Hobbes?"

"I beg your pardon?"

"I imagine you're not," Kate said, lifting another toasted and buttered crumpet to her mouth. "Not if you're a friend of my father's. He hates Nazis."

"Please be assured that I am neither a Nazi nor a Chinaman."

"Who's that funny-looking man in the picture over the fireplace, Hobbes?"

"That is the savior of your country, Miss. Winston Spencer Churchill. His lordship's uncle, as it happens. And he is hardly funny-looking, as you put it."

Katie was glad the funny man wasn't so jumpy anymore. Ever since she'd told Hobbes that her father was Angus McIver and that she lived in the Greybeard Light, he seemed ever so much more relaxed. He didn't even seem to be worried anymore that they'd gotten inside his castle. Or about Nicky and Gunner messing about with all of his boats and aeroplanes. Her father, Hobbes said, was a fine man and he was delighted to have his friend's charming daughter as a guest at Hawke Castle. He looked forward to meeting Nick and Gunner, too, as soon as he'd gotten the weary Kate some tea. Kate thought he was awfully nice, in a funny way.

Now, having tea before the fire in a massive hearth in the great hall of Hawke Castle, Kate had been telling her new friend of their recent adventures. He seemed interested in the chest they'd found, and very interested in Nazis, too, especially the German submarine that had given them such a ride. And how her brother had lassoed it, trying to find out how fast it'd go.

"I suppose you're not actually a Nazi, Hobbes. I can't imagine you in a strawberry patch, which is where they all hide, you know." She carefully lifted her cup, trying not to spill as she took a sip. "Mmm, yummy."

"I endeavor to give satisfaction, Miss," Hobbes said with a smile.

"Are you a butler, Hobbes?" Kate asked, looking at him quizzically.

"I beg your pardon, Miss," Hobbes said nonchalantly, although he'd never heard a more outrageous question in his life.

"I only asked because I thought butlers wore frock coats and striped trousers, not their underwear."

Hobbes barely suppressed a gasp.

"I assure you that I am not a butler nor are these my undergarments. This is my fencing attire. And this is my favorite tweed jacket which, while stylish, also provides a modicum of warmth in this drafty old pile. While perhaps not appropriate for tea, this is the wardrobe of choice for active swordplay. Now, about this pirate kidnapping your dog, I must say I–"

"He's really scary, Hobbes, with little skulls in his beard and a big sword and even his name is scary. Billy Blood. Isn't that a frightful name?"

Hobbes dropped his teacup.

It hit the stone floor with a tinkling crash and broke into a thousand pieces. Some of the tea splashed up on Katie's apron and her kneesocks.

"Oh! I'm terribly sorry, my dear, I hope I didn't–I hope I didn't–" Hobbes suddenly stopped and stood straight up. He looked Kate squarely in the eyes. "Did you say Billy Blood? I distinctly heard you say that name. Billy Blood. Did you say it?"

The warm smile had flown from Hobbes's face, replaced by a stormy look that startled Kate. It looked like thunder was coming next, maybe lightning.

"Yes, Billy Blood is his name. We met him at the Greybeard Inn last night after we found the treasure chest I told you about. I think he's bad," Kate said. "Nick thinks he's after our treasure chest and that's why he's kidnapped our dog. Is he a friend of yours?"

"Never could one man lay less claim to my friendship than William Blood. It is my life's great misfortune to know that vile kidnapper. Know what a kidnapper is, my child?"

"Someone who steals poor little children?" Kate replied, a furrow of worry creasing her smooth brow. "Steals them from their beds in the night?"

"That's Billy all right. A heartless thief of wee children, although he prefers rich ones to poor ones, my dear. He roams the Seven Seas, stealing the babies of wealthy parents! Holds them somewhere until exorbitant ransoms are paid. I thought we had lost sight of that vile kidnapper forever, but apparently we have not. This is grave news you bring, my dear, grave news indeed."

Hobbes didn't look well. All the color had drained from his face and his hands shook as he knelt and picked up the pieces of broken teacup.

"So he's back, is he? Well, well, well. Our old friend returns, does he? I suppose it's not enough that we have Germans to contend with, is it? Sailing about, spying on us, staring at us night and day?"

"Are you all right, Hobbes?" Kate asked. The man looked positively ill.

"Hmm? Bit of a shock is all, nothing really. I'm afraid we must go and see Lord Hawke at once. Hmm. Yes. Come with me, child!" Hobbes said, getting to his feet. "It is imperative that you tell Lord Hawke everything you know or remember about your meeting with this man Blood. How he looked, what he said, everything! Let's go!"

"May I finish my tea?"

"Sorry, my dear, we've not a moment to spare!"

He saw his fencing foil resting against the stone hearth and took it in hand as if he'd be soon in need of it. Then he took her hand and led her through the great hall, past many suits of armor standing at attention and the door to the little room that moved.

Just as they were walking past it, the door slid into the wall again and there stood Nick and Gunner. Gunner was holding the sea chest, and the cat Horatio was perched on his shoulder. Kate noticed that Hobbes was staring at the little group with the same bug-eyed stare that he'd first used on her. He'd forgotten to close his mouth again, too. Kate stepped into the lift and gave her brother a peck on the cheek.

"Hullo, Nick. In case you're wondering, this is not China and he is not Chinese, he's Hobbes," Kate said matter-of-factly. She noticed that Nicky's mouth was wide open too, and he was staring at her newfound friend.

"Captain Thor!" Nick said, still staring at Hobbes and standing riveted inside the little room. "So you are here! I saw your beautiful boat down there and I thought you–"

"He's not Captain Thor, Nicky, his name is Commander Hobbes and he makes the most wonderful tea and crumpets," Katie said. "He lets me call him just Hobbes. And he's not going to cut off my head with his sword, either."

"So you're Nick McIver!" Hobbes said, as if he'd been waiting his whole life to meet him. He stuck out his hand to Nick, shook it, and then practically pulled Nicky into the room, looking him over from head to toe. "I am so very happy to meet you, young Nick! I simply can't thank you enough for all the diligent work you've done for us! Your sister was just telling me about your encounter with a German submarine. I understand you attempted some kind of fix on her running speed? Most valiant piece of naval espionage, my boy! Worthy of some kind of recognition from the Ministry, I should imagine. Yes!"

"Captain Thor!" Nick exclaimed. "I'm so very happy to meet you, as well, sir! Ever since the day I first saw your splendid craft leaving the harbor I've been hoping to meet the man who owned her. And, of course my father holds you in the very highest–"

"Please, Nick," Hobbes said, taking his arm. "I am loath to interrupt what are likely expressions of kindness, but we were just on our way to see his lordship on a matter of some urgency. Please feel free to join us, both of you. Lord Hawke yields to no one in his desire for privacy, but in this case I'm sure he'll make a joyous exception. Indeed! Children in the house again!"

"May we bring him this sea chest, sir?" Nick asked. "This is my friend Gunner who is carrying it." Gunner smiled at Hobbes who nodded politely, but it was clear Gunner would have preferred to be anywhere at all but Hawke Castle. Nick smiled and continued. "This chest is why we took a chance and came here, sir. Lord Hawke being a world-famous scientific detective, I mean. Probably the only man alive who can solve the mystery of an old chest that looks so new, is what we are hoping."

"Quite true, quite true, I daresay it really doesn't smack of antiquity at all," Hobbes said, putting a finger to the side of his nose and bending to inspect it. "Not at all! It does not look a recent vintage, does it? Strange. Hmm, yes."

"Right, almost like it washed up on shore from another time, doesn't it, sir?"

Hobbes clasped his hand to Nick's shoulder and locked up his eyes with a warm smile.

"Indeed, you've done the right thing by coming here, Nick! We must bring it at once to his lordship's study. It most certainly has a direct bearing on a desperate case that Lord Hawke and I have been investigating for many years." Hobbes once more ran his hand over the smooth surface of the sea chest.

"The chest has my own name on it, too, Commander," Nick said.

"All very curious," Hobbes said, and bounded away.

They all struck off in hot pursuit of Hobbes who was galloping up the broad stone steps of the wide grand staircase that led from the great hall to the floors above. "Follow me!" Hobbes cried over his shoulder, taking the stairs three at a time and waving them onward with his whippy little sword.

"Lord love us all, will you look at this room, Nick?" Gunner said with a whistle of appreciation as they came to the end of a lengthy gallery that stretched high above the sea.

"This is the library," Hobbes said. They had entered a large circular room that was, in fact, the ground floor of the castle turret. "It's quite extensive, actually," Hobbes continued, "and takes up this and the three floors you see above you. It includes every volume on ancient military history and weaponry in existence and of course all the important works of English and world literature, science, and the arts. Including translations of many of his lordship's own works of forensic science, of course."

They all looked at the three circular floors of books spiraling around the open shaft up the center. Late-afternoon sunlight streamed down from windows somewhere high above. In the center of the library floor, there was a gleaming brass pole that seemed to disappear high into the ceiling four floors above. Hobbes saw Nick admiring it.

"It's an American firehouse pole," Hobbes said. "His lordship acquired it while on a visit to Chicago."

As Nick tried to imagine a fat English lord in a pinstripe suit sliding down a four-story fireman's pole, Hobbes opened the door to a small adjoining room with desk, chair, and a black telephone. He pulled the door shut and they could see him talking, rather urgently it seemed, through a window set in the door. He kept looking at Nick while he spoke, nodding his head, and soon emerged from the little telephone room wearing a happy smile.

"He'll grant you ten minutes, no longer," Hobbes said, pushing the lift button and gazing up as the slender mahogany carriage descended from the top floor. "It will be interesting to see how he reacts."

"What do you mean, Commander?" Nick asked.

"To the three of you, I mean." Hobbes replied, casting his eye over the visitors. "Outside of myself, his lordship's uncle Winston Churchill, and a handful of people at Buckingham Palace, my Lord Hawke hasn't uttered a word to a single living soul in more than five years. And, Nick?"

"Sir?"

"Call me Hobbes. Everyone does."

CHAPTER XIV

Lord Hawke's Tea Party

· 6 June 1939 ·

HAWKE CASTLE

"It's open."

A deep, gruff voice came from somewhere behind the thick carved double doors of Lord Hawke's private study. Hobbes opened them and silently ushered them all inside. The room took Nick's breath away. Circular, round as a compass, completely encircled in glass, it had panoramic views in every direction!

The floor, Nick saw, was a Mercator projection map of the English Channel inlaid in brilliantly colored marble. Nick found himself standing astride a compass rose inlaid in silver, and, looking west for the mainland of England, he saw its green marble coastline disappearing under Lord Hawke's large mahogany desk. Little Kate stood, one foot on the green coast of France, the other in the blue stone channel. A fleet of scale-model battleships and cruisers were arrayed across the floor. So, Nick saw, Hawke waged mock sea battles too, on this vast likeness of the Channel!

"I suppose I should introduce myself, shouldn't I?" Hawke

said, walking around a large round table set with silver and china. He was uncomfortable, Nick could tell, clearly unused to the company of strangers. "And then you can all tell me your names, won't you? I believe that's still how it's done, when uninvited strangers intrude on one's closely guarded privacy." He began filling his cup with tea and sat down, frowning, and folding his hands before him on the table. He was met with silence.

Hobbes looked stricken. "I'm terribly sorry, m'lord, but I thought you wished us to come up. We won't trouble you now, if it's not convenient, surely." Hawke looked at Hobbes for a moment, unsmiling, and then turned his gaze to the window, staring in brooding silence at the sea below.

"As you wish," Hawke said quietly.

"It's my fault, your lordship," Nick said, nervously. "We thought it was important to bring some things to your attention, and–"

"Yes, yes, come along, children. Gunner," Hobbes said, gathering them up, "his lordship feels perhaps another time would be best." Hobbes was already moving toward the door. "We'll set a proper time for a formal visit. I think that would be best."

"Yes," Nick said, backing toward the door. "Some other time. We'll come back some other time. Come along, Kate." Nick took his sister's hand and joined Hobbes at the door. They were all backing out the way they'd come in, pulling the door closed after them when Hawke finally spoke.

"No, no, no," Hawke said, turning to them, a pained expression in his eyes. "Don't go. Please. I'm terribly sorry. You must understand that I am not used to having anyone but Hobbes for company. You're all here, aren't you, so I insist that you have some tea. Please sit. I insist." Nick looked at Hobbes, who nodded, and they all returned to the table and took their places, staring at each other as the embarrassing silence deepened and filled the room.

"Well," Lord Hawke finally began, "as you may have guessed, I am Lord Hawke, the reclusive proprietor of this rather drafty old establishment," he said, smiling when they acknowledged his feeble joke. "Now, tell me who all of you are, won't you?" He looked at Hobbes. "Hobbes, you're exempted, of course," he said with a smile. "I already know who you are, don't I?"

Nick guessed that Hawke was making these small jokes in an effort to ease the strain of the situation and he found himself both grateful and impressed.

"I see you've all met Commander Hobbes. He's far too modest to tell you this, but he is the Royal Navy's most brilliant weapons designer. All of the experimental craft you must have seen moored in my underground basin are his work." Nick looked at Hobbes with the kind of reverence normally allotted to the gods. Here, then, was the genius behind the two-man sub! And the tri-motor seaplane!

"Who might you be, child?" Hawke suddenly asked Kate, swiveling his head in her direction. He had a fierce gaze, and you knew when he was looking at you.

"Katie McIver, age six," Kate said shyly, "almost seven."

"Ages, too? I'll excuse myself from that one, if you don't mind," said Hawke. "But, thank you, Kate. This poor room hasn't known the sound of children's voices in many, many years, I'm terribly sad to say."

A haunted, wounded look passed across his face and Nick had a sense of deep mourning about the man, of a heavy sadness filling the castle. Sorrow seemed to have settled in here, like dust on the chandeliers and in the draperies. Hawke, though hardly older than Nick's father, had the look of a man aged prematurely by grief.

Hawke was tall with sharply chiseled features, and wore long curly blond hair that brushed the collar of his loose-fitting white cotton shirt. He certainly didn't look anything at all like Nick had expected an English lord to look. Although he'd never met a peer of the realm before, Nick more or less expected them all to be short and rather plump, with red cheeks and wavy white hair. And wearing blue pinstriped suits with gold watch chains spangled across their waistcoats.

Lord Hawke looked, Nick thought–well, he looked more like one of the Three Musketeers! Behind his sadness, there remained a faint sparkle in his crinkly blue eyes, the look of someone who, once upon a time, had gotten a great deal of fun out of life.

"I'm Archibald Steele, m'lord," Nick heard Gunner say, interrupting his study of Lord Hawke. "Royal Navy gunnery, retired. Me friends call me Gunner, sir, and I'm most sorry to have intruded upon your privacy."

Archibald? Nick looked at Gunner, astounded. He'd never heard Gunner divulge his real name before.

"May I count myself among their number, Gunner, and call you that as well?" Hawke asked.

"I'd be honored, m'lord," Gunner said, smiling nervously. He still had the air of a man who was feeling lucky just because he'd not yet been shot at point-blank range. He hadn't wanted to come here, and clearly Hawke was making an enormous effort to be polite about their intrusion. In an odd way, though, Gunner felt that the man was glad they were there.

"Well, Gunner, have some tea and tell me more about this mysterious sea chest. Hobbes assures me it's something I should see, or I should never have subjected the three of you to my black moods and poor manners."

"It's here, m'lord, let me place it on the table," Gunner said, and he did, the muscles in his massive forearms bulging with the effort.

Lord Hawke looked at the chest for a long moment, running his hand over it, and then at Nick, and once again Nick had the feeling he was undergoing the careful scrutiny of Hawke's appraising eye.

"And you, of course, must be young Nicholas McIver," Hawke said, pausing before going on. "Although we've never met, I'm sure you've guessed our common interest in, shall I say, 'migratory birds,' Mr. McIver?"

Once again, a little joke to ease the terrible tension that still filled the room.

"Were you aware that your father and I were in fact, comrades-in-arms?"

Nick was both astounded and delighted. To be involved in such an important mission, keeping an eye on the Nazis for Churchill, and to possibly have the help of a famous detective such as Lord Hawke, and Hobbes too–well, it defied belief. "No, sir! What with all the island rumors, Gunner and I, why, we weren't even sure if you still lived here! Much less that you were one of Father's fellow birdwatchers!"

"I expect not! No one did! In fact, until today, Hobbes and I have been one of the best kept secrets in all England!" His face turned suddenly grave, remembering that a serious breach of security had just occurred. Two children and an old navy warhorse had just penetrated his impenetrable fortress. His manner turned deadly serious once more.

"Sadly, Nick, it's unfortunate that you've come here. This is a top-secret military installation. Our systems are all designed specifically to prevent just such intrusions as yours. But, now that you're here, you must swear yourselves to solemn secrecy. In the name of His Majesty, King George, I must have your sacred oath that you will reveal nothing of what you have seen or will hear today. Lives are at stake, including that of Commander Hobbes and your own father, Nick."

He looked at them each in turn. Katie and Gunner looked as if they had fallen off the planet and landed in a different world. And, in a way, they had. A top-secret naval installation? On an island where nothing ever happened?

"His lordship is correct. Do you so solemnly swear, upon your sacred honor?" Hobbes asked.

"Upon our sacred honor, your lordship," they answered as one.

"In the name of His Majesty the King," Kate added, in an awed little whisper. This, she thought, was secret-keeping at its very best!

"I only allowed Hobbes to bring you up here," Hawke said, "because there are three issues of grave importance. The first being the appearance, according to what Hobbes tells me, of William Blood on this island. Is this true?" he asked, looking directly at Nick.

"I'm afraid so," said Nick. "Although I just met him myself, the fellow has kidnapped my dog, sir."

Lord Hawke regarded him in solemn silence for a moment.

"I'm sorry," Hawke said. "You must all understand that Blood's appearance is an event of enormous significance to me personally. I will explain why that is so in due course. However, I understand that your encounter with Blood was preceded by the discovery of this particular chest. An officer's seagoing chest that would appear to be of the type common in the Navy in the beginning of the nineteenth century, and yet it has the finish of a brand-new one, doesn't it? Odd, I must say. And, finally, Hobbes and I have seen a dramatic increase in U-boat activity round the island in recent weeks. Apparently, Nick, there's an Alpha-Class lurking about?"

"Gunner and I were nearly able to put a clock on an Alpha-Class, sir," Nick said, with a mixture of excitement and modesty. "We estimate she was doing at least seventeen knots, your lordship. Submerged!"

"Seventeen submerged!" Hawke's eyes widened in amazement. "Do you hear that, Hobbes? Nick, I want you to give the commander a complete account of this submarine's performance. Did you identify her?"

"U-33, your lordship," Nick said. "May I borrow a pen to write it all down, sir?"

"I insist that you do so immediately, while it's fresh," Hawke said, handing the boy his own fat black Mont Blanc pen.

Commander Hobbes drew a sharp breath. "U-33. That's the one we've been looking for, your lordship! I knew she was cruising in these waters, I knew it! Well done, lad, splendid effort!"

"We'll need every scrap of information on her, lad," Hawke said, his eyes gleaming with excitement as Nick scribbled furiously. "And the sooner this new intelligence gets across the

Channel to Chartwell the better, eh, Hobbes? Tonight, if that's at all possible? Uncle Winston will be delighted!"

"Tonight, sir," Hobbes said, nodding in agreement. "*Thor* is fueled and ready."

"Let's turn our attention to this sea chest, shall we?" Hawke said, pulling the chest toward him. "Nick, be so kind as to tell me everything you can remember about the circumstances of its first appearance. Then we'll find out what's inside."

Nick found himself involuntarily taking a very deep breath.

I'm going to find out what's inside the chest, and it's going to change my life forever.

He told Lord Hawke about the discovery of the chest. About his shock at seeing his own name on the lid. And how surprised he'd been at its appearance when he'd noticed that, despite it's age, it was still flawless, shiny, perfect. Or, rather, that it had *become* so while in his possession.

"And you say Billy Blood appeared on the very night you discovered the chest?" Hawke asked.

"Yes, sir," Nick answered. "He was at the Greybeard Inn when we stopped in to get dry. It was cold and raining something awful and Katie's timbers were shivering something fierce. We thought Gunner might have a fire going, and he did."

"Gunner, you were there last night, you saw Blood when he first appeared?" Hawke asked. Nick noticed that he was making notes as everyone spoke.

"Appeared is the right word for it, your lordship, which it's just what they did, all right," Gunner replied, finally realizing that not only was Hawke not going to shoot them for invading his privacy, it looked like he was actually going to help them get to the bottom of all these strange goings-on! "They just appeared, sir, but I didn't see 'em do it. Popped-in, sort of thing. Out of thin air, m'lord."

"They? What do you mean?" asked Hawke. "They?"

"Well, there was two of 'em, wasn't there, m'lord? Plus the bird? See, it was a dark and blowy night, as your lordship will remember. And all my lads as usually likes to lift a pint down at the inn had stayed home with the missus to keep warm and dry. Place was empty as a crypt, nobody there but meself and me old tomcat, Horatio, and wind howlin' around the windows and down the chimney so I built us a nice fire, I did, sir. Horatio bein' a cat as likes his nice warm fire." Gunner stopped and took a look around to see if anyone was listening to his tale. Nick couldn't remember a time when Gunner'd had this much to say, but he supposed having such a famous audience as Lord Hawke encouraged him to loosen his tongue.

"Please continue, Gunner," Lord Hawke said, holding a match to his cigar and sending a stream of smoke from the corner of his mouth. "And please don't leave anything out, no matter how unimportant you feel it may be."

"Well, like I was sayin', custom was scarce last night on account of the storm, and I stepped out into the kitchen to ladle a dollop of cream into Horatio's bowl, him bein' my only patron of the evenin', and when I steps back, there's this swervy-looking polecat sittin' there, starin' into the fire and smokin' this long bony pipe. And his mate, lurkin' back in the shadows, like he didn't want no one lookin' at him."

Gunner paused and looked at his hands, trying to remember everything. Nick saw Katie shudder at this mention of Blood's companion and he shuddered himself at the memory of the man's horribly disfigured face in the firelight as Gunner resumed his tale.

"I didn't hear the door bang open or bang shut, nor even the rain blowin' in or blowin' out! Or, anythin' at all! But, there them piratical creatures sat, all cosy by the fire with that bright red parrot perched on the one's shoulder, whisperin' in his ear and–"

"Parrot! We didn't see any parrot, Gunner!" Nick said, leaning forward and grabbing Gunner's arm. He turned to Hawke. "Your lordship, I forgot to mention that there was a strange parrot guarding the chest when we found it! Bit my sister it did, too!"

"It doesn't really hurt anymore," Katie said, proudly holding up her bandaged finger for all to inspect.

"On my word, sir," Gunner said. "Blood had a parrot he did, big, red, nasty-lookin' bird, too. Shifty-eyed creature perched on his shoulder and talked a blue streak, too, though you couldn't make out what it was sayin'. Parrot talked right in his master's ear, he did, like he was tellin' him secrets!"

"I'm sorry, sir," Nick said to Hawke. "There was no parrot in the room when we saw Blood. Only a single red feather."

"He's correct, sir," Gunner said. "Now I recollect it, the parrot was flown from this Blood's shoulder when the young ones arrived. Never saw that bird again, either. Just disappeared, it did. Popped in, popped out. Blink of a ruddy eye, your lordship, that's how they navigate, these three."

"So, Hobbes, Bill's brought old Bones with him this time," Hawke said. "That's not good."

"Indeed he has, and Snake Eye, too, apparently," Hobbes added, his face clouded with a dark frown.

"Yes!" Nick cried. "That's right! Blood called the fellow hiding in the shadows, Snake Eye! Who is he, Commander?"

"Someone you never in this life want to meet again," Hawke said, placing his hand on Nick's shoulder. "If you can help it. I'm sorry, I must fetch some of our chronological equipment from my laboratory. Will you all excuse me for a few moments?" And with that, the famous detective stepped to the gleaming brass fireman's pole, leapt onto it, and dropped instantly from sight.

So much for plump little lords in pinstriped suits, Nick thought with a smile.

CHAPTER XV

The Mystery of Time

· 6 June 1939 ·

HAWKE CASTLE

Let's open the thing up, shall we?" Lord Hawke said. By the time Hawke had returned via the lift with the laboratory equipment, Gunner and Hobbes had moved the sea chest to a curved table next to the westernmost window. The dying rays of the sun caught the gleaming surface of the wooden lid. Nick was amazed to see how the old chest and its brass lock looked, even in this fading light. It looked, well, almost *brand-new*!

"The lock works will be left intact, of course, Hobbes?" Lord Hawke said. He was watching Hobbes's every move. Nick was surprised to see Hobbes's deft movements with the small precision tools as he proceeded to pick and pry at the shiny lock; it was like watching a master craftsman.

"Of course, sir," Hobbes said. "I assume we'll want to preserve its current chronology for time-dating in the laboratory this evening."

"Precisely, Hobbes. A step ahead of me, as usual," Hawke said, and took another deep puff on his pungent cigar. "I'm sure we'll find the lock works keeping track with the laboratory chronograph. The lock is attached to the chest, so it is traveling at the same speed, don't you think?"

"No question, sir. They'll be traveling together," Hobbes said through his clenched teeth. He was chewing on the tortoise-shell amulet that hung from around his neck, lost in concentration.

"Should we put the spectral chronometer on it, Hobbes–before we open the box, I mean?" Hawke asked, peering more closely at the lock. "Just in case?"

"Wouldn't hurt, m'lord," Hobbes said. He opened a mahogany case Hawke had brought from the laboratory and pulled out an odd-looking contraption. It appeared to be a sophisticated naval chronometer, but featured a number of strange dials, and had many-colored wires dangling from it. These wires were attached to two large brass clock housings with plain white faces and a red sweep second hand. In red type on the left face were the letters GMT. On the right, was the word FLUX. Nick stared at the contraption as Hobbes attached its wires by little clips to both the lock and the sea chest itself.

"GMT? That's Greenwich Mean Time, right?" Nick asked, feeling foolish as soon as the question was out of his mouth.

"Right-ho," Hobbes said, not even looking up from his work. "The exact time everywhere on earth as measured precisely up in Greenwich. A constant, as it were."

"And flux?" Nick asked. He noticed that the sweep second hand on the FLUX face began spinning wildly, too fast to see, the instant Hobbes attached its clip to the sea chest.

"A bit more complicated," said Lord Hawke. "Flux is simply

movement in time. Backward. Forward. Either direction, actually."

"Considerably more complicated, I'd say, m'lord," said Hobbes with a little laugh, inserting another copper wire into the keyhole of the lock.

"Excuse me, please, but what in the world is going on here?" Nick said, getting to his feet. The things he was hearing were making him doubt his own sanity. Nothing was making any sense, and it was a bit frightening.

"The chest has moved forward, Nick. But you just can't see it," Lord Hawke said, putting a calming hand on Nick's shoulder in an attempt to soothe him.

"It's moving in another dimension, lad," Hobbes said.

"It's moved forward in time, son," said Hawke.

"With respect, sir, it has *not* moved forward in time!" Nick said, his face reddening. "Because that is not even remotely, with all due respect to you both, not even *remotely* possible!"

"Sit down, Nick," Lord Hawke said kindly. "Sit down for a moment, and Hobbes and I will try to explain it to you."

"Do you know what the word 'flux' actually means, Nick?" asked Hobbes, gently placing the instrument on the table before Nick. The thin red needle was a spinning blur.

"I–I think so, sir," said Nick, taking a deep breath. "Change. Isn't that it, change?"

"Exactly," said Hobbes. "Change. It means change, and also, continuous movement. A constant state of movement. Along a sort of *track,* for want of a better word, called the fourth dimension, or, non-Euclidean space-time. Does that make sense?"

"That's what time is, Nick, *flux*. A constant state of

movement," Hawke said, pointing at the spinning FLUX dial. "Where is the needle now? When you say 'now,' what does that really mean, Nick?"

Nick looked at him, then at the red blur of the spinning second hand.

"It means *now,*" Nick said, "It means *right now,* doesn't it? I think all this is–is just too–I don't know what to think. I'm sorry." The boy rested his chin in both hands and stared sullenly at the spinning dial.

"I know how you feel, Nicholas," Lord Hawke said kindly. "I had precisely the same reaction the first time Hobbes explained the notion to me. Perfectly natural reaction. It is difficult to grasp."

"Thank you, sir," Nick said, straining to get his emotions under control. "I am terribly sorry. Hobbes, won't you continue?"

"*Now* is just a point in time, isn't it?" said Hobbes, hardly missing a beat. "And, as soon as you've said it, it's gone, laddie. It's long gone, boy. *It's moved.* It's somewhere else on the track. And the track has no end. Only points back there, here, and up ahead. And you can only see the point where you are, but that doesn't mean the others don't exist, does it? They're there, laddie, but you can only see them if you move! Here, let me try and show you–"

Hobbes pulled a scrap of paper from the drawer and extracted a black fountain pen from his pocket. He drew a line from left to right across the page and marked each end.

x

D________________________________E

"Time is that line, Nick," Hobbes said. "From 'D' the 'dawn of time' to 'E,' not the end, but 'eternity.' And 'x' is now. You can put an 'x' anywhere on the line, but the line stays constant. Each moment reaches backward and forward to all other moments. You can't see the time line, but everybody knows it's there. For centuries, men have known this, but it took Leonardo da Vinci's genius to enable man to move along the line, backward or forward. Do you begin to see that, Nick?"

"Or allow the objects to move to you," Hawke added, "like this chest you found on the beach, lad, like this chest sitting right here. It has moved along the track to you. That's how you came to find it there on the beach. Even as you so rightly said, it could *not* have washed ashore. It didn't, lad. It moved along the track. That's why we call it a 'traveler.' It's traveling through time. This traveler is a wooden box. But human beings can travel, too."

"But, that's not possible, is it? That's just not p-possible, is it?" Nick stammered, but he really didn't know what to believe anymore. He buried his face in his hands. He had the bewildering feeling he didn't know what was real and what wasn't anymore.

Hawke sat down and took Nick's hand in his, looking into his eyes with a depth of feeling Nick had not seen in them before. Even when the name Billy Blood had hung in the air above the table like a dreadful curse.

"Oh, it's possible, my boy," Hawke said. "Believe me, it is more than possible. It is real. Hobbes and I have been delving into the notion of time travel for years. But, until today, we simply didn't have the proper equipment. There is an entire laboratory in my cellar, filled with our complex and utterly failed experiments. But, don't worry, lad. It's all right.

After a while, this notion of traveling in time will become as real to you as sailing your boat around the island."

"How?" Nick cried, feeling the frustration welling up inside. "How can that be? Please tell me how that can be!" Time travel? It was unthinkable. Wasn't it?

The two men looked at each other and back at Nick.

"The answer is inside the chest, laddie," Hobbes said, gently, with real compassion for Nick's confusion and frustration. It was a frustration he and Lord Hawke had been living with for five long years. They could hardly expect the boy to just accept what they were saying at face value. Hawke put a consoling hand on Nick's troubled head. Nick lifted his head and looked into Hawke's eyes, which were clear and blue like a child's, and with a child's large, unblinking gaze.

"Why, you've found a time engine, you have, Nicholas McIver!" Lord Hawke said, in a jubilant whisper. "You've brought me Leonardo da Vinci's miracle time machine."

CHAPTER XVI

The Tempus Machina

· 6 June 1939 ·

HAWKE CASTLE

The sun was rapidly fleeing from the sky, leaving towering piles of purple clouds tinged with gold on the distant horizon. Most of the light inside the castle now came from the masses of chandelier candles above, and countless other candles on tall stands around Lord Hawke's tower room, all adding to the dreamlike quality of the moment.

The hasp of the padlock suddenly opened with a soft pop.

The lid of the chest was open! It seemed to rise a fraction, all on its own accord. There was a tiny noise of escaping air. Nick thought he might observe wisps of smoke or something seeping out around the edges, but there was nothing escaping from the box that Nick could see.

"Oh my goodness oh my goodness oh my goodness," Kate was whispering at Nick's side, and then she jumped behind her brother, peeking out from around him with eyes wide as Wedgwood saucers. Nick, too, felt himself taking rapid, shallow breaths, his heart pounding.

The lid of the chest rose another half inch.

"Leonardo da Vinci himself designed the wondrous instrument inside this chest, Nick," Hobbes said, bending to peer closely under the lid. "Herein, children, lies the culmination of mankind's ingenuity, realized almost half a millennium ago by the greatest mind the world has ever seen. A mind able to pierce the vale of time, the closest we've come to the mind of God, my dear children! The miracle of time itself lies within the simple machine inside this box!"

Hobbes gingerly lifted the lid of the sea chest. Hawke couldn't bear the suspense. He strode over to the window and gazed out at the sea.

They all leaned forward to peer inside in wide-eyed wonder, half expecting bolts of lightning or plumes of fire to blaze from the chest. Nick gasped. Gunner emitted a choked snort of some kind. Kate stood on tiptoes to get a better view.

The chest was full, near to the top, with water! No wonder it had been so heavy for its size, Nick thought.

"Ordinary seawater, I believe," Hobbes said, matter-of-factly, swirling the water with his index finger and then touching the finger to his tongue. "Yes, seawater. Hydrogen, oxygen, and an abundance of sodium. The only physical environment that will sustain the machine over a long period. The source of its power, too. Seawater, the very cradle of life, is the cradle of time as well! Splendid, isn't it?"

"Hobbes!" Lord Hawke barked in frustration, his face still to the window. "*Do we have the machine*, or *do we not have the machine?*"

"Sorry, m'lord," Hobbes said, rolling up his sleeves. He leaned right over the chest, peered into the murky water, and plunged one arm up to the elbow with a small splash, fishing around with a worried look on his face. "That's odd, I think it's not–wait a minute, here's something–I think it's just a, yes, that's it!" His face was lit with a huge smile as he plunged his other hand into the water.

And then he pulled a gleaming golden ball–a small globe, really–from the water, an orb that dazzled the entire room with its brilliance. Hobbes cradled it with both hands, lifting it up so that it caught all of the candlelight from the chandeliers above.

Nick couldn't tell if the ball was radiating light from within, or if its polished roundness was magnifying the many candles in the room, multiplying the candlepower a thousand-fold.

Kate squeezed his hand and whispered softly, "It's beautiful, Nicky, the most beautiful jewel in the whole wide world!"

"We have it at last, your lordship!" Hobbes exulted. "Leonardo da Vinci's ultimate triumph, the Tempus Machina! "

Hawke spun round and fixed his eyes on the brilliant golden orb.

"We have it, Hobbes," Hawke said, gazing at the shining thing with a look akin to reverence. "We have it indeed." He strode rapidly over to Hobbes and placed his hand on the shining ball.

"We have the Tempus Machina!" Hawke roared, throwing his head back and letting his full voice ascend into the dark reaches of the castle rooftop. His eyes were aglow and his whole body seemed to tremble. He looked to Nick like a man going instantly from darkness to light, his very soul lit by the gleam of the golden orb.

"Give you joy of the day, sir," Hobbes said. "It's been five very long years, your lordship."

Hawke nodded and reached out again to touch the still-dripping object in Hobbes's hands. It was as if he wanted to keep confirming with his fingers what his eyes told him was finally in his possession at last, Leonardo's triumphant victory over time itself.

"So, how does this thing work?" Nick asked, trying to get some normality back in his life by asking the only normal question he could think of.

Hobbes smiled. "Believe it or not, it is a masterpiece of simplicity, Nick. I'll show you in due time, but first I need to carefully examine the sphere's exterior to determine how it survived the voyage." Hobbes had put the machine on a velvet pillow and, with a large magnifying glass, was examining every facet of the globe.

"Voyage from where?" Nick asked.

"Why, from either the past or the future, Nick. We don't know yet. From the looks of the shipping container, though, I'd say the past," Hobbes replied, looking at the globe from a lower angle. "If you'll look closely inside the sea chest the globe arrived in, you'll see that it's lead-lined, with an inner lining of glass. A technique quite common one hundred and fifty years ago. And, as Lord Hawke has already pointed out, it's an early nineteenth-century naval officer's chest. I would imagine it was sent to you by just such a person, wouldn't you agree, your lordship?"

Lord Hawke was watching Hobbes's inspection, puffing thoughtfully on his cigar. Now that he possessed the globe, he appeared to have not a care in the world.

"Quite right, Hobbes. This Captain McIver of the H.M.S. *Merlin*, Edinburgh, as it reads on his chest, is very possibly a

The Tempus Machina

distant ancestor of yours, Nick. Has some reason to contact you, perhaps. From the looks of the carvings and insignia on the chest, he would appear to be someone serving Lord Nelson in actions against the French fleet. The Napoleonic Wars, as we refer to them now. Many a famous encounter with the French took place in these very waters, as you may know. Some brilliant actions were fought not two miles from this shore." Hawke pointed his cigar to the west. "Right out there," he said.

"Yes," Nick said, turning to look out the window to the sea, "I know."

And, at that exact moment, a gleaming black periscope silently broke the surface of the moonlit sea, not two miles from the entrance to Hawke Lagoon. Its hooded eye rotated left, then right, forty-five degrees. Below, another eye, a human eye, was watching, fixated on the blazing lights coming from the tower soaring above Castle Hawke!

"You think the chest was *sent* to me?" Nick asked, incredulously, and Hobbes smiled.

"I think it's the most likely possibility, yes. Kate told me, I believe, that you and Kate liked to sail or play along that particular stretch of coast almost every day. So, the odds of you personally discovering it were almost one hundred percent. A rather ideal place to send it, too, for someone calculating the odds. Hidden, accessible only by sea, and deserted most of the time, except for you and your sister." Hobbes had a faraway look in his eyes, and Nick could sense him working it out in his mind. "Yes, Nick, I think it was deliberately sent to you personally."

"Jip is really the one that found it," said Katie. "While he was chasing that mean old parrot."

"Jip," Nick said, looking suddenly at his sister, his face going pale in the candlelight.

Jip.

"What time is it?" Nick asked, a rising note of panic in his voice.

I suggest we meet at the deserted shanty down by the old wharf at six this evening.

"About half past seven, I imagine," said Hawke taking a puff. "Why?"

"Half past seven!" Nick cried desperately. In all the excitement, he had somehow lost track of time and his appointment with Billy Blood. How stupid could he be? "Blood said to meet him near the wharf by six if I ever wanted to see Jipper again! He'll kill 'im, I know he will! Six o'clock! We'll be lucky to get there by nine! How could I have been so stupid? Poor Jipper, he probably thought I didn't care about him, he thought–"

"It's all right, lad. Calm down," Hobbes said, chuckling softly. "I wouldn't worry about it, now."

Nick's face reddened with anger.

"Of course, you wouldn't worry about it!" Nick cried. "He's not your dog!" Nick lowered his eyes, not wanting them to see his pain and anger. Hawke put his hand on Nick's shoulder, and after a moment, Nick looked up at him. "Sorry, sir."

"That's not what Hobbes meant, Nick," Hawke said, pointing his cigar at the golden ball sparkling in the candlelight.

"Time simply has a different meaning for you now. Instead of you being a slave to it, time is now a slave to you. It's on your side now, lad. Time is on your side." Hawke patted his shoulder and walked back to the window to puff his cigar.

"You've got all the time in the world now, Nick," Hobbes said. "All the time in the world. You need never be late, or early, for anything again."

"My mum would like that," Nick said with a shy smile.

Perhaps this strange machine might come in handy after all. He felt a sharp pang at this thought of his mother. His parents were nearing London by now, in a desperate bid to save their dear old lighthouse home.

The boy sighed, and returned his attention to the object. He had problems of his own, of a more immediate nature. But, if Hobbes was right, and the "tempus machine" or, whatever they called it, really did work, why, then, he still just might be able to rescue his dog. He still had time, they said.

All the time in the world.

"I'm sorry, Hobbes," Nick said quietly. "I didn't mean to get angry and shout at you. I'm just so worried about that old dog. He's a sweet old dog, really, hasn't got a mean bone in his body. And I think Billy Blood is capable of anything, anything at all!"

Hobbes sat beside the boy and put his arm round his shoulder, speaking gently into his ear.

"That he is, lad, that he is. But don't you see, now that we have the machine, so are we. Capable of anything! We'll get Jip back for you, lad. Don't you worry," Hobbes said. "We'll rescue Jip, and we'll rescue little Annabel and Alexander, too. Don't you worry, lad."

Nick looked up at him.

"Annabel and Alexander? Who are they, Hobbes?"

Hobbes looked at him, searching his eyes. He glanced over at Lord Hawke, smoking by the window, and lowered his voice even more. "You don't know?"

"No," whispered Nick. "Can you tell me?"

"It's the worst possible tragedy, lad," Hobbes whispered. "And it's the reason his lordship and I have secluded ourselves from the world for all these many years, working in absolute secrecy, and with all the scientific knowledge we can muster, to solve the mystery. The one mystery his lordship has never been able to solve. And the most tragic."

"What mystery, Hobbes?" Nick whispered. "What happened?" He'd heard all of Gunner's stories of mysterious disappearances at Hawke Castle, but had always chalked them up to idle rumors and gossip, gossip being the only thing on his island more plentiful than cows.

"The disappearance of Lord Hawke's two young children, lad. The abduction of little Annabel and Alexander. It accounts for all the gloom of sadness that lies over this poor house."

Nick gasped. "But that's terrible! There've been no end of rumors, of course, but please tell me what really happened, sir."

"It happened one night just outside this very room. Over five long years ago, now, right out there on that terrace overlooking the sea. It was a stormy night, terrible wind and rain were whipping across the sea, and his lordship had taken the children out on the terrace to watch the storm come up the channel. Little Alexander, he loved lightning, loved to see it, wasn't afraid of it like most children, and he–" Hobbes stopped, choking back his emotion. "I'm sorry, lad. Anyway, I called his lordship in from the terrace to read an important telex just in over the wire from London. The children pleaded with their father to stay outside and watch the storm. He agreed. When he went back outside to rejoin them, well, they were gone. Gone in a heartbeat."

"Hobbes, I'm so sorry," Nick said, his voice trembling. "I had no idea."

"So we searched the rocks below for days, and the sea, too, thinking they'd somehow climbed up over the rail and–but we never found them, lad, not a trace. One instant they were there, laughing and playing, the next instant–well, we never found them."

"Hobbes, I feel terrible. Here we've invaded Lord Hawke's privacy and reminded him of–"

"Lad, listen to me. Don't you understand what's going on here tonight? Why do you think his lordship is so jubilant? You have brought him hope, Nick! Hope that he can find his children and bring them safely home! He's been waiting for this moment for five long years, lad! With your machine, he finally has a chance!"

"With the machine, you say? So you think the children are–" Nick furrowed his brow, trying to accept all that he was hearing. "You think the children are lost in time, Hobbes."

Hobbes looked at him, his eyes alight.

"Not lost, lad. But, they are somewhere in time all right. We think Billy Blood has them!" Hobbes looked up to see if Lord Hawke had overheard his conversation, but Hawke remained at the window, hands clasped behind his back, content.

Nick understood, and lowered his voice. "But, why, Hobbes, why? Why would Blood travel all the way to the future to kidnap Lord Hawke's children?"

"Past, future, makes no difference to him. And it's the oldest motive of all, I'm afraid," Hobbes whispered. "Money. Ransom money. Lord Hawke is sole heir to one of the last great fortunes in England. Billy roams the earth, amassing riches and power wherever he finds them. He finances all of his evil schemes with the enormous ransoms he demands for kidnapped children. Since time is no object to him, obviously, he saw a way to get at the Hawke fortune by coming to the future and kidnapping his lordship's children."

"He's still holding them for ransom?"

"The ransom was paid, many times over," Hobbes said darkly. "In full. The children were never returned. Billy holds them captive in the past. He will keep raising the ransom until the Hawke fortune is completely depleted. That's why we have got to find them first! It's the reason his lordship and I have dedicated most of the last five years of our lives to solving the riddle of time travel. It's a race against time, lad. We've vowed to rescue Annabel and Alexander and destroy their infamous kidnapper before his lordship's money runs out. We were getting close, too, and then you appeared with that miraculous sea chest–" Hobbes was startled by Lord Hawke's hand on his shoulder.

"I say, Hobbes, take a look at this!" Hawke had noticed something they'd missed in the excitement of opening the chest. Fastened inside the lid of the chest was a small parcel, wrapped in what appeared to be oilskin, and tied with a bright purple ribbon. He removed it and handed it to Hobbes.

Hobbes untied the outer ribbon and carefully removed the oilskin covering. Inside was a long sheet of heavy foolscap, all rolled up and tied with a scarlet ribbon. Hobbes untied the ribbon and spread the paper on the table next to the golden globe. Nick saw that there were hurried scrawls of ink down the length of the thing. Hobbes took the magnifying glass and began to examine them.

"What is it, Hobbes?" Hawke asked, leaning over to get a better look.

"Why, it's a letter, your lordship!" Hobbes said. "It's dated 3rd October, 1805, and was written at sea!"

"May I read it as well?" Nick asked.

Hobbes regarded him with a smile.

"I should say so, lad. *It's addressed to you.*" Hobbes handed the magnifying glass to Nick, who bent to see if this could possibly be so. It was. The letter, to Nick's astonishment, was addressed MASTER NICHOLAS MCIVER, GREYBEARD ISLAND.

From above, in the darkness high above the flickering candles, came a fluttering sound, a sound of large wings beating against air. They all looked up, and saw nothing. But they *heard* something. A sound that chilled them all to the bone.

A human voice, issuing from the throat of a bird: *Letter for Nick–squawk–letter for Nick–squawk.*

And with a great flapping of wings the bird escaped through the open window of the castle's observatory at the top of the turret.

"Bones," Hawke said. "Damn his eyes. He knows we've got the Tempus Machina!"

"Winging his way to tell Blood even now," Hobbes said, watching the dark shadow flapping over the shining sea.

CHAPTER XVII

Captain McIver's Letter

· 3 October 1805 ·

AT SEA

Nicholas,

I write in great haste with much to say and beg your forgiveness for the informality of this message. My command, Merlin, *forty-eight-gun English man-of-war, is gravely threatened. We are afire and sinking. If we do not reach England two days hence, the future of Admiral Lord Nelson's entire fleet of twenty-seven ships of the line is in gravest jeopardy.*

Merlin *was badly holed below the waterline this morning in an engagement with the French frigate,* Bellemère, *under the command of Admiral Rambouillet. We are pumping furiously but the sea is winning this battle. We have lost many hands, our fore topsails and mizzen topsails were blown away. Half our cannons are gone or unfireable and there is fire in the forward powder hold. The second officer believes he can extinguish the fire before she blows, that is, if we don't sink first!*

We find ourselves trapped. The cove on your island, where we hoped to make our repairs, is closed to us by seven vicious tentacles of reef. We were able to limp inside the haven, but now are unable to sail ourselves out. We are in dire need of someone with expert knowledge of these reefs and local waters as no reef is marked on our chart!

Our only escape route is a deepwater channel to the southeast, down around the southern tip of Greybeard Island, where stands Castle Hawke. But that way lies the Mystère, *a seventy-four-gun French frigate under the command of William Blood, a traitorous rogue who once sailed under me as second in command. This dog now sails for our enemy Napoleon, but will sail under any flag as he is the most piratical and evil creature on the high seas.*

The safe return of Merlin *to England, now so close to home after six months on station in the Leeward Islands, is vital to an English victory. We possess crucial intelligence gained from a captured Spanish spy about an almost certain alliance between France and the king of Spain. Admiral Lord Nelson must have this knowledge before the fleet sails for France three days hence! We have reason to suspect the navies of both our enemies are laying a fatal trap for Nelson and the fleet.*

We must reach England and forewarn Nelson!

Our situation is desperate. Our only hope is the golden ball you will by now have discovered in my chest. With this letter, I am bequeathing it solely to you. It is an instrument of great antiquity and power which was one of two captured when we sank Valais *off Antibes in early June. We later learned the two instruments were en route to Emperor Napoleon himself. Blood was able to steal one of the machines from my cabin during his mutiny. He has sworn to deliver both to Napoleon in return for a fortune in gold and command of the entire French fleet against England, the traitorous dog! A warning: To gain the second golden ball, and with it the means to defeat England, William Blood will do anything!*

Anything.

Although you may scarce credit it, the ball enables its owner to travel through time. This makes it a formidable weapon but, should both machines fall into the hands of Blood, all would be lost! Then his power would be limitless and put him beyond the reach of anyone! I have entrusted it to you, and placed you in peril, only because of the extremity of our situation. If we go to the bottom, Nelson and the fleet will sail into a deathtrap. And Blood will recover the second time machine and so rule the seas unchecked. As long as one machine remains in responsible hands, honorable hands, we have at least a prayer. Now, Nicholas, it is in your hands!

My second officer and navigator, now lost in battle, showed me its ease of use. Open the ball along its "equator" and you will instantly learn its secrets.

I used the machine this morning to locate you and can vouch for its safety and dependability. I'd use it, too, to travel to England and warn Nelson, but I won't desert my post with my ship and shipmates in such a perilous state.

If you are inclined to come to the aid of your king, country, and our beloved Admiral Lord Nelson, my ship the Merlin *is located off Greybeard Island, 49 degrees, 2 minutes latitude by 2 degrees, 2 minutes longitude.*

You must enter that exact location into the machine.

The time here is four bells in the forenoon watch, third October, year of our lord, '05.

We must warn Nelson!

Hurry.

Your most affectionate ancestor,

Captain Nicholas McIver

Nick finished reading aloud and looked up to see everyone staring at him. Were they all just as flabbergasted as he was? He started to say something but realized he'd been struck speechless by the amazing letter. If you could credit it, and he was beginning to, he was being asked to come to the aid of an ancestor from the last century and help navigate a burning man-of-war over what were certainly the Seven Devils!

No one in England knew those reefs as well as he did! If they succeeded and then managed to escape Billy Blood, they could reach England in time to save Admiral Nelson from a French and Spanish ambush! Nick McIver of Greybeard Island coming to the rescue of Admiral Nelson? For once, words failed him.

Lord Hawke rose from the table and began pacing rapidly by the window, asking questions and issuing instructions to Hobbes. Nick noticed that he paced with a heavy foot, hands clenched behind his back, head down, like a captain on his quarterdeck upon the eve of battle.

"Do you know these reefs the captain is speaking of, Nick?" Hawke asked.

"Yes, your lordship, very well," Nick answered. "The Seven Devils. They spread out from the base of Gravestone Rock. Just last week I was forced by weather to sail *Stormy Petrel* into the cove that lies inside them. And, at any rate, it was necessary to learn the reefs because I do a lot of sailing in that area. I'm sure it's the cove he mentions in the letter. Sandy Cove, it's called, and as treacherous a stretch of reef as there is, lies around that cove, sir. Twists and turns like a razor-backed serpent."

"And how did you 'learn the reefs,' as you put it?" asked Hawke.

"I swam them, sir, in the mornings when I wasn't helping my father to build the sloop. I used a diving mask and was able to map every square meter of reef. It took most of last summer, but I did it," Nick said, smiling. "There are ways for any vessel to get in and out of that reef, sir. You just have to know where the problems are!"

"You mapped them, these reefs?" Hawke asked. "Do you still have this map?"

"Oh, of course, your lordship. I use it all the time! It's in my chart locker on the *Petrel.* She's moored now at your dock, down in the lagoon. It's how we came to be here, sir, begging your pardon. By sea."

Hawke cast a sharp eye at Hobbes. "By sea, Hobbes?"

"Seagate was opened accidentally, m'lord," Hobbes said. "A silly accident."

"A happy accident, I'd say! We must prepare to depart at once, my dear Hobbes, per Captain McIver's instructions. I shall accompany young Nicholas to the *Merlin* in an attempt to rescue Captain McIver. We will need weapons, of course."

"What would be appropriate, m'lord?" Hobbes asked with some excitement, weapons being one of his favorite topics. "Perhaps the .35 caliber gravity-feed machine gun I designed for you, sir? The Maharaja of Jaipur affair? Chaps at the War Office rejected it as too radical, I believe they called it."

"Radical! Ha! We quite approve of the radical around here, don't we, Hobbes? Still, the .35 might be a bit unsportsmanlike for a mission of this nature, don't you think, old chap? Simple pistol or sword for me, I should think," Hawke replied. "Sword perhaps a more sporting choice than a pistol, but we'll need both. Yes, swords and pistols definitely for this sort of work. Do you fancy a sword, Nick? Had any fencing at all, at your school, anything of that sort?"

Hobbes smiled in the direction of Nick, both of them finding the idea that fencing might be on the curriculum at the tiny island school the silliest notion. But Lord Hawke was ardent about the sport and simply assumed everyone else was, as well.

"His lordship was three times fencing champion up at Oxford, you know. Nineteen twenty-two was your third victory, wasn't it, m'lord?" Hobbes asked. Hawke waved the question aside.

"Hobbes only mentions it because *he* was my fencing tutor," Hawke smiled. "But, please, back to business. Have you done any fencing at all, Nick?"

"I'm afraid not, your lordship, never," Nick said. He remembered Billy's bone-handled dagger in his jacket and felt for it. Still there. Good. He just might get the chance to return it to Blood. In person, if he was lucky.

"A sword for the lad in any case, Hobbes. One never knows," said Hawke, still pacing. "There could be close-in work, before this is over."

"Pistols, swords. Very good, sir," Hobbes said.

"Can I go, too?" Katie asked. "Back to the olden days?" She'd been so unusually quiet, they'd almost forgotten she was present. Hawke smiled at her.

"No, Kate, not this trip, I'm afraid. Perhaps the next," Hawke said, looking out at the quiet, moonlit sea. "I say, I've got a splendid idea! Hobbes, the moon is out and I've seldom seen the channel so peaceful. Lovely night for a fast nip across, I should think. You've got young Nick's report on the Alpha sub, and if you left immediately, it could be in Uncle

Winston's hands in time for his critically important speech to Parliament tomorrow evening!"

"Very good, sir," Hobbes said. "And, perhaps Gunner and Kate might accompany me? Should be a most pleasant trip, over and back?"

"Oh, yes!" Kate squealed, clapping her hands together. "Oh, can we go, Gunner, please?"

"I–I suppose we could, little missy," Gunner said, looking perplexed. "So long as the commander doesn't feel we'd be a bother."

"On the contrary, I should be glad of your company, Gunner," Hobbes replied, picking Kate up in his arms. "I'll provision *Thor* for a two-day voyage, stock the larder chock-full of cookies and crumpets! That way we can take our time coming home."

"Oh, won't it be fun, Gunner?" Kate asked, her arm around her new friend's neck. "Please say we can go!"

Gunner smiled at Katie, but he looked troubled, too. He cleared his throat to gain everyone's attention.

"If I might, your lordship," Gunner said, "I think I could be more helpful to you and the young master on yer rescue mission. I've got some twenty years of experience in naval matters of this kind under me keel and I think with me gunnery I could help get some o' the *Merlin*'s cannonades back in firin' order, sir, if I could be so bold, your lordship, as to toot me own horn, sir. Also, as I knows how to hand, reef, and steer any vessel that floats as well, your lordship, I'd like to offer me humble services."

Hawke stopped pacing and looked at Gunner. Gunner felt those appraising eyes of Hawke's that Nick had felt earlier. "The child was placed in your charge while Angus and Emily McIver are in London, Gunner," he said, looking at little Kate now happily perched on Hobbes's shoulders. "And that's a serious responsibility. Still, I suppose Hobbes would make an eminently suitable guardian while we're off to the past, eh, Hobbes?"

"Indeed, I'd be delighted," Hobbes said, bouncing Kate up and down on his shoulders. "I think the two of us can manage well enough. But, before you go, there's a Ministry letter inside my jacket pocket that I think you should read, your lordship. Nick gave it to me for safekeeping, sir. Bit of trouble for our friend Angus McIver, I'm afraid."

Hawke extracted the letter from the inside pocket, scanned it quickly, and replaced it in Hobbes's jacket.

"Dreadful business, dreadful," Hawke said. "So that's why they're off to London. Well, we must find a way to help, mustn't we, Hobbes? And we shall, we shall!"

"Have you made a decision then, sir?" Gunner asked, his eyes full of hope. "Can I join the expedition?" Hawke regarded him closely as Nick went to stand beside his friend and lend his support.

"I believe Gunner would be a great help to us, sir," Nick said, earning Gunner's undying gratitude. "He truly would! And, I'm sure my parents would not object to Katie being left in the care of someone like Commander Hobbes, sir."

Hawke's face broke into a broad grin and he clapped both Gunner and Nick on the back.

"Capital, dash it all! I think it's a capital idea, Gunner, a splendid notion! I don't know why I didn't think of it myself! Yes, I must admit you look a man who'd bring a great deal of gunpowder to the party, as they say. What is your weapon of choice, may I ask?" Hawke asked.

"That would be anything at all makin' good use of powder and lead, m'lord."

"Marvelous!" Hawke said. "Well. It's the three of us, then! All for one, as I believe that D'Artagnan fellow used to say!"

"And one for all!" Nick added, embarrassed as soon as he said it. And, unable to stop himself from adding, "And all for Jipper!"

"I beg your pardon?" said Hawke. "Jipper?"

"My dog, Jip, your lordship. I'm afraid he's been harmed . . . or worse. It's just gone eight o'clock and my meeting at the Old North Wharf with Billy Blood was two hours ago. If we can go back a hundred and thirty-four years with this machine, surely going back two hours can be done first, sir?"

"Of course we can go to the wharf, Nick," Hawke said. "It would make an excellent dry run. Give the machine a shakedown cruise, as it were. But I must warn you not to expect to find Jip there. I know Blood. He wants to ransom Jip. He's going to demand the chest and the orb of gold in exchange for your dog. But he'd never bring the dog with him, lad. He's keeping him somewhere else, until he gets the chest, I'm sure of it."

"There's nowhere on this island where he could hide that dog from me, sir. Nowhere!" Nick said, the steely resolve strong in his voice. "I'll find my dog, I will, you can bet on that!"

"Nick, I don't think Jip's on the island anymore," Hawke said. "I daresay I'm quite sure he's not, in fact. It wouldn't be Billy's way. No, I warrant you'll find your dog under lock and key aboard Blood's frigate, *Mystère,* Nick, in the year 1805. That's where we'll find your Jip. Still and all, I'll gladly go to the wharf first, if it will ease your mind, my dear boy."

"It truly would, sir," Nick answered solemnly.

"Right then, Hobbes. Open the machine!"

CHAPTER XVIII

Das Kapitän's Cabbages

· 6 June 1939 ·

OFF HAWKE POINT

Silence, you idiot!" the captain hissed in the darkness. "Can't you see I've got the sonarphones on?"

"Sorry, *mein Kapitän*!" came the meek reply from somewhere amidst the whispered chatter of the darkened submarine control room.

"Ach! Now I've lost him! *Schweinehund!*" he said. "I want absolute silence!"

Suddenly, it became deadly quiet and still inside the steel hull lurking beneath the mirrored moonlit surface of the sea. The only noise was the constant *ping* from the radar screen, a ghostlike green oval in the shadowy red light of the control room. The screen showed a jagged point of land, jutting into the sea, in brilliant detail. On the German naval charts, that point of land was marked Hawke Point, and it was here that U-33 had been spending most of her time lately.

Like everything else aboard the submarine, the sonarphones the captain was wearing were the most advanced available from German scientists. U-33 was also equipped with highly experimental turbopowered engines, which converted hot exhaust gases into supercooled liquid propellants that drove a giant turbine aft. It took four of the giant engines to power the massive submarine.

"Project Crossfire," a top secret German Kriegsmarine program to develop new submarine propulsion systems, had produced the magnificent engines, capable of more than triple the horsepower of conventional submarine engines.

The power plants were coupled to an even more radical breakthrough, the Hydro-Propulsion system. This entailed water entering the sub at the bow, being superheated, then fed through an impeller, supercooled, only to be expelled at great force from the stern. To Berlin's delight, the design almost doubled the sub's submerged running speed.

The only remaining question was, could U-33's steel hull survive double the stress-loads of the high-output, high-torque, high-speed Crossfire propulsion system?

U-33's mission to the Channel Islands was, in part, a shakedown cruise to assess the new Crossfire system's impact on a conventional sub hull. Her other mission, known only to a few men on board, was to confirm the existence of a network of English spies on tiny Greybeard Island. Spies who'd somehow been getting highly accurate information about Nazi naval movements in the Channel to Hitler's nemesis, Winston Churchill.

Churchill's speeches in the British Parliament were a daily source of irritation to the Führer, and he wanted the flow of information to the old bulldog stopped, at any cost. That's why U-33 spent most of her time lying off Hawke Point, the believed base of the espionage group.

Finally, the experimental U-boat was to scour the island coastlines and map them for possible infantry landing sites. Berlin's plan for the German invasion of these tiny English islands was already in the final stages. Hitler planned to launch his invasion of the English mainland from these four islands, so it was imperative he capture them first.

The new sub, entrusted with all these important missions, was the pride of the whole German Navy–the largest, fastest, deadliest undersea weapon Germany had yet produced. She was officially called U-33, but her crew had already given her a nickname that looked like it was going to stick.

She was called *Der Wolf,* a tribute to her skipper, Wolfgang von Krieg, the "wolf" himself.

Von Krieg was watching and waiting, his eye glued to the black rubber eyepiece of the periscope. Framed in the center of his lens was the dark outline of Castle Hawke, sitting high above the pounding black sea on its rocky cliffs, lit by jagged flashes of lightning from an approaching squall. The lights at the top of the castle tower had been burning since sundown, which was unusual. The eye knew. The eye was here night after endless night. Waiting for something, anything. Watching.

The human eye blinked away a tear, but it wasn't sadness or even fatigue that caused that solitary eye to water. It was cabbage.

"Ach! Zose cabbages! Zose cabbages!" the shrill voice of *Kapitän* von Krieg reverberated throughout the silent ship.

It was Monday, cabbage night aboard U-33. Pungent vegetable smells permeated the length of the vessel, from the torpedo rooms fore and aft to the control room amidships. Even a submarine this advanced was no place for a sailor with a sensitive nose. And the pungent smell of boiled cabbage now seemed especially powerful amidships where von Krieg stood with his eye to the periscope. *Kapitän* von Krieg, while not a sensitive man, had an extremely sensitive nose.

"I smell zose cabbages!" von Krieg thundered, though his first officer was standing immediately behind him. His number one on this voyage was a short, jumpy little man named Lieutenant Willy Steiner.

It was his job to be two steps aft of von Krieg and he had been the first officer to keep the job for more than six months. Was it because he was the only man who could tolerate the captain's constant abuse? Or, as gossip had it, because "Little Willy," as von Krieg called him, had powerful friends in Berlin? There was even a shipboard rumor, so far limited to the officers' mess, that Willy was an SS officer personally sent by Hitler to keep an eye on the sometimes explosive von Krieg.

It was no secret to anyone aboard U-33 that her captain was something of a loose cannon. A dangerous thing aboard any vessel. But especially aboard an experimental submarine on a highly secret mission that might well determine the outcome of the war.

Baron Wolfgang von Krieg, or "Wolfie," as he was known in civilian life, was the only son of one of Germany's richest and most powerful men, Count Helmut von Krieg. Tall, powerfully built, and quite handsome when his features weren't clouded with drink, Wolfie had been a notorious character in Berlin society. With his striking blue eyes and blond, almost white hair cut close to the skull, he had cut quite a dashing figure in ballrooms in every corner of the Fatherland.

Sent to university at Oxford against his wishes by his

half-English mother, the rebellious, arrogant boy had been shunned at school and had developed a great hatred for English people. A hate that was almost as strong as his love of French wine. A brilliant student, he'd nonetheless been accused of attacking a college Don in a drunken rage and been sent home to Germany in disgrace. The story that followed him home to Berlin was that he'd sliced off the Magdalen Don's ear with a fencing foil.

The von Kriegs had built Germany's most powerful arms and munitions empire. Their loyalty and support of Hitler's Third Reich was critical to the Führer's plan to bend all of Europe to his will. The von Krieg factories, deep in the Ruhr Valley, were operating twenty-four hours a day producing everything from bombs for the Luftwaffe air corps to long-range 88-millimeter cannons for the army. As Germany took up the weapons of a world war, it was with the powerful arms of von Krieg.

Wolfie knew that, and had taken every advantage of it to advance his naval career. His most glittering prize thus far had been the command of U-33.

"Why do I smell cabbages, Willy?" von Krieg asked, more pleasantly now, his way of keeping his assistant slightly off guard.

"It's Monday night, *mein Kapitän,*" Willy said.

"I know that, Willy," he said, his eye still glued to the eyepiece. "And what difference does that make?"

"None, sir, of course, except that Monday night is cabbage night," Willy said mildly.

He could almost feel von Krieg go rigid with anger at his scope. He had noticed that it didn't take a great deal to get this reaction from his captain. The captain had a hair-trigger temper and Willy often noted his captain's outbursts in the little black book he kept locked in a safe in his tiny cabin. A black book he kept for Hitler's eyes only, at his leader's orders.

"U-33's mission is critical to me personally, and I don't want this headstrong young captain to botch it, do you understand?" Those had been the Führer's parting words to Willy, and, not being suicidal, he took them to heart.

"It vas cabbage night, Little Willy, until I gave strict orders that there would be no more cabbage nights! You know how I despise cabbages! That is why I forbid anyone to cook this peasant food on my ship! Do you forget my orders so easily?"

"Of course not, *mein Kapitän*, but tonight is also Chief Torpedoman Ober's birthday and the cook thought that–"

"You say the cook thought? Surely I misunderstand you. Are you trying to tell me that our cook can think? For he surely cannot cook!" von Krieg hissed. "Listen carefully to me, Willy. I will say this only once."

Von Krieg made a fierce effort to control his violent temper. "I want you to go to the aft torpedo room."

"Aft torpedo room, *mein Kapitän*."

"*Ja,* the aft torpedo room. And I want you to arrest Torpedoman Ober."

"Arrest him, *mein Kapitän*?"

"Am I speaking too softly, Lieutenant?" Von Krieg had still not removed his eye from the periscope lens. "Yes! I said arrest him, you *idiot,* for disobeying a direct order!"

"*Jawohl, Kapitän* von Krieg!"

"Arrest him. And then I want this impudent torpedoman loaded into aft torpedo tube Number Four," von Krieg said.

"The torpedoman into the torpedo tube, *mein Kapitän*?" Willy shook his head in wonder. His captain was entering uncharted waters of madness. Hitler was right. This man needed watching.

"Into the tube, Willy. Into the tube! And then I want you to offer Torpedoman Ober best birthday wishes from *Kapitän* Wolfgang von Krieg, do you follow? Yes? Then seal the tube and prepare it for firing. Do I make myself perfectly clear, Willy?"

"Seal the man in the torpedo tube?" Willy asked, aghast. He'd done some terrible things himself, but such cruelty to an innocent man was too much even for him. "*Kapitän,* please! You must understand that it was not Torpedoman Ober who–"

"Willy!" von Krieg shouted and Willy knew there was no point in continuing.

"*Jawohl, mein herr!* It shall be done immediately!" Willy saluted the captain before leaving the control room, but von Krieg failed to notice. His periscope had just picked up something interesting at Castle Hawke. A room of some sort, atop the tower, had been ablaze with light all evening. And now those lights were beginning to go out.

And, at the base of the cliff below the castle, a powerful shaft of white light was visible, pouring through what appeared to be a thin seam in the rock. Was there some kind of secret inlet there? Something he wouldn't have noticed by day? An entrance to a hidden lagoon, perhaps?

"Achtung!" von Krieg shouted, though there was no need for shouting in the tiny control room. "Bearing zero-five-zero, heading left nine-two-five! Mark! All engines ahead flank speed!"

"All ahead flank, *mein Kapitän*!"

"So, Hawke, you English swine," von Krieg chuckled to himself, his eye pressed up against the lens of his periscope, "I believe perhaps I have finally discovered your little secret spy nest! *Ja,* the secret back door of Hawke Castle itself!" He smiled at his little joke. "So this is how the great Hawke flies in and out of his lair unseen!"

The sub lurched forward as the powerful Crossfire engines, four massive screws and the hydro-propulsion impellers did their job in perfect tandem.

"And *Der Wolf* will be waiting by the door for your next appearance, my lord," he added, chuckling to himself.

Little Willy had returned to the control room from his distasteful mission at the stern of the ship and now stood rigidly at attention. *"Heil Hitler!"* Willy saluted.

"Heil Hitler," von Krieg returned half-heartedly, eyes still riveted to the scope. "Tube Four is loaded as I ordered, Willy?"

"Aft tube Number Four loaded and armed for firing, sir," Willy said, morosely. The Führer would not be pleased to learn that U-33's torpedo tubes were being used, not against Germany's enemies, but to send an innocent German sailor to an unspeakably horrifying death.

"Fire!" Krieg shouted.

A crewman pushed the red button on the fire control panel. They heard a muffled roar from the rear of the ship. "Four away, *Kapitän*!" the crewman said, as the men around him stared in stunned silence. Every man in the control room knew it could have been anyone of them lying terrified in tube Four, waiting to be ejected with terrible force beneath the sea. With this mad captain at their helm, this promised to be a long and dangerous cruise.

"Happy birthday, Torpedoman Ober," von Krieg sang softly to himself at the periscope. "Happy birthday to you! Happy birthday to the English fishies, and the meal they make of you!" Chuckling, he pressed his eye again to the scope, trying to peer through the sea mists that now shrouded Castle Hawke. "And as for you, Lord Hawke . . . you will surely be next to feel the terrible wrath of *Der Wolf*!"

At that moment, in the crosshairs of his periscope, von Krieg was transfixed on this, his first glimmer of light and hope. The light escaping from the base of Hawke Castle meant that his suspicions had been correct. There was some kind of passage there, even if it was not visible by daylight.

"Well, well, Lord Hawke, it seems you've finally left the light on by the back door," he said to himself. "Yes, I think you've finally made a little error. And guess who is here to make sure you pay dearly for it, *ja*?"

CHAPTER XIX

Tempus et Locus

· 6 June 1939 ·

HAWKE CASTLE

Ah, there it is!" Hobbes exclaimed.

"There what is, Hobbes?" Hawke asked.

"Sorry, m'lord. I was referring to the Tempus Machina. I've managed to get the machine open. Quite interesting, actually."

"Open! I daresay, Hobbes, really!" Hawke said, crossing to the table in a bounding stride. The golden ball now lay in two halves on the velvet pillow, like two halves of a large golden orange. "I mean to say, the Tempus Machina, open at last, and all you can manage is 'Ah, there it is'? Really, Hobbes! You do try one's patience."

"It separates along the equator, with a reverse clockwise twist which threw me for a few moments. Sorry, sir. Although, you'll remember, Leonardo did many things backward. His mirror-writing, of course. As you may know, Leonardo da Vinci kept all of his journals written backward, so anyone attempting to read them could only do so by holding them before a mirror. Ha! The man wrote backward as easily as mere mortals write forward."

No one was really listening to Hobbes's history lesson. They were all much too captivated by the glittering interior of the four-hundred-year-old machine. Nick had no idea what he'd been expecting to find inside the machine–whirling atoms, perhaps. Actually, the device resembled an exquisite piece of jewelry. Delicate scrolled writing surrounded an engraving of the sun and its nine planets on one half, and there was a pyramid with what appeared to be Greek symbols on the other.

"I say, Hobbes, there seems to be some of your backward writing here, surrounding the figure of the solar system. Have a look, will you?"

"Nick," Hobbes said with some excitement in his voice, "hand me the mirror you'll find in that top drawer, please."

"Latin, I assume, Hobbes," Hawke said, as Hobbes held the mirror to the beautiful machine. "What does it say, Hobbes? Blurt it out, man! You do push one to the limit at times."

Nick looked at the backward writing reflected in the small mirror.

Nunc Mihi
Mox Huius
Sed Postea Nescio Cuius

"Now Mine, Then Theirs, But Forever After I Know Not Whose." Hobbes intoned the words, sounding like the voice of antiquity

itself. "Well, we know whose, don't we? Leonardo's Tempus Machina now belongs to young Nicholas McIver!"

Nick felt himself flushed with excitement, looking now at a number of jewels set in the golden faces of each half, like buttons. Unlike the scholarly Hobbes, Nick didn't know a lot of Latin. It was, in fact, his weakest subject at school, but he knew that the engraved words "Tempus" on one half, and "Locus" on the other stood for "Time" and "Place."

"Now, the 'Tempus' half seems to be a perpetual calendar," Hobbes said. "And, as you can see, this dial is showing today's date and time, exactly. Quite amazing, isn't it? Ticking along for four hundred years! Now, I imagine if I press this gemstone–an emerald, I believe–the calendar will advance–"

He pushed the emerald, and indeed the minutes, hours, and days started racing by, gaining speed until they were nothing but a blur. Nick noticed that, eerily, the machine made no sound at all.

"Hobbes, please be careful! Are you sure you know what you're doing?" Hawke said, peering over Hobbes's shoulder and clearly alarmed as time raced ahead on the machine.

"Fairly elementary, your lordship," Hobbes replied, nonplussed. "The genius of Leonardo, if you will. Ah, now that we've got time moving, I wonder how in the world we get it to stop!"

"Good lord, Hobbes! You're jesting, of course!" Hawke said. "You don't know how to stop it!"

"This stone here," Hobbes said calmly, "a ruby, I believe, should stop the acceleration. A brake, you'd call it in an automobile. Let's see if I'm right, shall we?"

Hobbes pushed the tiny ruby and immediately the spinning days and hours began to slow until they could be read again, and then they stopped. Nick would never forget the date where the machine stopped.

1 April 2079

It took his breath away. The machine had sped ahead a hundred and forty years into the future in the very blink of an eye!

"I say!" was all Lord Hawke could muster. "I daresay I'd feel a great deal more comfortable if you'd just return us to today, Hobbes. Really, let's not rush headlong into this, shall we? Can you get us back to today's date?"

"Certainly, sir," Hobbes replied. "Although the machine can not possibly take us anywhere without the two halves being rejoined, so I shouldn't concern yourself too much about experimenting with it. I would imagine this middle stone is the reset button. "Let's find out, shall we?"

Hawke let out a sigh when Hobbes pushed the middle jewel, a diamond, and the days began to spin slowly backward to a stop. They all noticed with great relief that the machine had stopped where it had started, on today's date. Nick looked at his watch. Same exact time as was showing on the machine. To the second!

"I must say, Hobbes, guessing the functions of the various gems is rather a neat trick."

"Not really, sir." Hobbes smiled. "Seventy-two percent of the civilized societies on earth have designated the colors green for 'go' and red for 'stop.' Leonardo, the original time traveler, would surely have discovered that fact in his travels to the future. I imagine he chose the red ruby for stop and the green emerald for go as his way of saying to anyone coming into possession of the instrument, 'You see, I've been to the future.' "

"A bit of an inside cosmic joke is what you're saying, Hobbes?"

"Precisely, sir."

"And this bottom half," Nick said, "it sets the geographic locations?"

Hobbes studied this lower half for a few moments.

"Indeed! One must assume that this dial here is a global positioning indicator. Notice it uses standard latitudinal and longitudinal numerals. Now, if I'm correct, the figures here should change if I walk over to the window, shouldn't they?"

Hobbes carried the device over to the window, studying it intently as he walked. "Yes," he exclaimed, "the machine is tracking with me as I walk, even this minute distance across the face of the planet! Look here, here is my new position!" Hawke and Nick practically ran to him to see for themselves.

"Astounding, Hobbes!" Lord Hawke said. "So this dial is the machine's current location, correct? Where we are standing now?"

"Precisely, my lord. That is to say, precise within a radius of, oh, a few feet. Maybe less, considering how it tracked my position as I walked to the window. I really don't know what the margin of error is, sir. Nick, would you plot Hawke Castle's position on the maritime chart you'll find in that drawer, please?"

Nick found the chart and quickly located Hawke Point. "All right, Commander, zero-two degrees twenty-four minutes longitude by forty-nine degrees twenty-five minutes north latitude."

"And the machine's reading, Hobbes?"

"Precisely the same, your lordship!"

"By Jove, Hobbes! You've cracked it!"

"I endeavor to give satisfaction, m'lord."

"Is that it, then, Hobbes? Can we at long last go find that scoundrel Blood?"

"One final thing, m'lord," Hobbes said, picking up one half of the globe in each hand. "Please remember. You enter the desired time of arrival in Tempus. And the desired destination in Locus. Then one must screw the two hemispheres together again to actually activate the machine."

"Time and space rejoined is what you're saying, Hobbes."

"Precisely, my lord. And, sir, before you depart, might I mention the historical protection issue? Not that you need reminding, m'lord."

"Historical protection issue, Hobbes?" Hawke asked, momentarily puzzled. "Ah, of course! Splendid point, Hobbes!"

He turned to Nick and Gunner, a deadly serious expression in his eyes. "We are about to venture into the past, gentlemen. In so doing, we incur an enormous responsibility to history. It is our obligation, you see, nay, our sacred duty to protect the flow, and to abide by the Law of Unintended Consequences."

"Protect the flow?" Nick asked. Hobbes smiled at Nick.

"By going back in time, you have it in your power to change the whole course of human history, Nick. This could have unforeseen and disastrous effects on mankind if the time traveler does anything to dramatically alter the precious flow of history."

"We can still help the captain, can't we?" Gunner asked.

"A relatively minor historic event," Hobbes replied. "Yes, you can help Captain McIver, Gunner. I'm talking about interfering in major events. The lives and deaths of significant historical figures, for instance. Do I have your solemn vow you will avoid this at all costs?" Hobbes asked his two fellow travelers.

Nick and Gunner nodded in silent agreement.

"Right! Our first stop, then, Hobbes?"

"The shanty, sir, any time prior to Nick's six o'clock appointment this evening, sir. I've taken the liberty of entering the coordinates for the Old North Wharf. You should arrive within or near the shanty. Shall I enter five-fifty to be on the safe side, sir?"

"Excellent! And Captain McIver's frigate?"

"Your next stop. Mr. Blood will be most unpleasantly surprised to see you, I should imagine, my lord."

"Yes, I suppose he shall. We shan't be gone too long, I wouldn't imagine, old boy. To do so might, as my hero Sherlock Holmes was fond of saying, generate too much unhealthy excitement among the criminal classes. Take good care of this pretty young lady, won't you, Hobbes?"

"Indeed I will, sir," Hobbes said, "My nursemaid skills are a bit rusty, but I think they'll come back to me. And now, sir, as the French are so fond of saying, *'Bon voyage et bonne chance!'* "

CHAPTER XX

Pigs and Stowaways

· 3 October 1805

H.M.S. *MERLIN*, AT SEA

Two thunderous raps sounded at Captain Nicholas McIver's cabin door. It was Old Ben's knock.

"Just a moment, Ben, I'm writin' the log! Can't jawbone and scribble at the same time, damn your eyes! If we ain't sinkin', I'll thankee to keep that door between us." He heard a grunt and the door stayed shut.

Captain McIver sighed, and looked back down at his half-written ship's log entry. Frowning, he picked up his quill once more. He'd been in the middle of describing the morning's ferocious engagement, the near fatal encounter with the Frenchman Rambouillet, and *Merlin*'s current precarious state. His ship was afire and sinking, and this entry could well be McIver's last, he knew, depending on how events worked out in the next few hours. The sounds of muffled chatter and movement of his men upon deck above his head was reassuring at any rate. Still floatin', weren't they? Couldn't Ben give a moment's peace?

Old Ben, so called because of his prematurely white hair,

stood outside his captain's door that morning on one good leg and one wood peg, polishing his tooth. He was the proud possessor of a lone tooth that had been fashioned from an old musketball in a spectacularly unsuccessful piece of shipboard dentistry. Ben was quite prideful of it however and kept it polished to gleaming perfection.

Now that the captain had put Mr. Stiles in charge of dousing the fire and plugging the holes the French cannonballs had made, the peglegged steward had been told the captain was to be disturbed only if it was necessary to give the order to abandon ship. Or, as he had told Ben, if "anything unusual" should happen.

Unusual? Ben, to his complete befuddlement, no longer had any idea what his captain meant by anything unusual. Was the fact that McQueeney, the gunner's mate, was nightly rumored to be threatening to steal the captain's blue gig and take a score of feverish deserting rats with him *unusual*? Or that Slushy, the cook, said ghosts were turning his tureens arsy-versy behind his back? Or that someone, maybe the boatswain himself, had let all the pigs loose and that wild porkers were even now terrorizing the barky's sick bay? *Unusual?* The word no longer had meaning on this vessel, at least in Old Ben's opinion.

Ben turned to the man beside him, a cold, shivering British tar they'd just plucked from the sea. They'd found the half-drowned sailor drifting by, clinging to what had once been some kind of dory, now reduced to floating rubble. The man claimed to have recently escaped from Blood's flagship, *Mystère*. The question to Ben's wary mind was, was this fellow surprising or unusual enough to present to his captain?

"Hold up there, shipmate," Ben said to the shivering wretch. "Whilst I ponders just how unusual my skipper may perceive your tale to be!"

"Unusual?" the poor man croaked. "Blood's got himself a floatin' prison out there, I tell you! A bloody seagoin' jail! Kidnapped children, dogs, horses, and that ain't the worst of it! Got Lord Nelson's own niece held captive, down in that hellhole of a brig deck! Lady Anne herself? That ain't unusual enough for the likes of you?"

Ben frowned, and raised his hand to rap again on the captain's door. Admiral Lord Nelson's own niece now held as Bill's captive? Surely that was newsy and unusual!

But ever since the blasphemous turncoat Billy Blood had mutinied against Captain McIver and all his old shipmates, everything on board this blasted vessel had been unusual, Ben thought. Mr. Alex Griswold, the midnight watch, had sworn up and down the deck that Blood frequently appeared out of thin air on the quarterdeck beside him. Once he'd even grabbed the helm and put her hard over for a towering iceberg on the port side of the barky! Then he'd disappeared just as ghostlike as you please. Of course, Mr. Griswold was a wee bit overly fond of his grog, as were many of the hands who ended up standing the lonely hours of the graveyard watch.

"Cap'n, may be I have somethin' the least bit unusual out here!" Ben shouted, rapping on the door, having decided the news that Billy had captured Nelson's beautiful niece was worth disturbing the captain over.

Unusual? McIver wondered, trying to concentrate on his log. He doubted it. "Blast it, Ben, leave me be! I've got to finish me log!"

The captain of the *Merlin*, too, was no longer clear as to what constituted strange or unusual on this blasted vessel. He had decided, for instance, that he'd best not mention to Ben that he was expecting a visitor from another century. As loyal as Ben was, he wasn't sure Ben could keep such a fantastical secret. You couldn't stop shipboard rumors, of course, but you needn't fan the flame.

In fact, no one on the ship, or indeed in the entire Royal Navy, knew about his letter to the future or, indeed, the unworldly powers of the magical golden ball. Should he unburden himself of his secret in the ship's log? There was only one other man on the Seven Seas who knew of the ancient machine's power, and he wasn't a man at all. He was the lowest form of life, lower even than a traitorous dog.

A turncoat mutineer named Captain William Blood.

Blood had stolen one of the two precious golden balls from his former captain the night of his treacherous mutiny. In fact, the betrayed captain had come upon Billy in his cabin during the robbery itself and it was the confrontation and scuffle that had led to the mutiny. McIver had put a pistol on Billy and made him put the time instrument back into the sea locker. Billy did so and then fled to the quarterdeck, where his fellow mutineers were waiting. Unfortunately, he had the other, second, machine safely in the folds of his jacket.

McIver and First Lieutenant Mitchell Stiles were able to put down the mutiny that dreadful night, but not without a lot of bloodshed. The scuppers had run red with the stuff, and, unfortunately, Billy Blood had managed to escape with his life, and the second of the two miraculous time instruments.

With the Tempus Machina in his possession, Blood could roam the earth, travel through time and space to wreak havoc wherever he went. However, having only one of the two golden orbs put Old Bill at a grave disadvantage. It meant, McIver knew, that whenever and wherever Blood traveled, he would always be looking over his shoulder.

McIver, or whoever possessed the second orb, would give Bill no rest, no peace. Blood knew whoever had the second orb would follow him to the ends of the earth, to the very boundaries of time itself, to regain possession of both devices.

The man who owned both of Leonardo's miraculous machines would be all-powerful. Captain William Blood was determined to be that man, no matter what it took.

But Captain Nicholas McIver was equally determined that such a catastrophe must never happen.

Captain McIver suspected that once Billy had gotten wind of the machine's immense power, the temptation of possessing both machines had brought the truly dark side of Blood's character to the fore.

Billy possessed one of the most brilliant military minds in the Navy and there were those who'd once believed he'd rise through the ranks to First Sea Lord. Some even said he'd go as high as Prime Minister. Now, they'd all be happy if he went to the devil.

There was only one soul alive who could help McIver. A kindred spirit, a distant great-great-grandson, and *he* wouldn't be born for another hundred and twenty-two years! But the captain's letter and the infernal time machine might bring the lad running, at least that's what McIver hoped.

Suddenly, the cabin door blew open with such violence it

almost flew off its hinges. Stiles rushed past Ben and the poor drowned rat beside him, into the cabin.

"What in life–" the captain shouted, turning to see his first officer, not Ben, bounding in.

Stiles, a tall, handsome officer who always wore his long sandy brown hair in a carefully braided pigtail tied with a black velvet ribbon, stood before his captain. His blue jacket bore not a few decorations for heroism and was normally immaculate; now he was soaked to the skin and covered with black soot from head to toe. McIver looked up, startled. The first officer's face was so blackened that the whites of his deep green eyes seemed to pop out of his head.

"Sir!" Stiles said, much out of breath. "Begging your pardon!"

"Close that door, will you, Lieutenant?" the captain said, seeing Old Ben's anxious face peering through the opened door. "In case of bad news, I'd like to be the one as spreads it," said the captain, calmly, "not Old Ben."

Calm in any sea was McIver's trademark in the service and it had served him well. The first officer closed the door on the scowling countenance of the steward kept waiting outside.

"We'll just wait here, thankee kindly, Lieutenant," Ben said with as much sarcasm as he could muster as the door closed on them.

"All under control then, Mr. Stiles?" McIver said, eyeing the man carefully.

"Afraid not, sir!" the young lieutenant said. "Fire's out, sir, finally, but the barky's taking far more water than we can handle with the pumps as are still working. She's down a good two feet by the head, sir, in this last hour! If we keep taking on seawater at this rate, she'll go to the bottom within the hour!" Down by the head meant the bow was two feet lower in the water than the stern–an unhealthy state for any ship to be in, especially the one under your own two feet.

"An hour! Blast it, Mr. Stiles. I saw where she was holed. She couldn't be shipping that much water that quickly!"

"With respect, sir, there was a second hole we didn't see at first on account of all the water she'd already taken on. It's just below the one you saw, sir, a gusher!"

"A second bloody hole! Well, blast it all, Lieutenant!" McIver cried, his face reddening. "Redouble your efforts! Plug them, man! You've got crew lazing on deck, for all love! Get them below with buckets, all hands! I'll not see my ship go down, sir. Is that perfectly clear, Lieutenant?"

McIver knew, as every good seaman knew, that the best pump on a sinking ship was a scared sailor with a bucket.

"Aye, aye. Bucket brigade, sir, at once!" said Stiles, but he made no move to leave the cabin. The man was clearly troubled.

"Is that all, Lieutenant?"

"A bucket brigade won't be enough, sir. With all due respect, Captain, I'm afraid there's only one way out of this," the lieutenant said, still standing rigidly at attention, fumbling with his three-cornered hat. "Perhaps if we got the barky–that is, if you would consider it, sir, uh–"

"Spit it out! I don't care where a notion comes from if it's a good one, Lieutenant," the captain said. He then added, more calmly, "Speak your mind. And please stand at your ease, Lieutenant."

"Thank you, sir," the lieutenant replied, and leaned forward earnestly, putting his two fists down on the captain's desk. "We need to get under way at once, Captain. If we can press on all available sail, and get her heeled over hard to port, the holes on the starboard side will both be above the waterline and we can make our repairs, sir. Shouldn't take the carpenters more than twenty minutes once she's not taking water."

The captain stared at the lieutenant, thinking it over.

"Only a thought, sir," Stiles said.

"A damn good one, by my lights. But what about these infernal reefs we seem to have gotten into? They're like the toothsome tentacles of some giant sea creature! They're everywhere I look! To get her heeled over enough to make repairs, she's going to need running room. She'll need sea room, some deep water under her keel. There's precious little of either in this cove, Lieutenant."

"That's one of the problems, sir."

"And the other, Mr. Stiles?" the captain said, standing up from his writing desk.

"The masthead lookout reports a sail due north, sir, hull down and headed this way!"

"One of ours?" the captain said, allowing a tiny light of hope to creep in. "An advance ship for Nelson's fleet?"

"Afraid not, sir. It's Blood's flagship. Since we're not comin' out, he's comin' in. With a full press of sail, even his topgallants, sir. He's flying over the water. And his *Mystère* is a lightning fast sailer when she's on her wind."

"How long have we got, Lieutenant?"

"We'll be in his cannon range in less than an hour, sir. Already close enough to read his signals. Lookout reports

Blood's run up our own Union Jack, the one he stole off the *Merlin*'s stern. He's flying it, sir, he's flying our own flag upside down from his royal topmast! Upside down, Captain!"

"The dog! I'll–"

"That's not all, sir," Stiles said. "He's run up signal flags, sir. Masthead signalman took the message and just sent a boy down. Here it is, Captain." Stiles handed the folded scrap to the captain, wincing at the sooty smudges he'd left on it.

McIver opened the message and stared at the four words scrawled there.

LADY ANNE IS MINE.

The captain crumpled the paper into his clenched fist and kicked the nearest chair halfway across his great cabin. He started to say something, thought better of it, and forced himself to regain his composure. This was the gravest affront yet to Nelson, and the great admiral of the British fleet would be most aggrieved. The beautiful Anne was Nelson's dearest relative on this earth.

"Anne? So, he's got Nelson's own niece in his brig now, has he? He'll use her as a pawn to lure Nelson out, won't he? Well, we'll just have to find a way to get her back, we will. Anything else, Mr. Stiles?"

"That's all, Captain."

"We've no choice, then," McIver said, anger and resolve hardening his voice once more. "We've got to stand him down! We'll go out and face him undergunned and undermanned and two holes in her bottom, to boot! How's our rigging? No matter! Give the order to run up every inch of canvas she carries! All abroad! Mains'ls, jibs, tops'ls and stuns'ls, royals, too! And run out every cannon that'll still hold powder. Tell every gun crew to double load! We can't just sit here and wait for that vile creature to come send us to the bottom, can we, Lieutenant?"

McIver raised his glass and peered through the stern window for a long moment. Blood was coming. Whether or not his desperate gamble with the letter to the future would pay off, he knew he had to act now. They had not a second to lose.

"Aye, 'tis Blood, all right," the captain said, collapsing the telescope with a sharp snap. "Beat to quarters, Mr. Stiles!"

"Aye, aye, Captain!" Stiles shouted and ran from the cabin to carry out his captain's orders. In seconds, the captain heard the muffled thunder of the drummer's rolling drumbeat, calling the men to quarters and then the scurrying of hundreds of feet overhead. He could feel the ship above and all around him springing back to life with the promise of a fight with Billy Blood! There wasn't a soul aboard who didn't have a score to settle with Bill.

"Ben! Ben!" the captain shouted to his steward who came racing in straightaway with his peglegged gait, the sodden stranger in tow. "Pray, come pour us some grog, man," McIver said heartily. "We'll need a bit o' sustenance afore this day is over! We've another fight on our hands, old son! Hello! Who's this poor wretch?"

"Aye, Captain, a splash of grog by all of us!" said Ben. Never one to shun the offer of a wee dram of rum, he quickly pulled three hammered silver mugs from the swinging rack over the captain's head. "Plucked this poor devil from the briny, we did, and he's fresh escaped from Billy's *Mystère*. Was originally a bosun's mate on *Reliant,* sir, till Bill sent her to the bottom a fortnight ago. He claims Blood's holding Nelson's own niece aboard that brig, sir. If that don't top all! Tell the captain if that ain't what you claim!"

"My c-compliments, Captain," said the shivering sailor, and then he collapsed in a puddle on the floor without saying a word. Ben gave him a sharp kick to see if he was dead. He moaned once, so Ben figured he hadn't yet departed.

"No news to me, anyhow, Ben, and get this fellow to a medico," McIver said, cocking a sympathetic eye at the shipwrecked sailor. "I already know Bill's got Anne, blast you. I thought you had news, man, something out of the ordinary for me!"

"This ain't *news,* sir?" Ben asked, shaking his head in wonder. He poured a healthy measure of rum into each mug, taking his time. He couldn't imagine how the captain already possessed such information. "Well, if Nelson's niece bein' held prisoner ain't news enough, I got more powder in me hold," he said hopefully.

"Speak up, Old Ben, speak up," the captain said, quaffing his own hearty swig of rum and the passed-out sailor's as well. "What blasted other news have you got?"

"Pigs, sir."

"Pigs?"

"Aye, pigs. Well, it's pigs, sir, is how I found out," Ben said, enjoying the sharp bite of the rum. "Ah, nothin' I likes better than a hearty breakfast! To your very good health, Captain!" McIver frowned and waved his mug impatiently.

"Pigs, you say? What about the rummy creatures?"

"Escaped their confines, sir."

"Porkers on the loose? And an action coming? That's all we need!"

"Aye. Y'see, someone loosed them squealin' porkers out of their hold, sir," Ben said. "They was terrorizing the sickbay. Causing a terrible unholy ruckus down there. Knocked over the surgeon and one poor bloke broke his crutches tryin' to escape from 'em! So, while you was in here scratchin' in yer log, I went below to gather 'em up and put 'em back as where they belongs, in the pig locker, and that's when I discovered 'em, sir."

"Hell's bells, Ben, discovered *who*? This poor devil on the floor? Is he dead?"

"No, not him, the stowaways, sir, if you can credit it."

"Stowaways! You mean–" the captain sputtered, blowing out a fine spray of Barbado rum, and stopped in midsentence as if the rest of the grog had gone down the wrong pipe. He put his handkerchief to his mouth and waved to Ben to continue. "Spit it out, man, spit it out! Stowaways, you say?"

Ben swiped his own kerchief across his rum-spattered jowly cheeks. "Beggin' yer pardon, Cap, it's you as is spittin' it out–"

"Blast it all, Ben, get on with it! Stowaways?"

"Aye, Captain. Three of 'em. Bleedin' stowaways all, smellin' o' pig, too! Don't know how they managed to avoid discovery all this time we been at sea. I figure it was them as let the pigs out in the first place. I wouldn't want to be bunking in with all those pigs myself! But I put the porkers back inside and locked 'em all up together, stowaways and pigs alike, nice and cosy. One of the three, a mere boy he is, asked for a word with you, sir. Said he was here 'cause of a letter from *you,* Captain! Ha! Touched in the head, I'm afraid, sir, less of course the boy can walk on water like our blessed Lord, sir." Ben sat back, happy to get off such a good one, even if the captain seldom acknowledged his rapier wit and sense of life's absurdities.

"A boy, you say, Ben! A boy! How old?" McIver asked, a ripple of excitement running down his spine. It had to be young Nick! Why, who else could it be?

"No more'n twelve if he's a day, sir," Ben said chuckling. "And here's the humorous part, Cap'n, guess what flag he's claiming to sail under? Says his name's Nicholas McIver! Don't that top it all?" Ben held his sides, shaking with mirth. Things had gotten so queer on this old barky, you just had to laugh.

"Damn it all, Ben! Half-dead sailors drownin' here on me floor and wild porkers terrorizing the sickbay! Stowaways in the pig locker!" the captain cried, still sputtering rum as he got to his feet. He leveled a hard look at his old companion.

"Ben, for all honesty, man, why didn't you tell me all this immediately?"

"Because, Captain," Ben replied, casually draining his mug and returning the look with an easy smile, "you said you was to be disturbed only if something *unusual* happened."

CHAPTER XXI

A Bump in the Night

· 6 June 1939 ·

ABOARD *THOR,* AT SEA

Racing with the moon, my dear girl!" Hobbes exclaimed above the impossibly thunderous roar of *Thor*'s twin engines. They were cutting a huge swath across the glassy sea, and twin plumes of foaming white water were thrown to either side of the knife-edged bow. "Quite the thing, isn't it? Glorious!"

He was right, too. The silvery moon, when it wasn't half hidden behind a few wandering clouds, was racing alongside the burnished luster of the dark mahogany hull, a watery, shimmering reflection of the moon above, speeding along beside them over the gleaming sea.

"Faster, Hobbes! Faster!" Kate shouted above the din, the cat Horatio cradled in her arms and her little nose pressed against the portside window. "See, no matter how fast we go, that old moon goes just as fast!" She turned to look at Hobbes and he saw her eyes shining with exhilaration in the greenish glow of the instruments. *Thor*'s tremendous power often had this effect on first-time passengers, Hobbes observed with a certain satisfaction. He'd designed the big launch with military objectives in mind, but few things were more fun than racing her across a flat, starlit sea.

"Can't we ever beat that old moon, Hobbesie?"

"Can't beat physics, my dear girl," the commander said, lighting up one of the fat Montecristo cigars he always allowed himself on these crossings. "Not without your brother's time machine at any rate." He laughed at his own little joke and ruffled her curly red hair. "We'll leave that duty to Lord Hawke, I suppose." He eased the throttles forward, and the boat surged ahead.

"I'll bet we could beat *Stormy Petrel*, though," Kate said. "She never ever goes this fast! Even when the mean old Nazis were tugging us along behind their submarine."

Hobbes glanced over at the greenish dial of *Thor*'s knotmeter. Pushing thirty knots, he saw. "Is this speed frightening you, Kate?" he asked, easing back on the throttles. He felt a keen responsibility for the child's safety in the wake of Gunner's departure to the past. "I don't want to scare you, you know."

"Oh, Hobbes, don't be so silly!" Kate said. "I never get scared too often. Besides, you could never scare me. You're the very best nanny in the whole world!"

"Nanny?" asked one of Britain's most heavily decorated naval commanders.

"Oh, yes! And, ever such a funny one, too!"

Funny? Hobbes had never in his life been described as being even remotely funny. Or a nanny, either. But, somehow, he found himself oddly grateful that this small person could consider him so. He'd grown rather attached to her already.

"Why, thank you, dear" was all he could manage. "I seldom

think of myself that way, you know. An occasionally amusing naval person, perhaps. A funny nanny, almost never!" he said, smiling, and the little girl giggled.

He was enjoying himself enormously, after all. He'd forgotten how much joy could be found in the company of children. Most especially one as full of Mrs. Barker's beans as Kate McIver. "Pass me that chart, dear."

Ninety miles across, roughly. *Thor* could manage the crossing to Portsmouth in just over three hours if the weather held. He looked at the faint glow of his wristwatch in the darkness. They had about two hours to go. His contact, an elderly fisherman named John Cory, was waiting in a darkened dory just off the harbor mouth. He'd be expecting Hobbes to arrive with his weekly intelligence packet at the stroke of midnight. Hobbes leaned forward to gaze at the sky above the raked windscreen. Clear enough. They'd make it, if he poured on a little more coal.

"Hold on to your hat, my dear!" he shouted to Kate, and firewalled the twin throttles. *Thor*'s powerful twelve-cylinder Allison engines roared, and her huge eight-bladed bronze propellers bit, and launched her forward, throwing tremendous cascades of white water to either side of her bow.

"Oh my goodness!" Kate exclaimed, looking astern at the churning wake as *Thor* leapt forward in the water. "Look, Hobbes! We'll beat that silly old moon yet!"

Hobbes settled back into the deep leather cushion of the captain's chair. A nice, uneventful crossing was in order tonight, he thought. Yes, he'd had quite enough excitement for one day, thank you.

The "departure" of the three time travelers for one thing.

Kate had been able to talk of little else while *Thor* made ready to slip out of the lagoon. In the glow of the instruments, Kate's eyes had been still wide with the memory of the time machine's breathtaking magical powers. No one had known quite what to expect when the two halves were rejoined, of course, neither the ones leaving nor the ones to be left behind.

"One final thing," Lord Hawke had solemnly announced, in the last seconds before departure. "It is important that I ask each of you here tonight to swear on your sacred honor that you will reveal to no one the existence of this machine. It can be a powerful force for good, but as Hobbes has explained, there is also great danger in tampering with so vital a force of nature as time. It is now up to those of us here gathered to protect this great secret in order that we may also protect the precious flow of history."

Hawke looked at each one in turn, studying their faces in the flickering candlelight. "Do you each so swear?"

"I so swear," each had replied, and solemnly bowed their heads.

After a final check to ensure the proper time and destination numerals had been entered into each half of the machine, Lord Hawke had said, with a surprising good humor and nonchalance, "Well, Hobbes, I suppose we'll be popping off, now! If you please, Nicholas?" And he held out his hemisphere to Nick.

Nick held his Locus up to Lord Hawke's Tempus and felt an instant vibration in his half of the machine, running up his arm and suffusing his entire body. He noticed that the metal surface became extremely cold, almost too cold to hold on to, burning his fingers. He felt a tugging sensation coming from Lord Hawke's half, much like the feeling of a powerful magnet, as if the two hemispheres couldn't bear to be apart. He held on and, hesitating just for a moment, touched his half to the other.

Time and space rejoined went through Nick's mind and he took a deep breath. He knew the two halves had to be screwed tightly together in order to function. What he didn't know is what would happen once that was accomplished.

"Rotate your half counterclockwise, Nick!" Lord Hawke said, his eyes alight and a look of keen anticipation on his face.

Nick, his hand shaking ever so slightly, did so, and felt the machine lock securely. The vibration stopped instantly, replaced by a gentle pulsing, a warming of the metal surface, and the tiniest sound from within the reformed globe, what sounded like a faint shimmering of tiny bells, and then he felt that his whole being was shimmering as well. Each individual cell seemed to be lighting up and humming within him, a warm feeling, not unpleasant at all, but he had cried out, "What's happening, Hobbes?" and heard Hobbes shouted reply, "It's called 'ionization,' Nicholas!" and then Hobbes wasn't there anymore, he was someplace else. And Nick McIver?

He'd been ionized.

"Are they gone, Hobbes?" Kate had asked, her face still buried against Hobbes's waistcoat, not daring to look.

"Oh, yes, dear Katie, they are well and truly gone!" he had replied, somewhat overcome with emotion himself. It was hard to come to grips with what he'd just seen.

"What was that light when they left, Hobbes?" Kate asked

now, her face still bathed in the eerie glow of *Thor*'s interior. "I could see it, even with my eyes closed hiding behind your back! Like when you lie on the beach and stare at the sun with your eyes closed! And that noise, like a million tiny bells at once–"

"Yes, wasn't it magnificent?"

"What *was* it?"

"Difficult to describe, Katie. It was as if, well, one moment they were all three standing there, as solid as the chair you're sitting in, hands joined around the machine, and the very next instant they were all three alight, as if every living atom of their beings had become the tiniest of fireflies, millions of them, don't you know, but forming the general shape of their bodies, glowing as pure and brilliantly as stars for a moment, and then they began winking, winking one-by-one until, finally, they had all winked out! Every single one! And it was just you and me, alone in the room!"

"Christmas! Wasn't it something, Hobbes!" Kate exclaimed, giddy with the memory.

"Oh, it was something all right, Katie," Hobbes agreed. Suddenly, he sat forward and peered through the windscreen. He thought he'd seen something out there in the darkness, but he couldn't be sure. A looming black shape on the horizon and then it was gone. Impossible, of course. Nothing would be just sitting out here in the dark without running lights to make itself seen. Hobbes shook his head to clear the cobwebs.

As often happened on these crossings on clear nights, the powerful thrumming of the engines below his feet and the cozy glow of the instruments sometimes lulled him into a semi-hypnotic state. This wasn't reckless, he told himself, at this time of night the channel was usually devoid of traffic. Normally, he enjoyed a relaxing few hours, puffing on his big cigars. But tonight, with his dear little passenger, he knew he couldn't allow himself to be anything less than completely alert. He tossed his half-smoked Cuban out the window.

"All strapped in, Kate?" he asked.

"Oh, yes, Horatio and I are perfectly–" She never finished the sentence.

At that moment, the mightly *Thor* struck something in the water. She struck it hard. Hard enough to stagger the big yacht, and send a shudder through her from stem to stern.

Kate, strapped in, didn't move, but Horatio flew from her arms and bounced squalling off the windscreen, and the commander was thrown forward from his seat, up against the helm, and then fell to his knees.

"Oh my goodness!" Kate said shakily. "What happened, Hobbes?"

"We appear to have hit something, dear," Hobbes said, getting quickly to his feet and rubbing his bruised shoulder with one hand, pulling the two throttles back with the other. The big boat slowed and settled immediately. Hobbes leaned forward, peering through the windscreen. "Though I can't imagine what it might be! Nothing at all out here. It's open water. Still, it's the oddest thing, though, I thought I saw something, just before we–"

"Are we going to sink, Hobbes?" Kate asked, fear creeping steadily into her voice. "I–I'm not the best of swimmers, you know, and that water looks awfully dark out there. And deep. If we do sink, Hobbesie, will you–"

"Of course we're not going to sink, my dear. That was just a bump in the road. We'd have to hit something a lot harder than that to put a hole in a big boat like this. Can't fathom what it was, however. Very odd, indeed." Hobbes put both engines in neutral and bent down beneath the wheel to open a locker.

Although he had no idea what they could possibly have hit out here in the open channel, whatever it had been was sizable. He listened carefully for the sound of incoming sea, and was grateful to hear nothing. His groping hands finally found the two items he'd been looking for in the locker and he handed one of them up to Kate.

"Still, I'd like you to put this on while I go forward and inspect the hull."

"What is it, Hobbesie?" Kate asked nervously. "Why does it have this little whistle attached?"

"It's a life vest, dear. You use the whistle to . . . to–oh never mind. Here, I'll show you how to fasten it and then I want you to stay right here with Horatio while I go forward, all right? Nothing to worry about, I promise. I'll go up on the bow and make sure all is well. Sit tight, won't you, dear?" He switched on his flashlight and made his way to the rear of the darkened pilothouse. "Shan't be a moment, I promise."

"But why do I need a life vest if we're not sinking?" she asked as he stepped out into the cool night air. Certainly a reasonable question but he didn't have time to answer it. Whatever they'd hit, they'd hit it hard, and he needed to reassure himself that Kate would not be needing her life vest.

As soon as he left the cozy warmth of the pilothouse and stepped out onto the aft deck, he knew for sure that his lovely evening sail was not going to go exactly as planned. He swung the flashlight's beam over the deck and paused for a moment, looking up into the night sky.

The moon was gone, for one thing. And the air was cold and wet, he could feel it damp on his cheek. The temperature had dropped at least fifteen degrees in the hour or so since they'd left Greybeard Island astern. And what the devil had they hit, he kept asking himself, following the little pool of light he shone on the deck and making his way carefully forward along the starboard side of his yacht. What was out there? The teak decks were a bit slippery in the damp air.

Inside the the pilothouse, he could see Kate still in her seat, stroking her big white cat and tooting on her whistle. Seeing him smiling at her through the window, she looked up and waved her small hand.

Certainly not a good night for naval adventures, he thought, waving back at her. Not a good night at all. He followed the pool of light forward, beginning to worry that he'd made a grave error in deciding to bring the child along.

He'd designed a fixture on the bow, where one could mount either a fifty-caliber machine gun or the powerful searchlight that was mounted there tonight. Hobbes threw a switch at the base that illuminated the thing, snapping and crackling, and suddenly the whole foredeck was bathed in strong white light. He swung the big light to and fro. No structural damage on deck that he could see, which was not surprising. Whatever they'd hit, they'd hit it quite low and head-on or just to starboard. He tilted the big light down at the most forward part of the bow, where the long pulpit extended beyond the bow, out over the water.

Kneeling between the twin anchor rodes out on the pulpit, the commander craned his upper body out over the starboard side, flashlight in one hand and the other hand clinging to the lifeline.

He was shocked at what he saw.

A huge ugly gash, running the entire length of the starboard bow, just above the waterline! Carefully, he played the light from one end of the laceration to the other. It didn't appear deep, thankfully. But fresh wood was exposed, and some kind of black paint marred the beautiful mahogany finish of his beloved boat. Still, the hull appeared intact, he saw to his relief. Whatever they'd hit, they'd struck it a glancing blow. He scratched at the black smear and some of the stuff came away on his finger. It wasn't paint exactly, but some kind of strange substance, and very odd indeed.

Curious, most curious. He rubbed the black, gummy stuff between his fingers. He'd never seen anything quite like it. What could that have come from? He squinted his eyes, looking out across the dark water. Floating out there, somewhere, was something that could cause an unwary vessel terrible damage. An old buoy or floating marker that had broken loose from its moorings? Not big enough. He stood at the starboard rail and swept his light over the water, thinking of the strange shadowy shape he'd seen just before the collision.

Nothing but the black empty sea, now.

Hobbes extinguished the powerful searchlight and turned back toward the pilothouse where little Kate sat waiting. Looking up, he was startled by what he saw. A halo of soft greenish white light now surrounded each window of the cabin. And that meant only one thing: Fog was rolling in.

A bad one. A pea-souper. As he ducked back inside, Kate piped him aboard with two toots of her life vest whistle and gave him a brave little smile.

"I'm glad you're back, Hobbesie. I was beginning to be a tiny bit scared. It's getting a little spooky out here, isn't it?"

Hobbes climbed back into his seat, nodded in the darkness, and stared out into the swirling fog. It was getting thicker by the minute.

Not precisely the word he would have chosen, he thought, tugging his collar up round his neck, but she was exactly right.

It was getting a little spooky out here.

CHAPTER XXII

In the Pigsty

· 3 October 1805 ·

H.M.S. *MERLIN*, AT SEA

Lord Hawke shoved a squealing pig out of his corner with a gentle nudge of his boot and smiled at his two comrades and fellow time travelers.

"Not quite the hero's welcome you'd expected, is it Nick?" he said, casting his eye about the small ship's hold full of pigs. "Hardly a stateroom worthy of Mr. Cunard, I must admit. Still, the *Merlin*'s yet afloat and one really must admire the machine's pinpoint accuracy. There's a lot of ocean just beyond that planking! We could just as easily have arrived out there, I suppose, if we hadn't entered the location correctly. Hobbes is a genius, I must say! Are you a swimmer, Gunner?"

"I float a little, your lordship," Gunner said, settling down in the straw beside Lord Hawke. He'd pulled his blunderbuss from its hiding place under the straw and was now using his handkerchief to polish the barrel. "And I might have preferred the briny to this accommodation. It ain't swine that bothers me so much as that infernal goat. If they keep us locked up in here with that wee beastie all night, I'll likely wring his neck just to keep him silent."

In addition to the dozen or so squealing pigs in the hold, there was one goat on board, much prized for her milk. She apparently bunked with the pigs, which was unfortunate for the three new arrivals. She'd been bleating loudly ever since the peglegged sailor named Ben had locked them in with her and gone off to tell the captain about the stowaways.

Despite Gunner's repeated attempts to soothe the loudly bleating beast, it would not be still.

"No need to strangle the poor thing, old chap," Hawke said. "I imagine the good captain will come running, once he learns a lad's suddenly appeared on board, claiming to have the name of McIver. Meanwhile, just give our noisy friend this." He pulled a large Cuban cigar from the crocodile case he carried in his coat and handed it to Gunner. Gunner stared blankly at the cigar in his hand, dumbfounded.

"All due respect, m'lord, I own I've never seen a nanny-goat as could smoke cigarillos."

Hawke smiled. "Not for smoking, dear fellow, for eating. Unwrap the wrapper leaf and offer her a bit of loose tobacco in your open hand. She'll be most obliged and probably a trifle more relaxed, I daresay."

Gunner held out his hand with a little pile of tobacco and the goat munched it greedily, nudging Gunner's hand for more. In a matter of moments, the animal had dined to its delightful sufficiency, consumed the entire cigar, and retired to the far corner of the stall, mercifully quiet for the first time.

"Ha!" Gunner said, delighted. "I never! A nanny goat as likes a good cigar!"

"She probably smelled them in my coat," Hawke said. "And quite a good nose for a young goat, too. This is good Caribbean leaf I brought along for the voyage. All goats love tobacco, you know, but this one's an aficionado!"

It seemed to Nick that Hawke and Gunner were awfully lighthearted at the moment, considering the terrible disappointment Nick had suffered at the Old North Wharf.

They'd arrived exactly at five-fifty, about twenty feet from the shanty. A little bewildered at first, they'd pinched themselves and stamped their feet and shouted to see if they'd actually made the time journey intact and unharmed. Then, bursting into laughter with sheer delight at what had happened, the three of them had embraced each other. Lord Hawke and Nick had actually jumped for joy at their safe and painless arrival.

"Give you both joy, by Jove, we've done it, lads!" he cried. "Lord, we've done it, haven't we! The machine works perfectly!"

Nick felt for the machine, sewn now into a pocket inside his jacket. Still there, a comfortable round presence, still warm from recent use. Nick had almost come to think of the machine as a perfect little work of art. Something made by man so perfectly that it had somehow become part of nature. Something in such complete harmony with the natural world that it was not bound to any one space or time. It simply had the ability to *flow* like a timeless river or sands across a vast desert. And those who touched it had that ability, too.

Truly, the beauty of the machine was its incredible simplicity. Still, Nick thought, it was strange how they had come to think of their travel as "departing" and "arriving." It really wasn't like that. Rather, it was like the sensation of watching a motion picture. In a dark theater, you see a character in one room and then in the blink of an eye you see the same character standing on a cliff overlooking the sea. And it seems perfectly normal.

That's the way it was with the machine. You blinked your eye in one place and opened it in another. There was of course the warm tingling sensation, but it was actually quite pleasant. It was as if you were standing on the steel deck of a great ship directly above the giant engine. The vibration simply took over your body. In a way, the thrumming sensation made you feel intensely alive. And the sound of the shimmering bells when both hemispheres were joined was quite the loveliest sound Nick had ever heard from a man-made object. As pretty, almost, as the patter of lightly falling rain on *Petrel*'s rooftop.

Suddenly, Nick had found himself outside the shanty. Lord Hawke had drawn his saber, Gunner had primed his blunderbuss, and Nick had kicked open the old wooden door which hung from one hinge. He had little hope of finding Jip on the other side because if Jip were inside, he'd be barking loudly by now. Inside the shanty there was only deathly silence. They entered the door in single file, their eyes slowly becoming accustomed to the dank gloom.

Nick took a deep breath. Would Billy suddenly leap down from the rafters and try to murder them all? Was Jip lying in a dark musty corner of the shanty, hurt and unable to alert him? Was it all nothing but an evil trap, using Jip to lure Nick and his friends into Billy's clutches?

Hello, Nick–squawk–Where's Jip?–squawk–Mystery. Mystery. Hello, Nick.

Blood's red parrot, Bones. Somewhere up in the dark reaches of the shanty roof, squawking in his evil-sounding speech. Gunner raised his blunderbuss and swung it around in the dim light. "Where is he?" Gunner cried, unable to see anything, wheeling about. "I'll have no more of this insolent magpie!"

"Hold on!" Lord Hawke said in a firm voice. "Here's a lamp." He lit an old oil lantern hanging by the door. It threw a weak yellowish light that pierced some few yards into the murky shadows. It was enough light to see that the shanty was empty. No Jipper, just as he'd feared. Nick saw Gunner's eyes, wide and searching for the supernaturalistic bird. There! On a rafter, some fifteen feet above them, they could make out the shadowy red figure of the parrot.

"Don't shoot him, Gunner," Hawke said. "I think he's trying to tell us something. Blood left him here for a reason, perhaps. He may be a messenger." Lord Hawke stood under the bird and shouted up to it.

"Where's your master, parrot?" Hawke said. "Where's Blood?"

Squawk–Mystery. Mystery–squawk–Hello, Hawke. Hello, Hawke.

"Good bird. Where's Jip? Where's the dog?"

Squawk–Mystery–squawk.

Gunner raised the blunderbuss to his shoulder.

"The only mystery here is why I've allowed the foul creature to live this long! Say your prayers, parrot!" Gunner shouted, and pulled the big bronze trigger. The ancient weapon exploded, spewing orange flame and hot lead, brilliant in the gloom. The noise was deafening in the small shanty and white smoke filled the air. When it cleared, they saw the parrot sitting just to the left of where Gunner had fired. It seemed to be picking something from its wing with its beak. Lead shot, perhaps. Had it somehow moved just outside the pattern of the blast in the instant of firing? Impossible!

"I missed him at this range?" Gunner cried, incredulous, reloading his weapon. "Not on your life, I'll warrant! I could give a sparrow a haircut at fifty yards! I'll get you this time, buzzard!" And he raised Old Thunder once more.

"No!" Hawke cried. "Leave him be, Gunner. The bird may be telling us the whereabouts of Jip and Blood. Let me talk to him, please!"

"Parrot! Listen to me!" Hawke said, as if talking to an unruly child. The bird looked down, fixing its bright eyes on Hawke.

Hawke. Hawke–squawk.

"Parrot *parley français*? Parrot speak French?" Hawke said.

Whee–squawk–Speak Frenchy, whee–squawk–Whee.

"He says *oui*. He says yes!" Hawke exclaimed. "Now, listen carefully lads. Parrot! Say 'mystery' *en français!* Mystery *en français!*"

Squawk–Meestair. Meestair–squawk–Mystery–squawk.

"You were right! Blood's got Jip on his flagship, the *Mystère*!" Nick cried. "The French parrot is simply translating *Mystère* to 'mystery' because we're English! You were right, Lord Hawke. We've got to get to the *Merlin*!"

And so in the flickering yellow light of the old oil lamp, and with Billy's French-speaking parrot watching from above, they'd opened the machine once more and inserted the correct Locus and Tempus for *Merlin* that Captain McIver had given them in his letter. Then, in a glimmer of fireflies and a shimmer of bells, they'd disappeared....

And arrived in this pigsty in October, 1805.

Now the door swung open and the sailor with the pegleg and the polished silver tooth jumped into the room.

"You say you're Nicholas McIver, boy?" the sailor said, a smirk on his face.

"That's me, all right!" Nick said, getting to his feet and brushing the straw and hay from his breeches. They were all dressed in simple cotton garments, trousers, shirts, and coats. Still, the visitors from the future must have looked a bit odd to the one-legged sailor.

"Unusual, ain't it, boy, you havin' the same name as our captain?" Pegleg said, eyeing Nick from stem to stern. "Bit unusual, I'd wager. And just who might these two fine gentlemen be?" he asked, raising one bushy white eyebrow, and putting his hand on the hilt of his sword, just in case.

"Hawke is my name," said Lord Hawke, brushing the hay from his knees and rising as well. "And this is Mr. Archibald Steele. Did you offer our compliments to your captain, my good fellow?"

"Aye, that's why I'm here, ain't it? To escort you three stowaways directly to the captain's cabin," said Ben, clearing a path through the squealing pigs with his boot. "Normally, we just throws stowaways overboard, but captain's orders is to bring you to 'im without yer feet going up on deck and without so much as a whisper to a living soul. Step lively, too, we've a couple of holes in our bottom with an enemy vessel bearing down on us. The air'll be filled with enough hot lead to singe yer eyebrows presently! Most of our cannons was knocked out in a little skirmish with the Frenchies this morning! Mind yer heads, mind yer heads now. What's wrong with that goat? He looks a bit greenish around the eyeballs, don't he?"

"Oh, he's all right," Gunner said. "Maybe he ain't used to such fine Cuban cigars is all."

Ben just looked at him and shook his head. Tabaccy-smoking goats? Just what was this old barky coming to?

CHAPTER XXIII

A Skirmish in the Dark

· 6 June 1939 ·

ABOARD *THOR*, AT SEA

Clang. Clang-clang. Clang.

Somewhere out in the fog, not too distant, Old Number Seven chimed its mournful toll. Hobbes listened carefully, glancing down at his chart. Yes, it was the ancient bell-buoy that marked the outer approach to Portsmouth Harbor. Despite his blindness inside the soupy fog, his vessel's damaged bow, and his running at greatly reduced speed, they'd likely make their offshore meeting with John Cory's trawler shortly after midnight. At worst, perhaps an hour late or so, Hobbes saw, by the glow of his wristwatch in the darkened pilothouse.

Passing Old Number Seven to port, Kate said he'd better come outside and see this.

"See what, Kate?" Hobbes asked through the opened window. "Your old friend the moon?"

Kate, who'd gone to a berth below to sleep for most of the journey, had awoken feeling slightly queasy and Hobbes had sent her out on deck to get some air. The fog had lifted somewhat, and Hobbes already had the powerful searchlight illuminated so Cory would see them coming. Katie, her red curls blowing in the cool breeze, stood at the starboard rail feeling much improved and happy to see a bit of the moon back on the water.

"Racing with the moon again, are we Kate?" Hobbes asked cheerfully. Happy to be safely across, he intended to spend the night moored in Portsmouth Harbor. A sunny morning's crossing back to Greybeard Island would be great fun for Kate. Off by eight, he'd have them home for luncheon at Hawke Castle by noon. Kate's face appeared at the open window.

"No-o, not the moon exactly. Something's happening out here, Hobbesie."

Something's happening? Not liking the sound of that one bit, he pulled back on the twin throttles and brought the big boat to a standstill. Throwing the engines into neutral, Hobbes pulled on his old officer's pea jacket and stepped out of the pilothouse into the cool night air. "What is it?" he asked, joining her at the rail. He'd brought his electric torch and he flicked it on.

"The sea. I think it's exploding," Kate said. "Look!"

Hobbes swung the beam of light out over the blackness and was amazed to see a huge mound of boiling white water growing from the surface of the sea, not fifty feet away!

"Whatever could it be, Hobbes?" Kate asked, eyes wide with wonder. "It's not some kind of sea monster, is it?"

It was something monstrous, all right. First, that heaving mound of foaming white water that kept getting bigger and higher, a rising shape that always reminded Hobbes of the sea's surface when a massive depth charge had detonated deep. The mushroom shape rose now, and expanded until it looked like it would indeed explode, and the water all around them was afroth and alive like some giant sea creature was about to make its appearance. Then the roiling sea did explode and a massive ugly black snout of steel surged majestically into the foam-blown sky at a forty-five-degree angle, water pouring off her sleek dark sides in sheets, her diving planes flashing in the moonlight.

Why, she's enormous! Hobbes thought. He'd heard rumors, of course, but this was simply beyond belief. What had they built? An underwater battleship?

"Oh, my," Kate said, "a giant submarine! Oh, my goodness, Hobbes!"

"Goodness doesn't have anything to do with these fellows, my dear," he said. "Our friends the Germans, you know."

"Nazis, Hobbes?" Kate asked, leaning forward over the rail to peer at the monster. "Real live Nazis?"

"I'm afraid so, Kate, I'm afraid so," Hobbes said, raising the binoculars that hung from a strap round his neck.

The conning tower broke through the surface, the whole of the stunning machine still rising at that impossible angle, so unlike anything a boat should be able to do, and Hobbes saw the red swastika and the U-33 legend and knew he was finally face-to-face with the pride of the Kriegsmarine, an Alpha-Class submarine!

He devoured her with his binoculars, hardly able to believe the extraordinary size of the thing. Elated, Britain's most celebrated naval designer and clandestine espionage agent suddenly realized he had just been handed an early Christmas present. The only unfortunate part, he thought, putting his arm round Kate's shoulders, was that he was currently employed as a nanny. Nannies and Nazis weren't likely to be a healthy combination.

The broad bow came crashing down into the still-boiling sea. Instantly, three or four dark figures appeared up in the brilliantly illuminated conning tower, staring across the water at *Thor* with binoculars of their own.

"I wonder what they could possibly want," Hobbes said, and then he was blinded by a powerful searchlight beam coming from somewhere on the forward deck of the U-boat.

"It hurts my eyes, Hobbes, I can't see!" Kate cried. Hobbes bent down and put both hands on the little girl's shoulders.

"Listen, my child," he said. "I'd dearly love it if you'd go below to the galley now. Put the kettle on for me, please, and get out those lovely sandwiches we made at Hawke Castle. I'm famished. Take Horatio with you, and give him a nice bowl of milk. Hobbes will be down in a bit. After I find out what these rascals are up to. Run along now, darling, won't you?"

Kate nodded her head and turned from the rail after giving one last look at the huge black submarine. Nazis, she thought, and far from her mother's strawberry patch, too. "Horatio!" she called. "Come along, you naughty cat, we're going to make a nice midnight supper for Uncle Hobbes!"

She wasn't afraid of Nazis. Why, her own mother didn't even believe in them!

"Turn that bloody light off, why don't you?" Hobbes shouted across the water as soon as the child was gone. "You're blinding me!" There was no answer, but in a moment the light was extinguished, which meant at least one person on the sub spoke English. A few smaller spotlights along the base of the sub's tower were illuminated and trained on *Thor.*

"Ahoy there, vessel *Thor*!" said a heavily accented voice in English floating over the water. "German vessel *Wolf,* here! Do you require assistance?"

Assistance? What kind of assistance could he possibly require from a German U-boat? "No, I do not," he shouted across the water. "Do you?"

There was some hesitation on the conning tower bridge as they sorted that one out, and then one of them said, "We are following you all night! We are making sure your hull is intact after our collision!"

Collision, had he said? Hobbes thought immediately of the ugly scar on his bow. Yes, that was it. He must have somehow collided with the U-boat, lying at periscope depth, an hour or more outside the entrance to Hawke Lagoon.

Or, he thought, his mind taking a darker turn, the giant U-boat had *collided with them!* Hobbes's mind was racing. Perhaps there had been a simple accident, as the Germans claimed, and they were simply acting according to the international rules of the sea. Or had they lain in wait as *Thor* emerged from the lagoon, tracked them, and then staged the collision in an effort to–what–sink them?

No, there could be nothing in that, he decided. That would be an act of war, and their two countries were still at peace, at least for now. So, the more likely thing, he decided, was that the Germans meant to "accidentally" disable his vessel and prevent her crossing.

He and Lord Hawke had long known that Berlin wanted to get its hands on them. Operating entirely undercover, the

Skirmish in the dark

two of them had done enormous damage to German espionage and Gestapo operations inside Germany, and on the continent as well. So far, they'd managed to outwit the Germans at every turn. They remained one of England's best kept secrets. He'd made this weekly run to Portsmouth for almost a year, with nary a hint of trouble. But, what if the Nazis had somehow now identified them? What if–a voice interrupted his thoughts.

"I am *Kapitän* Wolfgang von Krieg!" said a strong voice over the water. "Can you hear me?"

"Yes, I can," Hobbes replied. "Quite well!" The sub was drifting closer and sound traveled quite well over water anyway.

"You appear to be sinking! We are sending a boarding party over to assist you!"

He wasn't sinking. He'd been going forward belowdecks every twenty minutes or so, climbing into the anchor locker under the bow deck, to inspect the hull and had seen only a tiny trickle of leakage from the collision. But now a party of men had gathered near the bow of the U-boat and appeared to be lowering a large rubber raft into the water.

He also noticed, with some discomfort, that a sailor was manning the sub's five-inch deck cannon and had swung its ugly barrel around toward *Thor*. These boys were serious, he thought. The sub had also maneuvered her bow around toward his boat. Lit up like a Christmas tree, he was now a sitting duck for her forward torpedo tubes as well as that deck gun.

"Thank you, Captain, a boarding party won't be necessary!" Hobbes shouted back from the rail. "My vessel is intact and I am proceeding to my destination."

After all, there was nothing preventing him from simply going into the pilothouse, engaging *Thor*'s powerful engines, and leaving this bloke sitting on the surface while he raced off for Portsmouth Harbor.

Nothing, of course, except that five-inch deck gun and the six forward torpedo tubes.

"We insist!" came the captain's voice. "Do not attempt to leave, please! We are boarding you!"

Please? Hobbes decided to see just how polite this fellow could be. "Cheerio, chaps!" he called, smiling into the light and waving good-bye, as if he hadn't heard this last bit about boarding. Turning from the rail, he began to walk aft toward the pilothouse entrance. For a moment, opening the door, he thought he'd successfully called the Nazi's bluff but then four words floated across the water that froze his heart solid.

"Torpedoes away, *mein Kapitän!*"

Hobbes ran back to the starboard rail, grabbing onto it with a death grip. He saw two white torpedo trails in the black water, racing from the bow of the U-boat directly toward him!

"Are you people insane?" Hobbes screamed. "Have you lost your minds, I–" The twin trails were inside twenty feet. It was over.

He squeezed his eyes shut, unable to bear seeing the end. The few remaining seconds were interminable. He thought of Hawke, and how utterly he'd failed him. He should have known they couldn't outwit the Germans forever! He thought of Nicholas and Gunner, too, and finally he thought with overwhelming sadness of the little red-haired girl, waiting for him to come down to tea. He waited for the explosive sound that would mark the beginning of silence and the end of peace.

Nothing happened.

No explosion. No anything. Only some strange beeping noises coming from the water just below where he stood at the starboard rail! Hardly daring to breathe, Hobbes opened his eyes and looked down at the water. And gasped.

There were two small silver objects, hovering in the water, not five feet from *Thor*'s hull! A pair of blinking red lights just above the nose of each silvery tube looked like nothing so much as the eyes of some ungodly metallic fish, staring up at him! And their tails were afroth in churning water, some kind of propulsion system. He stared at the two cylindrical objects, dumbstruck. They defied comprehension. Torpedoes that stopped and looked at you? Blinked?

"*Tigersharks!*" cried a loud, German-accented voice from the conning tower. "Our newest type of radio-controlled torpedo! Don't vorry, zey von't bite you! Unless of course, you try to run! Let me show you!"

Suddenly, the two small torpedoes reversed themselves and backed away from his boat. Quite astonishingly, they then turned away from each other and raced off in opposite directions, one around his bow, the other round his stern! In a flash, they were back, passing each other within inches as they looped in deadly circles around *Thor*, around and around.

"All right, all right!" Hobbes cried. He obviously had little choice in the matter, and he was desperate to get the two Tigersharks away from his boat and little Kate as quickly as possible. "Call off these little monsters and tell me what you want!"

"We want only to assure ourselves that your vessel is seaworthy, *Thor!* Please believe us!" The rubber boarding raft, with three men aboard, was already halfway across the distance.

"Yes, yes. Fine! Permission to board!" he replied, his eyes never leaving the tiny torpedoes as they raced full speed toward each other and stopped less than two feet apart. Suddenly, their red eyes began blinking very rapidly and then they both nosed downward simultaneously. Two powerful but muffled explosions occurred seconds later, and a pair of small mushrooms appeared on the surface. If I live to tell the tale, Hobbes thought ruefully, the boys at Advanced Weapons will be building an English version of the remote-controlled Tigershark torpedo by summer's end. If only there were a way to learn what other little secrets the Alpha sub contained, he thought. And perhaps there was.

Feeling grateful to have a solid deck still under his feet, Hobbes went to the stern, and hung the folding mahogany ladder over the transom so that the Germans might board his boat.

Trying to look unhurried, he ducked into the pilothouse. Opening a locked drawer hidden under his seat, he took out two items, an American snub-nosed .38 Police Special, which he stuck into the waistband of his trousers, and the new packet of Nick's Alpha intelligence for Winston Churchill.

He dumped a box of .38 cartridges into the oilskin document packet. Knowing these fellows might search his boat, he went to the window opposite the Nazi raft, and flung the weighted packet into the sea. It made a small splash and sank instantly. When he turned to check on the Germans, they were coming up over his stern.

The first over the transom was a big blond-headed fellow

in a black sailor's uniform. He had an ugly submachine gun slung over his shoulder. Not a good sign, Hobbes thought, as a second man appeared. This fellow was shorter than the first, quite round, and seemed unarmed and harmless enough.

"Everything's ready, Hobbes," a small voice behind him said. "Aren't you ever coming down to tea?"

"Oh, quite, quite," he said, turning to her, smiling. "Sorry, dear girl. It's just that we appear to be having a few uninvited guests." He motioned toward the stern and Kate saw two men in black helping a third come up the ladder.

"Nazis!" she cried. "Oh, Hobbes, wait till I tell Father! I'm meant to keep an eye on them, you know!"

"Yes, well, you've certainly got a front-row seat now, my dear," Hobbes said, his mind racing furiously. "They're Nazis, all right, the question is, *who are we*?"

"What? What do you mean?"

"Shh, speak softly, dear," Hobbes said, lowering his voice to a whisper. "I mean, I'd rather not have these chaps know who I really am, dear."

He took her hand and quickly led her back down the steps into the main salon where she'd laid the tea. He wanted them to appear as relaxed as possible. He bent to Kate's ear and whispered, "You see, it might be bad for me if they find out who I really am. And I don't have the foggiest notion of what to tell them."

"Oh, that's easy enough, Hobbes," Kate said brightly. "Just say you're my papa!"

Hobbes didn't know whether to hug her or kiss her. Bending to pick her up in his arms, he did both. He was whispering his hastily put-together plan in the child's ear when he saw the sailor with the submachine gun coming down the steps.

He put Kate down and smiled at the chap.

"Hello," the young submariner said with a shy smile. "English not so good, but my name is Ingo. Everyone all right?"

"Hello, Ingo!" Kate said. "I'm Kate. I'm almost seven! Are you a real Nazi? Want to hold my cat?" She held Horatio up to him and the sailor took the big cat in his arms, just as the other two Germans were stepping down into the warmly lit salon. Ingo looked at his superiors sheepishly, and handed the cat back to the little girl, picking up the black Sten gun once more.

"Good evening," said the taller and rounder of the two men. He didn't look like Hobbes's idea of German submarine officers at all. "I am Dr. Moeller, ship's surgeon aboard U-33, and this is my assistant, Klaus."

His English was good, but thickly accented. The man had heavy pink lips and Hobbes was astounded to see him picking his teeth with a long, shiny instrument that was obviously a surgical instrument of some kind, a scalpel!

Hobbes eyed the two men carefully before answering. Everything about them, their black leather jackets, their steel spectacles, said "Gestapo," the vicious German secret police.

"I'm certain there's a reasonable explanation for all this trouble you fellows are going to, Doctor," Hobbes said, looking Moeller in the eye and smiling.

"But, of course!" Moeller replied, through rubbery lips. "We've been sent by our commanding officer to ensure that your vessel is seaworthy following our unfortunate collision! Common marine etiquette, is it not?"

"Your captain says you've been following us for nearly

three hours, Doctor," Hobbes replied mildly. "Clearly, *Thor* is seaworthy. Now, tell me precisely what it is that you boys really want."

"I want," the little German said, with a cruel twist of his lip, "first of all to know your names."

"Kate McIver, aged six and three-quarters!" Kate said, stepping forward, and putting out her hand, which the doctor awkwardly shook. "Nice to meet you! Are you a real Nazi, too? My mother doesn't believe in Nazis, but you seem real enough. This is my daddy, not my mommy. And this is my cat! Isn't he pretty? We all live in a very drafty old lighthouse on Greybeard Island. It's called the Greybeard Light! Perhaps you've heard of it? Say hello to Horatio!" She held up Horatio. The doctor, with a look of utter disgust, took him and handed him to Klaus.

"Yes, yes, Doctor," Hobbes said, picking Kate up in his arms. "My family and I keep the Greybeard Light. My name is Angus McIver."

"Ah, but of course," Dr. Moeller said, stroking his chin. "A lighthouse keeper. I should have known that by the size of your yacht. I think perhaps I should defect to your country so that I, too, might enjoy this luxurious life of the English lighthouse keepers who live in such castles and have such yachts. You don't object if Klaus takes a look around your beautiful boat, do you? Just to ensure her seaworthiness?"

"Be my guest, Klaus old boy," Hobbes said with a smile, looking down at the little red-faced German with the thatch of orange hair over each ear. Klaus didn't look like a fellow who knew one end of a boat from the other.

Hobbes said, "Bow's up that way, stern's back there. Don't

trip over any ropes, chappie." He laughed and put Kate down. "Kate, dear, why don't you take Ingo into the galley and offer him some tea?" Ingo seemed a nice enough chap, Hobbes thought, a boy barely out of the naval academy. Kate seemed to have taken to him, too.

"You are not amusing, Mr. McIver," Dr. Moeller snarled after Klaus had gone forward and Kate had led Ingo by the hand aft into the galley. "And I must warn you. Do not make the mistake of trifling with me. It will have most unpleasant consequences."

He twirled the gleaming scalpel round his fingers deftly and slipped it into his pocket. "You see, I'm quite a terrible surgeon. Perhaps the worst who ever lived," he said with a laugh. "Why, before I retired, I was known as the 'Butcher of Berlin.' Amusing, no? It's why my, how shall I call them, my current 'employers,' find me so useful during interrogations."

"I'm sure they do," Hobbes said, managing a chilly smile. Gestapo all right, assuredly capable of any atrocity. But it wouldn't do to show fear. Hobbes knew this from a few previous encounters with the German secret police.

"Listen, what exactly can I do for you, Doctor? Before you reply, I should make it clear that I am not accustomed to having my boat rammed at sea, nor of having uninvited guests come over my stern at midnight. Please state your business as briefly as possible and then my daughter and I will be on our way."

"We have reason to suspect that you're an English spy, Mr. McIver," Moeller said, pulling back his jacket so that Hobbes could see the big black Luger in the holster under his arm. "We have certain information about this vessel. And, we know for a fact that you and your daughter were visitors at Hawke Castle this evening. The home of Lord Richard Hawke, I believe. He is someone my superiors would very much like to talk to, Mr. McIver. But we're happy to start with you. Assuming you are not Lord Hawke himself?"

Hobbes regarded the man with an icy stare. "Listen to me closely, little fellow. I have no idea who or what you're talking about. You are threatening me. Our two countries are not at war. Not yet, anyway. Are you yourself personally declaring war on England? Do you have that authority? If not, you're merely a foreign criminal, engaging in criminal trespass inside English territorial waters. I can easily have you arrested, you know, I'm very chummy with the local constabulary."

"So, you deny knowing Lord Hawke?" Moeller asked, his hand closing on the grip of the Luger.

"In a word, yes," Hobbes replied coolly. "And leave that cannon right where it is unless you plan to use it. Makes me tremble just to look at it. You see, old chap, I'm absolutely terrified of unpleasant little Nazi policemen who carry unpleasant big German firearms and sail around the Channel in the middle of the night bumping into people and terrifying the seagoing population."

"You are lying to me, Mr. McIver," the German said, and pulled out his pistol. "I believe you perhaps are not who you say you are. Yes! I believe you are Germany's most wanted spy himself, Lord Richard Hawke!"

"Don't be absurd! I wouldn't know a spy from a seagull," Hobbes said. "And I'm not going to answer any more of your ridiculous questions. You can of course kill me where I stand, but it wouldn't look too good in tomorrow's London *Times,* do you think? 'German Agents Murder English Lighthouse Keeper at Sea off Portsmouth!' Might cause an international stir, old chap, bit of a flap in Berlin, too, I might imagine!"

At that moment, Klaus returned from his inspection of the damage to the bow. "You were correct, Herr Doktor," he said. "I sadly must inform the Englishman that his vessel is sinking and must be abandoned. A pity, isn't it?"

Sinking? But that was impossible! Hobbes turned and saw a steady flow of green seawater flooding into the main cabin from the companionway. His beloved *Thor* was going to the bottom and there was nothing at all he could do about it. Suddenly the German plan was clear as Waterford crystal.

He looked at Klaus and the little orange-haired German smiled at him with crooked teeth.

"Ever been aboard a German submarine before, Herr Lighthouse Keeper?" Klaus asked.

The German was unable to decode the strange gleam that came into the Englishman's eyes. Had he been able to, he would have feared for his life.

The Germans had just unwittingly invited the most dangerous fox in England into their henhouse.

CHAPTER XXIV

Captain McIver's Cannonball

· 3 October 1805 ·

H.M.S. *MERLIN,* AT SEA

"It's them three stowaways from the pig locker, Captain," Old Ben said, stomping in on his peg, and ushering the three strange figures, with small ceremony, into the great cabin at the very stern of McIver's crippled frigate.

"Thankee kindly, Ben," the captain said, rising from his table and looking them over. "They don't look a too dangerous lot. You can leave 'em here and go tell Lieutenant Stiles his presence is requested, if you please."

Ben shook his head with uncertainty, but withdrew from the cabin pulling the door closed behind him, unhappy about leaving his captain alone with these scalawags.

The captain regarded the new arrivals silently, taking their measure, and Nick used the brief moment to look around his quarters. It was difficult to believe he'd arrived in such a splendid place!

Sunlight was twinkling out on the blue water beyond the leaded-glass stern windows, throwing a checkerboard pattern of yellow light across the burnished paneled walls and the polished wooden floor. But it was a large gilt-framed portrait on the wall that got Nick's immediate attention. Why, it was an exact duplicate of the one that hung in his own kitchen! With one glaring difference. The admiral in the lighthouse had a jagged hole in his belly, and this fine fellow had none!

The stern-looking fellow in the portrait very closely resembled the living man who now stood before Nick, a huge grin on his bearded face. The captain, Nick noticed, was not a tall man, not much taller than Nick himself, with a shock of brown hair and kind blue eyes that were quite merry considering his current predicament.

"McIver?" said the captain, squinting at Nick. With all the hope in the world in his eyes, you'd have thought him a father beholding his long-lost son. Which in a strange way, Nick was. "Are you McIver, lad?" he asked.

"McIver," said Nick, breaking into a laugh at the sheer impossibility of the scene. "And you the same, sir?"

"Aye, lad, a McIver," he said. "To the very last drop of me briny blood, and fiercely proud to say so, sir!" The captain took Nick's hand in both of his, peered into his eyes, and then all but enveloped the boy in his arms, squeezing him with pure joy. "You've come, haven't you, you've come for all love!"

Lord Hawke extended his hand to the captain. "Lord Richard Hawke, sir, an honor to meet you. I apologize for coming along uninvited, but I've a personal interest in this chap Blood you mentioned in your letter. Young Nicholas was kind enough to allow me to accompany him on this adventure. I hope to resolve a long-standing grievance with William Blood. And in so doing possibly aid you in your current dilemma. Please consider me humbly at your service, sir!" Lord Hawke bowed deeply from the waist and the little captain did the same. Nick had never seen grown men bow to each other before, but in this otherworldly setting, it seemed ever so normal.

"I am most grateful for your friendship and your aid, Lord Hawke," Captain McIver said. "Captain Blood has many enemies, it appears. And the enemy of mine enemy is my friend. The *Merlin,* sir, is honored by your presence!"

"My honor, sir," said Hawke. "And may I introduce our friend Mr. Steele, whom we call Gunner. He is here to offer every assistance, as indeed we all are, sir."

With great cheer he then turned to Gunner. But the big man had walked to the stern windows and was leaning out through the opened panes. He was marveling at the view below, the heaving stern and the screeching white gulls whirling above the sparkling blue sea.

Gunner turned and beamed at the captain, taking a few steps toward him before stopping short, twisting his old hat in his hands.

"Captain McIver, if I might," said Gunner, his eyes full of strong emotion, "I was chief gunnery officer in His Majesty's Navy for near thirty years, and I never dreamed to have the honor of standing in such a holy place as this, nor shaking hands with so noble a personage as yourself, sir. It is my very great pleasure now to salute you, Captain, and proud of the hallowed glory you stand for I am, sir, and the blessed and honored traditions as what you fellows bestowed down to us in the service, as we tried to uphold in our poor way, Captain. It will be my great honor to fight one last sea battle standing by your side, sir!"

Nick looked at Gunner in some amazement. He thought Gunner was going to get all watery around the eyeballs, and indeed he was close, but his lifelong friend managed to get his hand up to his brow in a stiff and proper salute.

The captain returned his salute with great ceremony and a smile of good cheer on his own face as they, too, embraced. In a moment, all four burst into loud and happy laughter at the simple wonder of the occasion. Two old sailors who had journeyed through time itself to find each other in this moment. It was either destiny or a trick of destiny which had brought them all together and it really didn't matter. To those gathered in that sunny cabin, it was magic itself.

Captain McIver wiped something from his eye and then coughed politely to get their attention.

"Now, afore we all go giddy as schoolgirls, and I'm guilty as the lot of you, I ain't ashamed to say, pray come to this window and look at what's upon us, will you? Why I called upon your kindness, Nick, and begged you use that infernal machine–look there off our starboard quarter!"

The captain handed Nick a long brass telescope, just the kind that hung over his bed at the lighthouse. Nick raised it to his eye and his heart skipped a beat as he grasped the focus ring with his thumb and forefinger. Strange. The glass felt oddly familiar! There were two raised letters there and he knew exactly what they would be before he looked; he held his breath as he turned the instrument over to see.

"NM!" He was holding the same spyglass he would inherit a hundred and thirty years from now! The glass of his ancestor, Captain Nicholas McIver, now standing beside him.

"Ahem!!" the captain said, interrupting Nick's stunned

reverie. "There'll be time enough to unbosom ourselves once we've seen the last of that despicable rogue. There! D'ye see him, lad? Do you see that devil flying over the sea?" Nick put his boot up on the velvet cushioned banquette that lined the window and braced the long telescope, elbow on his knee. He drew a sharp breath. He couldn't believe the image in the glass! A full-blown man-of-war coming straight at him, hard on the wind! All her snowy white sails were set and full, main to royals and stunsails, throwing white water to either side of her bows, sun gleaming from the rows of brass cannons set along the length of her bright red topsides and–he stopped, blinked his eye, and looked again–it couldn't be!

"Why, she's *red*!" Nick exclaimed, examining her hull more closely through the telescope. Indeed the big frigate was painted bright red from stem to stern, with golden quarter-boards on either side carved in the shape of striking serpents. There was a massive figurehead under her bowsprit, also done in brilliant gold. It was the figure of a woman whose long flowing tresses, Nick now saw, were actually masses of writhing golden snakes!

"What is red, Nick?" Hawke asked. He and Gunner joined Nick at the open window. "What is red?"

"The *Mystère*! Blood's flagship!" Nick said, not wanting to relinquish the glass. "Stem to stern, she's painted bright red!" But all Hawke could see with the naked eye was a small black flyspeck on the horizon, a ship, hull down, headed their way across the shimmering ocean. She was maybe an hour away, Hawke noted, maybe less.

"Aye, she's red all right," said the captain. "If you can credit it, a ship o' the line, as red as a sailor's eye when the rum pot's dry. She was once Nelson's, you know; we lost her in oh-three off Gibraltar. Now, she's a disgrace to any seagoin' man the world over, she is. A red frigate indeed! A direct affront to Lord Nelson's proper black-and-white checker and the natural ways of the service. Bill had her up in dry dock down south at Les Lupes last winter, and done up in such a frightful shade of crimson as makes a man turn his head away in disgust. We hear even the little Frenchman Bonaparte himself is outraged at the tartiness of it. But that's Billy Blood for you, and that's him comin', lads, in his blood red *bateau*, and he means to send us to the bottom!"

"What's your exact situation here, Captain?" Lord Hawke asked, looking at Billy's crimson abomination flying toward him in the lens of the spyglass. He felt a stab in his heart when he realized that little Alexander and Annabel could well be held captive aboard that very vessel. He was close, now. So very close. "Any changes since you wrote the letter? It would seem the fire aboard is under control. No smell of smoke in the hold."

"Aye, and not a moment too soon, either," McIver said. "Them flames was lickin' at the door of the powder hold, too. But we snuffed it, all right. Our problem ain't fire now, but water. She's holed like I said, two of 'em below the waterline, sir. My first lieutenant, Stiles by name, says she'll swim for maybe an hour or so. And there's our real dilemma, sir."

"Blood's long cannons will reach us before then, won't they?" Hawke asked, and in the glass he could see them, run out for battle, three decks of them, gleaming in the sun.

"Aye, and if we sit, we sit like a duck," McIver said. "And I ain't never been one for sittin'. So, we shall fly, sir! As I've a meeting with Nelson himself three days hence at the Palace of St. James in London, we shall verily fly! I must be there no matter what transpires in these next hours. The very future of England is at stake, sir!"

"Are you at liberty to explain it, Captain?" Hawke asked.

"Aye. We've a Spanish spy aboard, a slippery one known out in the Americas as Velasquez. We captured him when we sank the galleon *Conquistador* just after she'd put into Barcelona on her way back from the Gulf of Mexico. Still full of Spanish gold, I might add, most of which now lies in our hold. But, more important, there also lies Señor Velasquez. He was carrying documents that proved an unholy alliance between Spain and France, although Spain has solemnly promised King George she'd not enter this war! Politics, sir, murderous politics and scurrilous deception."

McIver produced a scrolled piece of paper from within his blue greatcoat and spread it on the table. The bottom half was blackened and charred. It was scrawled in Spanish, with an English translation in a rough hand below.

"We found this on 'im, too. Tried to burn it, he did, but I snatched it from 'im just in time. A plot, as you can read here, to lure Nelson's fleet down off Cape Trafalgar and into a trap laid by both enemy navies combined, over fifty of their bloody frigates and galleons just waitin', lickin' their cowardly chops! In any event, the entire British fleet is at grave risk!"

"May I inquire as to your scheme, Captain?" Hawke said. "To reach England in time? Your flight plan, so to speak?"

"Flight plan?" asked the captain, clearly puzzled.

"Bad joke, sir," Hawke replied, with an embarrassed smile at Nick. "No aeroplanes for a hundred years. Sorry."

"Not at all, sir," McIver said, pulling a chart from the drawer. "Here it is. You see, I can't run behind this big rock because of these blasted reefs all round. And I can't sit because we're badly holed and sinking. So we're throwing up every square yard of canvas she'll carry and going out to meet Blood. The only way to plug those two holes is to get her heeled over to port. Get the holes above the waterline and the ship's carpenter will have her right in jig time. We'll be seaworthy again at least. Outgunned and outcanvassed, sir, but never outwitted!" McIver laughed, and slapped his knee.

Gunner spoke up. "Have you been able to repair much of her gunnery, sir?"

"The lads are hard at it now," the captain replied. "But we lost more cannonades than we can afford, Gunner. Any help you could give us there is welcome."

Gunner nodded. "I have your permission then to go on deck and parley with the gunnery crews?"

"By all means, sir, by all means! But, pray, not in that costume! You fellows scared poor Ben witless with those outfits! As soon as Lieutenant Stiles has a moment to spare, I intend to explain your presence to him in some credible fashion and then have him get you each a set of these nankeen trousers and blouses. Then your appearance won't be such a distraction to the ship's company. There are several hundred men up there, Gunner, with one thing on their minds. Avenging Blood's treachery. They'll take any help any of you can afford them. But they won't have time to ask too many questions. Now, look."

The captain unfurled another massive chart and spread it across his table. "See, we lie here, by my mark. To the east, the reefs here and here and that large nasty rock blocking our escape north, round to the lee of the island. The whole infernal coast is treacherous! Ought to build a lighthouse right here, is my opinion!" He pointed his stubby finger to the spit of land where Nick now lived.

"A lighthouse there on the point would be a fine idea, Captain," Lord Hawke said with a grin that only Gunner noticed. "You should suggest it to the Admiralty, sir."

"Gravestone Rock," Nick said absently, although it wasn't marked as such on the chart. It wouldn't acquire that name for more than fifty years, he realized, after it had claimed the lives of hundreds of poor sailors. Then, a lighthouse *would* be built and the dreadful loss of life would cease. The lessons of history, his mother would call it, were often painful.

"So, you'll advance out to the north here, Captain?" Hawke said, tracing the route with his finger. "Where Blood waits. And then what? Engage?"

"That's what Blood will expect, certainly," said the captain, rubbing his chin. "Billy knows I've never been shy of a fight. Don't forget, he served under me as second in command for over ten years of this miserable war. He'll be expecting me, as is my custom, to come right in and trade broadsides at close quarters."

"But not at all what you intend, I take it," said Hawke.

"No, my lord, not what I intend at all. Wounded as we are, though Blood doesn't know how badly, that's a fight I cannot win," he said. "No, I intend a feint. I'll fly straight toward him as if I'm preparing to engage, you see. At the last possible moment I plan to tack right up under his bow, get off one ripplin' broadside with the port guns, and then a swift tack about as if we're goin' around to give him a taste of our starboard cannons! But me plan, sir, is *not* to complete that maneuver, but rather to tack away, make a run for it northwest, to Portsmouth, and hope for the best."

Hawke took a breath, not at all sure it was proper for a civilian to question a captain in His Majesty's Navy about his plans. On the other hand, McIver had sent an urgent request for assistance, so he chanced it. "Captain, surely he has a firepower advantage, not to mention speed! Why not–?"

The captain raised his hand. "Aye, he has both, to be sure. But he won't shoot until we engage, and in any event, I don't plan to stick around and let him splinter us. I'm going to run and run hard for England, sir! In the time it takes him to discover my intent, and get under way, we'll have opened up some sea between us. Even still, he could catch us. But I'm going to lighten up this barge, sir. I'm going to heave every single cannon, and every single ball of lead shot over the side. Stores, too. Water, beer, and salt pork, too! Lightened, we'll fly, sir! We'll fly to England with empty stomachs and full hearts, sir, but we will warn Nelson of this dreadful treachery!"

"Begging your pardon again, sir," Hawke said carefully, "but why not just use the Tempus Machina to travel to London and warn Nelson? It seems logical enough, sir."

"And leave my crew, my sinking ship, sir? And avoid the long-awaited showdown with this dog Blood? I think not, sir, and I'm sure upon reflection you would withdraw that question!"

McIver was red and fuming and Lord Hawke quickly saw the error of his ways. He bowed deeply in apology for his insult. He remembered that in this era duels and bloodshed had resulted from far less, for these were affairs of honor, not logic.

"My deepest apologies, Captain. I was substituting expediency for honor and so disgraced myself by my insult," Hawke said. "I am truly sorry, sir!" He was relieved to see the captain quickly return to a less warlike posture.

"It is history most ancient, m'lord," said McIver, realizing the man had made an understandable mistake, hailing, as he did, from another time.

Hawke continued, "But, in all events, Captain–and again, forgive my ignorance–why would Blood hold his fire until we sail out to engage? Why not start pounding us as soon as his long guns can reach us?"

It was a good question, but the captain had an equally good answer.

"Quite right, m'lord, but even Billy Blood is not so despicable as to fire upon an enemy sitting like a duck dead in the water. No, I warrant he'll hold his fire until I–"

"GET DOWN!" Gunner screamed. "Everybody hit the deck!!" He dove from the window where he'd been standing and tackled Nick from behind, pulling the boy to the floor with him. He couldn't believe it! He'd been watching Blood's approach in the glass, seen a tiny puff of white smoke on the *Mystère*'s red bow, and then, incredibly, a cannonball, that's what it was, growing ever larger in the lens! It was bounding toward him across the water like a skipping stone, skimming off the tops of waves. It appeared to be headed directly at the *Merlin*'s stern!

"Lord, Gunner, what's the–" McIver started, himself diving for the floor, but at that instant the huge lead ball smashed through the glass and lead of the stern window, missed the captain's head by a whisker and, showering him with glass, tore through the great cabin and slammed into the bulkhead where hung the admiral's portrait.

They all regarded the portrait from the floor in shocked silence. Nick, openmouthed with wonder, rose and stood before the painting in stunned silence. The admiral, with his generous belly swathed in navy blue and bright brass buttons, now had a jagged hole right in his middle! Nick stuck his fist through the hole. It fit perfectly! Courtesy of the French cannonball, this painting was now a perfect match for the one currently hanging over the McIver kitchen hearth! Now, he thought with a smile, he alone would know the secret of the famous hole in the admiral's belly. This *was* the exact picture now hanging in the lighthouse.

"I say!" Lord Hawke said, getting to his feet and picking pieces of broken glass from his clothing. "That ball had to have traveled well over two miles! Quite extraordinary, what?"

He was quite jolly about it, in fact, and seemed to be happy that the battle with Billy Blood seemed finally to be joined. A high red color suffused his cheeks and his eyes were alight. Here, surely, was a man who dearly loved to clear life's decks for action and lay on with a will.

Captain McIver got to his feet, swearing a blue streak, and put his fist through the hole in his aged relative. "Aye. And now the scurvy dog has holed me own grandfather, Admiral Noah McIver! Whatever cannon can Blood possess that can fire a ball that far? Nothing I know of can fire a ball a tenth of that distance. Some infernal piece of artillery he picked up roaming around in the future, I'll wager you that!"

"Desperate situation, Captain," Lord Hawke said, moving to the stern window and raising the telescope. "He's got some advanced weaponry on board. My opinion is that we can't advance into such fire, and if we sit, as you say, sooner or later, we sink. Whether Blood sinks us, or the ocean does it for him, doesn't much matter."

"Aye, aye," said McIver, a worried look clouding his brow. "He's trapped us, all right. He'll pound us as he closes, then sit just outside the range of our cannonades and pick us apart like ducks at a shooting gallery at Scarborough Fair. Blast his turncoat hide!"

Gunner had gone to retrieve the spent cannonball and now he entered the cabin and held the ball up, inspecting it closely. "It's not the cannon he picked up in the future, Captain, it's the powder. Look at these flash burns on the ball. Nitro."

"Nitro?" asked the captain, taking the ball and turning it in his hands.

"Aye, nitroglycerine," Gunner replied. "An explosive ten times more powerful than black powder, sir. It will be developed about fifty years from now. He's gotten hold of some and is adding it to his powder supply. That's why the ball reached us so easily. He can fairly pepper us at will, sir, and, by the looks o' this, that's just what the rogue intends!"

CHAPTER XXV

The Windowless Submarine

· 7 June 1939 ·

OFF PORTSMOUTH, ENGLAND

Do you think Nicky and Lord Hawke are having as grand a time as we are, Hobbes?" Kate whispered.

"Oh, I imagine they are, dear, although I do hope their boat isn't sinking!" Hobbes pulled the collar of Kate's jacket up around her ears. There was still a chill in the night air. He glanced back over his shoulder at the doomed *Thor*. She was settling rapidly down by the bow now, as seawater flooded her forward compartments. He turned away, unable to bear the sight of her slow death.

They were aboard a large black rubber raft, an inflatable, with three wooden thwart seats. Hobbes and Kate sat in the bow, Klaus and Ingo were just behind them on the middle seat, paddling, with Dr. Moeller and his Luger sitting silently in the stern. Hobbes could not help marveling at the towering superstructure of the submarine growing ever larger on the moonlit sea. The U-boat had to be three times again as large as the biggest British sub. The thing was monstrous.

The three Germans had been silent since boarding the raft

and Hobbes could only wonder at their true intentions. He couldn't prove it, but he was sure Klaus was responsible for their predicament. He'd had ample time alone up in the bow, after all. There were any number of ways to open a gaping hole in *Thor*'s wooden hull. But, why? She was lost, at any rate. He was worried about their personal safety, especially the child's. But what could he do? They had no choice. They had to accept the doctor's offer to return them to Greybeard Island aboard the U-boat.

But what would happen to them once they were aboard the black monstrosity ahead was anybody's guess. He needed a plan, and quickly.

Surely, he reassured himself, no peacetime German submarine captain would allow any harm to come to two innocent English civilians. Ingo seemed a nice enough fellow, but both Moeller and Klaus were beneath contempt. Luckily enough, though they suspected he might be an English agent, they had no idea who he really was. Certainly not that he was a British naval commander engaged in his weekly mission, ferrying crucial intelligence to Churchill!

Or, he thought with a smile, someone with a keen professional interest in the latest German submarines. Only days ago, he'd have been glad simply to catch a glimpse of one of these things through his binoculars. Now, he was about to board one!

Indeed, Britain's foremost naval intelligence expert was stunned to find himself minutes away from a six- or seven-hour passage aboard the most closely held secret in the German Navy! As an invited guest of the German Navy itself! Hawke would love the poetic irony of it, he thought, and wondered again how his dear friend was finding life in the early nineteenth century. Both had embarked on a remarkable pair of adventures, though the success of either was far from guaranteed.

Somehow, he had to find a way to turn this incredible opportunity to his advantage without endangering Kate. He was considering the beginnings of a promising scheme when Klaus spoke up, in German. One more thing the arrogant little Gestapo agents didn't know about him, Hobbes thought with a smile, was that their friendly lighthouse keeper spoke fluent German.

"If he is a spy, Doctor, perhaps this is not so good an idea after all. To take him aboard our most secret submarine."

"*Dummkopf!* If he is a spy, you idiot, he won't live to tell anyone about it. I'll make sure of that. If he convinces Colonel Steiner that he is who he claims to be, we'll simply return the two of them to their little lighthouse and continue our search for this elusive Hawke."

"*Ja,* this is true," Klaus said. "Fancy yacht for a lighthouse keeper, though, isn't it? I couldn't find any papers on board her, but still I think he's lying. What's he doing at Hawke Castle if he's not in league with Hawke?"

"If anyone can find that out, it's me and Little Willy, isn't it?" the doctor said, and for some unpleasant reason they both erupted into laughter.

So the Germans had finally identified Hawke, Hobbes now knew, just as he'd always feared they might. He took Kate's hand and squeezed it gently. He had the outline of a plan but somehow he needed to tell Kate about it before they reached the U-boat. She looked up at him, smiling bravely.

"Horatio is very excited about going for a submarine ride, Father," she said. "And I guess I am, too! I'm sorry about our pretty boat, though."

"Thank you, dear. I'm sorry, too." He looked back once again at *Thor* and winced at the sight of her. Her bow was angled down at a precipitous angle and all of her cabin windows had gone dark, seawater having now shorted out her electricals. It wouldn't be long before her stern came up and she slipped beneath the waves. He turned away, unable to bear the sight of her, and whispered in Katie's ear. "Listen carefully to Hobbes now, all right? We're going to play a secret game when we get aboard the submarine, won't that be fun?"

"I love secrets, Hobbesie," Kate whispered back. "What are we going to play?"

"Spy," he said, and quickly began to outline his scheme, glad to see the child nod her head in understanding.

In a few moments, all of Hobbes's whispered plans were interrupted by the rubber bow of the raft bouncing gently against the great hull of the submarine. He looked Kate in the eye and another brief nod of her head said she understood exactly what to do.

Hobbes reached out to grab a line dangling from the U-boat, and when he touched the hull, he discovered the steel sides were sheathed in black rubber. It explained the ghastly mess on his bow, but what was it for? Sound deadening, perhaps, to help her avoid the British destroyers' listening devices? Yes, another brilliant notion for the Advanced Weapons chaps at Portsmouth. The loss of *Thor* might prove a small price to pay for such valuable intelligence. That is, if he should live to tell the tale.

"Home sweet home!" Klaus said in English, and then he laughed.

Moments later, Hobbes stood atop the submarine conning tower with Katie in his arms. He paused for a last breath of the sweet air, looking down sadly at his sinking vessel from this great height. *Thor* had only minutes to live. "Are you all right, Kate?" he whispered in the child's ear. "Can you remember everything Daddy told you?"

"Yes, Daddy, I remember. But I am a little sleepy, I guess," Kate whispered back. "Do they have beds on submarines?"

"I'm sure they do, dear," Hobbes said, and then they were all silent, waiting for a crewman inside to acknowledge Ingo's one-two knock on the hatch and open it.

At their feet, the main hatch cover opened with a loud pop and a waft of dank air. Someone's hand swung it up and open. A strange reddish light streamed up from the round hatch. A bald head, glistening with sweat, emerged and looked somewhat suspiciously at Ingo, then at the two strangers he'd brought back to the sub. Ingo barked at him and he backed down the steel ladder, motioning for Hobbes to follow.

Hobbes took a deep breath and a last glance at *Thor*. Her stern had come up at a steep angle and most of her bow was already under water. She was not long for this world. With Kate still in his arms, he turned away and stepped down onto the first rung of the ladder.

Descending slowly into the warm, stale air of the sub, Kate carefully cradled in one arm, he took the rungs of the ladder carefully and deliberately. Ingo was following behind them, with the cat Horatio in his arms. Klaus and Dr. Moeller had gone to the bow for a quick smoke, it seemed. He had already decided that he would kill Moeller if he so much as laid a hand on Kate.

Hobbes sensed many pairs of eyes below, watching them descend. He couldn't worry about it. He could think only of how best to get them out of this predicament alive. Luckily, the plan he'd feverishly formulated while being rowed across to the submarine seemed like it might succeed. He'd need Kate's help, of course, but if she was half the little actress he thought she was, it just might work indeed.

When they were finally standing at the base of the ladder, the crewmen in the control room gathered around, craning their necks to get a good look at this great curiosity, an Englishman and his daughter.

Hobbes knew it was time for his performance to begin and that executing his bold scheme would take every ounce of his ingenuity. He gave Kate a kiss on the cheek, and then turned to the crew.

"My daughter and I would like to thank everyone aboard for your great kindness," Hobbes said. "Indeed, had you not been here to rescue us, we–" Kate was tapping his arm.

"May I ask them a question, Papa?"

"Certainly, dear. Anything you'd like," Hobbes said, and saw Kate turn and favor the crewmen with her most winning smile.

"Well, I was just wondering if this old boat had any windows," the little girl asked sweetly. "Because if it does, you ought to open one of them up right away! It's dreadfully stinky in here, don't you gentlemen think?"

There was a loud burst of laughter from all those crewmen who understood English, and then more as they translated it for all those who didn't. Hobbes knew his idea couldn't succeed without Kate's help, but the little girl astounded him. She was every bit as good an actress as the popular young American star, Shirley Temple. Together, he thought, they had a chance. A slim one, perhaps, but a chance.

"Silence, you fools!" Dr. Moeller shouted as he descended the ladder. "Silence! Where is Colonel Steiner?" he asked a crewman standing at the periscope. "We have brought him a little surprise. Here is the Englishman whose powerboat we spotted leaving the castle earlier!"

Suddenly, a short, stubby officer with close-cropped blond hair and steamed-up glasses stepped from the shadows into the pool of red light. He elbowed men roughly aside to get to Hobbes and then addressed him directly.

"I'm terribly sorry about the loss of your vessel," the man said to Hobbes. "I am Lieutenant Steiner, second in command aboard this submarine. I understand our unfortunate accident has had tragic results. Fortunately, of course, we were nearby and able to offer safe passage for you and your daughter back to Greybeard Island."

"Of course," Hobbes replied, eyeing the man carefully. "Very fortunate. You'll forgive us, Lieutenant. This adventure has been most upsetting. My daughter is very sleepy. Do you have a bed where she might rest?"

"Indeed," Willy said. "I'm sure this is all most distressing for both of you. I will arrange sleeping accommodations for our voyage back to the island. We are preparing to dive now and should have you home by tomorrow morning."

"Most kind, Lieutenant. We're very tired."

"Ingo!" Steiner called. "Won't you show our guests back to

their stateroom? I believe Chief Torpedoman Ober's quarters, sadly, are now available. Twin bunks, as I remember? Small, but you and your daughter should be quite comfortable for the overnight crossing."

Suddenly, a loud klaxon horn wailed loudly throughout the ship and red lights mounted on the various bulkheads dimmed and then began to flash rapidly. Kate grabbed Hobbes's hand as they felt the deck beneath their feet pitch forward at a sharp downward angle.

"*DIVE! DIVE! DIVE!*" shouted the officer of the deck and Kate looked up at Hobbes with a mixture of worry and excitement.

"We're going under the ocean now, aren't we, Daddy? I hope someone remembers to close all the windows!" Kate said, earning another titter of laughter from the control room audience.

"Yes, darling, we're submerging. Isn't it exciting? Thank you, Lieutenant, for your generosity," Hobbes said, as Kate yawned right on cue. "It's been a long night. You're not offended if we call it an evening?"

"I would be offended if you do, but only because I've some hundred-year-old schnapps in the wardroom and no one to share it with. Will you allow Ingo to show your lovely daughter to your quarters while you join me in the officers' wardroom, yes?" Hobbes looked at Kate. He could tell she was going to be fine. If he didn't know better, he'd swear she was actually having fun.

"Are you quite all right, little Kate?" Hobbes asked, ruffling her curls. "Do you mind if Father has a quick schnapps with the lieutenant?"

"Don't worry about me, Father. I'm fine." She stood on tiptoe for a kiss, and Hobbes, who of course had little experience with fatherly things, wasn't quite sure how to go about it. Placing his hands on her shoulders, he bent and kissed the top of her head.

"Good night," he whispered, "and thank you."

"Good night, Papa," she said and, with the white cat in her arms, looked up at Ingo with a smile. Hobbes was grateful that she seemed to have found a new friend in the young submariner. Holding Ingo's hand, Kate made her way past all the admiring glances of the crew. Clearly, she'd already won their hearts. So far, so good, he mused.

"Shall we adjourn to the wardroom, Lieutenant?" Hobbes asked cheerfully. "I've a weakness for schnapps that I'm sure you can understand. An occupational hazard among lonely lighthouse keepers!"

In the wardroom, Hobbes sat at a round table covered with dark green baize, while Willy poured them each a healthy dollop of fruit brandy from a heavy crystal decanter. Hobbes took a sip and murmured his appreciation. "I'm glad you like it," Willy said, and delicately placed a fragrant yellow cigarette in a long black holder. He then lit it, politely blowing the smoke away from Hobbes's face as he did so.

"Excuse me, how rude of me! Would you like a cigarette as well?" Willy said, sliding the pack across the table to Hobbes. "They're quite good, Egyptian in fact. I buy them from my man in Cairo. Egyptian Deities they're called."

The little officer was strutting back and forth with the cigarette holder stuck at a jaunty angle in his teeth. Hobbes was sure he imagined that the effect was quite grand, but in truth Hobbes was having difficulty suppressing a laugh. He was reminded of the popular moving picture star Charlie Chaplin in the film *The Great Dictator*.

Suddenly, the German stopped, pivoted on his boot heel, and regarded Hobbes with an expression meant to convey authority, but which struck the British commander as comically absurd.

"Your real name, sir, if you would be so kind?" said Willy behind a cloud of exhaled smoke and in his best imitation of upper-class English speech.

"Not at all," Hobbes said with an even smile. "My real name is Angus McIver, as I told your two minions before. And your real name, if you'd be so kind?"

The man gave him a hard look and considered his words carefully before he replied.

"Steiner is my real name, Mr. McIver," Willy said. "Lieutenant Steiner, as you may observe from my uniform insignia. But that is only my naval rank. In the SS, I am a full colonel." He watched Hobbes's face for a reaction to his revelation about being Secret Service. When none was forthcoming, he continued. "You may call me Colonel Steiner. Yes, Steiner. From the German word *stein*, meaning stone, or rock in English. A stonemaker. Strength that endures, wouldn't you agree, is the quality of rock?"

"Strong, but exceedingly dense, wouldn't you also agree?" said a smiling Hobbes.

Reaction was swift. Willy pulled his sidearm from the leather holster under his shoulder, not the Luger on his hip, but a small, evil-looking automatic, and leveled it between Hobbes's eyes. "Insult me once and you see what happens!

Do it again and you are merely an early English casualty in a war that hasn't even started yet! No stones, no matter how dense, will mark your watery grave, McIver! Do I make myself entirely clear?"

"Entirely, sir. I'm sorry," Hobbes said smiling. "I was only testing you. I've learned what I needed to know. You are clearly not a man to be trifled with, Lieutenant Steiner."

"*Colonel* Steiner," Willy said, irritated.

"I'm sorry, I said 'lieutenant,' didn't I?" Hobbes said. "Foolish of me. Only a fool would mistake you for a mere lieutenant."

Willy smiled, flattered, and said, "You are an intelligent man, Mr. McIver. Obviously perceptive. Cultured. I find it odd that such intelligence and good breeding is wasted in a remote lighthouse in the English Channel–odd, and, how shall I say this, difficult to believe?"

"A lot of time to read, I suppose. One does pick up a good deal in books," Hobbes replied, cautiously. "Such is the life of the poor lighthouse keeper. But of course, I had no choice, Colonel. You see, I inherited the bloody thing. In my family for generations. Yes, five generations of lighthouse keepers. Ah, well, such is life."

"You're not happy there, Mr. McIver?" said Steiner. "In your cozy little lighthouse? It is quite pretty, standing up there above the sea. We often use it as a navigational landmark."

"I've been happy," Hobbes said, taking a deep breath and plunging ahead with his bold plan. He had, after all, nothing to lose and England would soon have a war to win. "At least, until recently. Now, I find myself involved in–other–activities. More interesting. More, how shall I say this, more *exciting*."

The German stopped in his tracks and looked at him.

Hobbes saw that his dangling hook, if not set, was at least poised above the little Nazi in midair like a fat mayfly above a swiftly rising trout.

"Precisely what do you mean by that, Mr. McIver?" he said, leaping to the bait just as Hobbes had hoped he would.

"I mean, Colonel Steiner, that I am an English spy. I mean that I am in fact the ringleader of a little band called the 'Greybeard Spies.' Heard of them?"

"Very interesting," Willy said slowly. "A spy, are you? We shoot spies, you know. Any reason at all why I should not shoot you now, where you sit?" Once more he aimed the automatic at Hobbes.

"Just one," Hobbes said. "I'm for sale."

At that moment, the door banged open and a large bleary-eyed fellow careened into the room. "Ah, *mein Kapitän*," Willy said, "let me introduce you to Angus McIver, whose yacht we unfortunately sank this evening."

The submarine captain said not a word, but stared at Hobbes with a malevolence he'd rarely seen. And it wasn't just hatred for the English Hobbes saw in those eyes. It was something else. What was it? Familiarity! Yes. Hobbes had the distinct feeling he'd met the man somewhere before. But where? Who was he?

"Sorry about your boat," the captain said, and staggered back to the door. "You should watch where you're going. Come to my cabin when you and Dr. Moeller are done with the Englishman, Willy," he said, and pulled the door closed behind him with a loud metallic bang.

"Charming fellow," Hobbes said mildly, and drained the balance of his glass of schnapps.

CHAPTER XXVI

In the Nick of Time

· 3 October 1805 ·

H.M.S. *MERLIN,* AT SEA

I have a map here, Captain McIver, of the entire reef," Nick said, pulling the scrolled paper from inside his jacket. "I made it myself so I can vouch for its complete accuracy." Hawke, who'd been watching the relentless advance of Billy Blood from the stern windows of the English warship, hurried over to the table where Nick and McIver stood.

"A cartographer, too, are ye, boy?" asked the captain, chuckling. "Aye, you've that salty McIver blood coursin' through yer veins, lad!"

Nick unfurled the handmade map and placed it on the table but the edges kept curling over, making it impossible to read. He pulled the knife from his inside pocket and used it to affix an edge of the map to the wooden table. He saw the captain wince and feared he was reacting to Nick's casual treatment of his expensive officer's furniture.

"That's Bill's dagger," the captain said, squinting his eye and staring at the bone-handled knife. "Wherever did you get it?"

"He stuck it in my front door with a letter announcing he'd stolen my old dog, Jip," Nick replied, feeling a jolt of anguish as he realized how much he missed his beloved dog. He wondered if Jip were even now imprisoned aboard the crimson frigate bearing down on them.

"He stuck it in my front door once, too," said Captain McIver, ripping open the bodice of his shirt and revealing an angry red scar about six inches long down his breastbone. "Although there weren't no ransom note stuck with it. Old Ben thought it was the end when he found me that night, but the ship's physic just stitched me up and made me drink nothing but fine port wine for a week. Good as new in three days!"

"How'd it happen?" asked Nick.

" 'Twas the night of that bloody mutiny," said McIver, "when I caught old Bill here in my cabin and breaking into me locker to get his hands on those infernal time machines. I managed to get a pistol on him and get one of 'em aways from him and got that dagger in the chest for me trouble. Knocked over that oil lamp there in the scuffle, which lit them draperies and the whole cabin went alight with flames. Bill's own coat caught fire. That's when Ben rushed in and old Bill Blood, he lit out of here with only that second golden ball hid under his arm like a snake with his tail on fire!" The captain chuckled a bit and continued, "But, pray, let's hear more of your plan, Nick. Lord knows we need one, and soon." He looked toward the window. "The flaming snake returns upon us relentless now, don't he?"

Nick nodded, flattening out his chart so all could see.

"You'll forgive me, Captain, but your current chart is woefully inaccurate as regards our present position," Nick said, getting down to business. "This is a chart I made of these waters by diving on each reef and noting the dimensions, depth, and exact location of each and every one. You would have no way of knowing this, sir, but from our present position there is an escape route to the north here, twixt the island and the large Gravestone Rock as we call it in my time. I've used it as an escape route many a time myself aboard the *Stormy Petrel,* running from a blow."

The captain bent down and followed the path of Nick's finger through the bewildering maze of reef. He nodded his head, scratching his bearded chin and considering what Nick said. It did look possible. Nick dipped the quill in the captain's inkwell and retraced the route in black ink. Old McIver nodded, and noticed that, once inside the lee of the large rock called Gravestone on Nick's chart, he'd be protected from Billy's murderous short carronades. Then, he could bear north around the northern tip of the island, safely out of the reach of Blood's long guns. Still, something about the plan was troublesome.

"Looks wide enough for the barky to pass through, boy, but how deep is this water here and here?" he asked, pointing to critical spots on the chart. "This here barky needs a good ten feet 'neath her keel, lad. Or you'll be guttin' her on sharp reef."

"Runs to two fathoms all the way through, Captain," Nick said with a smile. "No one would believe it, that close in to shore, but that's what she is, sir. Perfect escape route." Nick was understandably excited. Here he was, a mere boy in his twelfth summer, and he was helping a captain in Nelson's Royal Navy plot his escape from a murderous pirate. He couldn't help but marvel at the turns his life had taken this strange summer. If only he had his dog back, his life would indeed be perfect. Eventually, they'd have to fight Billy Blood, but right now they had to buy enough time to get McIver's ship back in fighting trim. And his plan did just that!

It was too wondrous for words. He wondered if, at this very moment, he was writing history. Or, perhaps, rewriting it! Lord Hawke had mentioned "protecting the flow of history," but when he thought about that too much, his head hurt. So he tried to push all such thoughts away, and decided it didn't much matter as long as he did what was right. He saw the captain scratching his beard, tracing and retracing Nick's escape route.

"Maybe we could fly that way, couldn't we?" the captain mused. "But then, so could he, couldn't he? Blood?"

"No, sir, that's the beauty of it," Nick said, grinning. "You're looking at absolutely the only chart of this reef in existence. Blood couldn't possibly have one, no matter where he traveled in time! No coastal survey could ever afford to take the time to map it the way I did that summer. As you can see, there are more twists and turns and dead ends in here than that great maze at Hampton Court! We'll have a good head start on him, and without us to follow or the use of this chart, he'll run afoul of something before you can trim your jib staysail, if you've got one, sir."

"Aye, we've got a jib staysail. And it's a good plan you've got, young Nick, and one that makes me proud to be your old relic of an ancestor. My very heart is warmed just at the sight of you, son. As I have not yet married, I didn't expect the pleasure of gazing upon my future progeny, lad. I bless my stars."

Nick felt the color rising in his cheeks. "Thank you kindly, sir. I, uh, never expected to have the honor of meeting you either, sir."

"But," the captain said, shaking his head sadly, "there's one little mayfly in this perfect pie, lad."

"What is that, Captain?" Hawke asked, poring over the chart to see what Nick could have possibly missed.

He thought Nick's plan was not only brilliant, but it was their only way out. To attack Blood now, in their condition, leaking badly and with half their cannons out of action, was suicide. In Hawke's mind, they desperately needed to buy time to return the *Merlin* to her fighting strength before even considering a close-in action with *Mystère*... Nick's plan did just that.

"Well, I'll tell you what, boys, and here's the thing," the captain said, clearly uncomfortable with delivering the bad news when the brave trio had come so far to be of help. "It just won't work. I don't know what kind of boats you're sailing out there in 1939, but a three-masted barquentine of the kind on which you're now floatin', well, she ain't built to skip around and tack on a farthing like what you be askin' of her now, no. She's seakindly all right but she ain't no trick flea from the sea circus. No, sir. She's pretty as you please on her wind, but when you ask her to perform certain navigational miracles, well, she'd never sail her ways through that serpentine escape route, never in your life, sir. No, she'll sink first, I'm afraid."

As if to punctuate the captain's death sentence, and perhaps put another nail in all their coffins, they felt the sickening thud of another of Billy's nitro-powered cannonballs slamming into the *Merlin*'s hull. Hawke shook his head, staring despondently at the chart and the pathway through the reef that Nick had marked with the captain's quill in deep black ink. The captain, they plainly saw, was sadly right. With these twists and turns, and with the fluky winds this close in to shore, there was no way the big old barky could tack her way through and out. Even the brilliant Nelson couldn't sail his way out of this one. No, they'd have to stand and fight, and a lopsided battle it would be, to a fare-thee-well.

There was a heavy and deathly silence in the cabin. Only the sound of running feet above and the muffled thunder of the crew rolling a heavy cannon from one rail to the other signaled that the *Merlin* was not yet ready to strike her colors and surrender.

Nick, elated only moments before, now felt the cold claw of Billy Blood tightening around his heart. He remembered the sound of tinkling silver skulls and Blood's hooded eyes that rainy night at the Greybeard Inn, and in Billy's eyes the look of sheer evil that shone there in the firelight.

Nick knew somehow that this was now his fight to win or lose. He placed his chin in his hands, leaning over the chart on both elbows, staring at the puzzle with all his might, willing his mind to come up with some escape from the pirate's crushing grip. He thought hard. And then he thought harder.

He couldn't shut out the ticking of the old longcase clock in the corner of the cabin from his ears. He shut his eyes, though, and thought as hard as ever any boy ever had. Then, when he did think of it, it was so simple that he hesitated to blurt it out, for fear of sounding foolish. He took a deep breath. "Captain, sir! Could you step over here for a moment?" Nick said, excitement in his eyes.

"What say you, Nick?" McIver asked. "You look fevered!"

"We don't have to *sail* her out, Captain!" Nick cried, leaping to his feet. "No, sir! We'll *pull* her out!"

The captain and Lord Hawke stared at him.

"You said pull her out, lad?"

"Aye! Tow her! You must have a few gigs or jolly boats on deck, Captain," Nick said, excited as the plan took full hold of his mind. Four seaworthy craft and strong men to row them?"

"Aye, we've got four jolly boats. Two slung forward and two aft," the captain said. "For socializin' round the fleet and rowing the crew away should the barky sink. I, of course, go down with the *Merlin*," he added proudly. "In that unhappy eventuality."

"Well, that's it, then!" Nick cried. "We'll *tow* her through the reef with the jolly boats!"

Hawke looked at Nick, weighing the plan.

"Bless us all, I think he's cracked it, Captain!" Lord Hawke said with a broad smile. "Yes! We'll hitch *Merlin* up to all four jolly boats and pull the old girl out! Let's fill all four launches with the stoutest lads and strongest arms we've got, Captain, with four stout lines to the *Merlin*'s bow, and tow her through the reef."

The captain stared at him and then at Nick and then a huge grin spread across his face.

"It may work, lad, it just may work, God love you!" He beamed with pleasure. "But one thing. How do we get all the lads rowing together in the right direction? It demands a bit of witty navigation to be sure!"

"I've thought of that, sir," Nick said brightly, "and I think there's a way. What if I climbed up to the crow's nest at the very top of the fore topmast? I could see the whole reef from there and I could direct the fellows in the jolly boats. I'd take my chart, of course, but from that height, and in this strong sunlight, I could *see* the dark blue path through the reef clear enough, couldn't I?"

"Aye, you could, Nick," McIver said. "And I could post a man at the base of the mast and another out on the bowsprit. You could shout out the directions down to them and they could call them out to the lads rowing the jolly boats!"

The two of them looked at each other, grinning, and then at Lord Hawke who now stood at what was left of the smashed stern window with the spyglass trained on Billy's red frigate.

Looking at Blood's bizarre flagship, he tried in vain to shut out all thought of Annabel and Alexander, but to have them so near and yet unreachable caused a deep and wounding pain in the middle of his heart. But, knowing such thoughts would only distract him as they prepared for the coming battle, he pushed them aside.

"I'd say you've got about twenty minutes to get those boats lowered away and pulling, Captain," Lord Hawke said. "This *Mystère* is clearly a fair devil for speed and she's run out every last cannon into firing position. Billy's spoiling for a fight, sir, and closing fast!"

"Aye," McIver said with a wink, "I'd say the lad here arrived in the nick of time!"

CHAPTER XXVII

Kate Saves the Day

· 7 June 1939 ·
U-BOAT 33, AT SEA

"Let me see if I understand your wildly improbable little tale correctly, Herr McIver," the German SS officer said as he took a seat at the wardroom table. His glasses had steamed up while Hobbes had been talking, but Hobbes could feel those froggy eyes staring. At least he hadn't summoned Dr. Moeller and his nasty little scalpel, Hobbes thought with some relief. "Ready?" Willy asked.

"As you wish, Colonel."

"You've been a lighthouse keeper all your life."

"Correct."

"A lifelong resident of this insignificant little island."

"Sadly, yes."

"Hmm. But, recently, you grew bored and became involved in more–how did you say it–more *exciting* activities. Such as spying, I believe. Care for a smoke?" Willy asked, taking a yellow cigarette from the pack and then shoving it across the table. "No? You don't smoke? I find it calms the nerves a bit." He pulled a gold cigarette lighter emblazoned with the SS black enameled death's-head insignia from his pocket. "You seem nervous, Mr. McIver."

"Wouldn't you be nervous?" Hobbes asked, his eyes averted from Willy's for a moment, considering every possible aspect of what he was doing. His plan was brazen, and for that it might work. But the little Nazi was clever. Hobbes knew he'd have to be careful. And lucky.

Steiner said, "I suppose I would be. So. You are the ringleader of something called the 'Greybeard Spies.' You monitor all German naval activity in your vicinity. Warships. U-boats, that sort of thing. You were on just such a mission tonight when we had our little accident."

"Indeed I was."

"And now, because of some government mix-up or other, you're being thrown out of your lighthouse. You wish to come over to the side of Germany. You are willing to betray all of your colleagues, lead us directly to them, in fact, in return for money."

"It wasn't a mix-up. My country has betrayed me! Thrown my family to the wolves! Taken my home from me! It's not just that I need the money, though I do, it's that those fools in London *deserve* to lose this war!"

"And that's your story."

"That's the truth."

"I see," Willy said, getting to his feet. "I see. How unfortunate there is no proof." He walked over to the door, shaking his head, and pulled it open. "*Ingo! Kommen Sie hier, bitte!*"

In an instant, Ingo, who'd been standing guard outside, appeared in the doorway. Willy quickly whispered something in his ear, which sent Ingo running, then shut the door and returned to the table. His face was a mask, hiding whatever he was feeling.

"What are you doing?" Hobbes asked, trying to hide his own nervousness behind Willy's blue cloud of cigarette smoke. "What was all that about?" He sensed this was not going well at all. His plan, which had seemed so simple, now seemed wildly improbable, even to him. Hearing his own lies played back to him by Willy, they sounded ludicrous. How could he have been so foolish? Was Willy having him taken away to be shot? Or worse, summoning Dr. Moeller and his scalpel to take over the interrogation?

"Relax, Angus. It will only be a moment." Willy sat back and smoked quietly, regarding the Englishman through a blue haze.

But the moments stretched out, and Hobbes could not relax. He felt a thin sheen of perspiration on his forehead as he tried to imagine what he might do if the doctor appeared at the door with his gleaming scalpel at the ready. It would be impossible to overpower both of them. Even if he did, where could he run to?

"Hullo, Papa!"

His mouth dropped open. Katie! The man had sent for Katie! "Are you mad?" Hobbes said, lunging across the table for Steiner.

Willy snapped his fingers and Ingo immediately cocked the submachine gun. "Ingo, please ask Mr. McIver to be seated and shut up," he said, and Hobbes fell back in his chair, his eyes on Kate. How could he have been so stupid as to allow the child to accompany him on the cross-channel trip? But it had seemed such a lovely moonlit evening, such a–

"You will remain silent throughout my questions, do you

understand?" Willy said to Hobbes. "Please. I merely wish to ask the child a few questions and then she'll be returned to your cabin unharmed. I advise you to keep silent during this, Angus. It is, believe me, your last and only hope."

Hobbes sat back feeling drained and defeated. He'd miscalculated badly, that much was obvious. Willy was far shrewder than he'd imagined. And now look where he'd got them. Poor Kate. He'd never forgive himself for what he'd done.

"Are you comfortable, child?" Willy asked softly. "I'm sorry to wake you, but I need to ask you some very important questions. If you tell me the truth, it will be a great help to your father."

"I always tell the truth," Kate said, covering a yawn with her little hand. Hobbes's heart flew to her, watching her rub the sleep from her eyes with her tiny fists. Ingo had placed her in a chair directly opposite him. She was wearing a crewman's pullover as a nightgown and was wrapped in a blanket embroidered with dark red swastikas. The effect was startling, but at least she was warm.

"Good," Willy said. "Now tell me, dear girl, what does your daddy do for a living?"

"He's a birdwatcher."

"A birdwatcher! How interesting! Here I thought he was a lighthouse keeper." Willy shot a glance at Hobbes. "So, he watches birds all day, does he?"

"Oh, no. That's just his hobby. His real job is a lighthouse keeper. We live in the lighthouse, too. It's fun."

"I see. What kind of birds does your daddy watch when he goes out? Mollymawks? Gooney birds?"

"Gooney birds?" Kate laughed. "Don't be silly! He watches birds like you!"

"Like *me*?" Willy asked, and Hobbes had a hard time not smiling at the little German's reaction.

"Sure! Birdwatching's our secret name for Nazi-watching. You're a Nazi, aren't you? Papa's hobby is keeping an eye on the Nazis. Mine, too, actually. You and Ingo are the first ones I've really talked to. Spying is fun. Why, I'm spying on you right now! Fun!"

"Yes, I see," Willy said, rubbing his chin. "Fun."

"Right. Sometimes it's not fun. One time my brother and I didn't see a single periwinkle all day. But every day we write down whatever we see or find out about you old Nazis and then we send it along to the King," Kate said.

"The King," said Willy.

"Or, somebody like that. I'm not really sure. We're very angry with the King, you know. I'm sure Papa told you."

"No, I didn't know. Tell me about it, dear," Willy said. "Why are you so angry?"

"Oh, it's terrible! Some mean old people in London don't think we should be birdwatchers anymore, so they are throwing us out of our house. We won't have anywhere to live. I've never seen my father so upset. I'm sad, too. We don't like the King anymore. We like you."

Little Willy regarded Kate for a long moment as she favored him with the sweetest smile Hobbes had ever seen. Finally, he rose from the table and stood wiping his glasses, looking from father to daughter. "Ingo," he said softly, "you may return Miss McIver to her cabin."

"Good night, darling," Hobbes said to her as Ingo lifted her from the chair. "Daddy will be there shortly." He sat back breathing an inward sigh of relief. She'd confirmed his story in every detail. It had been the most amazing display of courage and grace he'd ever witnessed.

"A most convincing performance," Willy said, smiling at Hobbes. "It's a pity you have no physical proof of all this, however. No evidence. Yes, most unfortunate, I'm afraid to say. Ingo, will you ask Dr. Moeller to join us in the wardroom? Thank you."

Ingo, with Kate in his arms, paused at the door, looked back at the Englishman and saw that all the color had drained from his face. The poor little English girl's father plainly knew he had just received a death sentence. Or, rather, something much, much worse.

"Jawohl, mein herr," Ingo said, "I will send Herr Doktor immediately." He turned to leave, an expression of great sorrow on his face. Hobbes waved good-bye to Katie, thinking it was perhaps the last time he'd ever gaze at that sweet face. "*Danke,* Ingo," Willy said. "Herr Doktor is a genius at extracting the truth when there is no actual proof of a story, Mr. McIver."

"Did you show him the letter, Papa?" Kate said, as she was being carried out. "The letter?" Hobbes asked in a shaky voice. "What letter?"

"The one from that mean old minister in London, of course. The one you're keeping for Nicky, Daddy," the little girl said. "It's in your pocket, remember?"

The letter! Of course! He had the official notice from London, the one that expelled Angus McIver and his family from the Greybeard Light. He had the physical proof the Nazi had demanded right here in his pocket! He withdrew it and slid it across the table. Then, he said a silent prayer.

"There's your proof," Hobbes said.

Kate had perhaps just saved his life.

CHAPTER XXVIII

A Landlubber Aloft

· 3 October 1805 ·

H.M.S. *MERLIN*, AT SEA

Nick leaned far out over the starboard rail of the *Merlin*'s bow, towering high above the heaving blue sea. He took a deep breath of the tangy salt air. It was fine to be stepping out onto the sun-drenched deck, like stepping out into a world he already knew, but one found only inside the pages of his books. He took it all in and found it not wanting in any aspect.

The acres of billowing white canvas above, the worn blue coats of the officers on the quarterdeck below. The sun-bleached white nankeen trousers of the barefoot swabbies, and their long pigtailed hair and flashing golden earrings. And then the breathtaking scarlet-clad Marines, forming up for battle amidships. It was these same Marines, Nick knew, who would swarm over the side of the enemy vessel should the captain decide to board it.

It was a riot of color and activity that washed over him and seeped inside his pores. Under his bare feet, he felt the warm wood of the pristine caulked decks, holystoned to gleaming white perfection. He felt the warm sun on his face, heard the sails snapping and billowing overhead. It was as fine, he thought, as he'd always imagined it would be. And Nick felt, in an odd way, that he'd come home at last.

Clearly, he thought, this was the life he'd been born for. He looked proudly down at his new blue jacket. It wasn't really new, it had been Lieutenant Stiles's own jacket when he'd been a midshipman. It was a bit tattered and torn, and Stiles had apologized when he'd offered it, but Nick had never been so proud of anything as he was of that poor blue coat.

He smiled to himself. He knew of boys who had run away to sea, yet it had never occurred to him that he might one day do it, too. But maybe– A loud voice at his very ear interrupted his thoughts.

"Ahoy, there, jolly!" said the young Lieutenant Stiles, now standing next to Nick at the rail. He cupped his hands and shouted down to the young ensign standing in the stern of this last jolly boat to be lowered away. She was now rowing for the other three, rowing for all she was worth. "Form up now and all ship oars! Await my signal! Look lively, now, our old friend approaches on the fly!" With a quick look over his shoulder at *Mystère,* hard on the wind, Stiles turned to Nick and smiled. "And still he comes, the devilish creature. Ready to go aloft, lad?"

"Aye, aye, sir," Nick said, happily. "Up the ratlines through the lubber's hole to the top foremast?"

Stiles looked at him quizzically. "You appear to know a good bit about this old barky and the ways of the sea, Nick. Was you a cabin boy once in His Majesty's service?"

"No, sir," Nick replied. "Book learning, mostly. Me mum's a

right devil about book-reading, sir. And I've a small sloop of my own, which I've sailed, mostly right over–" He caught himself. He'd been about to point to the Gravestone Rock and the point where the Greybeard Light would stand in about a hundred years' time. "Right over there," Nick said guiltily, moving his pointing finger so that it was pointed away from the island and vaguely toward England.

"So, well enough, and up you go then, Nick," Stiles said, easily hoisting the boy up to the ratlines leading up to the first yardarm of the foremast. "Handsomely now, lad, handsomely now!" Nick climbed easily, his bare feet sure of each step on the rope ladder. The lieutenant climbing up beneath him was impressed. "What's this sail we be passing here, Nick the sailor man?" Stiles asked with a laugh as they climbed.

"Too easy, sir," Nick said, looking back down at the lieutenant. "That's the foresail, sometimes called the course. Everybody knows that!"

He heard the lieutenant laughing out loud below him and pulled himself up onto the lower yardarm, waiting for Stiles to join him. "How'd I do, sir?" he asked, reaching his hand down to Stiles and giving him a friendly but unnecessary pull up. Then they were standing side by side on the bottom crosstree near the thick wooden mast, some thirty feet above the deck.

Nick could see the whole northern coast of his island from this height, including the towering rocky point where one day his lighthouse would stand. Far to the south, jutting out into the sea, was the hazy silhouette of ancient Hawke Castle itself. Surely Hawke himself had seen it, and Nick wondered how passing strange that must feel to his lordship.

Stiles was still laughing as they stood there, pausing for the moment on the crosstree before resuming their climb upward to the masthead. "I should have known any relative of our beloved captain would have saltwater in his veins! Scampered up them ratlines like you was born to it!" Stiles now pointed aft to a small sail set between the upper mainmast and the mizzenmast at the *Merlin*'s stern. "Now, name me one more sail, that one there aft, and I'll give you a gold piece, young Nick!"

"That one?" Nick squinted into the sunlit maze of white canvas. "Mizzen topgallant staysail, I believe, sir."

"You believe correctly, boy!" Stiles said, and dug a small gold napoleon from his trouser pocket and flipped it to Nick. Nick caught it but the toss was a bit wide and Nick had to reach out for it, and when he did he felt his foot slip out into space and suddenly he was grabbing at air and saw the sickening sight of the deck spinning far below.

He knew instantly that he'd made a grievous error and was going to fall.

"Watch it, lad!" Stiles cried and bent down and instinctively shot out a hand, watching in horror as Nick lost his balance completely now and tumbled out into space.

All Nick saw was the spinning deck coming up to meet him.

He felt a scream rising in his throat as he pitched forward into the air, a heart-stopping plunge, and then a violent jolt as he felt the lieutenant clutch his collar and yank him upward.

He looked down between his dangling bare feet at the tiny figures running to and fro on the deck far below, saw the sun sparkling on the sea on either side of the boat, saw the white gulls swooping through the rigging below him. Then, he heard a loud ripping sound, as of cloth parting, and he felt the hand-sewn seams of cloth under his arms starting to give. He shut his eyes–

Nelson the Strong, Nelson the Brave, Nelson the Lord of the Sea.

And felt himself being lifted swiftly upward. The lieutenant's instantaneous reaction, and the strong blue fabric of the midshipman's jacket, had saved his life. Stiles had grabbed him at the last instant and had been strong enough to stop his fall. With a sharp upward motion, Stiles lifted the boy quickly back to the yardarm, and not a second before the material of the coat would have finally given way.

Nick's wildly swinging feet finally found the solid spar of the crosstree, but his legs were shaking so badly he wasn't sure he could remain standing. Breathing hard, and pushing down the panic, he grabbed a line and held on, literally, for dear life. He looked down at the deck and saw the crew still scurrying about, unaware of the barely averted tragedy above. He looked at Stiles. He'd only known the man for half an hour and already he owed the young lieutenant his life!

"Thank you, sir, for saving my life," Nick said, breathing hard. "I'm–I am terribly sorry about my–I don't know how I could have been so–" He felt under his arm for the comforting round shape of the Tempus Machina and was glad he'd stitched the inside pocket closed. "So stupid, sir. Now I've gone and torn your beautiful jacket. But I'll sew it, sir, I'm handy with a needle and thread and–"

He half-expected the lieutenant to be angry, but instead

found him to be smiling and shaking his head from side to side in merry-eyed amusement.

"Which you know the names of everything aboard the barky it seems, but someone's forgotten to learn you the most important rule of all, I see," Stiles said.

"I know. I promise you, it'll never happen again, I swear it," Nick said, deeply embarrassed. "I was so amazed at everything and having so much fun, I guess I just–"

"Never you mind, lad," Stiles said, putting a hand on Nick's shoulder. "Just remember this always–especially up here in the rigging, too. One hand for yourself, and one hand for the barky. It's how young towheaded seamen like meself end up old-grey-headed seamen like our beloved Nelson! Are you steady now, boy, on yer pins?"

"Yes, sir, I believe that I am."

"Then, let's get up top, shall we?" Stiles said, and the handsome young officer started up the ratlines as easily as a monkey might move from tree to tree. Nick started up after him, still shaky, but realizing that time now was precious.

They had to get the *Merlin* through the reef and inside Gravestone Rock in a hurry. He looked across the wide blue water toward Billy Blood's *Mystère* and was shocked at how large she loomed on the horizon. Nick climbed as fast as he could. Occasionally, he dared to peek below and watch the tiny figures down on the deck grow smaller and smaller as he approached the very top of the foremast. It took not a little courage to keep moving up, especially after what had almost happened. But he climbed with a will, knowing it was his duty to the ship and her crew.

When they had finally reached the top of the mast, with only the whirling seagulls for company, Nick was breathlessly surprised. Both at the towering height, for he could see now for miles in every direction, and also to find that there was no crow's nest! Certainly not like the ones in his books! No place at all, it seemed, where he could sit and call down his directions. "But where am I to sit, Lieutenant?"

"Why right here, young Nick," Stiles said, and Nick saw that he'd rigged a strong manila sling from the masthead where Nick could hang comfortably if somewhat precariously, swaying with every motion of the boat. "Will this suit you, lad? I use suchlike myself all the time."

"Well, I think it's splendid, sir!" Nick replied climbing up into the sling and pulling the chart from his jacket. In fact, the sling was quite comfortable. "May I borrow your glass as well?"

"Begging your pardon, Nick, but my thought was to remain with you up here till we got through the reef. I could use the glass to confirm your chart and then shout your directions down to the bosun, Willick, whom I've stationed below at the base of the mast. He knows my commands and can easily pass them on to the bowsprit."

"Well enough, Mr. Stiles," Nick said, unfurling the chart and pinpointing their location in the lagoon. He looked out across the blue-green water and could easily locate a deeper blue channel winding through the reefs. Escape meant a twisting serpentine route indeed, but it looked as if they just might slip through.

"Are you ready, Nick?" Stiles asked.

"Aye, sir," Nick said, looking from his hand-drawn chart to the reef and back to the chart. "Here we go. Please take us dead ahead three hundred yards. Then have the crews execute a fifteen-degree turn to starboard when the great rock is dead on their port beam." He was calculating in his mind the forward momentum of the ship and how he would have to anticipate each turn a good hundred yards before it occurred. It was going to be trickier than he had imagined.

Stiles cupped his hands and shouted down to the bosun at the base of the mast: "All boats dead ahead! Three hundred yards and listen for the call! The great rock will be dead on your port beam! Then, execute a turn hard a' starboard of fifteen degrees! Smartly now, lads, smartly!"

The bosun, Willick, called out Nick's directions to the burly hand who was straddling the tip of *Merlin*'s bowsprit, and he in turn shouted orders out to the four ensigns in charge of each jolly boat. At once, Nick saw the oars on all four boats flash with splendid precision, saw the four lines to *Merlin*'s bow spring tight, creating a mist of seawater round the ropes, and felt the huge vessel respond, slowly at first, and then quite smartly as she overcame the moment of inertia.

Suddenly, he was rocking to and fro in his jury-rigged seat high above *Merlin*'s decks. He felt a cool breeze on his face, and smiled as the barky surged forward, in tow behind the four jolly boats.

She was moving precisely where he'd intended, right into the mouth of the blue water channel that led through the Seven Devils! He felt a chill run up the length of his spine. It was the same route he'd taken the *Petrel* through, and even with her shallow draft, the passage had always been tricky.

At least the channel was clearly wide enough for the beamy warship. Although the last thousand yards or so would

"Hard a'starboard on my mark!"

be the most devilish, for they were lined with shoals and outcroppings of jagged rock that were invisible even from Nick's perch in the sky, he believed it was going to work. Now, if only they could outrun Blood by a sufficient margin to conceal their route from the *Mystère*'s navigator!

"Hooray!" cried Nick, with joy in his voice. "All ahead, two hundred yards more! Watch that shoal as she bears on your port beam!"

"All ahead two hundred by the mark! Mind the shoal as she bears to port, lads!" shouted the lieutenant down to the bosun. Nick heard the muffled call of Willick on the foredeck and then a loud cheer went up from the crews of the jolly boats, all shouting in unison, "Hooray, hooray, the *Merlin* away!" The crews rowed as if their very lives depended on it, which well they did.

Stiles reached up the mast to Nick's swaying makeshift sling and gave Nick a hearty slap on the shoulder. "I knew you was a capital hydrographer by the looks of your handmade chart, but I had no idea you was such a fearsome navigator, Nick."

It was at that moment that the boy saw the first plume of white water jet upward from the sea about twenty yards from the lead jolly boat. Cannonfire! Blood had marked their plan and now his chaser cannon was in range of the escaping *Merlin*! The four slow-moving jollies would be sitting ducks for the *Mystère*'s long-range twenty-four-pounders!

Another jet of white water erupted into the sky, this time only yards in front of the jolly boats rowing desperately for safety. Blood was calibrating their range. Nick knew Blood understood his only hope was to prevent the four boats from rowing *Merlin* into the protected lee of Gravestone Rock. Once behind that massive tower of black granite, the *Merlin* would be safe from Billy's deadly cannonfire. Nick looked back and saw successive white puffs and spurts of flame from the *Mystère*'s bow. The chaser cannon with a nitro load! A lick of flame again and then he saw it, a heartbreaking sight.

A jolly boat was hit! Nick saw a ball tear a piece of stern away and saw a man rowing there thrown with the splintering wood into the sea. The boat was badly damaged but still seaworthy and the crew bent to it with a vengeance. The crew in the stern reached for the injured sailor, but he slipped from their hands and beneath the waves.

Nick blinked, unable to come to grips with what he'd seen. Death in war was going to be far more terrible than anything he'd been preparing himself for. Reading about battle, it's pain and destruction, was scant preparation for the real thing. He'd just seen a man die!

Nick now noticed the speed of *Merlin* increase as the frightened sailors realized Blood had found their range. The safety the great rock promised was only a small distance across the water, perhaps only a thousand or so yards more to go, but who knew how many twists and turns they must execute to get there? However many it would be, faster was better when you faced such merciless cannon fire. So they rowed on with a fierce will. Their faint cries, urging each other onward, floated up to Nick at the masthead. His prayers went out to them.

"Nick! Press on with it, lad! Where away the next turning?" cried the lieutenant below him, happy to be in the thick of it once more, but mightily concerned at the dreamy expression that inhabited Nick's face. He'd seen it before on the faces of boys getting their first taste of battle. He knew it was a mixture of fear and rapture. You could easily lose your edge on the thing. And your life shortly thereafter.

Nick forced himself to push down the image of the sailor slipping beneath the waves and back to the formidable task at hand. Stiles was right. The safety of all of them, every man and boy on board, was in his hands at this moment. He saw the dark blue channel snaking to starboard ahead and confirmed it on his chart. To execute the turn ahead at this faster speed, they'd have to commence it immediately. He'd missed the call. Was it already too late to get the big slow-turning ship around?

"Hard to starboard on my mark!" Nick cried in desperation. "Mark, now!" He gasped as he saw the severe right-hand turn approaching much too rapidly for the equally slow-turning jolly boats. They could never form up for such a tight turn so quickly.

He heard the faint voice of Willick pass the word to the bowsprit man and then suddenly his heart lifted as he saw how quickly the four boats' masters got their crews back-paddling and spinning their boats, pulling mightily for the proper angle of approach. The four crews had become one in heart and mind and muscle, and it was a beautiful thing to behold from the great height of the foremast.

The *Merlin* herself slowly came starboard and round behind the jollies, led through the maze like a placid horse through a twisting canyon to water. She would follow, in her fashion, but follow she would. Now, the abrupt turn to the right. She came round at the last instant, but still she came round! The escape was working, if only Blood didn't sink their very saviors rowing the jollies. Three more difficult maneuvers through the shoals and they'd be inside the lee of Gravestone Rock. Beyond the deadly fire of *Mystère*'s twenty-four-pounders loaded with nitro, and headed for open sea! And, then, on to England and Nelson!

They had less than a thousand yards to go. And on came *Mystère*. Racing to catch them, she was being led right into their trap!

Nick heard a rapid series of enormous thundering explosions below and saw that *Merlin*'s own portside cannonades were now spouting jets of fire and smoke and lead. The *Merlin* had entered the action in earnest now. He felt the powerful aroma of cordite filling his nostrils, could actually make it out on his tongue, his first real taste of battle, wafting up into the rigging, and he saw his best friend Gunner below, running from gun crew to gun crew, urging them onward.

Another series of thunderous booms almost immediately from the *Merlin* and a huge cheer went up from her crew as fire licked from the muzzles of *Merlin*'s guns, and giant plumes of white water nearer and nearer Blood's flagship marked the accuracy of their efforts. Gunner had whipped the crews into shape in short order it seemed, and his skill and knowledge were clearly paying off.

Another turning in the reef ahead! He'd almost missed it, distracted as he was observing the now raging battle from his post in the sky! *Stay sharp!* he told himself, and said out loud, "Hard a'port on my mark now!" Truly it was loud enough to be heard by the jollyboat crews without Stiles or Willick! "Steady, steady, on the mark, hard to starboard, NOW!" he roared, and the crews responded with a will.

The number of plumes around them had increased, and one more ball had struck the hull of a jolly boat causing terrible damage but no injury that he could see. The jolly boats now were nearing the shelter of the rock and every second counted.

Nick set his jaw in fierce determination and concentration. This last five hundred yards of serpentine blue water was the most dangerous of all! He knew only too well the jagged outcroppings of reef and shoal that lined the passage and, indeed, they were circled in red on his chart. One there now to port! "Starboard five degrees on my mark!" he cried. "Mark, ho!" and Stiles shouted out the command below, "Mark, and mind the shoal!"

It was then that Nick felt the air around him rent by a terrible WHOOMPH! He knew that Blood had figured out the two men aloft must be directing *Merlin*'s route through the reefs. Now he had turned his guns on Nick and Stiles in desperation. The jollies were entering the lee of the rock and Bill's only hope was to blind or extinguish the eyes that guided them. He was gaining rapidly now, and Nick hoped it was only a matter of moments before Billy ran afoul of the reefs. If not, well–

Another ball tore the air inches above his head, carrying away a mass of sail and rigging and heavy tackle. The noise and violence of it was terrifying. Nick forced himself to ignore it and call the next turning at the top of his lungs, "All ahead fifty now, and then port ten degrees on the mark. And, mark!" He looked down at Stiles and saw the man smiling up at him.

They were comrades under fire, his smile seemed to say, and this young stowaway was certainly proving his mettle! "Ahead fifty, port ten, and mark!" Stiles shouted below. And that's when the nitro-powered cannonball struck the mast mere inches below Nick's sling and his world turned upside down.

The horrible cracking sound of hot lead smashing through the heart of stout timber, splintering it instantly to pieces, was in Nick's ear as he found himself jolted in the sling, hurled upward for a terrifying instant, and then falling only to be jerked up sharply as the sling wrapped itself round his right ankle and held him there like an upside-down puppet dangling from a string. Would the sling hold? If it didn't he'd surely plummet headfirst to the deck below!

He could feel the blood rushing to his head. Would he pass out? Could he reach the mast and haul himself up to the remaining crosstree? No, he was hung too far out to reach it. If he could swing his body, maybe he could reach that shroud! He looked down. Maybe Stiles could pull him close enough to–but Stiles was gone!

The lieutenant had been clinging there to the upper mast, standing in the ratlines just inches below Nick's sling. The ball must have hit him directly when it tore the masthead away! Nick let a sob escape from deep in his heart, and then whirled himself in fury so he could see Blood's *Mystère.*

She was bearing down on them in earnest now and he could clearly see her crimson topsides and golden quarterboards, and the Jolly Roger snapping from the top of her top foremast. And below the skull and crossbones, Blood was flying the English Union Jack upside down! It was a clear and deliberate insult to the *Merlin*'s captain and crew. A crew that now included Nick McIver and his new friend, just injured or killed by Blood's murderous fire.

Stiles dead? It wasn't possible! They'd only just become fast friends and besides, the young lieutenant was much too great a hero to die here, merely helping a boy tow an old boat off a reef. The tragic loss tore at the wildly pumping heart that leapt in Nick's chest, but there was scant time for grief, he knew. He had to finish what he'd set out to do and there'd be time enough for mourning later.

Nick snarled in anger and hurt at the loss of his friend and whirled himself back to regard the jolly boats. Although he was hanging upside down, he found he could still see the proper channel. He was cheered to see the lads had properly rowed on, probably even unaware of what had just happened at the masthead.

The great rock was so near! There were two more difficult turns and then the barky would be safe behind the mountain of granite. He could feel the weight of the Tempus Machina, sewn inside his shirt, pulling the shirt down around his neck. If only he could keep it from falling down over his head and blinding him! He had a job to do, and the crew was counting on him. He looked for the next turning, holding the shirt out of his eyes to see.

Nick cupped one hand to shout and looked downward at Willick, and saw that the bosun was starting up the ratlines to rescue him. "No! Stay there! Only two more turnings!" he shouted to Willick, who paused and nodded his head in understanding. He had to be there to relay Nick's commands to the bowsprit.

Nick tried to focus on the spinning reef. For a second he was motionless, and he saw again the dangerous tentacle of rock that snaked out from the base of Gravestone. It had almost snared the *Stormy Petrel* and it would now surely rip the bottom out of his ancestor's ship.

It was invisible to the crews in the jollies. They were stroking right over it now in the shallow draft boats, with the barky just behind. In two seconds it would be too late!

"Hard to starboard now lads, five degrees on the mark! And, mark!" Nick cried downward to the bosun with the roar of blood filling his skull. He saw the crews turning the barky, pulling hard, maybe enough to avert disaster. Just then, another cannonball tore through the canvas of the fore topsail, just inches below Nick's wildly swinging head.

He felt its breeze, as they said in the service, and he was still smiling. French cannon shot was pounding the English barky now. All those balls splashing in the water around her had roiled the sea, causing *Merlin* to roll and pitch wildly.

Nick was sure someone onboard the viciously roaring *Mystère* had him in the sight of his spyglass and was directing cannon fire at the dangling boy navigator swinging wildly by his heels high in the rigging! Oh, it was terrifying enough now for a boy born to peaceful times on a small English island, that place where nothing ever happened, and where all the fights had been trifling scuffles in the schoolyard.

You could stare down a mean boy who hurt your sister, and you could even break his nose if you cared to. But you could not stare down a French cannonball fired in anger, nor break its nose. A cannonball was a cold, fearless item, and he'd seen how they could kill a man in the blink of an eye.

Nick summoned the phrase that always gave him courage when he recited it. And if ever he needed to pull himself up, it was now, when his life was truly hanging by a thread.

Nelson the Strong, Nelson the Brave, Nelson the Lord of the Sea!

Another ball cracked the air nearby.

He laughed and twisted his body around so that he was once more facing the reef. Even viewed upside down, the dark blue pathway was clearly evident. Still, he shuddered when he heard the balls whistling through the shrouds. He was far more afraid of the heavy rigging falling from above, raining down all around him, than a little French cannonball. No one in the French Navy could hit a small boy swinging by his heels at a thousand yards. Not even Gunner was that good, and he was the best shot in all of England!

If they got him, it would merely be a lucky ball. Or a piece of jagged timber hurtling down from above. He was only a boy, a small target after all. You'd have to be awfully lucky to hit so small a boy, he guessed.

He laughed at the notion of a lucky ball. Luck was everything in war, he guessed. Luck, and fate, too, maybe. Nothing more.

How the thought cheered him, and still Nick fought hard to keep his concentration, though it was a desperate effort. Every time he managed to get the reef channel in focus, another ball would tear past his head or slam into the hull, and he would swing around, losing his fix on the next maneuver. He fought the motion, twisting his body this way and that until he was facing the reef, again.

And there, hanging by his heels among the shattered rigging and tattered canvas, with the acrid smell of cordite stinging his nostrils, the oddest recollection popped unbidden into his upside-down head. A memory from a childhood book: the match-boy who lost his arm to a French cannonball. But still he'd bent down to pick up his still-burning match from the deck with his one remaining arm, touched it to the gun's powder hole, and then laughed at the thunderous roar his cannon made. *Laughed!*

Hanging in the rigging, his comrade dead and the cannonballs flying, Nick had no idea what fate had in store for him, or even if he would live another minute, much less long enough to see the sun set this day. But moments before, in the heat of the battle's most dangerous hour, he knew he, Nick McIver, had done one quite amazing thing in this life.

He had laughed in the very face of danger!

It was the last thing Nick remembered before the upper third of the foretopmast, smashed by a thirty-two-pound ball, and wrapped in fouled lines and heavy tackle, came hurtling down from above and struck his head a horrible blow.

CHAPTER XXIX

Spies for Sale

· 8 June 1939 ·

U-BOAT 33, AT SEA

Hobbes was on an operating table. Wide awake. Couldn't move a muscle. And something was wrong with his nose. He couldn't seem to get air through it properly. A doctor leaned directly over him, his crazed eyes gleaming above the sweat-soaked surgical mask. He could hear the surgeon's muffled voice. *The tongue,* the surgeon said, *the tongue is next!* Then Hobbes had seen the gleaming scalpel flash, dripping with his own bright red blood. And, above the surgeon's mask, the mad, glittering eyes of Dr. Moeller! A scream was building in his throat, and then he woke up.

Fully awake now, drenched in sweat, Hobbes couldn't even dream of going back to sleep. He'd remained fully clothed in case of an emergency.

He lay rigid on the hard metal upper bunk of the U-boat's tiny cabin, the thin mattress providing scant comfort, staring at the cold steel bulkhead above. In truth, he'd missed a horrible appointment with the mad doctor by a mere whisker. If little Kate hadn't remembered the letter in his pocket proving his story, well, he shuddered to think about it. The quick-witted child had saved him from Dr. Moeller's wicked scalpel, and no doubt about it.

In the bunk below, Kate's soft breathing reassured him that, after her splendid performance in the wardroom, she was finally getting a good night's sleep. If only he could sleep himself, he thought, putting his hands behind his head, staring at a small panel in the bulkhead above his head. It was coated with moisture and seemed to be vibrating.

Odd, he thought, and placed the palm of his hand on the steel plate. It was ice cold. He pulled out his slim pocketknife and removed the screws that held it in place. The plate came away easily.

He lit his Zippo, held it up into the opened space, and peered at the submarine's normal tangled mass of wiring and conduits inside. But there was something else, something that caught his expert eye.

Two gleaming stainless steel tubes, one on top of the other, each about four inches in diameter. The top tube had started to smoke when he removed the plate and now he touched it. It burned his hand, not hot but cold. Supercold. He touched the bottom one more carefully. Room temperature. And it was thrumming with vibration. Fluid, perhaps seawater, was being pumped through it at extreme pressure. And they were superchilling it for some reason.

Then he saw the small metal sign above the valve atop the pipe coated with frost. He quickly scanned the German words printed above it in red. When he saw the word *Hydroschiffsschraube* he knew he'd hit the jackpot.

Hydroschiffsschraube.

Waterpropeller.

The much rumored hydropropulsion system! So that's what they called it, "waterpropeller!" Somehow, they were probably pumping seawater aboard at the bow, superchilling it, velocitizing it, and expelling it aft. No wonder U-33 had been able to keep pace with *Thor* all the way across the Channel! He was aboard the fastest submarine in the world! And he was about to find out what made it tick! He saw another valve just beyond the–

There was a muffled rap at his cabin door.

Quickly, he replaced the small plate, screwing the four screws back into place. "Yes?" he said with sleep in his voice. "Yes?" He feigned a loud yawn, and heard a voice say, *"Guten morgen, Herr McIver."*

A key turned in the lock and the door swung inward. It was a young seaman he hadn't seen before. The guard smiled down at the sleeping child and then up at Hobbes who turned and looked down from his bunk, rubbing imaginary sleep from his eyes. He hadn't slept a wink all night, but then he'd never needed much sleep.

"*Kapitän* von Krieg would like to see you, urgently," the guard whispered in English. Hobbes jumped down, pulled Kate's blanket up around her shoulders, and then followed the crewman the length of the sub. A lot of activity this morning, Hobbes noticed. Something was clearly afoot. The guard opened the door to the same wardroom where he'd been interrogated the night before. The British commander stepped inside and saw *Kapitän* von Krieg drinking hot coffee at the big green table and Little Willy strutting around puffing on one of his yellow cigarettes.

Von Krieg had the pale blue envelope from the Ministry in his hands. He was staring at Hobbes the way he'd done in the wardroom when they'd first met. He could again feel the man trying to place him. Had they met? Was it possible? Where?

"*Guten morgen*, Angus," said Little Willy. "Good morning! How did you sleep? Well, I hope. We've got a busy morning planned for you. We're currently about twenty miles north-northwest of Greybeard Island, running at flank speed. *Kapitän* von Krieg has decided to consider your kind offer of assistance, if, of course, you also convince him you're telling the truth." Willy's eyes bored into Hobbes's own. And so, he noticed, did the red-rimmed eyes of the tired-looking submarine captain. A rummy, Hobbes thought, part of his problem, an angry drunk.

In that instant Hobbes understood why von Krieg had been looking at him so strangely. Because he himself now remembered who this German captain was! No wonder the man had looked so familiar! The name jumped into the forefront of his brain with dreadful clarity.

Wolfie.

Of course! How could he have been so thick! Wolfie, the tall, arrogant German aristocrat who'd been the short-lived bane of the then-young Oxford fencing master. Hobbes remembered it all now, the angry fights over the prettiest girls, the carousing, the pub brawls at all hours when Hobbes would have to go and drag the boy by his heels from under a pile of shouting, brawling students.

And, of course, the infamous severed ear of the Magdalen Don that finally resulted in Wolfie's unceremonious dismissal from the college and return to the Fatherland. Hobbes had been the one with the unpleasant task of telling Wolfie he'd been sent packing back to Germany.

"Versuch?" the captain now said to Willy, holding up the blue Ministry letter. "Proof? This one letter is proof of the Englishman's foolish story?"

Hobbes nodded and turned to Willy for support, but the cagey SS man simply smiled and let him hang there. Wolfie, his arms folded across his broad chest, was still staring at him. Did von Krieg remember Hobbes, too? If he did, the game was up, it was as simple as that. He felt a trickle of perspiration make its way from under his arm and realized that perhaps it was warmer in the wardroom than he'd first imagined. He tried to gaze mildly at the captain, to give away nothing in his eyes. To get Katie and himself out of this alive, he had to remain cool, no matter what. If Wolfie recognized him, he was dead. They both were. He'd lived a full life and had no fear of dying. But the child? It was unthinkable.

"That is the letter I told you about, *mein Kapitän,*" Willy said. "I'll leave it to you to judge its authenticity." The captain, his eyes never leaving Hobbes, pulled the letter from its envelope, raised it to his bloodshot eyes, and began to read. Hobbes, his pulse racing, waited for his fate to be determined. He felt a shudder go through the hull of the submarine; or perhaps it was just the hull of his heart.

"Notice the gold Ministry seal and the London postmark, *mein Kapitän.* Is the letter not everything I promised?" Willy asked, a smirk he could not hide in his voice. "'Activities outside the scope of his duties'! In other words, spying! Amusing, isn't it? His own government doesn't want him spying for Churchill anymore than we do! He's our Greybeard spy all right!"

"*Ach!* Only if all zoze things in life are as they seem, *mein Colonel*," the captain replied. "But, perhaps he is telling the truth. If so, he just may be useful, *ja*, that's true."

The captain folded the letter, stuck it back in its envelope and nodded to Willy, silently admitting that the letter was acceptable proof of Hobbes's story. He then looked at Hobbes, those narrow-beamed eyes searching his face again.

"But now, Englishman," the captain said, "you must whet my appetite with more information. I'll decide if it's significant enough to bother with keeping you and your daughter alive."

"Oh, it's significant all right, Captain," Hobbes said, mentally breathing a huge sigh of relief. He was still in the game. And it was time to turn up the heat. "Have you fellows by chance ever heard of a man named Richard Hawke?" he asked, a disingenuous smile on his face.

Willy stopped his pacing and almost fell over backward. The captain coughed into his fist and muttered, "I may have heard dis name before. It's possible."

"I should think so," Hobbes replied coolly. "Those two goons you sent over to sink my boat told me you spend every waking moment staring at his castle through your periscope." He was gratified to see the captain's jaw drop.

"They *told* you that?" Wolfie exploded. "They–the 'Tweedle Twins,' those idiots! I'll have them shot! I'll have them tortured and shot! I'll–"

"Tweedle Twins?" Hobbes asked, confused and amused at the same time.

"Yes, yes, that's what *das Kapitän* calls Dr. Moeller and Klaus, my two little Gestapo agents. The Tweedles, 'Dee' and 'Dum.' It fits, doesn't it?" Willy took another deep sip of his steaming coffee. He seemed to be positively enjoying himself.

"Ah, yes," Hobbes said, with a twinkle in his eye. "But which one of them is 'Dum'?"

"Why, *both of them*, Angus!" Willy said, exploding with laughter and a spray of hot coffee across the table.

"So, you *have* heard of Lord Richard Hawke, Captain?" Hobbes said pleasantly.

"Yes, yes, yes, of course I have heard of him!" Wolfie said. "Now what about him? Besides the fact that *der Führer* wants him dead?"

"I work for him," Hobbes said, his eyes shining, for this was his favorite part of the game. Spinning the web. "Hawke controls a vast number of English spy rings operating in this part of the world–in France, for instance and Spain. Greybeard's is only one of the smallest cells. I am its ringleader, but I am also Hawke's personal courier. You must have wondered how a simple lighthouse keeper could afford such an elegant craft as *Thor*?"

"We planned to ask you about that, if you lived long enough," Willy said.

"She belongs to Hawke, Lieutenant," Hobbes said with a smile. "Lord Hawke he is, and he has more money than sense, if you ask me. Have you ever known titled people like that? At any rate, I use his boat to ferry information around the Channel. I was on just such a mission tonight, planning to report a couple of Luftwaffe squadrons we'd recently observed patrolling off the coast of Jersey. Messerschmitt 109s escorting Junkers Su 390 heavy bombers."

Willy nodded and looked at Hobbes thoughtfully. "He's

correct, *mein Kapitän.* Last week, I heard Air Marshal Göring mention just such a Luftwaffe mission to Hitler in the Reichstag staff meeting."

Hobbes sat back and waited for all this to sink in. The crisis was passing perhaps, but certainly not the danger.

"This Hawke you speak of, Angus," Willy said. "Does he trust you?"

"As much as he trusts anyone allowed inside his secret base, Lieutenant."

"Colonel! I am Colonel Steiner! How many times must I remind you?"

"Sorry, Colonel Steiner."

"Secret base! What secret base?" said an excited Willy, pushing his perpetually steamy round glasses up on his nose. Willy could hardly believe his luck. The man could be a goldmine of priceless information! Even the captain would now have to admit his instincts had been correct.

"Why, Hawke's lair, of course," said Hobbes. "Surely you've heard of it! The secret submarine base at Hawke Castle?"

"So Hawke Castle *is* the base!" von Krieg said, pulling out one of his charts. "Just as I thought! Congratulations, Willy, it seems we're about to crack Berlin's most urgent assignment after all! We'll be famous, I tell you, famous."

"I'll want names, naturally, everyone, everyone!" Willy said, actually licking his fleshy lips like a man sitting down to a gourmet feast. "Are you still prepared to do that, Angus? Betray countrymen, betray your many comrades?"

"Pay me enough money, Colonel, and I shall introduce you personally to every spy on Greybeard Island! Including Lord Richard Hawke himself! Because I plan to sail your lovely submarine right up to Lord Hawke's bloody front door and invite you and the lads inside for a cup of tea with England's most notorious spy himself."

"*Wunderbar! Wunderbar!*" Willy shouted, dancing around the wardroom table, expelling clouds of purple smoke.

"We go see then, Willy," the captain said, leaning back in his chair with a smile. "We go and see if the *Englischer* lighthouse keeper is telling the truth. If he can get *Der Wolf* inside this Hawke's lair. If not, well, that will be too bad. For both you . . . and your lovely daughter!"

"I'll get you inside, all right, Captain," Hobbes said quietly. "Don't you worry about that. Just set your course for Hawke Lagoon!"

CHAPTER XXX

In the Sick Bay

· 3 October 1805 ·

H.M.S. *MERLIN,* AT SEA

"Who are you?" Nick asked one of the faces floating hazily just above his own. There was a glow of flickering light swinging to and fro above him, and faces were swimming in and out of it, in and out of the heavy gloom.

"He's the ship's surgeon, Nick," said yet another face floating into the light. "You're alive, Nick, I knew it, for all love!" This face he thought he recognized. Yes, of course, it was Lord Hawke. But who was Lord Hawke?

"Keep still lad, lay back and rest," the Lord Hawke face seemed to say. "Don't talk now." Talk? About what? All he wanted to do was sleep. Sleep forever. His head hurt him something awful, and he couldn't remember why.

"Where am I?" Nick asked, and felt a terrible bolt of pain in his temple. He groaned and tried to sit up. Then he felt someone's hand on his shoulder and felt it gently press him back against the pillow. He closed his eyes. Above him in the gloom was that strangely bright, swinging light, and it hurt his eyes terribly.

"You're in the *Merlin*'s sick bay, Nick," Lord Hawke whispered quietly. "You've been asleep for some time. We weren't at all sure when you'd wake up." Nick saw that his face broke into a broad smile. "Or even *if* you'd wake up."

Lord Hawke saw Nick squinting in pain at the light, and he took the ship's lantern hanging above the boy's berth and placed it on the deck, dimming the already soft glow in the sick bay. Most of the wounded men were sleeping, as it was the middle of the night. The only sound was the soft moaning of one sailor who'd finally lost his right leg to the bone saw only an hour before. The surgeon had given the man a large dollop of monkey's blood and a leather bit to clench in his teeth when the pain became unbearable, but it hadn't helped much.

Hawke was glad Nick hadn't been awake to hear the sounds of the poor sailor going under knife and saw, or his pitiful wails when his stump was plunged into boiling pitch to seal the wound and stop the bleeding. Hawke himself could barely stand it, but at that point, mercifully for all concerned, the sailor had fainted. There were one or two other sailors here in the sick bay, men who probably wouldn't live to see the sunrise. But everything that could be done to ease their pain had been done.

"Are we safe?" Nick asked, although he wasn't sure why. Something about cannonballs buzzing by his ears and splintered timber crashing down from above. And Stiles, yes, his poor friend Stiles who'd been with him in the rigging when the whistling balls had started flying. The memories started returning and Nick choked back his feelings. Stiles was dead. Blown out of the rigging into a watery grave. A hero's death, at least, Nick tried to console himself, the pain in his heart far more acute than the wound to his head. "Safe at last, sir?" Nick asked.

"Aye, we're safe all right, lad," said the whispering voice of the surgeon. "Which is in no small part thanks to yerself, boy, thanks to yerself." The elderly ship's physician reached over and patted Nick's hand, which had lain motionless upon his chest since they'd carried him down here many hours earlier.

"What happened, sir?" Nick asked, his voice painfully weak. And, quietly, Lord Hawke told him.

The *Merlin* had ghosted northward behind the great rock just moments after Nick had been injured. To the great relief of the crew, the shadow of the towering rock fell across the *Merlin*'s decks and the hands looked at each other in amazement. They'd done it! Thanks to the heroic boy at the masthead, they had navigated the reef and were safely behind the rock!

Suddenly, a great roaring cheer had gone up from the hands, all lifting their eyes skyward to the small boy hanging by his heels high in the rigging. He'd done it! He'd seen them through! Even the crews out in the four jolly boats were on their feet, whooping for joy and throwing their hats into the air for the brave lad at the foretop masthead.

But when the boy didn't respond to their wild cheers, but just hung there limply, twisting in the wind, Hawke instantly knew something was dreadfully wrong. He'd grabbed the nearest shroud and started up. In a trice, four or five hands also shot up the shrouds nearest the foremast and they had all reached the gravely wounded and unconscious boy in seconds. The first thing they noticed was the dark blood matting his curly yellow hair. It was a head wound.

It didn't look good. Hawke had seen battlefield wounds as bad as this. And they'd been fatal.

They had handed Nick gently, unconscious and bleeding profusely from the head, from the uppermost crosstrees down to the deck. The sailors handled his limp form with great respect, even awe. Hawke's heart swelled with pride. After all, to the ship's company, Nick was only a twelve-year-old stowaway. Yet he had saved them all from the specter of death and certain defeat, that they might fight another day.

One of the men removed the bandanna from his own head and wound it around Nick's to staunch the bleeding. Hawke was touched at the reverence even the lowliest hand bestowed on poor Nick as he lay motionless on the sun-bleached deck. Some removed their hats and bowed their heads, praying, or more likely, paying their last respects.

Gunner had knelt on the deck beside the boy, cradling Nick's head in his arms and wondering if his young friend was even aware that he was dying a hero's death. He'd always yearned to be a hero. It was the only thing he'd ever wanted, far as Gunner knew. And now . . .

"You can't die yet, boy, you just can't!" Gunner whispered, and lifted Nick gently in his arms and cradled him to his chest. Then, his eyes brimming with tears, Gunner had sadly carried Nick below.

And now in the sickly light of the lanterns of the sick bay, they heard the doctor's first happy words.

"You're a right lucky one, Nicholas McIver," the old surgeon said. "Hardheaded, too, you are! Lots of blood with head wounds, and yours was a sharp blow to the side of your temple. Stitched it with catgut so you'll have a nice piratical scar, lad. One as charms the gentle sex. Now, had you been looking up and seen the blow comin', well–"

The room fell into an awful stillness. Death was still hovering in the gloom and even the sleeping must have felt it. Just then, a cheerful voice full of life broke the silence.

"Oh, he's a lucky Jack all right!" said a familiar voice in the bunk right next to Nick's. "As lucky as they makes 'em! Boneheaded, but a right fine navigator, too!" Nick turned his head to see who it might be, a smile already breaking across his face.

Lieutenant Stiles!

Nick rolled on his side and stared in disbelief at the heavily bandaged figure lying in the next berth. His heart leapt for joy.

"Why, Mr. Stiles, I thought you were–I mean, I reckoned you had been–" Nick stammered at the miracle of seeing his friend still alive and seemingly healthy. "I didn't think I'd ever see you again, Lieutenant."

Nick sobbed, and realized that hot tears of relief were pouring down his cheeks and that he didn't care who saw it. Some tears, he guessed, were justifiable.

"It was a close article for me, too, Nick," Stiles said, and smiled up at Lord Hawke. "I was blowed right into the boiling sea! But for your friend here, me dear old mum would've been reading me name in the black-border lists in Hyde Park. Aye, I was lucky to have an angel such as Lord Hawke to look out for me. Why, Nick, you should have seen it! The great Hawke flew down from the barky's rail and delivered me up from the sea, just like Gabriel himself! Swam through a hail of lead to save me, he did, too!"

Now, in the gloom and sour air of the sick bay, the young lieutenant stretched his hand across the narrow space between his bunk and Nick's. Nick extended his hand across to Stiles, and felt the bond formed by that grip was strong enough to last an eternity.

"What's that noise, Lieutenant?" Nick asked Stiles. His senses were coming back into focus now and he was aware of a swishing noise just outside the hull at the head of his berth.

"That be seawater, lad," Stiles said. "Rushin' by the barky's sides. We're on the wind and sailing hard nor'east for England. See how she heels? The wind is fresh on her starb'rd beam and we've got our lee rail down. We must be making seven knots! Hear that bangin' and sawin' forward? Ships' carpenters fixin' those holes in her starboard bows now that we got her leaned over to port. Without such chance to get her heeled and patched, why, we'd be on the bottom by now! As it is, we'll be good as new afore daybreak!"

For the first time, Nick noticed the angle of the sick bay and the way all the lanterns were hanging. They were indeed heeled well over and making good speed. They'd made good their escape after all!

"Where's Gunner?" Nick asked, weakly. "Is he all right?"

"He's fine, son, asleep in a hammock they strung for him on the gundeck where he could be near his guns and his lads," said Lord Hawke. "He's been down here watching you, too. He was convinced you'd wake up eventually, and, thank the saints, he was right."

"And Jip?" Nick asked. "Where's my old dog Jipper?"

"Why, Billy's got him, Nick," Hawke said gently. "Remember? That's why we're here!"

"Where is Billy now?" Nick inquired in a low whisper. "Is he upon us?"

"Ah, I only wish we knew, lad," Lord Hawke said. "He tried to follow your route through the reefs just as we thought he would and got his ship hung up on a mighty mess of rock, we hope. By the time he gets her pulled off and repairs the hole in his bow, we'll have opened up a good stretch of sea between us and be ready to fight. If he didn't, well–"

"He's skittish as the four winds, that Blood," Stiles murmured, and they all fell into deep thought. Each trying to imagine what course of action the pirate might take. "When old Bill is after you, all you need is a trick or a miracle," Stiles added sleepily. Closing his eyes, he fell into a deep sleep, letting go of Nick's hand.

A moment later, Nick, too, was sleeping peacefully.

CHAPTER XXXI

The Fully Hatched Scheme

· 8 June 1939 ·

U-BOAT 33, OFF HAWKE POINT

"All engines dead stop!"

"All engines stop, aye!"

"Up periscope!"

"Up periscope, aye!"

"*Kapitän?* A question?"

"What is it now? I'm busy, Lieutenant!" von Krieg said, turning with the periscope so that his back was to Little Willy in the reddish gloom of the bridge deck.

"It's *Colonel*! Must I continually remind everyone on this boat of my rank? Please! We must work together now, whether we like it or not. Now, listen. I've been thinking–McIver does seem a bit too knowledgeable about the workings of a U-boat. Perhaps you are right about him. I, myself, have been suspicious all along."

"Of course I am right, you idiot!" von Krieg said, and turned to face the little man. "And, whether you are an idiot *lieutenant* or an idiot *colonel* is no matter to me! I am still *der*

Kapitän, lest you forget!" Hoping for a reaction, von Krieg got nothing but a mild smile.

"I'm curious. What are you planning to do with them–later?" Little Willy asked.

"After we have gained entrance to the castle, they will both meet with an unfortunate accident. The Tweedles will arrange something. Tragic. And, simple."

"Not the child, surely!" Willy said, for, despite himself, he had been completely charmed by the little red-haired girl. She had the entire crew wrapped around her finger. He couldn't imagine himself able to harm her, but, he reminded himself, this was war. Or would be soon enough, at any rate, when England finally awoke from its slumber.

"I am surprised at this weakness in you, frankly, Lieutenant. You know as well as I do what has to be done. She is a sweet little thing, but in war there are always civilian casualties; it is out of my hands. Both of them must be taken care of as soon as possible. Dr. Moeller will handle it. As you know, he actually has a fondness for such things."

Hobbes had left Katie, still sleeping peacefully in their little cabin, and was now making his way forward along the narrow companionway. Having returned to their cabin after convincing the captain of the truth of his tale, he'd finally grabbed a few hours' sleep. Now, he'd been summoned once more to the control room. Apparently, they'd made excellent time, and were now lying at periscope depth somewhere just off Greybeard Island.

He felt a trickle of perspiration run down his cheek and disappear inside the collar of his shirt. Tight quarters, he thought. It was hot inside a U-boat, and before this day was over, Hobbes knew, it was going to get even hotter.

Hobbes was about to embark on the single most significant gamble of his naval career, of his life. His own life, and Kate's, depended on how he handled himself for the next half hour. He stepped silently into the gloom of the control room and saw Willy and von Krieg at the periscope, so preoccupied that no one had seen or heard him enter.

"Looking for me, boys?" Hobbes said, brightly, stepping up behind the two German officers at the periscope. He felt an air of breezy confidence was called for this morning. It would take all his ingenuity, but he would do it. He had to do it.

"Ah, Herr Lighthouse Keeper!" the captain said, turning around and giving Hobbes the eye. "I didn't hear you enter." He looked at the man carefully for a moment and then returned to his periscope.

"Right here, *mein Kapitän,*" Hobbes said, stepping forward into the halo of hazy red light. He detested the way the captain kept looking at him like a bug under a microscope and yet there was little here and now that he could do about it. He needed perhaps an hour, and then it wouldn't matter anymore. He smiled at Willy. "And much refreshed after a few hour's sleep in such sumptuous accommodations, gentlemen!" Willy, unsmiling, eyed him carefully.

"Excellent! I gave you our best suite, which luckily had just become available. So, what do you think of our little underwater miracle, Herr McIver, now that you've spent some time aboard her?" The captain did not bother to hide the pride in his voice as he swiveled the eyepiece through ninety degrees.

"We now lie about a thousand yards directly to the south of Hawke Point. And yet I still see no entrance to this secret lagoon you described, McIver. And I've been looking for it for weeks."

"May I take a look at your approach to the point, Captain?" Hobbes asked.

"By all means, by all means!" said the captain, and he stepped aside to give Hobbes access to the periscope. Hobbes could feel the captain waiting for his next move, watching to see how the lighthouse keeper handled a sophisticated periscope.

"Sorry, Captain, I've never handled one of these gizmos before. Only seen them in movies, I'm afraid. Mind showing me how to do it?" Von Krieg looked at him, hard, for a moment, and then laughed. He was clever, this Englander, but not half so clever as he imagined.

"Not at all, Herr McIver. Hands go here. Turn this to focus. And your eyes go here," the captain said with an unreadable smile. "Of course."

"Thank you," Hobbes said, not trusting his eyes to look at the captain. He put his hands on the grips and swiveled the scope until the target came into view. At first he thought the periscope lenses were out of focus, the world looked so crazily distorted. Then he realized it was only his own sweat, stinging his eyes. He took a deep breath and kept his eyes glued to the scope where the Nazis couldn't see the nervousness that filled them.

"You see, Captain, the entrance is designed to be hidden, visible only from a very precise angle. We are now lying perpendicular to the entrance, at almost a ninety-degree angle," Hobbes said. "To enter the inlet, the submarine must lie parallel to the cliff face. And of course we must submerge to a minimum depth of twenty meters. May I have your chart for a moment? And perhaps a pen or pencil?"

"Why submerge at all?" asked von Krieg, handing him a pencil and the ship's chart. "Why not just sail into the lagoon on the surface?"

Hobbes, taken aback, tried not to show it.

"Well, first of all, the element of surprise, I should think," said Hobbes, a bit surprised that any sub captain would be brazen enough to just sail in on the surface into an enemy lagoon. "But it's also the only way a sub of this size can enter. Let me show you the correct method of entry on the chart, Captain. You'll see that I've drawn the configuration of the submerged entrance on the chart for you. It's a bit complicated, so I'll sketch out the whole thing."

Hobbes had designed the underwater entrance so that it was impossible to detect by the casual observer. But it was quite simple for him to sketch it now for the captain.

"This is the cliff face here," Hobbes said, drawing the outline of Hawke Point with his heavy black number-two pencil. "The fissure in the face begins here at the top and widens gradually down to the sea, as you can see. At a depth of twenty meters, you should have a good five meters of clearance on either side of the sub. If your navigator manages to put us in dead center." The captain nodded his head.

"So, we take her down to twenty and go in dead slow. *Wunderbar!* Did Hawke have this entrance designed for British submarines, I ask you?" von Krieg asked suspiciously. "I wonder."

"Not at all, Captain," Hobbes lied smoothly. "It's a natural rock formation. But you're correct, it does provide an almost ideal undetected entry for submarines. It is one of Lord Hawke's most closely guarded secrets. The first of many to be revealed, I assure you."

"*Wunderbar!*" The captain laughed. "A secret English sub base! Ah, Willy, wait until Berlin hears about this! *Der Führer* will have a parade just for us, no?" A huge grin appeared on the U-boat captain's face. "Bosun!" he shouted, and the big crewman with the short blond hair appeared instantly.

"Aye, sir!" the crewman said, snapping to attention.

"We are taking *das boot* through this hidden undersea passage in the rock," the captain said, excited now. "There is an opening here, see, just twenty meters below the surface of the water. We'll take her down, pass through this narrow opening, and surface just inside the hidden lagoon. As soon as we're up, I want a man on the five-inch deck gun and I want the two large rubber rafts deployed. One for Lieutenant Steiner, myself, and our two guests, and one for the good doctor and his assistant, armed with submachine guns. Also, I want both forward and aft torpedo tubes loaded and primed to fire! We are finally about to pay a surprise visit to the famous Lord Richard Hawke!"

"Aye, aye, sir!" said the bosun, snapping out a stiff-armed salute. "Heil, Hitler!"

"Heil, Hitler!" said the captain, with a half-hearted salute.

"Heil, Hitler!" shouted Little Willy, patriotic fervor filling his voice.

They both looked at Hobbes, waiting.

"Heil, Hitler!" the English commander said, clicking his heels and raising his right arm in the stiff-armed salute. Smiling approvingly, the Germans didn't notice Hobbes's left hand slipping into his jacket pocket. There, he felt for the two small buttons on his remote radio-controller and firmly pushed the one on the right.

And lowered the Seagate.

For better or for worse, they were going in.

CHAPTER XXXII

The Spanish Masquerade

· 4 October 1805 ·

H.M.S. *MERLIN,* AT SEA

All eyes were fixed on the eastern horizon as the distant burning star of fire inched up above the earth's dark rim. Rising, it sent its first brilliant, white-hot rays streaking across the heaving black wave tops, splashing color over the water's surface, radiant streaks of deepest blue. The sea air on their faces was cool, and carried a sharp bite of salt.

It was going to be a beautiful day.

No one had spoken for some time, not even an hour earlier when Nick had wordlessly joined Gunner and Lord Hawke at the port rail just aft of the bowsprit. Like them, Nick stared silently down at the dark, rolling sea, now shot with brilliant sunlight.

Both men knew why Nick was not in his sick bay berth, even though in the waning moonlight they had seen a dark stain of blood on the white bandage wound around his head. He'd come to the port rail for the same reason they all had. They'd all come to wait for Billy. And Nick again found himself thinking about courage, and the brave little match-boy.

Was he, too, going to prove himself courageous this day, a truly brave boy? As brave as the boys in stories who always stood and fought, and never ran? Never gave in. Never surrendered.

Near enough to Nick's own age, the match-boy was serving under Admiral Lord Nelson during the Battle of the Nile, aboard *Goliath*. Each gun crew had its "match-boys" and "powder monkeys." Powder monkeys ferried gunpowder from below and match-boys lit the powder in the "touch-hole" to fire the cannons. In times of close-range exchanges, when the huge warships were yardarm-to-yardarm and trading broadsides, keeping your limbs, much less your wits, about you was essential. It fell to these young match-boys to do both.

One day, the story went, during a pitched battle at close quarters, an incident occurred which had caused Nick to ponder the question of courage in earnest. A hailstorm of cannister shot and cannonball was tearing into *Goliath*'s canvas, rigging, and topsides with ferocious velocity and accuracy. The English ship's great guns were red-hot, bucking and roaring in response. There was more hot lead in the air than air itself. If you were a match-boy, you were right in the thick of it!

At the breech end of his cannon with a burning match in his right hand, the boy was waiting for the gunners to clean and reload, when a French cannonball from the opposing vessel severed his right arm. The ball took his dear limb most cleanly, leaving his entire arm hanging from the shoulder by only the slenderest thread of skin.

The boy looked from his grievously wounded arm to the

match that lay, still burning, on the deck. Smoke, fire, lead, and the screams of the wounded filled the air. The boy bent down, picked up the match in his good left hand, and put it to the touch-hole. The cannon belched fire and lead. His perfect ball tore away the royal topgallant mast of the French frigate. And this mere boy, no more than twelve years of age and in shock from the loss of his own blood, had laughed at the murderous effect of his cannon, and then gone off to the surgeon to have his arm attended to.

One arm hanging by a string, he'd fired his cannon and then he'd *laughed.*

Nick had never forgotten that laugh. Surely that was bravery itself, the laugh of a real hero!

"Sail, ho!" now came a faint cry from the masthead high above. Although they of course could see no such sail; at their level the horizon was still a pale empty orange line in the distance. Nick saw the masthead signalman come flying down a shroud to the deck, with nothing but his hands and his calves wrapped lightly around the line to control his fall. The man then scrambled aft to find the captain, the whole maneuver taking only a matter of seconds! "Sail, ho!" echoed the runner at the foot of the mast, cupping his hands and shouting this news to the officers on the quarterdeck.

"Where away?" said the quarterdeck.

"Hull down, and dead to leeward!"

"Hull down, dead to leeward, aye!"

And a moment later, they saw a small shadowy black shape on the pale pink line where the sea met the sky. As they watched, the shape grew steadily larger as she bore down on them. *Mystère* advancing into battle was the vision of menace.

Compared to their own warship, she was a monster. Enough to give even the bravest man, even Hawke himself, pause. But Hawke knew that this day the sure, swift sword of England was in their hands. And that *Merlin* was finally ready for a fair fight, a fight she had to win.

The captured Spaniard spy Velasquez, a noose around his neck and spilling his guts in order to save them, had revealed that Spain, in a treacherous secret alliance with France, planned to entrap an unwitting Nelson and his fleet, now lying at Portsmouth, by luring them down off Cape Trafalgar with a single small Spanish galleon known to be loaded to the gunwales with Incan gold.

If McIver failed to deliver Velasquez and his documents of treachery to Nelson, the unwitting sea lord and his fleet would sail on the next tide into the waiting arms of a combined French and Spanish Navy. It would be an unthinkable disaster for the English.

Finally, as the *Mystère* loomed ever larger on the horizon, it fell to Gunner to break the silence. "Yer feelin' a bit better, are ye, lad?" he asked Nick. "Seein' as yer up and about?"

"Aye," said Nick.

"No use in askin' if sick bay ain't the perfect place for the wounded young shipmate today?"

"None."

"Aye, I thought as much. Still, we won't be pepperin' each other from a distance today, Nick. We'll be boardin' her or she'll be boardin' us, grapnels'll fly, and then yardarm to yardarm we'll lie. Frenchies with sabers screamin' like banshees, mind you. Broadside to broadside, too, lad."

"I've read that's the way it's done," Nick replied softly,

staring out at Blood's looming black silhouette, every inch of canvas spread. "The way Lord Nelson does it anyway. Attack. Always attack."

"Lord Nelson ain't got a little sister waitin' for him in the next century," Gunner replied, spitting over the rail. "Nor a mum and dad, neither."

"Ain't got his best dog chained up and starving in this one, either, has he? On that bloody pirate's boat over there, I'll wager," Nick shot back. Lord Hawke coughed and put a hand on Nick's shoulder.

"Nicholas, listen to me. If you must remain on deck, I will understand. But I want you to stick close by Captain McIver," Lord Hawke said, a worried look clouding his brow. "He'll be by the helm, well protected by Marines. I must insist that you remain by his side throughout the engagement. No matter what happens to Gunner or me. Is that clear?"

"Aye, aye, sir," Nick said with a smile, feeling as if he'd just won the Irish Sweepstakes. He'd been sure Lord Hawke was going to make him stay below and miss the entire engagement. "I won't leave the captain's side, your lordship, I swear it!"

"See that you don't, lad," Hawke said seriously, and handed Nick a thick envelope sealed with wax. "Please sew this immediately into your pocket. Keep it safe with the time machine, Nick. If something happens to me, I want you and Hobbes to personally deliver both the envelope and Leonardo's machine to this person in London. We must not allow this machine of yours to fall into William Blood's hands. Do you understand, lad?"

"Aye, sir, I do," Nick said, and turned the envelope over in his hands. On it was a name in Lord Hawke's fine hand. It said simply, *George R.* George Rex, Nick realized in an instant. The packet was addressed to the King of England.

"I think it's time, your lordship," Gunner said, casting an eye at the sea and the steadily advancing red-hulled seventy-four. "By the looks of that spray off his cutwater, he's making a good ten knots! She fairly flies, don't she!"

Hawke looked out at Billy's position, nodded, and the three of them went aft to find the captain.

Nick kept expecting to feel afraid, but was aware only of a growing sense of excitement. He saw the bluejackets lashing huge rolls of thick canvas to the rails all along the port side. To what end? he wondered. And he saw that the main deck was curiously empty of sailors or Marines, and then he remembered Stiles saying they needed a trick or a miracle. Apparently they'd decided not to count on miracles.

"Ahoy there!" he heard the captain shout, his voice ringing with good cheer at the sight of Nicholas on deck. "Fine day, ain't it, young McIver? Glad to see the medico's nostrums has you up and about, lad. I am truly overjoyed!"

He was standing by the helm on the quarterdeck and next to him stood Mr. Stiles and a group of scarlet-coated Marines. Nick was most happy to see Stiles, another escapee from sick bay. The captain raised his long brass glass and swung it round to *Mystère*, spinning the little focus ring with the raised letters "NM."

"And so we find Mr. Blood returns!" the captain said loudly. "He'll find us in better health than he left us, Mr. Stiles! Strike our colors, Lieutenant!"

"Colors, sir!" Stiles replied, and they all looked aloft as the red and blue Union Jack fluttered down from the main topmast.

"Haul the Spanish ensign to the masthead if you please, Mr. Stiles," McIver said.

"Haul away, aye!" Stiles cried.

And they watched as the Spanish flag was hauled up on a halyard to replace the British, snapping in the breeze, to flutter at the top of the mainmast.

"What's going on?" Nick whispered to Stiles out of the side of his mouth.

"A masquerade party, Nick," Stiles whispered back with a smile. "A little trick the captain's preparin' for Bill. We ain't showin' him our true colors; instead we're dressing the barky up to look like a pretty Spanish señorita. See how all three masts is raked sharply aft in the Spanish fashion? Try to lure old Bill over close without him firin' them magical cannons of his. Here, put this on."

He handed Nick an odd-looking little sailor's cap, the floppy kind Nick knew the Spanish sailors wore. Nick noticed that they were all wearing them, even Captain McIver who had shed his blue officer's coat for a simple white blouse and a floppy cap.

"What's next?" Nick asked.

"Well, about now Billy's masthead lookouts will be reportin' a small Spanish galleon swimmin' in their direction. That's the way our aft-raked rig will appear in their spyglasses from this distance," Stiles said. "And since Billy's expectin' to meet up with just such a barky today, he may well credit it."

"What about when he gets in close?" Nick asked. "We won't look so much like Spaniards then."

"Aye, that's what them rolls of canvas lashed to the port rails is for. A señorita's costume disguise for the whole barky!" Stiles said and turned to the captain. "Let fall the portside canvas now, sir?"

"If you please, Mr. Stiles," said McIver, and on Stiles's order the crew cut the ropes. The thick canvas rolls unfurled all along the port side of the *Merlin,* from the rail down to the sea. Nick went to the rail to watch and saw that the canvas had been carefully painted with a blue and gold checkerboard pattern over blue topsides to resemble the side of a Spanish galleon. He noticed that the gun ports had all been painted to appear closed, adding to the deception.

Behind the painted canvas, the *Merlin*'s real gun ports were open, her cannons ready to be run out, and he saw gun crewmen gathering the canvas tightly to the hull and lashing it there to help the illusion. From a distance, Nick now saw, the *Merlin* would appear to be something she surely was not, a pretty blue and gold Spanish galleon!

Nick returned to the helm a few minutes later, smiling. It was a devilish good trick and it might just work! He saw that a dark-haired stranger with a full black beard had joined the officers at the helm. He was wearing a royal blue greatcoat with shiny silver buttons and a yellow sash across his chest, in the Spanish style. A blue and gold three-cornered hat perched atop his black curls. Then Nick saw that Stiles had his flintlock pistol stuck in the middle of the man's back.

"Allow me to present Señor Enrique Velasquez!" Stiles said

to Nick, bowing deeply and smiling. "Formerly a spy for the Spanish crown and recently promoted to captain of this here barky!" So, Nick thought, they were using the Spaniard as a decoy captain!

"Signal flags on the enemy red frigate, sir!" came a shouted voice from the masthead signalman who'd returned aloft with a spyglass to the rigging above. "He signals '*What boat?*' "

"What boat then, *Señor Capitán*?" Stiles asked Velasquez, prodding him with the pistol.

"¿El Condor, señor?" the man said, full of anger and loathing for his humiliating predicament. "Or, is it *El Diablo*? I forget, you know I–"

"Five seconds, señor," Stiles said, sticking the pistol up under the man's jaw. "Is about how long you've got to live."

"*Condor*." Velasquez said raspily. *"¡Es El Condor, señor!"*

"Aye," McIver said, and thought about it for a moment. "Send him '*El Condor* out of Catalonia,' " Captain McIver shouted aloft, and saw the proper signal flags run out immediately.

"He signals 'Welcome *Condor!* Rendezvous?' " said the lookout, and Stiles and McIver smiled broadly at each other. So far, it was working. The fact that Billy wasn't already firing his nitro-powered long-range guns meant the illusion was holding up. At least for now.

"Where's Gunner and the crew?" Nick whispered to Stiles. "Where are all the bluejackets and Marines?"

"They're massed belowdecks, waitin' for a signal," Stiles said. "No more talkin' now, lad, unless you speak *español*. Sound travels far across water."

They could see Billy's red topsides clearly now–he was

closing fast. In his rigging, the black skull and crossbones known as Jolly Roger flew, and the upside-down English flag. He had all his gunports open and they could see the gun crews at each station. They hadn't run them out yet. Blood might be fooled, but he wasn't taking chances, either.

"I'll hold fire until your signal, Captain," Stiles whispered to McIver.

"Aye, Lieutenant," he replied in a hushed whisper. "My signal will be 'God save the King!'"

"Aye, sir!"

Nick could see Billy tacking cautiously closer, not willing to commit, but clearly drawn in by the blue and gold topsides and the aft-raked Spanish rigging. Billy had furled his stunsails and royals now, and slowed the big seventy-four considerably. Nick could sense the presence of many enemy eyes watching them through spyglasses high in her rigging. The others must have felt the same because everyone pulled their Spanish caps down farther around their ears. Nick noticed that the sun had climbed about two hands over the horizon and that Billy was sailing right into its blinding glare. It was probably why he had not yet seen through the painted canvas draping *Merlin*'s hull.

A little miracle, Nick thought, and he'd take it, with God's blessing.

"Easy, lads, easy," McIver growled in a low whisper. You could feel the tension round the helm as Billy's flagship hove into view. She was now less than a thousand yards distant. She was magnificent there in the full light of the rising sun, with bright pendants streaming from her three mastheads and billowing clouds of white sail above her crimson hull.

Even slowed, she was still heeled well over, and throwing foaming white water to either side of her cutwater.

A glorious sight, but it felt to Nick as if every one of her seventy-four gleaming cannons would soon be aimed at his heart. It was hard to believe that such a breathtakingly beautiful vessel was bent on his personal destruction.

Below the quarterdeck, where Nick stood, he could hear the stamping and impatient murmurings and the jangling of swords of hundreds of anxious sailors and Marines, waiting for the signal to fire the rows of cannons hidden behind the canvas and eager to race up on deck and engage the enemy.

Gunner, in a brilliant strategy devised the night before, had put all the working guns on the port side and heaved the disabled ones overboard. *Merlin* could now only fight one side, but she'd be much quicker and more nimble than the big first-rater, a heavy seventy-four.

"*¡Hola! Hola!*" A shout of hello from a hand aboard the huge *Mystère* came drifting across the water. They were hailing the Spanish captain. Stiles again jabbed the spy Velasquez in the back with his hidden pistol and the startled Spaniard returned the shouted greeting.

"*¡Hola!*" Velasquez cried.

"*¿Buenos días, señor! Esta* El Condor?" said the Spanish voice, floating across from the French warship.

"*¡Sí, aquí es* El Condor!" Velasquez shouted in return, and the big red frigate tacked once more and crept in ever closer. Surely they could see the false paintwork now! But, no, she kept coming.

Nick could see the sun glinting off the endless rows of polished brass cannons on every deck of her massive hull. Like everyone else at the helm, he held his breath. Stiles, who felt some uneasiness from the jittery Spaniard standing at the business end of his pistol, started to say something, but it was too late.

Suddenly, without warning, Velasquez bolted forward for the port rail. Screaming like a man possessed, he started tearing wildly at the ropes that bound the canvas to the *Merlin*'s topsides.

"*¡Artificio! Artificio!*" Velasquez shouted across the water to the French as he ripped and tore at the lines supporting the painted canvas disguise. "*¡Decepción!* A trick! A trick!"

Nick saw the largest section of canvas fall away from the rail and into the sea as Stiles raised his pistol and took aim at Velasquez, but he knew it was already too late! Stiles fired and the Spaniard crumpled at the rail, clutching his leg. A dark bloodstain spread on his breeches, but he was not mortally wounded. McIver wanted him alive for the meeting with Lord Nelson. Seeing that he was still tearing at the lines that held the canvas, Stiles raised his pistol to fire again, but the captain shook his head no. It was too late.

The *Merlin* now lay unmasked, and, with the telltale black-and-white "Nelson checker" pattern now bared along her side, she was revealed for what she was, a battered English man-of-war, undermanned and undergunned and spoiling for a fight!

There was a shout aboard *Mystère* and then an instant later, a roar of powder and flash of flame from Billy's bow. A ball tore through the rigging over their heads, showering them with debris. Nick drew a deep breath. The sharp bite of gunpowder was becoming all too familiar. He heard another enemy cannon roar and *Mystère* came storming in under their lee now, rolling her big guns out as she came.

A rapid series of explosions, marked by flashes of fire and booming thunder along her massive flank, almost immediately hid the big red frigate in a cloud of roiling black smoke. Nick braced himself for the incoming barrage of iron shot but, miraculously, there was none.

The French cannons, fired in haste, had all been fired on the ship's downward roll, and most balls pounded harmlessly into the sea. Still, the battle was now joined, for better or worse, and Nick craned his head around, fore and aft, aloft and below, starboard to port. It was as if he couldn't possibly see enough, hear enough, *feel* enough. He was, he reminded himself, a hand, albeit an *unpaid* hand, on an English man-of-war going into battle under the magnificent broad pendant of Horatio Nelson, the heroic victor of the Nile and St. Vincent!

"Strike the Spanish ensign, Mr. Stiles, and show her our true colors! Haul our ensign, if you please," McIver said, his voice barely above a whisper. As the Union Jack fluttered aloft into the sun, the captain clambered up to the top of the rail, got up on his tiptoes, cupped his hands, and delivered the resounding battle cry. He'd donned the blue coat of the Royal Navy once more.

"God save the King! God save the King!" Captain McIver roared. "God save our bloody King!"

"Save the bloody King!" came the roaring answering cry, from one end of the ship to the other.

There came then a great rolling thunder of English cannon fire from the three decks beneath Nick's feet. The entire hull shook with the enormity of it, the unmistakable fury of a rippling broadside!

Every portside cannon was now firing in perfect sequence on an upward roll and delivering a devastating first strike! Gunner had done it, Nick rejoiced! Instantly the air on deck was full of boiling black gunsmoke, and across the water, through clear pockets in the thick smoke, the devastation was plain. Already the cries of the maimed and wounded aboard *Mystère* floated back across the water to Nick. Much of her upper rigging hung in limp shambles. The captain turned to him with a huge grin.

"I've never seen the like of it, Nick! Your friend Gunner has done it all right, finest ripplin' broadside as ever I saw!" And he turned back to the main deck and continued his battle cry, "At 'em with a will, now lads, England expects nothing less of you!"

There was no indecision now, no running behind a rock. Captain McIver was taking the fight right into the enemy's throat. With a roar of her men and a roar of her cannon, Nick heard and felt the *Merlin* exploding to violent life all around him. He could scarcely imagine the look of shock and rage on Billy's face when the painted canvas had dropped into the sea, exposing the English cannons now rolled out into the sun! Velasquez's desperate attempt to foil the plot had been too late after all! Billy had taken the bait and now he was paying the price for it.

The massive multiple explosions of the great cannons continued their endless rolling rumble beneath Nick's feet.

"Hear that, boy?" said McIver gleefully. "Give you joy, that's our dear Gunner down there! Has the lads tickin' like a fine Swiss clock! He's timin' our rolls perfectly, reloading on the downward, firing on the up! And, we've blasted old Billy a good one with that first broadside! That'll send Bill reelin', and no error! We've got a chance now, Nick, a fighting chance!"

Nick knew it was true. If *Merlin* was victorious this day, it would be in large part due to that first devastating broadside. Gunner had made good on his promise. Nick hoped it was an omen of things to come.

Captain Blood's *Mystère*, reeling and stunned by the surprise attack, could only watch in dismay as the English ship tacked abruptly behind her to windward and then raked her stern mercilessly. Now *Merlin* came slashing toward the French seventy-four's starboard flank, all of her forward cannons blazing. From where Nick stood, *Mystère* looked to be in total disarray. She was fighting back, to be sure, but it was a confused effort, bereft of any rhythm or symmetry. *Merlin* was running downwind now, and showing a great turn of speed.

On board the French warship, an unhappy officer stood on his quarterdeck.

"Mon Dieu!" said the bewildered French lieutenant, looking at the utter chaos surrounding him. "My God!"

The first officer on the massive French vessel was in fact in a state of complete confusion. Approaching battle into a blinding sun, he'd failed to recognize the trickery of *Merlin*'s painted side and suffered a devastating broadside in consequence. Now he heard the cry of "God save the King" float across the water and saw the enemy tack around and into him.

He was shocked to see all her hatches fly open and legions of shouting red-coated Marines surge up on her decks with a great cry of "Hurrah!" and begin forming up on the main deck. All around them, he saw, were bluejackets with cutlasses flashing in the sun, who now swarmed up and massed at the port rail breastworks, as everywhere English officers in blue coats urged them on. Sharpshooters with muskets were scampering up into the rigging and already firing at targets aboard his floundering French warship.

What was Captain Blood's plan *now*, he wondered. And where, pray, was the infamous captain himself? Hiding below in his cabin? Sporting with his captured English filly?

Mystère's stern lookout now called out a warning and the French officer went completely pale. The little English third-rater had spread all her canvas and was bearing down on him at an ungodly speed! Surely, even the wily English captain did not intend to heave to and attempt to *board* the much larger vessel? That would be suicide! The French crew outnumbered the English two to one! But what else could he be thinking, tacking right up inside *Mystère*'s lee? Where was Captain Blood? In his cabin sipping English breakfast tea with his English mistress of course. *Mais certainement!*

The French first officer found his Captain of Guns wandering the main deck in a daze. The man was bleeding from both ears and unable to speak. No wonder they weren't returning fire! No one had given the order! The first officer ran off like a madman, ordering every crewman he saw to fire at will. It wasn't textbook tactics, but it was effective. Finally, the French gun crews got off a deafening broadside, and the *Mystère*'s bow lookout smiled, happy to sniff a little French gunpowder in the air at last!

Order restored, the big French seventy-four now turned

all her starboard heavy guns on the oncoming English vessel.

Almost instantly, aboard the *Merlin,* the air was full of deafening blasts and thick black smoke as the two warships now traded blows at close quarters. Murderous amounts of iron shot were now ripping into *Merlin* and Nick saw the devastating effect it caused all about him, especially the splintered wood that exploded inward every time a ball struck the wooden hull. For the first time Nick noticed the wet sand spread on the deck underfoot and remembered its gruesome purpose–to soak up the blood of the dead and wounded so that the decks would not become slippery with the thick red stuff.

Merlin was coming up on Billy's stern quarter now, and Nick could only imagine how terrible the French broadside would be. He held his breath and waited as the seconds seemed to stretch into hours.

"Hard a'port, now, lads, hard a'port!" McIver screamed and lunged for the wheel himself, impatient with his helmsman. He put the wheel hard over and drove her straight for Billy's midships! Nick could see the shock on the faces of the Frenchmen now lining *Mystère*'s starboard rail. Did the English captain now intend to *ram* them? Would he dare sail right into the rain of hot lead and iron they were firing?

"Handsomely, now, handsomely!" cried McIver, pale blue eyes raised aloft, watching for the luff of his mainsail, spinning the ship's wheel lightly through the tips of his fingers. You could feel the effect of the mighty press of canvas aloft, feel it singing, shuddering throughout the huge wooden boat, feel it through your feet, Nick realized, you could feel it in your toes!

Nick watched the spectacle of McIver's performance in

awe; here then, and there was no other word for it, here then was a *mariner*. Here, then, was a *warrior*.

Ramming? All standing at the *Merlin*'s helm held their breath in anticipation of the captain's next move. It would not be unlike the great sea warrior McIver to attempt any maneuver at all. He had no qualms about ordering a tactic with even the slimmest chance of success if he felt it would ultimately serve the cause of victory. Stiles looked nervously at the rapidly diminishing distance between the two vessels.

"Captain, sir!" he cried. "With respect, sir, the barky can't survive a–"

"Ready about, Mr. Stiles?" McIver whispered to the loyal first lieutenant standing at his side. "On my signal, sir." And again McIver's hands were a blur, spinning the great wheel with his fingertips, his blue eyes focused on some point directly amidships of the French seventy-four.

"Ready, aye!" Stiles shot back, gladly relieved to learn of the impending tack, his eyes riveted on sail trimmers in the rigging, whose eyes were in turn focused on the rapidly diminishing angles of the two vessels.

It was the trimmers, standing barefooted on lines along the yardarms, who would now determine when the barky would stop and where. Everything hinged on their ability in the next few seconds. Sharpshooters high in the rigging of both vessels continued their deadly work and Nick was shocked to see a man standing just to the right of him fall to the deck without a sound, a small fountain of blood bubbling at his belly. Two Marines whisked the poor fellow below without a word. It shocked Nick to realize he'd probably never even learn the man's fate.

Still, *Merlin* continued to bear down on *Mystère* and the anxious crews who lined the rails on both warships braced for the collision. The silence at the helm was a roar in Nick's ears. He braced for the terrible, inevitable collision. On both ships, an unspoken question. Was the Englishman at the helm mad?

"Mr. Stiles, you may fall off five degrees, please, and back the main, on my signal, sir. Another fifty yards, sir. Steady as she goes." The captain was whispering repeated directions softly under his breath and Nick took a deep breath, bracing himself against the mizzenmast halyards. What was the captain thinking? A devastating collision was now clearly unavoidable! Nick saw a Marine next to him squeeze his eyes shut in fright. If the *Marines* were afraid . . .

Inside a hundred yards now and closing at full speed. Nick looked aloft at the *Merlin*'s clouds of sail, white and full of wind and drawing against the rich blue of the sky. He saw a single white tern circling high above the top royals and marveled at the bird's serene indifference to the bloody tragedy unfolding just below.

"Look alive, sir!" McIver whispered harshly, and Nick thought for a wild moment the captain was addressing *him*. "Mind your helm!" McIver had turned the helm over to his first officer so that he might concentrate on the multiple instant decisions he had to make in the next few seconds.

"Alive, aye," Stiles said quietly, gripping the wheel, his eyes on the sails and the scant few yards that separated the two giant warships. Nick closed his own eyes then. He didn't want to see it.

"If you please, Mr. Stiles," he heard the captain say, "back the mainsail now, and prepare to heave to. We'll take her up alongside now." McIver, a tremor of excitement lifting his voice now far above a whisper, now shouted, "Easy now, easy, on my order–heave to, sir, now!"

The *Merlin* had been sailing at hull speed straight for the *Mystère*'s starboard midships and had closed to within less than fifty yards! Nick still doubted a collision was avoidable, but at the last possible instant he heard McIver cry out, "Back the main and hard to starboard! Heave to, boys, heave to! I want her dead stopped in forty, thirty, twenty–douse all sail now!"

Nick opened his eyes.

Merlin steamed ahead, then staggered as the trimmers doused her canvas, as she lost her wind, as the cry "Heave to!" echoed across the water. The relief and the peace, however, were but momentary.

Merlin's intentions were now clear, she would board, and the enemy gun crews went to work again with a will. Great flashes of flame erupted every second and French cannons sent chain shot into the rigging and cannister shot and grape shot screaming across *Merlin*'s decks. The air was full of lead and death and choked with smoke and the cries of the newly wounded. Nick didn't even realize that he was screaming too, urging the *Merlin* on as they drifted into *Mystère*, almost within spitting distance now, and crews on both sides firing and screaming and wanting at each other's throats.

And *Merlin,* her helm hard over, spun beautifully at the last possible moment, her bowsprit nearly tangling in Billy's midships rigging. Having dumped her wind, momentum carried her forward and around until she was now yardarm to yardarm with the enemy vessel, perfectly positioned to board the party of Marines still forming up on her main deck!

The two warships were now ghosting toward one another, the gap of water between them a matter of feet and inches, and narrowing rapidly.

Nick heard a great cheer go up from the masses of men forming up on the main deck and saw a few redcoats leap up onto the breastworks on the *Merlin*'s boarding side and raise their cutlasses into the air. The *Merlin*'s crew surged forward with an ear-splitting yell. The scarlet coats were pressing forward, ready to go up and over the side as soon as the two vessels came close enough to rub shoulders and the grapnel hooks secured the boats together.

Only a few feet now separated the two vessels, and the crew of each for some reason abruptly ceased fire and simply stared at each other across the narrow gap of water, men lining both rails staring with a terrible mixture of fear and unbridled malice. To Nick, that silence seemed as loud somehow as the roar of cannons.

Nick felt a dull, jarring thud as the two ships met. A brilliant chill went up his spine as he looked into the face of the enemy. There were too many emotions at once for him to fathom. But they all shared a single name:

War.

Nelson the Strong, Nelson the Brave, Nelson the Lord of the Sea.

To his surprise, Nick found that he was repeating his chant rapidly to himself, over and over, somewhat breathlessly. "Board her, lads! Board her now!" Lieutenant Stiles was screaming to his officers from the rail, and Nick saw that the two warships were now bumping and touching, shoulder to shoulder. He felt the whole ship shudder under his feet each time the two big vessels collided.

Then a monstrous cry went up on both sides and the men of the *Merlin* surged up and over the breastworks and Nick saw the mass of shouting Frenchmen rise up in response, saw their striped shirts and caps and the flashing cutlasses and pikes in one hand, pistols in the other. They fired the pistols first, then threw the useless weapons down or at the enemy, there being no time to reload in the heat of battle. And to his horror he saw that the stripe-shirted enemy sailors were not only repelling the Englishmen trying to board *Mystère,* but that scores of them were leaping down onto *Merlin*'s deck and slashing the English marines as they waited to board. He saw a large number of the French who'd broken through now making for the quarterdeck where he and the captain stood.

The Marines guarding the helm fixed their bayonets and lowered their muskets.

"Repel boarders!" McIver screamed at his officers. "Beat 'em back, lads!" he said, pushing two Marines aside and pulling his cutlass from the scabbard. Then he was leaping down from the quarterdeck rail, wading into the very thick of the battle on the main deck. Nick watched his namesake smash into the massed French boarders, a cheer rising in his throat. Captain McIver didn't mind repelling a few boarders himself, it seemed, while he spurred his officers on. He saw the captain leap up onto the breastworks over the bodies of two dead Frenchies, waving his cutlass, shouting at his men to press forward, Lord Hawke among their number.

But, shockingly, it seemed to Nick that the men of the *Merlin* had now lost their will, been beaten back, their attempt to board the enemy vessel thwarted. French sailors now mounted the breastworks seemingly at will, and, save the brave English captain fighting now almost single-handedly, leapt unchallenged to *Merlin*'s deck. For the first time that day, Nick felt truly afraid.

He felt the reassuring hand of Stiles on his shoulder.

"Easy lad, easy," Stiles said. "Your friend Lord Hawke knows a thing or two about this dreadful game, I see!"

"But the French sailors, they–"

"It's a feint, Nick," Stiles said, bending to shout into his ear. "A ploy, lad! The captain and Lord Hawke is only luring them Frenchies aboard afore they commits our main body of boarders. See them now! The French officers think we've–"

A huge roar went up then from the *Merlin* and Nick saw the Frenchmen fall back as Lord Hawke himself leapt up to the breastwork to join McIver, followed by an enormous swelling mass of red-coated Marines! Like an angry swarm of bees, the *Merlin*'s men now rose up and over, slashing with pikes and cutlasses and firing their pistols point blank into the enemy before them, driving the striped shirts back to their decks or into the sea. A surging tide of Englishmen, which seemed to have the immutable force of nature behind it.

Nick climbed up onto a mizzen halyard block for a better view of the action, and his heart leapt in his chest as he saw his friend Hawke, England's greatest swordsman, fending off three of the bloody striped shirts at once! Lord Hawke had let one get behind him but he whirled at the last moment and fired his pistol into the man, blowing him backward into the gap between the two warships and into the sea. He whirled again, disarming one man and running the other one through. Nick soon lost sight of his two friends as Hawke and McIver leapt into the snarling mass of humanity on *Mystère*'s deck, but he was thankful to see at least ten redcoats right behind them as the two determined Englishmen waded in, no doubt in search of the quarterdeck and Billy Blood.

"Huzzah! Huzzah!" Nick cried, waving his Spanish cap and wishing he could be at Lord Hawke and the captain's side when they at last encountered Captain Blood. But he'd made a solemn promise to Hawke to remain at the helm and he intended to keep it, even though he no longer enjoyed the protection of the captain. He wondered how long the ring of Marines surrounding the helm would hold.

"Nick! Behind you, lad!" he heard Stiles shout. "They've broken through!" Nick whirled around to see.

Four of them! A small gang of French swabs had somehow broken through the ring of Marines on the quarterdeck and were coming his way. He saw the lead one raising his arm in a throwing motion and then an ugly steel dagger thudded with a loud thump into the mizzenmast barely three inches from his right eye!

Nick saw the man who'd thrown it laugh and raise his cutlass to summon the others forward. His bald head and face were horribly disfigured somehow, as if he had blood red scars around his eyes and nose, but as he got closer Nick saw that it wasn't scars, it was a grisly tattoo of some kind. Like snakes slithering round his eyes and up his nose.

Snake Eye!

Billy's strange companion at the Greybeard Inn!

Nick, in desperation, yanked the still-vibrating dagger out of the wood and saw the tattooed Frenchie smile a horrible grin, red rings dancing around his eyes.

"Bonjour, Monsieur McIver!" Snake Eye said to Nick, calling him by name in a thick French accent. "We meet again! I bring compliments of Captain William Blood! He said I'd find you here and he is still willing to trade your flea-bitten dog for this object in your possession. If you refuse, I have orders to bring the object itself to him along with your head!"

"I refuse," Nick said, and the words were out of his mouth before he could take them back. Jip was worth more to him than a thousand golden orbs.

"Allons!" the tattooed one shouted, and the gang of ugly swabs began closing in on the boy.

"Hello, Snake Eye!" Stiles said to the tattooed swabbie. "Which I was wonderin' when I'd see your ugly face again." Stiles leapt in front of Nick and raised his cutlass.

"Kill these English dogs!" Snake Eye screamed savagely. He motioned for his mates to attack, but they hesitated. Perhaps they too had met Lieutenant Stiles before, Nick thought.

"Up on me shoulders with you, Nick!" Stiles said, standing just below where Nick still clung to the mizzen, standing on a block. "We'll make short work of this paltry lot! Take this cutlass and watch me back, will you now lad? Hop on! We've seen 'em before. They ain't much!"

Nick took the cutlass and jumped down from the mast onto Stiles's broad shoulders, straddling his head as they waded toward the Frenchies. Stiles, slashing the air with one hand and challenging them to advance, shot one who was getting a little too close and then threw the spent pistol into the face of Snake Eye who howled in pain and fell to the deck.

Two of the others had crept up behind them and Nick whirled, slashing out with the heavy cutlass and lifting their hats for them. Stiles then spun about and in one blow knocked both their swords away, but Nick saw another dangerous turn of events just behind them.

Snake Eye, blood streaming from his broken nose, had found five more bloodthirsty comrades and they were closing in a circle around Stiles. Nick could see Snake Eye's tattoo clearly now, two thick red serpents descending down his forehead and coiling around his eyes, one of which was an empty black hole. The snakes then encircled his bloody nose and, to his horror, Nick saw that when the man smiled, the triangular heads of the two red serpents rose up and slithered into his nostrils!

So this finally was the murderous face of the enemy, Nick thought, so this was the true face of evil and death and war. No matter what happened now, he thought, at least he'd seen the genuine article in Snake Eye.

"Down and run for it, Nick!" Stiles shouted, realizing that he could never fend off this quarrelsome bunch with the burdensome weight of Nick on his shoulders. "And get below with you, Nick! Too hot on deck for young lads who's attracted the personal attention of Billy Blood this morning!"

"Run! Run where, sir?" Nick cried, looking around them. They were completely surrounded by grinning Frenchmen and Snake Eye was advancing one inch at a time, his one murderous eye riveted on Nick!

"Aloft!" Stiles shouted, catching sight of the dangling ratlines just above Nick's head. "Up the mizzenmast with you!"

Nick got to his feet on the lieutenant's shoulders and reached upward just as Snake Eye lunged forward with a shout. But Nick couldn't reach the hanging ratlines!

"Jump for it, lad! Now!" Stiles said and, sheathing his sword, he pushed Nick upward with both hands, feinting back as Snake Eye took a vicious cut at him with his cutlass. Nick caught the dangling rope with one hand, stuck Bill's dagger in his teeth and shot up the ratline like a scalded cat, having now learned a thing or two about getting aloft quickly.

Up the mizzenmast he went, pausing for a moment to look down. He saw Stiles whirling and slashing with a fierceness he could scarce credit in his friend and saw the Frenchies circling him, a pack of cowardly dogs, howling for blood.

From this height, a third of the way up the aftermost mast on the deck, he could see the entire battle. Although many of the gun crews were dead or wounded, the air was roiling with thick black smoke and cannons on both vessels were still firing at point-blank range, chain shot into the rigging, and lethal cannister shot across the decks. There was now a pitched battle raging on *Mystère*'s main deck, and he saw Lord Hawke and McIver fighting back-to-back in the very thick of it, though he could not tell who was getting the better of it. He heard something, a grunt, just below him on the mizzenmast and looked down.

Snake Eye was racing up the mizzenmast ratlines after him, a dagger in his teeth.

CHAPTER XXXIII

Nazis in Hawke Lagoon

· 8 June 1939 ·

U-BOAT 33, HAWKE LAGOON

A fine hard rain was falling inside Hawke Lagoon when the ugly snout of the U-33 broke the surface. *Der Wolf* had finally penetrated Hawke's lair. As the sub surfaced, Hobbes was sure everyone around him could hear his heart pounding inside his chest. He was so close now, so very close. If only his luck would hold.

Hobbes took one last look around in the muggy heat of the U-boat's control room, memorizing every aspect of it, recording it mentally for the lads of Advanced Weapons, in case things did not work out quite as he planned. The big blond bosun handed them each black rubber ponchos and they slipped them over their heads, Kate smiling at Hobbes and how silly he looked. Hobbes ruffled her red curls and gave her a big wink. Her performance aboard U-33 rivaled the finest ever seen on any West End stage. She had put her trust and her fate in her new friend and Hobbes was fiercely determined to prove worthy of that faith.

"Got your cat, my dear girl?" Hobbes asked, the two of them standing at the foot of the conning tower ladder.

"Right here, Father!" she replied, and opened her poncho to reveal Horatio cradled in one arm.

"So, Mr. Lighthouse Keeper," Captain von Krieg said cheerfully, "are you ready to pay your friend, the famous Lord Hawke, a surprise visit?"

"Ah, yes, Angus," added Little Willy gleefully, "it's always exciting when friends drop in unexpectedly." Hobbes saw a strange light in the SS colonel's eyes and hoped he saw it for what it was, only the glittering dream of future glory. He turned to face the captain who was pulling his black poncho over his head.

"I must remind you, Captain von Krieg, to do exactly as I say when we reach the dock," Hobbes said levelly. "The security measures here in the lagoon are extraordinary, as I have told you, both lethal and ingenious, and you must all follow my instructions to the letter."

"We are in your hands, McIver, aren't we, Colonel?" the captain replied. "Unless of course, you try anything foolish and then you and your daughter are in the hands of our Gestapo friends back there. Do I make myself perfectly clear, Herr, uh, McIver?"

Hobbes could scarcely imagine a worse fate for he and Katie than being left to the devices of the mad surgeon and his assistant. "It goes without saying, Captain," Hobbes said, and then for good measure added, "Heil, Hitler!"

"Heil, Hitler!" they all shouted, and pulled up the hoods on their ponchos. "Let's go!" Little Willy said, and bounded up the ladder like a wiry monkey. The rest followed and in a moment they were standing atop the conning tower in the pouring rain. The circular walls of glistening black granite towered all around them and because of the storm above, and the dense rainfall, midday was almost dark as night in the lagoon. The captain threw a switch and powerful klieg lights mounted around the conning tower lit up the length of the sub's black hull, raindrops hissing on its broad decks.

Hobbes said a silent prayer for Hawke, Nick, and Gunner, still visitors in another century, praying that they were safe.

Hobbes could barely make out the lights on his dock in the driving, needle-sharp rain as they climbed over the side and began their descent to the U-boat's deck. The fact that not all of the lights on the dock were illuminated was a good sign. Clearly, Hawke was not at home and expecting him. His plan still stood a chance of success.

Each of the black rubber rafts had two wooden thwart seats. Hobbes and Kate did as they were told and took the forward seat in the first raft. Von Krieg and Little Willy sat just behind them and took up the paddles. Hobbes craned his neck around and saw Moeller and Klaus climb into the second raft and shove off from the U-boat.

He noticed that the crewman manning the deck gun had it trained directly at him. Not a good sign, he thought. He heard the captain tell Dr. Moeller in German to stay behind his own raft and to watch every move the Englishman made. Then he too shoved off and began rowing away from the sub. It was a little over a hundred yards to the dock through pouring rain.

Hobbes took Kate's hand and squeezed it. There were many things he would have liked to say to her at that point, but he felt it was better and safer to just stare straight ahead in silence. So far, his plan was working beautifully. But it was far from over. Gradually, he saw the dark green line of the dock emerge through the grey curtain of rain. The only noise other than the rain on his poncho was the rhythmic sound of the paddles cutting the water, and it echoed inside the walls of the lagoon. Ninety yards. It was almost over.

Then von Krieg said something that chilled Hobbes to the very bone.

"Do you still have that scar under your left arm, fencing master?" the captain said pleasantly above the hiss of the rain. Hobbes froze.

"Scar?" Hobbes asked. "What on earth are you talking about?"

"Surely you remember? I gave it to you the first day I arrived in your quarters at Oxford," von Krieg continued. "You were trying to teach the awkward young German boy how to fence like a proper Englishman, remember? I lost my safety tip just as I was lunging for your heart, as I recall, and nicked your chest. Pity."

"You must have me confused with someone else, Captain," Hobbes said without turning around. "I haven't the slightest clue what you're talking about."

"Oh, I think you do. You know very well. Hobbes, isn't it?" von Krieg replied. "Or is it Commander Hobbes now? British Royal Navy Intelligence, as I recall from your last dossier in Berlin."

"I am sorry, Captain. You're mistaken. My name is Angus McIver. Surely you don't keep dossiers on lighthouse keepers in Berlin," Hobbes said, still facing forward and buying a little time.

He squeezed Katie's hand and she turned a fearful face up at him. He was glad she couldn't see what he was doing as he reached beneath his rain-drenched poncho and inside his jacket. All bets were off now. He was down to a few desperate chances. He felt the cold steel of his little snubbed-nose .38 police special. It was small enough to fit in the palm of his hand, but quite deadly at ranges such as this. It had been small enough to hide in the compartment above his berth.

"I've never made a mistake in my life, Commander Hobbes!" he heard the captain snort behind him.

"Are you calling me a liar, sir?" When Hobbes turned, he had the gun in his hand.

"Yes, as a matter of fact, I am," von Krieg said, looking with disdain at the small silver weapon in Hobbes's hand.

And Hobbes saw that both the captain and Little Willy had their big Lugers sticking out of their ponchos and pointed at the middle of his forehead. It was over. He'd never get off two shots fast enough and everyone knew it.

Von Krieg was smiling under his poncho, Willy's ferretlike face was hidden in the shadows of his own hood. Hobbes could sense he wasn't smiling. He was sure Willy was so filled with cold fury at Hobbes's deception that only a prize as desirable as Lord Hawke had kept him from exploding and killing Hobbes immediately.

The SS colonel sat rock still, seething, his finger tense around the trigger. Hobbes had made a fool of him in front of the captain. Hobbes knew then that he could expect not a trace of mercy, no matter what happened in the next few minutes.

Hobbes lowered his pistol. The look on von Krieg's face told him his charade was finally over. Which meant this was going to be a lot more difficult than he'd imagined. At any rate, they wouldn't dare shoot him until he got them safely inside the castle. The raft was no place to try anything, certainly not with Kate by his side. He casually tossed his pistol into the water and smiled as if it had all been only been a silly misunderstanding.

"Your name is Hobbes," the captain said coldly in his clipped German accent. "After Oxford, you took an advanced engineering degree and flew experimental aircraft for the Navy. After that, you joined British Intelligence and were stationed at various posts in Europe and South America, becoming station chief at Rio de Janeiro and finally returning to England. You then joined the Naval Advanced Weapons Group where you and your old friend Richard Hawke from Oxford got reacquainted, and the rest of course, is history. As are you, I might add."

Hobbes smiled. "Ah, well, Wolfie," Hobbes said, smiling at the captain's reaction to the use of his old university nickname, "it was worth a try, I suppose. All's fair in love and war and all that. You've got quite a file on me, I must say. When did you finally catch me out? Or did you know all along?"

"No, I don't think so, Commander," von Krieg said. "You see, I finally found a faded photograph in my sea chest last night. My fencing club at Oxford. And who do I see standing puffed up with pride in the middle of our little group? Why, my new friend the lighthouse keeper! I shared this photo this morning with Colonel Steiner and he agreed it was a remarkable likeness, didn't you Willy?"

Little Willy nodded inside his poncho but still said nothing. So they'd known his true identity all morning! Despite himself, he was impressed with their performance on the bridge of the U-boat and later when the sub was slipping through the hidden opening to the lagoon. Von Krieg had probably made Little Willy contain his anger at least until they were safely inside Hawke Lagoon. Hobbes saw that they were nearing the dock. He had come so close to pulling off his masquerade! Now he simply had to concentrate on keeping himself and Kate alive until they reached the castle itself. He wondered if the captain could control Little Willy that long. He prayed he could.

"Then I'm surprised that I'm still alive, Captain," Hobbes said. He knew the only reason they hadn't killed him yet was their intense desire to gain entrance to the castle itself. Once that was accomplished, his life expectancy would take a dramatic turn for the worse.

"The colonel here wanted, to put it delicately, to deal with you personally this morning, Commander," von Krieg continued, "but I convinced him otherwise. I said no, Willy, we've come this far. Let's allow the commander to show us how to penetrate the Hawke Castle security devices and then we'll deal with unpleasant matters after that."

Finally, a cold voice came from inside the shadowy hood of Willy's poncho, words sharp as razors.

"Take a deep breath, Commander," the SS colonel said. "And enjoy it. You only have a few left, I promise you." He cocked his Luger and Hobbes flinched involuntarily, waiting for the bullet. The seconds stretched out.

Hobbes stared at the dock less than fifty feet away. The time for false bravado had passed. His only hope was to keep the U-boat captain calm and stay alive until they were all on the dock. He said, "And the child, Captain?"

"We are not monsters, Commander Hobbes," von Krieg replied. "In the event that something unfortunate should happen to you, Dr. Moeller will see that the child is returned unharmed to her home." Hobbes stiffened and put his arm around Kate, drawing her close. Moeller would see her safely home? He didn't believe a word of it.

"Oh, look!" Kate exclaimed softly. "There's the *Petrel,* Nicky's sailboat!" Hobbes peered through the rain and saw the small white sloop moored alongside the dock, just as they'd left it. "I do hope my brother's all right. And Gunner and Lord Hawke, too," Katie said, as if she'd been reading his mind. Despite their own perilous situation, the three time travelers were never far from either of their thoughts.

Was Kate crying? He felt her shivering beside him, and kissed her forehead. "It'll be all right, my dear," he whispered to her. "Just stay close to Uncle Hobbes's side and do exactly as I say." She rewarded him with a brave smile and said, "I'm only cold and wet, not afraid. I learned how not to be afraid from my brother. Besides, I have to take care of Horatio for Gunner until he gets back."

The raft covered the last few feet through the hissing downpour and then they saw the dock ladder loom up out of the rain. The raft bumped gently against it. Hobbes reached up for the bottom rung and put his weight down on it as he stood. He had designed the ladder so that even five pounds of pressure on any rung silently triggered Hawke Castle's elaborate high voltage warning system. It was unfortunate that they'd found him out, he knew, but there were still a few surprises left, and a slim chance they could still survive this. He hoped that was true. The Tweedles, Fritz and Klaus, neared the dock.

"You and the child up the ladder!" the U-boat skipper barked, waving his pistol at Commander Hobbes. "Now!" Hobbes lifted Kate up until she got her feet on the bottom rung and she climbed up onto the dock. He followed her up and then glanced at the hidden warning light set into the rock fifteen feet above the steel dock. It was flashing amber. That meant he'd definitely activated the secondary security system. They had about two minutes before the light turned red. Von Krieg came up the ladder with one hand, the other holding the Luger pointed at Hobbes. The SS colonel followed, and in a moment the four of them were standing on the dock, waiting for Fritz and Klaus in the second raft to join them. Kate clung to Hobbes and he knew she was afraid, maybe not for herself but certainly for him.

Little Willy came directly to Hobbes and stood on his tiptoes so he could deliver a private message, out of Kate's earshot.

"How does it feel to be a dead man, Commander Hobbes?" Little Willy hissed from under his poncho. "Once we're inside the castle, Dr. Moeller will make sure you live just long enough to regret making a fool of me, and it will be the worst ten minutes of your life, I assure you."

Hobbes didn't answer the little colonel but looked over his

shoulder into the lagoon and held his breath, waiting nervously for the two Gestapo men to tie their raft to the dock and ascend the ladder. He wanted all four Nazis on the dock surface before the warnings commenced. He glanced up at the warning light above and could tell from the rate of flashing that he had about thirty seconds left until it turned from amber to red. "Tell them to hurry," he said to the captain.

"Come on, you idiots, hurry up!" von Krieg screamed at the two thugs, who, because of their weight, were having a difficult time getting up the small ladder. Hobbes was silently grateful to see the Tweedles leap as if stung and scramble up the ladder. Fifteen seconds. The amber warning light was silently flashing very rapidly now and Dr. Moeller was coming up the ladder first.

"Can I kill this lying English pig now, *mein Kapitän*?" Moeller asked as he clambered up onto the dock. He went up to Hobbes with his scalpel flashing, drawing the razor-sharp blade just under the commander's chin with a teasing motion. Von Krieg never had a chance to answer the monster's question.

The unseen warning lights now all began flashing red.

"You must leave at once!" boomed a voice from numerous loudspeakers mounted high above among the floodlights in the rocks.

Suddenly, the entire lagoon was lit up with powerful floodlights both from the rock walls surrounding them and under water. With the hissing lights and the rain, the darkness inside the towering granite walls was transformed into a brilliance of light and falling water. Hobbes felt they could all be standing under a cascading hundred-foot African waterfall at midday. A pleasant enough notion at the moment, and they were still alive.

The rain had softened a little now and, as it fell down into the floodlit lagoon, it turned to a fine white mist. Hobbes was glad that Kate, who had seen and heard all these warnings and lights before, was not unduly afraid, and she wisely held his hand and said nothing. The black hull of the U-boat loomed large out in the swirling white mist at the center of the green lagoon. Hobbes was glad to see that occasionally the sub was completely obscured by the clouds of mist. It meant the sailor manning the deck gun didn't have a clear view of what was going on at the dock.

The metallic voice rang out again, bouncing around within the mist inside the towering rock walls.

"This is a restricted area. This is a military facility, restricted to British government and military personnel. If you have not re-boarded your vessel and left this lagoon within five minutes, severe measures will be taken. Extreme measures."

"A military facility, is it? What sort of measures, Commander?" von Krieg demanded, putting his Luger right up under Hobbes's chin. "You never mentioned that this was a military installation!"

"I warned you both that there were security obstacles to be overcome, Captain. Now please be so good as to get that thing out of my face or you can forget getting off this dock and gaining access to the castle." Even though the Germans knew his true identity now, Hobbes knew he was still holding a few cards. If Kate weren't involved, he would have been a lot less polite.

Kate herself had no such qualms about polite behavior

toward the Germans, however. She didn't like the way the captain was treating her friend. She pulled the cat Horatio out from under her poncho and placed him on the dock.

"Don't you dare do that to my friend!" Katie screamed and kicked the captain as hard as she could, squarely in the shinbone. Von Krieg barked in pain as she drew her foot back to strike him again. He pointed his pistol at her curly red head.

"Kate! Leave the captain alone! He's not going to hurt us," Hobbes said, grabbing her away from him. He saw to his amazement that the little girl actually stuck her tongue out at the U-boat captain with the Luger an inch from her nose. He put his hands on her shoulders and stationed her safely behind his back.

"I repeat, Commander, *what kind of extreme measures*?" von Krieg shrieked, jamming the pistol once more in Hobbes's face.

"Ah, yes, I mentioned those, didn't I?" Hobbes said. "I don't want to shock you, Captain, but this dock is electrified."

"Electrified?" the captain screamed. "What do you mean electrified?"

"Surely you're familiar with electricity, Captain?"

"You now have four minutes," the recorded voice boomed again, echoing around and around the stone walls. *"The dock you are standing on is electrified to ten thousand volts. Now the power is off. In less than four minutes it will automatically be switched on. Anyone standing on or touching the dock at that time risks serious injury or death. Reboard your vessel immediately. This is your last warning!"*

"Did he say ten thousand?" Hobbes said. "Actually, it's twenty thousand volts, Captain. But it was felt that might be overly alarming." Hobbes smiled, enjoying himself for the first time in many long, unendurable hours.

"Twenty thousand volts!" Little Willy exclaimed. "My God, we'll all fry!"

Hobbes saw out of the corner of his eye that the doctor, and Klaus, too, had lost some of their taste for adventure. Both had turned deathly white and were edging back toward the ladder. The threat of twenty thousand volts tearing through your body usually had that effect on people, Hobbes noted with some satisfaction. He'd considered that very human emotion when he'd designed this system. Von Krieg swung his pistol around and leveled it at the plainly terrified Dr. Moeller.

"If you move a single step closer to that ladder, Doctor, I'll put a bullet in your fat cowardly back!" the captain said to the ashen-faced Gestapo agent. Hobbes noticed that they didn't move, but neither did they retreat away from the dock's edge. The two were rooted to the spot and plainly terrified. The Tweedles, at least, were out of the fight.

"Three minutes. Repeat, three minutes. Electrification of the dock area will commence in three minutes. Leave the area at once."

"*Kapitän,* please!" Moeller pleaded. "This is insanity! We'll all be killed!"

"Silence! How do you disarm this abominable system, Commander?" the captain said, turning his attention back to Hobbes. "It's most annoying."

"Right here!" Hobbes said, and hurried to the center lamppost where the *Petrel* was tied. There was a black control panel mounted on the post with a small lever on the left side. Hobbes pulled it down and the panel door swung open.

Inside, beneath a row of red flashing lights, were a number of switches and a button pad.

Hobbes began pushing the buttons. "Emergency manual override!" Hobbes said. "Fairly standard. First you punch in the code, then throw this switch. This switch will stop the alarm sequence and prevent electrification of the dock surfaces! Nothing to fear, Captain, I assure you!"

Hobbes threw the black switch to the emergency override position. The dock lights dimmed for a moment but then nothing happened. The wailing sirens continued, the red lights in the control box stayed red.

"Three minutes. Repeat, three minutes. Electrification of the dock area will commence in three minutes. Leave the area at once."

"It seems to be out of order, Captain," Hobbes said, turning ashen-faced toward von Krieg. "We'd best get off this dock immediately."

Von Krieg raised his pistol. "Try it again! If you're playing with me, Englishman, so help me, I'll–"

Suddenly, there was a loud splash in the water nearby and then another. The U-boat captain whirled around and saw both the doctor and his assistant paddling furiously, swimming for the submarine at the center of the lagoon.

Because of the underwater floodlights, their huge round bodies were perfectly illuminated. Von Krieg leveled his Luger at Klaus first and slowly squeezed the trigger. The muzzle flashed and the man reared up in the water and then a black stain slowly spread across the bright green water and Klaus fell quiet, floating facedown in the spreading pool of his own blood.

Hobbes heard a gasp of horror from Katie at his side and

put a protective arm around her, pulling her close and enfolding her in his poncho, shielding her eyes. It wasn't over, he knew. "Is he dead, Hobbes?" her muffled voice asked, and Hobbes's heart ached for this and all the suffering about to be visited on the children of the world. He held her tightly to him.

Dr. Moeller had stopped swimming and was dog-paddling in place, looking from his dead comrade to the furious captain on the dock, his face a contorted mask of fear. "Please, *Kapitän*! I beg of you, don't!" he wailed.

Von Krieg raised the pistol and took dead aim.

"You two miserable swine have laughed behind my back for the last time!" the captain shouted across the water. "So, you think I am a joke? You absurd Tweedle Twins who laugh over your beer at me? This is what happens to anyone who disobeys a direct order from the mightiest officer of the mightiest undersea navy on earth! *Die Kriegsmarine!*"

He shot the doctor right between the eyes. The Gestapo agent stopped paddling instantly and hung in the water like an enormous puppet with severed strings. There were now two black pools darkening the bright green surface of the water. Seconds later, three or four small black triangular fins could be seen circling the bodies, coming in closer with each pass. The twin pools of blood had brought them racing up from the bottom.

"My God, not sharks?" von Krieg said to no one in particular.

"I'm afraid so, Captain," Hobbes said. "Nasty creatures, but a highly effective deterrent, I daresay."

"Anyone else want to go for a swim?" von Krieg said, turning to Little Willy who stood ashen-faced and trembling five feet away.

"*Kapitän,* how do we know this is not all a trick?" Willy cried and he too was plainly wide-eyed with fear. The sharks now thrashing about with the two dead Gestapo agents in their jaws clearly hadn't helped his disposition much.

"Two minutes. Two minutes. Warning. Warning. Leave at once."

A loud klaxon horn now began wailing, deafening inside the high rocky walls. Warning lights atop each of the lamp-posts suddenly flashed on, throwing a harsh red glow across their faces and the glittering granite stone behind them.

"The entrance to the castle, Commander! Where is it?" von Krieg shouted at the top of his lungs. "Open it now, or you die! The child, too! Both of you, I swear it! Open it!"

"Von Krieg!" Little Willy shouted in a high whining voice. "Come to your senses! We'll all die if we remain here! It's a trap, don't you see? Hasn't he made enough of a fool of you? Let's go back to the U-boat and I'll make this English swine beg to tell us how to get inside! I have ways to make him talk, believe me!"

"No!" von Krieg shouted over the wail of the klaxons. "We're here now! He can get us inside now! We'll be heroes! Open the entrance now or watch the little girl join those two in the water, Commander!" Von Krieg lunged toward Hobbes and grabbed Kate, yanking her out of Hobbes's arms. He pulled the child to himself, his arm tightly around her and the Luger under her tiny chin. "I'll feed her to the sharks, I swear it, Commander!"

Hobbes desperately wanted to kill the man on the spot but knew that their lives depended on his complete and utter self-control at this very moment. He reached up and grabbed a wedge of protruding rock on the face of the wall.

"It's here. A lever in the wall disguised as rock–" Hobbes said, and pulled down on the short outcropping of rock. Suddenly, a whole section of the granite face of the wall began to move out and sideways. A smoky red light appeared around the edges of the hidden door. Then, it seemed to slow its movement. Von Krieg threw Kate aside and ran to the slowly opening door and clutched at it desperately. He was but inches from getting inside, inches from fame and glory in the highest echelons of the Nazi empire! Nothing would stop the man who was about to bring England's greatest spy to his knees!

"Look, Colonel! See for yourself!" von Krieg cried. But Willy hung back, edging closer to the dock ladder." Willy! Come!" the captain shouted. "It's open! Hawke Castle is ours for the taking!"

The crack in the door was open just wide enough for von Krieg to insert his desperate fingers. He pulled mightily. The granite-clad steel door began moving again. The captain gritted his teeth and threw his weight against the heavy door. Hobbes stood back and kept Kate well behind him.

"What's wrong, Hobbes?" the captain screamed. "Why isn't it moving? How do you open the bloody thing?" He braced his leg against the stone wall and heaved mightily on the door.

"Something must be wrong! It's stuck!" Hobbes said. "The hydraulic mechanism isn't working! I'm sorry, Captain, but we have to get off the dock immediately! There's no time to reset the system! We must get back aboard the raft and away from the dock!" Hobbes pulled Kate toward the ladder as von Krieg looked from the cracked door to the raft, enraged and confused.

"One minute. One minute. Final warning. This is your final warning. This structure is electrified to ten thousand volts. Remaining on the dock surface or touching the structure will now be fatal to any living thing, human or animal. Repeat. One minute."

A siren now began screaming over the wail of the horns. "Can't you see it's all a trick, Captain?" Willy shouted above the wail. "You idiot! He wants to kill us all! Stay and die if that's what you choose, but not me!"

Willy turned and leapt from the dock to the raft below. But he misjudged the jump and landed on the raft's rounded rubber side. Instantly, the raft flipped over and Willy, arms pinwheeling wildly, went screaming into the lagoon. The captain stepped to the edge of the dock. Roaring, he fired his pistol repeatedly at the shadowy figure clawing desperately through the brilliant green water and under the dock. He saw a black dorsal fin gliding toward the dock, and smiled.

Ah, well. The insufferable little SS colonel would not be returning with him to Berlin to spread his malicious lies about problems aboard *Der Wolf*'s first cruise.

He turned back to Hobbes who was shielding Kate behind him.

"Very well, fencing master, it's down to me and you," he said, keeping the Luger on Hobbes and moving to the ladder. "You think the arrogant Oxford don has again outsmarted the awkward German student? You think you've outfenced me once more? Well, we'll see about that." Von Krieg stepped backward onto the first rung of the ladder, keeping the gun on Hobbes.

"Don't do this, Captain!" Hobbes cried. "You can't leave a child to suffer like this! It's monstrous!"

"Good-bye, Commander. Tally-ho. *Auf wiedersehen, Katharina.*"

The captain descended the ladder with his back to the water, never taking the gun off Hobbes who was moving toward him, pulling Katie behind, shielding her with his body. The captain stepped carefully down into the raft.

"*Thirty seconds.*"

"Are you insane?" Hobbes cried. "Shoot me if you want, but you can't leave us here to die like this!" Hobbes lurched toward the ladder and the captain fired the Luger at his feet, the bullet ricocheting off the steel dock with a loud twang. Hobbes jumped back and he and Kate pressed their backs against the stone-covered door. Kate was trembling uncontrollably.

"Stay back! Away from the edge or I will shoot you both!" von Krieg shouted, untying the mooring line to the raft. "It's over, Commander! I'm taking my submarine back home to Germany now. But I'll be back, I promise you, with more men and equipment. And then I shall blast my way into this castle over your toasted body! Until then, I look forward to watching you die of your own devices!"

Standing on the thwart seat, he pushed off against the ladder and the raft skidded away from the dock.

"For God's sake, take the child!" Hobbes cried as Kate pressed her head into the folds of his poncho, her little arms clasped around his legs.

"*Fifteen seconds.*"

"I'm afraid our route back to Berlin doesn't pass by her pretty little lighthouse. Sorry!" The captain had seated himself on the aft thwart seat and was stroking away from the dock with an oar in one hand, the Luger pointed at Hobbes and Kate in the other.

"*Ten seconds.*"

"*Auf wiedersehen,* Herr English Fencing Master!" Hobbes heard the captain cry through the mist. "Pity you're going to miss this glorious war! I might even have enjoyed dueling with you on a slightly larger scale!"

"*Five seconds.*"

Hobbes squeezed Kate's hand. The captain was about fifty yards away, his eyes glued to the two figures left standing on the dock in the swirling mist.

"*Four seconds, three, two . . .*"

There was a sharp crackling noise, as if lightning had struck the dock, and every light in the lagoon dimmed low and seemed to sputter on and off while the piercing siren wailed a single high note that filled every living ear with pain.

Abruptly, it stopped.

"*One.*"

Hobbes and the little girl crumpled to the rain-soaked dock.

A hundred yards away, the U-boat captain shipped his oars, stood in the middle of his raft, and regarded the tragic scene on the dock with grim satisfaction. He felt a twinge of pity for the child, but none at all for his three comrades, nor his former Oxford instructor, still full of his old English arrogance and treachery.

He knew that this was just the beginning, the first act in a great drama of war now unfolding. He'd have many more opportunities to avenge the honor of his Fatherland, so cruelly treated by England after the Great War. Now Germany was rising up, and before this war was over, the whole world would cower before the might of the master race. Or be ground to bits beneath the heels of its hobnailed boots.

And he, as the triumphant Admiral Wolfgang von Krieg, would lead the world's most powerful underwater armada of super U-boats! Yes, on to glorious victory over the enemies of the Fatherland! He raised his stiff right arm in a farewell salute to his old adversary as the raft floated farther out across the lagoon, through the spreading black pools of blood.

He picked up his oars and rowed slowly into the mist and his waiting submarine. There was no longer even a trace of the two cowards, Moeller and his assistant, nor of Little Willy, and this too was satisfying. The voyage home would be much more pleasant without the three bothersome passengers who'd died here in the Hawke Lagoon.

Before the thick wet fog completely obscured the dock, he noticed that all the sirens had ceased and that all the floodlights had been extinguished. The lights on the dock posts, barely visible to him now, had returned to normal; a few pale yellow halos in the mist as the dock at Hawke Lagoon finally receded from view and he was alone on his raft, pulling on his oars for his submarine. The Englishman who'd humiliated him? Fried to a crisp. He felt another brief twinge of remorse for the little girl, perhaps, but then, this was war.

On the darkened dock itself, there was no sign of life.

And then a small whispery voice broke the stillness.

"Are you dead, Father?"

"I don't appear to be. How about you?"

"I'm completely alive, thank you. A little cold, I guess. Is the scary part quite over now?"

"Quite over, I should think. Be still for another moment

and I'll check." Hobbes slowly raised his head up an inch so that one eye could see beyond the forearm where he lay with his head on the cold wet steel of the dock.

He saw his old nemesis and his raft disappear into the solid wall of white mist that now blanketed the sub. He heard, too, a muted exchange in German between the sub and the raft and then a horn somewhere inside the sub and the muffled rumble of the U-boat's two powerful Crossfire engines roaring to life.

"Is that mean old captain gone, Father?"

"Yes, the captain seems to have gone back to his submarine. I don't think he'll be coming back," Hobbes said quietly. "You may call me Hobbes again, by the way, dear. I think our little spy game is over now, thank heavens."

"Oh. Right. I forgot," Kate said, lifting her head and staring into the misty lagoon. "The captain thinks we're dead, so he's leaving, isn't he, Hobbes? Going back to Germany?"

"I believe that's his plan, yes," Hobbes said, and rolled over on his shoulder so he could reach down into his trouser pocket. He pulled out the small metal boxlike object and rolled back onto his stomach. Propping himself up on his elbows, he regarded the strange little box. It had a small toggle switch and two small lights, one of which was flashing green.

"What's that, Hobbes?"

"Ah, this," Hobbes said. "Just that little gadget I invented, my dear. I believe I may have shown it to you when you first arrived at Hawke Castle. It's a radio-wave remote controller. Watch this!" Hobbes flipped the toggle switch to the up position and the light flashed red.

For the first time in days, Kate saw a huge smile spread

across Hobbes's face. "Ah, yes, I do believe the opening round of this coming unpleasantness just went to England, my dear. Our friend the captain is going to be most unhappy!"

"Why? What does that little box do?" asked Kate. "I forgot."

"Opens and closes things at a great distance, for one thing," Hobbes said with a smile. "By flipping this little switch here, for instance, I just closed the Hawke Lagoon Seagate. Unbeknownst to our friend Captain von Krieg and his crew, an impenetrable thirty-foot steel mesh curtain is at this very moment rising across the entrance of the lagoon. The captain and his U-boat are now the permanent guests of Hawke Lagoon, whether they like it or not! Can't get inside the castle, I daresay, and can't get outside the lagoon, either! Completely trapped!"

And Hobbes rested his head on his arm, allowing himself the first full, happy laugh he'd had for days. He rolled onto his back and let the light rain fall on his face and just let the relief of laughter come. "We've just caught the biggest enemy fish of all, my dear Kate! And the war hasn't even started yet!"

"That's good, I suppose. Can we go inside the castle now, Hobbes?" Kate asked. "When you're finished laughing, I mean?"

"Certainly, my dear, by all means!" Hobbes replied, wiping tears of joy from his eyes and sitting up. "It's most unpleasant out here, isn't it? Allow me to escort you up to the castle's main hall where I shall promptly get a roaring fire going and brew you a pot of fresh hot tea. I may even have a nice warm sweater that will fit the brilliant young Kate McIver! Has anyone ever told you that you are a magnificent actress, my child? I don't believe I've ever seen anyone play dead quite so convincingly, you know! The way you crumpled in a heap, ah, it was inspired! Simply inspired!"

Hobbes was still laughing when he jumped to his feet and pulled Kate up. He went to the partially opened door and pushed the rock lever all the way up, and then pulled a second jutting rock downward. The massive stone and steel structure slid open silently and Kate saw that it was as thick as a bank vault, three feet of solid stainless steel behind the rock.

Beyond it was another red-lit passage like the one she and Nick had taken, leading into the castle. She hung back, looking a little sadly into the mist hovering over the lagoon. She'd never seen anyone die before, and no matter how horrid the three German men had been, she wasn't sure they deserved the awful thing that had happened.

"Hobbes? Why weren't we electrified like the loudspeaker said?" Kate asked, still looking back over her shoulder at the lagoon.

"Oh, that," Hobbes said with a smile and an arm around her shoulder. "You see, actually there *is* no electrification, dear. I had it all removed a year or so ago when I discovered that the warnings alone were quite sufficient. No reason to actually physically *endanger* anyone, you know, if it's not necessary! That's my view of it, anyway!" With great good cheer, and in keen anticipation of the telephone calls he was about to make to Naval Operations in London, Hobbes pushed her along ahead of him.

"You know I wasn't really *acting* like I was dead on the dock, Hobbes," Kate said, stopping for a moment to pull the dripping poncho up over her head.

"No?" Hobbes replied. "You weren't playing dead, still as a poor churchmouse?"

"No, Hobbes, I was *thinking*!" Kate exclaimed, looking forward to the hot tea and the warm fire. "I was thinking very hard!"

"And what were you thinking about, dear?"

"Crumpets! May I have a crumpet with my tea, Hobbes?"

"My dear, you may have dozens!"

"And go to China in the little room?"

"All the way to China and back, if that's what you'd like!"

Kate skipped away, Horatio hot on her heels, as the massive door to the lagoon swung shut behind them and Hobbes's merry laughter followed her all the way down the passage.

CHAPTER XXXIV

Snake Eye and the Kingdom of Lost Children

· 4 October 1805 ·

H.M.S. *MERLIN,* AT SEA

"Can't run, boy! ! I'll catchee! I'll catchee!"

Snake Eye was right on his heels, coming up the ratlines after him and screaming like an angry banshee. Nick, terrified of looking down, was streaking upward, fist over fist. The image of a howling one-eyed man, with a viciously curved dagger clenched in his teeth was driving him up the mizzenmast more rapidly than a fifth-year midshipman gunning for promotion to lieutenant.

Nick shot up the ratlines to the first yardarm and no one in His Majesty's Navy had ever done so more smartly. He paused a moment to catch his breath and looked up to the masthead, wondering how high Snake Eye would follow him. Shocked, he saw a dead sharpshooter hanging in the rigging just above, blocking his path farther aloft!

He heard another inhuman wail from the mast below, and cast a nervous eye down between his feet. Snake Eye had stopped only a few feet below and he grinned up at Nick, taking the wicked dagger from his mouth.

Nick stared openmouthed as the fellow stuck out his long pink tongue, grasped it between two fingers, and then sliced off the tip of the organ with the serpentine dagger! Holding the little pink morsel of bloody flesh aloft, he threw his head back, opened his mouth, and dropped it down his gullet. Only then did he look at Nick with his one good eye and grin, blood trickling down his chin.

"Sharp, ain't it?" he said, putting the dagger back in his mouth and climbing.

Nick could go no higher, could go no lower, and had seconds to decide what to do. He took a deep breath. There was nothing for it but to step out onto the slender crosstree, high above the deck. He'd seen the surefooted crew do it with ease but the idea of doing it himself sent his pulse racing. He kicked off his boots as he'd seen the riggers and trimmers do. Barefoot, he edged out gingerly onto the wooden yardarm, trying to avoid looking down as Stiles had taught him. If he looked down, he knew he was a dead man. He took three steps, breathing rapidly, and froze, unable to take another step.

And then Snake Eye, too, was up and after him, hauling himself onto the same first yardarm. Snake Eye clung to the mizzen spar, the curved dagger glinting in his mouth, and Nick could see him trying to decide whether or not slitting Nick's throat was worth stepping out onto the narrow crosstree, thirty feet above the deck. If Snake Eye came for him, Nick tried to imagine jumping, but, even if he survived the fall, he'd be jumping into a mass of slashing swords.

So he edged toward the end of the yardarm, his toes clinging desperately to the narrow beam, one inch at a time, one foot in front of the other, one eye warily on Snake Eye. To his horror, he saw the man start to move out along the yardarm, and he had murder in his red-ringed eye.

Nick reached the outer end of the yardarm. Snake Eye was still moving cautiously along the crosstree, now less than fifteen feet away. Unless he thought of something quickly, Nick knew it was over. He looked down and was surprised to see the rolling sea below! He hadn't realized the crosstrees extended this far beyond the ship's gunwales below!

And there, too, was the majestic stern of Billy's warship *Mystère* bobbing and rolling just off the end of his own yardarm, the sun reflecting back from a hundred panes of glass in her stern windows.

Nick saw a glint of hope, too, in those panes of glass. Because of the vast difference in size between the two warships, the many towering stern decks of *Mystère* rose so high above the sea that her stern quarters were just opposite the *Merlin*'s lower mizzen yardarm where Nick now stood!

When the two ships rolled toward each other, Nick realized, the tip of his yardarm and the windows of the enemy vessel would be only a few yards apart! He could almost reach over and touch the *Mystère*'s red hull! If only he could–

Then he saw it. The largest of the stern windows amid the rows and rows of lead-paned glass was open! Nick knew it was his only chance. If he could time his jump precisely, he just might be able to dive right through the window of the French frigate! Whatever awaited inside could scarcely be worse than the tattooed wretch edging ever closer to him now. And, besides, his dog was on that frigate, and hadn't he come all this way to rescue him?

He didn't have to worry about it long, because at that

moment a howling Snake Eye was about to lunge for him, the vicious dagger raised above his head! All at once, the two boats rolled near each other and Nick saw his one desperate chance. Crossing himself, he leapt for the open window, away from Snake Eye's flashing blade, waiting for the searing pain even as he jumped. But it was Snake Eye who screamed in pain, his arms pinwheeling, wavering unsteadily on the yardarm, looking down to the deck to see who could shoot a dagger out of a man's hands at thirty feet, taking three of his fingers with it.

Down on the quarterdeck was Gunner, a broad grin on his face.

And a smoking blunderbuss in his hand. Snake Eye had just been introduced to Old Thunder. Now the two warships were beginning to roll apart, rapidly widening too far for Snake Eye to follow Nick through the open window. A shrill scream of anguish and rage was forming on his lips when the ship suddenly pitched and Snake Eye's bare feet lost their precarious hold on the wooden yardarm.

The man tumbled into space, helplessly waving his bloody hand, screaming all the way down. Gunner, who had more pressing matters to attend to, never even saw where the one-eyed pirate landed. Nor did he care.

Nick must have closed his eyes because when he opened them he found himself inside the most splendid room he'd ever seen, a magnificent space. He'd happily landed on a soft, cushiony banquette of silk pillows of every size and color. The settee wrapped around beneath the great sweep of stern windows of what could only be Billy Blood's great cabin itself! Even the roar of cannons overhead couldn't drown out its splendor.

Twin statues of blackamoors flanked either side of the banquette, holding intricately filigreed oil lanterns, and the brilliant stern windows were hung with thick velvet draperies of deepest claret. All the cabin furniture seemed made of gold and covered in red silk. There was a huge white marble bust of Emperor Napoleon standing on a massive golden table studded with jewels.

"Well, and what kind of bird might this be?" a lovely voice asked, "who has flown through my window?"

When Nick looked up to see where the musical voice had come from, his heart caught in his throat. There, in the shadows of the cabin, stood the most beautiful woman he'd ever seen in his life. He climbed down off the banquette and approached her. She smiled at him with flashing emerald eyes, but didn't move. She seemed to be resting her back against one of the four varnished columns that divided the cabin and supported the deck above.

"Who are you?" he asked, admiring the long deep red curls falling over the creamy white silk of her dress and bosom.

"You speak English!" she said. "Are you from the *Merlin*, I pray?"

"I am, indeed!" Nick said, pulling up his tattered bandage which kept drooping over one eye. "My name is Nicholas McIver."

"Indeed!" The beautiful woman laughed. "Well, small world and no error! He's come to save me, he has! Nicholas McIver, the *Merlin*'s skipper, as I live! One of my uncle Horatio's most famous and courageous captains! I'd no idea you were so young, Captain McIver–upon my word, I did not!"

"Oh, no, not her captain, ma'am, but surely one of her crew," Nick said proudly. "Her captain is my, my–"

"Your father?"

"Not my father, but my–" Nick stammered. What *was* the captain to him, after all? "He's my, why, he's my uncle! A rather distant uncle, in fact," Nick said, smiling at his small joke in spite of himself. "Who, may I ask, are you, ma'am?"

"I am Lady Anne, but you may call me Anne, if I might call you Nick?"

"Then it's you! You're his niece, aren't you! Lord Nelson's niece! You're the one we've come to rescue, you and all the kidnapped children!"

"And arrived in the nick of time, too, young Nick! I'm to be executed this very evening."

"Executed? Surely, you can't mean–"

"Listen! There is no time for talk! You must leave here at once!" she admonished. "Billy Blood could return at any second and he would surely kill Captain McIver's nephew just as he plans to kill me!"

"But why on earth should he kill someone as–as cordial as you, ma'am?"

"Because I won't betray my uncle or my country, no matter what he threatens." She looked at Nick fiercely, with fire blazing in her green eyes, and said, "Nor will I obey him or submit to his lewd advances. I care only for the poor children he holds so cruelly below! So he threatens to kill me tonight. As soon as he's sunk your poor uncle!"

"Well, then, we must run!" Nick said.

"No, *you* must run," she replied. "I cannot move from this detested place! You see, Billy Blood has chained me here for the duration of the battle. He then intends either to shoot me or hang me, and, frankly, I prefer the rope!"

Nick looked behind the post and saw thick iron manacles on her thin white wrists. He could see instantly there was no hope of removing them. Not without a key.

"Don't worry! My friend Lord Hawke and Captain McIver are leading a squadron of Royal Marines against this vessel," Nick said. "Captain McIver's somewhere up on deck now, ma'am. I'll try to find him and bring him here. He'll find a way to help you."

"That is most kind of you, Nicholas McIver," she said. "I should be eternally grateful to you, sir! But, first, you must free those poor children from their dreadful dungeon. If this ship should go down, there'd be no hope for them, trapped below."

"I will do it, ma'am," Nick said, "as soon as I can find them!"

"Run to my cabin, Nick," Anne said. "As fast as you can! My companion, Sookie, is there. She and I have been helping the children as best we can, stealing food from the galley, nursing the sick. Sookie will lead you to the children. They call her Sookie la Douce. Sookie the sweet."

"However might I find your cabin?" Nick asked hurriedly.

"It's in the fo'c'sle, Nick, just below the main deck! But you must run across the main deck to reach the bow! From the sound of it, that is where the worst fighting is. You must run as fast as you can and keep low. The fire must be murderous! Down the steps in the fo'c'sle, at the bottom, first door on the right! Knock three times. Sookie will let you in! Hurry, Nick, hurry!"

Nick ran to the door, peeked through the crack, and saw

that it was free of sentries or guards. "I'll be back, your ladyship!" he shouted.

"Godspeed!" the beautiful Lady Anne replied as he dashed out the door and down the dimly lit corridor. He had a feeling about this beautiful woman in his heart that he couldn't quite account for. He felt quite fluttery, like there was a thrumming of bees inside his head and chest. The strangest feeling! Warm and slightly dizzy in the knees. Not at all an unpleasant sensation, he noticed. Whatever could it be? But he had scant time to consider, and he dashed up the steps to the main deck.

Emerging on deck from the dark stairwell into the smoky light of day, the boy stepped into hell itself.

The air was choked with a roiling black cloud of burned gunpowder, and heavy clumps of rigging and tackle were raining down from above. The awful noise of falling rigging and roaring musketry and cannon made him clasp his hands over both ears.

He saw that the air was full of lethal flying splinters of wood caused by the terrible impact of incoming English fire. They were firing the carronades, the short-barreled "smashers" used for close-in exchanges. But the jagged pieces of timber were the cause of far more horrible injuries and deaths than the cannonballs themselves. It wasn't so much the enemy's lead, but small pieces of the boat itself, blown to bits inward, that usually killed or maimed. He shuddered at the dangerous route he now must take.

He had no choice but to proceed across the awful scene of devastation. Somehow he'd get forward to Anne's cabin and find Sookie. The children must be freed or face a horrible death by drowning.

Calculating what might be the least dangerous route, he darted across the battle-engulfed main deck, hurrying forward toward the fo'c'sle at the bow, hands clamped to his ears. The noise of battle was deafening. If only he could cover his eyes as well, he thought, and shut out the horrible sights as well as the terrible commotion.

Nick raced across the main deck for the steps down to Anne's cabin. He was forced to leap over many wounded men, lying on the deck and writhing in pain from horrible injuries, and the boy tightened his hands over his ears as he ran. It was a vain effort to shut out the dreadful screams of the wounded.

His eyes were shocked by more blood than he'd seen in his life, running pools of the stuff, sticky and darkening, and masses of heavy rigging and tackle were still crashing down on the decks every time an English cannonball found its mark. Glancing upward, Nick saw that the sails hung in tatters and that most of the French vessel's fore topmast had been shot cleanly away.

The English seemed to be giving as good as they got, he realized, and was cheered by the thought. He sprinted the last fifty feet forward, dodging the falling debris and stepping quickly over the wounded. He could see his destination through the black smoke–only about twenty feet more to go!

Just then a French crewman who'd been crouching at the base of the foremast, drunk and plainly terrified, shot out his hand and grabbed at Nick's trousers as he passed by. "Let go of me!" Nick cried, desperate to escape this awful scene, but the man only grinned, showing his ragged yellow teeth, and grabbed with one badly burned hand at Nick's leggings. With the other, the poor sailor raised a half-empty rum bottle to his parched lips. Nick saw to his horror that half the man's face was missing. Torn away by grapeshot, it was a miracle the poor fellow was still alive.

Nick ripped himself away and ran the rest of the way to the fo'c'sle. The men on deck were too preoccupied with their own blood and thunder to notice a small and terrified boy trying only to stay alive another thirty seconds.

Dashing down the darkened steps, he paused at the first cabin door.

And heard his own dog Jip barking on the other side!

"Hullo? Open up!" Nick cried, pounding three times with his fist on the door. "Sookie! I've come from Lady Anne. You've got my dog! Open the door!" The door swung open and then a great black shape was flying at him and knocking him to the deck, paws on his chest and barking and lathering his face with sloppy wet kisses.

Jipper!

"Good boy! Good boy!" Nick cried hugging his dog and staring wide-eyed at him, his eyes filling with tears. He could never remember such a feeling in his heart as he felt at that moment, staring up into the fine brown eyes of his noble companion. "Did you think I'd forgotten you, boy? Did you think Nick would ever forget about his old Jipper? Good boy, *good boy*!" And Jip barked right in his face, saying hello in his own moist way.

"So, his name's Jip, is it?" said a tall, dark-skinned woman with smiling eyes, looking down at him. "We've been callin' him Marmaduke after her ladyship's father, the vicar. He's your dog? We rescued him from the brig and been takin' care of him ever since."

"He sure is and I thank you most kindly, ma'am!" Nick said, laughing and turning his face this way and that to avoid Jip's wet tongue. "Billy Blood stole him from me and I've come a long way to get him back!"

"Seems like Billy has a habit of stealing people's dogs. And their children, too! Who are you?"

"My name's McIver, ma'am," Nick said simply. "Nick McIver."

"Ha! I'm Sookie and don't be callin' me ma'am, Nick."

"No, ma'am," Nick said, rolling Jip off of his chest and getting to his feet. "I need to find the children. The stolen children aboard the vessel–can you take me to them?"

"I surely can, boy. Must be thirty or forty of 'em down in that smelly hold. Billy's holding most of them for ransom. Kidnaps 'em from all the lords and ladies of England, he does, been doin' it for years. You listen to Sookie and stay away from that pirate, boy, or you'll end up down there in the brig with the rest of 'em!"

"Down where?" Nick asked with a growing sense of excitement. "Where's the brig?"

"You want to go there now? 'Cause if'n you do, you come to the right place."

"Tell me, Sookie," Nick said, "are there perhaps two children down in that brig with the surname Hawke? Annabel and Alexander Hawke?"

"Annabel and Alexander!" exclaimed the dark-skinned lady. "Why I nursed those two babies like they were my own! Sure, they're down there all right, and crying every night for their poor father. I did what I could for them, but they were so afraid they'd never lay eyes on their father again because they'd been away from him so long. You know him, their father?"

"I do, Sookie! You must take me to the children at once, please!" Nick cried, his heart leaping with joy for Lord Hawke. Sookie stepped outside the cabin door and made a beckoning motion with her arm, heavily laden with golden bracelets.

"This way to the kingdom of lost children, Nick McIver!" she shouted, and raced off down the narrow corridor.

Nick and Jip followed Sookie deeper and deeper down into the damp and foul-smelling bowels of the ship, where the sound of the battle raging above was barely heard and lanterns were few and far between. Nick stumbled in the dark more than once over objects unseen, lying in his path.

Still, they passed no one, only a few scurrying rats and a few poor souls who'd been grievously wounded and were wandering about below, dazedly in search of someone to attend to them. No one seemed the least interested in a woman and a small boy with a big black dog. Deeper and deeper they descended, and the smell of the bilge below was as bad as that of blood above.

They came at length to a long dark passageway that ended with a heavy oak door. Two black lanterns hung on either side, sputtering candles glowing dimly inside. Atop each lantern stood the huge black metal figure of a crow or some kind of bird, it's wings spread as if it were about to take flight. Curious, Nick stood on tiptoe to examine the bird figure atop the nearest lantern. It wasn't a crow, he saw, it was a parrot. And it wasn't black, either. It was dark shiny red. It was a replica of Bones, Blood's parrot, the eyes and ears of his master, Nick thought, and a fitting pair of sentries for this terrible place.

"This is it, child!" Sookie whispered to Nick. "Captain Blood's dark kingdom of little lost babies! And, if you ever see a bird like that parrot on this boat, cover your eyes! Billy's bird, that is, and it can pluck your eyeballs clean from the sockets before you can blink!"

Sookie pulled Nick down into the shadows, to a crouching position away from the door. "Sssshh!" she said, a pretty brown finger to her lips in warning. "You wait here for my signal!"

Sookie rapped on the thick wooden door once, then twice, then once again, and it creaked open to the coded signal. A waft of damp, fetid air rushed out. Behind the door, Nick caught a glimpse of a dark passage between rows of iron bars, a gloomy space lit by guttering candles hung every few feet or so. This was a place that had never known the briefest ray of sunlight.

A large, sullen-looking sailor stuck his ugly head out and Nick ducked down out of the pool of lamplight. He clamped his fingers around Jip's muzzle to keep him silent because an enormous rat had just scurried out the opened door and right beneath the big dog's nose.

"Philippe!" Sookie said to the guard. *"Le capitaine est mort! On vas fêter, maintenant!"*

"Le capitaine Blood, est-il mort?" Philippe cried, and he threw back his grizzled head and laughed, then wrapped his beefy arms around Sookie, lifting her into the air with joy. He put her down and raced past Nick, eager to join the celebration on deck. The captain, Nick thought, was obviously not a very popular figure aboard this vessel.

"Billy's dead?" Nick whispered, incredulously, rushing to Sookie's side.

"Course he ain't," Sookie whispered to Nick. "I just told

him everybody on deck was celebrating the death of Billy Blood. A trick! See him run? Everybody will dance at that vile demon's wake, child, including Miss Sookie herself, soon as he really is dead! Come along, now, the children are right inside here, Nick!"

"Bonjour, mes enfants!" Sookie cried, entering the gloomy brig. "How is everyone this fine day?"

"*Bonjour, Sookie! La Douce! Bonjour!* Rain or shine? Rain or shine?"

"Shine today, children, lots of shine up there today!"

"Shine! Shine! Shine! Shine!" the children behind bars cried in sad unison.

The children all began chanting happily in singsong, beating their little tin cups on the iron bars. It was clear to Nick that Sookie was a much-loved fixture of the children's brig, their only connection with the world of sunshine they'd left behind. On both sides of the shadowy candlelit passage, they stuck their tiny faces through the bars and smiled at her as they went by.

Sookie was marching Nick and Jip straight to the end, past the rows of iron cages with the pale outstretched arms. She stopped only at the very last one on the port side. There was a small candle in a holder on the wall of the cell and it cast its flickering light on two small bodies, huddled together on the straw-covered floor.

"May I present Monsieur and Mademoiselle Hawke!" Sookie announced, and Nick was heartbroken to see the two beautiful children dressed in tattered rags and sleeping on a pile of matted straw. He put his face between two bars and peered into the shadowy light of the tiny cell.

Alexander and Annabel. Looking just like the photograph he'd seen of them in Lord Hawke's study. Sookie had been telling the truth. Still, something was odd about the way the children looked, and Nick couldn't quite put his finger on it. They looked exactly as they had in the photograph and yet–yes, that was it! Five years had elapsed and the children had not aged at all! Strange, but wasn't everything?

Though they had been held in captivity for nearly five years, they both appeared to be about five years old, the age Hobbes had said they were when they'd been kidnapped! They'd been trapped, not only aboard Billy's red prison ship, but also in time itself! In some way, Nick realized, the clock stopped when you took a trip with the time machine. He could hardly wait to tell Hobbes about it when they got home.

"May I go inside?" Nick whispered to Sookie.

"Don't see why not," Sookie said. "I stole the master key from Philippe after he went to sleep last night!" She pulled a large key from somewhere deep in the folds of her apron and inserted it into the rusty iron lock. The creaky door swung open.

Nick dropped to his knees in the musty straw beside the sleeping children. They were so peacefully unaware of the madness raging on deck above them he almost hated to wake them, but he knew he must. He reached out, brushing the straw away from their foreheads, damp with perspiration in the foul closeness of the brig.

"Wake up, Alexander," Nick said quietly. "Wake up, Annabel!"

Their eyes opened slowly and they looked up at him, yawning and rubbing their fists in their sleepy eyes.

"Are you quite awake now, children? Then listen carefully,

will you? I'm a friend of your father's," Nick said, gently. "We've come to take you home to Greybeard Island."

"Home?" Annabel said. Their eyes widened and glistened in the flickering candlelight. "To our home? Hawke Castle?" They looked at each other in openmouthed wonder and it was plain they could hardly believe it.

"Our father?" Alexander said, in a small, disbelieving voice. "You know our father?"

"Very well, and he misses you both so terribly," Nick said, picking bits of straw from their hair and smiling. "If I tell you something, will you promise to do exactly as I say?" They nodded yes, their big round eyes gleaming in the candlelight.

"Listen carefully, now. Your father is aboard this very ship," Nick said, and both children's hands flew to their mouths and they regarded him in wide-eyed wonder.

"He's here? Our papa?" they cried in unison, and their eyes filled with tears of hope and longing.

"Yes, he's come to rescue you from this terrible place," Nick said. "But you and all the other children must remain here in the brig until he has dealt with Billy Blood. It's very dangerous up on deck now where your father is. I must hurry and see if I can help him–"

"Oh! We must see our daddy, Sookie! We must!" Annabel cried, clinging to Sookie's long skirts. "Why, Alexander and I–"

"Please listen, Annabel!" Nick said. "You'll see him soon! But only when it's safe. Sookie, will you help me? I want you to unlock all the cells and gather all the children in the passageway. But you mustn't let a single one leave the brig until you hear from me! As soon as Billy has surrendered *Mystère* to Lord Hawke, you shall have my signal!"

"What will the signal be, child?" Sookie asked. Nick frowned. He hadn't thought that far ahead.

"I'll send Jip!" Nick turned to Jip, pointed at Sookie, and asked the dog, "Where's Sookie, boy, where's Sookie?" Jip jumped up and licked the brown woman's face and Nick knew the dog would be able to find her anywhere.

"You be careful now, Nicholas, and don't you let ol' Billy or his devilish parrot get hold of you," Sookie said, hugging Nick. "These poor babies been sufferin' down here a long time, a very long time! I've waited years for the day they's set free!"

"Today's that day, Sookie, you have my word on it!" Nick cried, and calling Jip after him, he ran out of the cell and disappeared down the gloomy corridor.

"We'll keep belowdecks all the way aft, boy," he said to Jip. "It's a little too hot for the likes of us up on deck right now!"

CHAPTER XXXV

Merlin Victorious

· 4 October 1805 ·

H.M.S. *MYSTÈRE,* AT SEA

But all was strangely quiet on deck when Nick and Jip emerged from the aft companionway, Nick blinking his eyes in the bright sunlight. He looked around the big French ship's aftmost deck and saw that the deck was almost deserted, save the dead and wounded. The cannons on both vessels had ceased their roar and forward he could see a press of sailors from the two warships gathered on the quarterdeck below, with an occasional cheer in French or English rising from their midst.

He heard, too, the vicious sound of two cutlasses ringing against each other with a determined fury. A brutal swordfight, from the sound of it. He looked aloft and saw the battle-torn French flag still fluttering at the top of the mizzen. So Billy had not surrendered!

In the typical manner of most French first-raters, there was a small pilothouse here on the poop deck, and it gave Nick an inspiration. From its roof, Nick realized, he might be able to look down on the entire quarterdeck unobserved. He quickly rolled a nearby barrel up against the back of the small house, clambered atop it, and then pulled himself up onto the roof, Jip right behind him. He inched forward on his elbows until he could lift his head just enough to peek down at the frenzied scene on the quarterdeck below. The crews of both vessels were pressing aft from all over the ship, trying for a glimpse of the action taking place at the helm. Nick, lying atop the pilothouse roof, was perfectly positioned to observe the battle taking place not ten feet below him.

The great sea battle had come down to a two-man war. Captain William Blood and Lord Richard Hawke were locked in a death struggle.

Blood was a spectacle, wearing what must once have been magnificent finery, white silk breeches and a great flaring white satin captain's coat, but now all this flummery was torn and soiled with black powder and red blood. Hawke had a terrible gash down his right cheek and his shirtfront was soaked with his own blood. Still, he had his cigar clenched in his teeth and he held his left hand rigidly behind his back, fighting Blood in a classic dueling fashion, but with more fury in his face than Nick would have thought possible.

He parried Blood's wicked blows each and all and thrust his cutlass again and again at the darting pirate. Despite Hawke's genius-like finesse with a sword, it was immediately clear that this was the fight of his life, as Blood brutally laid on three resounding blows in quick succession.

"It's finished, Hawke, surrender!" Billy cried, advancing. "There's not a swordsman alive who can best Billy Blood! I'll cut yer bleedin' heart out and eat it for me supper!"

"I think you shall go hungry, then, sir!" Hawke cried,

slashing forward. "No, no! It's the brave kidnapper of women and small children who's finished, Blood!" Hawke said, deflecting a tremendous cut which would have surely split him to the chine had he not intercepted it with his sword in time.

"Look! Even your own crew has little stomach left for you, Billy Blood! See how they stand idle, waiting to see their captain's blood run in the scuppers!"

Hawke, in a brilliant dancing parry and lunge, laid on a powerful blow and a great clang of iron rang out across the deck. It was true. The men had all fallen silent, weapons at their feet, watching the battle with rapt attention. McIver, having dispatched the last pockets of resistance on deck, had now ordered a few Royal Marines to keep their muskets leveled at the few Frenchmen who'd not yet thrown down their arms. This, in case they had any rash notion of coming to Billy's aid.

"Lying dog!" Billy screamed, his face flushing bright red with furious blood. He charged at Hawke like a wounded rhino, bellowing at the top of his lungs. Hawke raised his cutlass to defend the ferocious blow, but Billy stopped short at the last instant and spun on his heel, whirling his body completely around and striking with huge force at Hawke's upraised cutlass. The sword was brutally ripped from Hawke's hand and went clattering across the deck.

A cold hand gripped Nick's heart as he saw Hawke retreating, completely defenseless against the murderous Billy, and stumbling backward, tripping over the wounded men lying about the deck, arms and legs akimbo.

A Marine leveled his musket at Billy, but Captain McIver pushed the barrel aside, shaking his head. It was Lord Hawke's fight, win or lose. Honor dictated that he finish it, an affair of honor, after all.

"Captain Bonnard!" Billy said, pausing to shout at his captain of French Marines. "Why have your men ceased fighting? To watch this pitiful coward die? I order you to attack! Kill these English dogs, starting with this pathetic mongrel!" He started for the weaponless Hawke. But then Bonnard suddenly blocked his path to the defenseless Englishman.

"I will take no more orders from you, Captain Blood," Bonnard said, stepping forward and drawing his own blade, and a cheer went up from his tattered crew. "We've hardly a soul left with a will to fight, a fire rages near our powder magazine, and we are grievously holed below the waterline. Any fit captain at all could have seen this mighty ship to victory today, sir, but you have precious little fitness in that regard. We had no chance. We have suffered you long and long enough, sir! Enough! You are unfit to command this vessel, and I intend to negotiate her surrender on behalf of my crew. Throw down your sword, Blood, you are under the arrest of the Imperial French Navy! Bosun, strike our colors, we are surrendering the *Mystère* to–"

"Mutiny, is it then?" Billy threw back his head and laughed. "I'll slit all your mutinous French throats afore I'm done, but I'll begin with this English swine!" He swung his hateful gaze and his sword on Hawke, then lunged forward, his blade aimed at Hawke's heart.

"Lord Hawke! Up here!" Nick shouted, and everyone turned to see a small boy standing atop the pilothouse with a large black dog. He pulled the cutlass Stiles had given him from his waistband and threw it to the empty-handed Hawke. Hawke laughed as he reached up to catch it, but Nick's toss

"It's finished, Hawke, surrender!"

was short and the sword clattered to the deck at Hawke's feet. Nick saw Hawke bend to retrieve it and Billy use the moment's distraction to circle in toward Hawke, his sword poised for a murderous blow. Hawke was coming up with Nick's sword as Blood's blade was coming down, and the flat of Billy's sword caught Lord Hawke hard across the shoulder blades, driving him down to the deck. The sword flew from Lord Hawke's hand, landing a good ten feet away. Nick drew a sharp breath.

Now!

It was only about ten feet from the roof down to the quarterdeck and he timed his jump perfectly. Nick landed squarely on the shoulders of Captain Blood, straddling his head as he'd done with Lieutenant Stiles. Nick clamped both hands over the enraged pirate's eyes and hung on for dear life. Blinded and snorting, Blood whirled about, staggering over the bodies of the dead and wounded on the deck. He clawed and shook the tenacious boy who was clinging to him, tormenting him, but Nick held on.

He saw Jip still up on the roof, barking loudly at the scene below. "Find Sookie, boy!" he cried. "Find Sookie!" and then he felt himself flying through the air and crashing to the deck as Billy finally ripped him from his shoulders and flung him like a rag doll to the blood-washed decks.

"Found your mange-ridden dog, have you boy?" Billy sneered, striding over and planting one of his gleaming Hessian boots squarely in the middle of the boy's chest. "Then you must give me Leonardo's little gold ball, mustn't you? That was our bargain, wee swabbie!" Blood poked the tip of his razor-sharp blade at him, prodding Nick's jacket. "It's on your person, ain't it, boy? That's what me bird Bones tells me–"

He slashed Nick's thin blue coat right through the pocket and the golden ball spilled out upon the deck, rolling away as Nick tried desperately to grab for it, and in a flash Blood's hand darted out like an inhuman claw and clutched it. Billy uttered a howl of delight, raising the brilliant object up into the sun.

"At last I've the both of them! The twin orbs of eternal power," Billy shouted gleefully, staring at his gleaming prizes. "Which of the Seven Seas does William Blood not now singly command? Come, you mutineers, come all and witness a force of nature no man can conquer! We'll yet throw these pathetic Englishmen into the sea! We shall rule the world!"

"No!" Nick cried. "The machine is mine!" Nick was clawing at Blood's leg, trying to rise from the deck, but Billy had pinned him with his boot, painfully pressed now in the middle of Nick's stomach. Nick could only twist frantically like a spider impaled.

Nick reached inside his jacket for the bone-handled dagger Billy had stuck in his front door. *Perhaps I can return it to him in person,* Nick remembered thinking. He plunged the dagger deep into the fleshy part of Billy's calf. Roaring in pain, Billy didn't see Hawke coming up behind him.

"He said the orb belongs to him, Blood," Lord Hawke said, the point of his cutlass in Billy's back. "Return it to him now."

"Your tongue has wagged its last, Hawke," the pirate said and whirled to face Lord Hawke. Billy lunged first, his blade going for Hawke's exposed gut, but this time it was Hawke who spun on his heel in lightning fashion, whirling his body with his flashing cutlass outstretched, and then an awful sound Nick would never forget, the awful sound of steel on flesh and bone, of steel *through* flesh and bone.

There was an enormous howl of pain and Billy held up a bloody stump of an arm.

On the deck, Blood's still-twitching hand, bloody fingers clenched around the shining golden ball. Hawke knelt and pried the Tempus Machina free. Then he handed it back to Nick.

There came a look then in William Blood's eyes when the smoldering fires of hell, always within, seemed to lick out of his very eyeballs, to singe the air, even the beard of Lord Hawke. Billy swore that foul oath at Lord Hawke then, the one that would be whispered among sailing men for years, and dashed up the steps to the afterdeck. He was running for his life from the angry press of sailors, English and French mutineers both, who now charged after him. Nick saw Billy bolt into the stairwell aft of the pilothouse. It was the same stairwell Nick himself had used upon leaving Nelson's niece.

"Lady Anne!" Nick cried out to Captain McIver above the excited tumult. "She's a prisoner in Billy's cabin, sir! He swore he'd kill her for sure, Captain!" Nick shuddered at the thought of the beautiful woman, helpless before Billy's fury, and saw McIver's own face go white with rage. How could he face Nelson if Anne were killed?

"Show me the way, lad, show me the way!" the captain shouted. He followed the boy racing aft, taking the steps up to the poop deck three at a time.

There was a gaggle of bloodthirsty sailors, both French and English, pounding at Billy's heavy cabin door, screaming for his head. But above those screams could be heard the terrified cry of a woman pleading for her life. They heard, too, the enraged snarls and howls of something more animal than human: Billy. Nick's breath caught in his throat. The door was too thick. Were he and the captain too late?

"Attention!" Captain McIver said in his booming voice, and the rowdy sailors all immediately came to order. "I want this door destroyed in five seconds or less. Make that 'less.' "

Four French sailors formed up and, in one furious blow, visited their years of suffering under Captain Blood upon his thick oak door. It splintered inward on their first smashing attack and the sailors tumbled into the great cabin with Nick and McIver right on their heels.

"Search this cabin!" McIver ordered the men, his own eyes scanning desperately for Nelson's niece and Billy Blood. But Nick had seen at the stern windows in that last moment a glimmering golden light, as of a thousand shimmering fireflies, and knew their search would be fruitless. He saw Lady Anne collapsed on the banquette, her head bowed and sobbing, her dress ripped and torn, a bloody stain at her white shoulder.

"She's been hurt!" the captain shouted and rushed to her side.

The captain sat beside her, and began applying a homely bandage he'd made from his torn shirt to Lady Anne's shoulder. "I don't think it's at all serious, Lady Anne," he said soothingly, "but this should hold you until I can get you to the *Merlin*'s surgeon. Are you all right, my dear girl?"

"I–I think so, Captain. Thank you. And I'm eternally grateful to this handsome young gentleman, too," she said favoring Nick with a lovely smile. "Did the pirate escape?"

"He's gone, Captain!" a crewman cried, bursting into the

cabin. The French sailors had been searching the lower decks in vain for Billy Blood, against all hope. "He's escaped!"

As Nick knew, Billy Blood, of course, had not fled to another deck, but to another place or time. And escaped the punishment Nick knew he so richly deserved.

"Billy's got away, Captain," Nick said, eyes downcast.

"Ease yerself, son," McIver said softly. "What escape can there be for the creature? Wherever can he run? France? He's lost their most powerful warship for them! The little Corsican emperor will have his head in a basket at the guillotine for that one, sure! England? There's a king's ransom on his vile head there, too! The Seven Seas? No, he's not escaped, lad, he's doomed to wander the ages, missing his good right hand, reviled by all who encounter him. Besides, you've still got your golden orb, Nick. Wherever Bill roams, so, too, can you and Lord Hawke. He can't escape your justice, lad, and that's a good thing."

Billy's gone–squawk–he'll be back–squawk–Billy's gone–squawk–back back back.

Bones. The parrot fluttered his bright red feathers and then the terrible bird was gone in search of his master, flown out the open window.

On the *Mystère*'s quarterdeck, the French Captain of Marines, Bonnard, went down on one knee and presented the sword of surrender to Lord Richard Hawke. Hawke accepted, in lieu of the captain, smiling at the men assembled around the helm, removing his now well-chomped cigar from his lips. "Let him run, the devil. There's no hiding for him on this ship. Or, anywhere on this earth!"

He turned to the French captain. "Captain Bonnard, on behalf of *Merlin*, Captain Nicholas McIver commanding, and His Majesty's Royal Navy, I accept your surrender. I will present your colors and sword to my captain forthwith." Hawke bowed deeply and Bonnard did the same. "You are a gentleman, sir," Hawke added, as Bonnard handed him the tattered French ensign. "It has been my honor to do battle with you."

The French struck their colors and now every English heart lifted, as the flag of England fluttered against the blue sky at *Mystère*'s topmast.

Hawke stepped up onto the binnacle and raised the surrendered flag of France into the air and an explosion of cheering voices from the *Merlin* and the decks of the *Mystère* rose up to meet him. It was a sound he'd never dared dream of hearing, but one that would stay with him always. His own men were cheering the English victory, the Frenchmen celebrating their liberation from the evil tyranny of Captain Blood. And they both appeared to be waiting for some kind of speech from Hawke. Everyone on deck had suddenly gone stone silent.

"My brave shipmates and comrades, I hardly know how to thank you for–"

"Father! Father!" A tiny voice pierced the silence in a way that made Hawke's heart leap into his throat so fast he could not get another word out.

"Oh, Father, yes, it's really you!"

And then Hawke saw the sea of sailors part and two small ragged children race across the deck toward him, led by a big black dog. Suddenly, tears of the purest joy were coursing down his cheeks and he leapt down from the binnacle and ran to them, falling to his knees as they approached him, hardly able to believe his eyes. Annabel and Alexander! Yes, it was true! And suddenly his two wee children were once more in their father's long-lost arms, all three of them laughing and crying at the same time, hugging each other as if they might never let go.

"Oh, Daddy, is it really you?" Annabel said, hugging him around the neck as tightly as ever she could. "We didn't think we'd ever see you again!"

"Yes, Father," Alexander exclaimed, as Lord Hawke kissed both of his wet little cheeks and brushed the hair back from his forehead. "However did you find us? We missed you so terribly, terribly much! And we were so afraid you wouldn't know where to look for us!"

"I had a great deal of help, son. More than I can ever repay," Hawke said, pulling the two children to his chest as tightly as he could, thinking then of Nick, and Gunner, and of course his dear Hobbes and all they'd done to make this most wondrously joyful reunion possible. Looking up, he saw a radiant Caribbean woman with massive golden rings in her ears standing over them, the brilliant smile on her face shining down on the happy little family.

"So, you're the papa, is that so?" she asked. "Well, well, I been their mama for the longest time and I know better than anybody how happy they are to see you. Just as handsome as they said you might be, too!" Sookie threw back her head and laughed. "My, my! What a joyful day!"

"You took care of my children all this time?" Hawke asked, smiling at Sookie.

"Oh, yes, Daddy, she truly did!" Annabel exclaimed.

"Them and a lot more where these two come from," Sookie said, laughing. "Have you put paid to that loathsome pirate yet?" Hawke nodded that he had. "Well, now old Billy's gone, just you watch this! You ain't never heard a ship explode like this, Lord Hawke. No matter how many sea battles you've been in!"

Sookie inserted two fingers into her mouth and let out a piercing whistle. Hawke heard loud barking and saw the big black dog bounding back across the deck and disappearing down the dark stairs of the midships companionway. Instantly, there was a shrill explosion, just as Sookie had promised. Not of cannon or gunfire, but of children's laughter! All about the decks, hatches popped open, doors were flung open, and small shaggy heads emerged, blinked in the brilliant sun, and shouted for pure joy.

From every corner of the vessel they poured, children of all ages, filthy and dressed mostly in rags, but all of them now laughing and singing and leaping about from the sheer wonder of being in the open air again, of being in the warm sunshine once more, of being free. There were animals, too, released from captivity. Dogs and cats, goats and pigs, and birds of every description. Hawke was amazed to see a number of brilliantly colored tropical birds fly up out of the hatches and perch up in the rigging! He even saw two Shetland ponies with two near-naked boys astride them, go trotting across the deck! And still the children poured from the bowels of the ship, bursting forth from every hatchway like laughter itself.

Soon enough, hornpipes and harmonicas, fiddles and fifes appeared, and the sound of children singing cheerful rhymes and sea shanties could soon be heard from stem to stern, as on the *Mystère*'s crowded decks, and even spilling over to the *Merlin,* a great many French swabs and English jack-tars and happy children whirled each other about under the noonday sun in an endless swirling jig.

Lord Hawke, standing on the poop deck beneath the fluttering towers of war-torn canvas, with one of his laughing children in each of his arms, looked down upon this joyful scene and turned to Sookie at his side.

"Ever see such a sight in all your life, Sookie?" he asked her, letting his eyes gaze over the bobbing and dancing heads on the decks below, to the forward end of the great vessel and then up into the rigging where now scores of brilliantly colored birds of yellow and blue and green, every exotic shape and hue, were singing their songs of the deep Amazonian rain forest to the children dancing gaily below.

"No, for all love, I surely ain't, sir," Sookie replied, shaking her head in wonder. "Children are truly the light of the world, your lordship."

Her laughter floated lightly out over the children's happy faces like the sweetest music of all time.

CHAPTER XXXVI

A Glorious Farewell

· 4 October 1805 ·

H.M.S. *MERLIN,* AT SEA

Just then there was a tapping at Captain McIver's cabin door, and Hawke pulled it open with a gallant flourish. Hawke knew who it must be. He saw Nick and the captain standing outside the door, huge grins on their faces. The captain removed his black officer's hat and bowed deeply from the waist. He'd changed into his best uniform, blue coat over snow-white breeches, and someone had given young Nick a cockaded black hat as well. Nick removed it, smiling widely, and imitated the captain's dramatic bow.

"Back already, are you, then?" Hawke asked, his eyes alight with happiness. He stepped aside so they might enter. "And a good thing, too! These two children here are chafing to go home." Since the great victory, Hawke, Gunner, and the children had been in the captain's great cabin aboard the *Merlin,* busily preparing for the voyage home.

"And me as well," Gunner said. "Homeward bound, at last! Was yer final mission a success, lad?"

"Aye, Gunner! What a treasure we have here!" Nick said,

holding up his golden ball. “We used the machine to return every single one of the those poor children to their parents and relations! Feel the machine, Gunner, it’s still warm from so much use!” He laughed and threw the golden ball across to Gunner who caught it easily and rolled it between his hands in delight. “Has there been a happier mission than ours, Captain?” Nick asked his traveling companion.

“Aye, it was joyous! Never in life have you seen such glee as young Nick and I were greeted with! Them poor parents, scattered all over God’s creation! Why, they’d given up hope, they had. Believed they’d never set eyes on those little ones again. And suddenly, here’s an old sea captain and a wisp of a boy as comes walkin’ up the lane with their wee children in tow, and rappin’ upon their very doors! Aye, most couldn’t speak for the tears of joy they shed, am I honest, Nick?”

“Aye, Cap’n, it was the most fitting end to the most perfect day, sir,” Nick said softly, remembering. “Especially climbing up the pyramid, sir.”

“Pyramid! What’s the boy talking about, Captain?” Hawke asked.

“Ah, yes,” McIver said, his face wrinkling in a merry grin. “Our last little one. Turned out to be a pharaoh’s boy! Bloke by the name of Ramses, his father was, had this amazin’ pyramid right by the River Nile. I don’t speak much Egyptian, but you’ve never seen a happier pharaoh in all your days!”

Then Hawke and Gunner erupted into delighted laughter, clapping Nick and the captain on their backs and cheering, a warm glow of happiness across all their faces. The machine was finally being used for good, rather than evil, in this world.

"Now, come, I've but a moment to bid you farewell, my dear friends," Captain McIver said. "We must fairly fly to England if we're to catch Lord Nelson before he sails!"

He stood back looking down at them, hands on his hips, favoring the three time travelers with the warmest of smiles.

"I've neither sand enough left in me glass, nor poetry enough in me heart to tell you what is welling in me full breast," the captain said. "But I'll warrant it's the fortune of my life to have stood shoulder to shoulder with you three these recent hours. Each of you is as brave and gallant a man as I've encountered on any sea, and I include you when I say that, Nicholas McIver, for indeed you've distinguished yourself as the match of any man who fought this glorious day!"

The captain opened his arms then, and Nick ran into them, pressed his happy head against his dear ancestor's broad chest, his own arms around the captain's shoulders, holding on to him as if he would never let go. "It's been my honor, sir," Nick said, stifling a sob.

"Come, come!" the captain said, pounding Nick heartily on the back and tousling his hair with enormous affection before pulling away for the door. "No parting tears! This brave band will be joined again, afore two shakes of a nanny goat's tail! Let us get you lowered away, so that the barky may race for England's shore and Nelson's ear!

"Come, children, we're going home!" Hawke said, and a freshly scrubbed Annabel and Alexander leapt from their seats beneath the stern window and ran to their father.

Captain McIver paused at the door and turned to the travelers with a mischievous little grin on his ruddy face. "Now, I hope you'll forgive us. Mr. Stiles and meself couldn't resist a little send-off as befits your noble efforts on behalf of the old *Merlin*! I'll see you on deck when yer done with yer preparations!" And so the captain took his leave.

"Have you entered our destination yet, Gunner?" Lord Hawke asked.

"Where do you want to arrive, your lordship? The library or the kitchen?" Gunner said seriously, looking at the chart and punching numbers into the glittering Locus half of the jeweled instrument. He was seated at the captain's small desk, deep in concentration, beneath the sun-filled open stern windows. The sea air, at last clear of gunsmoke, had that fine bite of salt a man loved to fill his lungs with.

"You've gotten so handy with that infernal thing, have you, Gunner?" Hawke laughed, stowing the fancy French sword of surrender into his sea bag. McIver had insisted he take it, and Hawke had been deeply touched.

It was Gunner who'd first raised the problem of how they might suddenly disappear from the vessel without causing Captain McIver all sorts of inconvenient questions. And he had been quick with a solution. "Whyn't we get them to lower us away in that little sailin' skiff, say we've unfinished business back on the island and don't want to be no inconvenience, and–"

"And, soon as we're over the horizon, use the machine to return to Hawke Lagoon in nineteen thirty-nine!" Hawke had exclaimed. "It's brilliant, Gunner! That way, no questions, and the captain's sure to make it to London in time for his meeting with Lord Nelson!" Hawke was laughing to himself. They were actually getting quite good at this rummy business of time travel!

"I've entered the Locus and Tempus, your lordship," Gunner said. "We can all go home now!"

So the three travelers, their kits slung over their shoulders and the children in the arms of Lord Hawke, with Jip barking loudly and bringing up the rear, marched up the broad staircase to the *Merlin*'s quarterdeck and stepped out into the brilliant sunshine once more. Nick blinked his eyes twice, stunned by the pageant he saw arrayed before them.

Every man of the *Merlin,* it seemed, was turned out on deck. And all three hundred or more crewmen were dressed in their best Sunday whites, and the officers in their fine blue coats sparkling with decorations and all in a line; and, on the main deck, a squadron of crimson-jacketed Marines in tight formation with silver muskets raised in the air. And, beside them, a corps of drummers dressed with magnificent battle drums, who now launched into a stately military tattoo that rolled across the decks.

"What's this?" Nick whispered to Gunner, for he could hardly believe this was all somehow related to their departure.

"I ain't at all sure, Master Nick," Gunner bent to whisper back, "but it's got all the earmarks of a twenty-one-gun salute!"

Nick saw the captain and Lieutenant Stiles now standing in front of the other senior officers formed up along the quarterdeck rail. All Nick could see under the row of black silk officers' hats was a row of pearly smiles. The ship was under way again, and had a fine heel to her. Looking aloft, Nick saw clouds of freshly repaired white canvas towering above, pulling hard for England. She was a fine, weatherly ship and, if this breeze held, she'd have no trouble completing her do-or-die mission. Astern, about a quarter of a mile in the

Merlin's wake, he saw the giant red *Mystère,* under a mountain of sail, now a prize sailing under English colors, and throwing a fine white spray off her bows.

On a signal from the lieutenant, a four-man squad of red-coated Marines formed up around the travelers, and Nick understood that they were going to escort them through the mass of humanity to the starboard rail amidships. There, he could see the captain's gig already slung from davits.

"Squad, ho!" bellowed the Captain of Marines standing next to Stiles, and the squad formed up around them, one in front, one in back, one on each side. At a barked signal, they began moving at a quick clip past the officers toward the steps leading down to the main deck. Nick found that he had to step lively in order to remain in proper formation and saw Mr. Stiles grinning broadly at his feeble efforts at naval decorum. Both Stiles and the captain were staring straight ahead as he approached, and Nick was struck to the marrow to see first Stiles, then McIver's hand snap smartly to their brows.

Surely, they weren't saluting *him*?

Taking no chances, Nick raised his own right hand in salute as he passed his two new friends, and saw the officers all fall in behind them as the group made its way through the sea of sailors to the starboard rail. He heard hearty murmurs of congratulations as the crews parted to let them through, and saw broad smiles on every face. There, hung between two davits, was the captain's beautiful little gig, and they'd dressed her proper, too, with a big Union Jack hung aft, and colored signal flags up her forestay to the masthead and then down to the stern, fluttering gaily in the stiff southerly breeze.

At the rail, Hawke's gallant little squad did an about-face

and they turned to view the Marines formed up mid-deck, muskets at the ready. Lord Hawke lifted the two children up into the small sailboat, into the hands of a waiting crewman who'd help them lower and get under way. Jip leapt up into the boat to be with his new friends, little Alexander and Annabel. Then the three travelers stood ramrod straight at the rail as the captain and his first officer approached them. Nick saw that the captain was carrying something, a small triangular cloth package with a thick vellum envelope lying on top.

With a whispered thank-you, Captain McIver gave the envelope to Lord Hawke and then, looking straight at Nick, with a crinkly smile playing about the corners of his merry blue eyes, bent forward and placed the little cloth bundle into Nick's hands. He whispered something then, just loud enough for Nick's ears only.

"Magnificently done, Mr. McIver!" said the captain, and, turning to the Captain of Marines, gave the order to fire.

At the sound of the first gun's powerful explosion, a huge roar went up from the assembled crew, an enormous, swelling cheer that rose up to fill the air, a rising cheer that was soon joined by hundreds of sailors' hats and caps flung high up into the rigging, only to float and fall and be flung up again and again as the drums rolled and the big guns fired one after another until all twenty-one had fired. The flag-bedecked little skiff with its passengers was lowered away and was soon some half mile away on the rolling blue sea, hull down and hard-bound for the southern coast of Greybeard Island.

Only then did Nick look down at the small, folded bundle that lay in his lap. It was a torn and shredded old gift he'd got, much blackened with gunpowder. A thoroughly ragged old thing, he noticed unfolding it, a gift that had seen far, far better days. But, he knew at that moment, it was the thing he'd forever cherish above all else in his possession.

The battle-torn flag of France, so recently hauled down in surrender, and now a thing of tattered glory.

CHAPTER XXXVII

Landing at Hawke Field

· 8 June 1939 ·

AT HAWKE CASTLE

It was cold, windy, and rainy up on the tiny runway. An unseasonable chill tore at the thin summer clothing of the small gathering waiting there for an aeroplane to descend out of the fog and clouds in that waning hour of sunlight before darkness fell.

Lord Hawke's runway, nothing more than a thin ribbon of grass far above the lagoon, stretched out along a high, rocky point adjacent to the castle itself. Hawke Field, as Hobbes jokingly referred to it, was unlighted and unsuitable for night landings, so Hobbes had placed four powerful searchlights at either end of the grass runway. A low, rolling fog had flooded in off the Channel. The searchlights, aimed straight up, formed great columns of light in the foggy evening sky.

Landing at Hawke Field, as Hobbes never tired of telling his flying Navy friends, was just like landing on an aircraft carrier, only half as long and twice as narrow. And now, with the fog, and a sticky crosswind whipping across the field, Hobbes saw it would be even more difficult than usual. He didn't envy the Royal Air Force pilot who'd probably be flying the group from War Command over from the mainland.

Hobbes and Katie were there waiting, of course, feeling the bite of the wind's chill, but much restored by an afternoon in front of the blazing fire, sipping Hobbes's lemony mandarin tea and eating scores of homemade crumpets with raspberry jam. Hobbes had first placed a call to Kate's mother to say all was well and ask her to join them for dinner at Hawke Castle.

Hobbes had then rung the naval attaché in London. The excitement crackling over the wire from the Whitehall war offices about the captured U-boat was near delirious, and the attaché had promised to dispatch an inspection team immediately to Greybeard Island. Since Hobbes knew that "immediately" by sea meant twelve hours minimum, he reminded the attaché that Hawke Castle possessed the only private runway among the islands, albeit a grass one, little more than a skinny cow pasture, but adequate enough for light military aircraft.

And that to arrive sooner, rather than later, Hobbes had added, was probably a good idea when you had a fully armed Nazi U-boat penned up in your goldfish pond. And an enraged German captain who by now must surely be going quite mad, that is, if he hadn't been quite bonkers already!

It had been a quiet afternoon, sitting cozily by the fire as the rain whipped round the castle, and Hobbes and Kate had chatted happily, discussing their submarine adventure in minute detail. Laughing aloud, they imagined the look on Wolfie's face when the nose of his mighty submarine bumped up against the massive steel curtain of the underwater Seagate. And then realizing that he couldn't even blast his way out, that his deadly torpedoes were useless in such a small, confined body of water! It wouldn't take long for the captain to conclude that the torpedo's concussion alone would kill everyone aboard the sub.

"A pig in a pokey?" Kate asked, stoking Horatio's silky fur.

"Something like that, my dear, a poke, I believe is the term."

"Will Nicky *ever* come back, Hobbes? Do you think his adventure was as grand as ours? What do you think he's doing right now?" Kate said, her mouth forming a perfect little "o" as she yawned and slowly fell over on the massive settee, her red curls spilling onto the yellow silk cushion of the spacious sofa. Her eyelids fluttered and closed, and she mumbled sleepily.

"Sailing?" she said with a yawn. "He's always sailing or, or–" The child was fast asleep. Hobbes, deeply relieved at the outcome of his gamble, and in a state of numbing exhaustion himself, hardly noticed he'd lost his audience.

"Well, my dear, I'm sure he's–that is to say, I'm quite sure that he is perfectly all right, but I must say–" And then Hobbes too yawned sleepily and gradually slipped off, his head falling back against the worn needlepoint cushion of his chair, admiring the lovely play of the firelight licking into the shadows of the ancient room. It was lovely to be home, he thought, so very lovely to be home.

He felt a hand on his shoulder and a distant voice gently repeating his name. It was a familiar voice and he tried to place it.

"I say, Hobbes old thing, are you quite all right?"

"What?" Hobbes said, realizing that he must have tottered off to dreamland himself. He cracked one eye and saw the child still on the sofa. "What's that? Ah, yes, my dear, now, where were we? Your dear brother, was it? Hmm, yes, well, he's probably right now engaged in a bit of fancy swordplay with some nasty Frenchman or other and–" The room felt awfully warm, he thought, and he really ought to get up and open a window but he was so frightfully sleepy, having lain awake all night on the tiny submarine cot and–

"Hobbes! I say, Hobbes!" Hawke whispered, squeezing Hobbes's shoulder. "We're right here, old man, wake up! We've returned!"

"What?" said Hobbes. "Who's there?"

Hobbes opened his sleepy eyes just enough to see them. He saw a few dim figures in the light of the flickering fire and that of the golden stream of late afternoon sun, slanting through the gathering storm clouds and pouring down from the windows high in the castle wall. Lord Hawke, it looked like, but was it? Could it really be?

"Returned, have you?" Hobbes asked sleepily, trying mightily to surface. He saw little Kate, still fast asleep on the settee opposite, and remembered the cozy conversation and the startling fact that he had an angry German U-boat captain penned up in his lagoon.

"Returned, Hobbes!" Lord Hawke said. "All of us!"

"We did it, Hobbes!" Nick said, patting the drowsy man on the shoulder with far too much enthusiasm. "We helped Captain McIver escape from Billy! He's on his way now to warn Lord Nelson about the bloody Spaniards!" He laughed and then Hobbes, aghast, felt a wet tongue licking his hand and looked down to see a large black dog at Nick's side. "We got Jipper back, too, Hobbes? Isn't it wonderful?"

"Quite, quite," Hobbes said, pulling his hand away from the overly affectionate canine. "Dogs? Spaniards? I say!" said Hobbes, completely befuddled. "Is that you, too, Gunner, lurking there in the shadows?"

Gunner stepped into the light, his twinkling blue eyes sparking behind the little gold spectacles. Nick didn't believe he'd ever seen his old friend so happy.

"Aye, Hobbes, and glad I am to be here! We gave it to 'em, though, sir! Dressed the barky up like a pretty Spanish señorita and lured old Bill in for as lovely a ripplin' broadside as ever you could hope for!" Gunner said, and he too patted Hobbes affectionately on the shoulder. "It was textbook gunnery, sir, hundred-year-old textbook with a touch of the twentieth century thrown in for good measure, but pure textbook it was!"

"My word! And you, your lordship, are you quite all right?" Hobbes asked, squinting up at Hawke in the dim firelight.

"Quite all right, old chap," Hawke said, lighting a brand-new cigar and puffing away with enormous good cheer. "Nick here got a bit of a tap on the head and some devil nicked me on the cheek, but I've done worse shaving myself! Gunner here got off without a scratch, although I can't say the same for the French chaps on the other end of his blazing broadsides, ha-ha! Capital show, really, Hobbes. I'll fill you in completely this evening. I've invited Nick and Gunner to join us for a jolly victory dinner tonight. Oh, and there'll be two extra settings for dinner as well! Roast joint of lamb, perhaps, with mint sauce! Our best china and silver, I should imagine, old boy, and ice cream, too, lots of ice cream!"

"Two *more,* sir? Ice cream! But who–"

"Terribly sorry, old man, perhaps they should introduce themselves!" Hawke laughed, his eyes sparkling with joy at the surprise he was springing on Hobbes. A small figure stepped forward out of the shadows.

"Hullo, Hobbes," the little boy said, and stuck out his small hand. "Do you still remember me? I'm Alex."

Hobbes blinked back the tears rapidly filling his eyes as he leaned forward to peer closely at the small figure standing before him. It appeared to be, for all love, Master Alexander, looking precisely as he had the night Hobbes had last seen him five years earlier, out on the terrace, waiting for the electrical storm. It wasn't possible, but it was the very boy standing there! Alexander Hawke!

"I missed you, Hobby," the boy said softly.

"Oh, I missed you too, Hobby!" Annabel said, leaping right up into his lap. "I missed you so very, very much!" Alexander then jumped up on Hobbes's knee and now *two* children were excitedly hugging Hobbes around the neck, kissing him and giggling and squealing with delight.

"Oh. Oh, my!" Hobbes said, sputtering and looking completely astounded. "Annabel! Alexander! I say, I mean, really!" He looked up at Lord Hawke and Nick saw that Hobbes's eyes were glistening in the firelight. The man put his arms around both children and squeezed them to his breast, trying to convince himself that he was not still sleeping and that this wasn't all some perfect dream of life as he had always dearly wished it to be.

"The children are home, Hobbes!" Hawke cried. "Don't you see? The children are home at last!"

"Two extra at table tonight, your lordship," Hobbes said, laughing. "And every night after that until they tire of my cooking, I expect!"

"Oh, Hobby, don't worry about that," Annabel said. "We're used to eating gruel every day!"

"Then you shall find Hobbes's cooking suits you exactly, my darling daughter!" Hawke exclaimed, picking her up and throwing her into the air.

And, for the first time in many long years, swelling peals of children's laughter rang out through the long silent halls of Hawke Castle.

Now, on the windswept runway, Hobbes tried to wrap Kate and the two children inside his flapping mackintosh as they all stood waiting by the hissing searchlights. Nick and Gunner were kneeling in the tall, wet grass, trying to get one light relit, and joking happily about the plight of the Nazi U-boat captain, sitting below in the lagoon. The aeroplane was already a good half hour overdue, and Hobbes was beginning to feel a bit nervous.

"Don't worry, Hobbes, they'll be along shortly, I expect," Lord Hawke said, himself looking nervously at the sky. "Who precisely did you say was coming over?"

"The naval attaché, certainly, sir," Hobbes said, "and the usual assortment of submarine technicians and engineers, I imagine. And he mentioned the possibility of an admiralty bigwig or two. Certainly no one as high up as the First Sea Lord, I don't expect, but perhaps an admiral or two. They are frightfully excited about the whole thing in London, as I explained to you, sir."

"As well they should be, Hobbes!" Lord Hawke exclaimed.

"It's only the most remarkable sea catch of the century, old boy. Don't be so modest! Not the First Sea Lord, eh? I must say it would be jolly to see dear Freddy."

They heard the aircraft before they could see it. A droning hum growing louder in the cloud bank to the northwest.

"I expect that's them now, sir," Hobbes said.

"Quite sure, old chap? Not Lucky Lindbergh in his *Spirit of St. Louis,* you don't suppose?" Hawke said, chuckling.

Hobbes usually ignored Hawke's feeble attempts at humor, but given his friend's joyful mood since the return of his children, he replied, "Perhaps, your lordship, or possibly the Red Baron in his Fokker triplane!"

The silver aeroplane descended out of the clouds on its final approach to the airstrip, its nose and wingtip landing lights creating three downward white shafts in the fog. Hobbes was surprised to see that it was a De Havilland twin-engine light bomber, a larger plane than he would have thought necessary for the small inspection party, and a lot of aeroplane for the short, narrow runway. At any rate, a bit dicey for any pilot in these conditions.

"Flash that lantern three times, please, Nick," Hobbes ordered, and Nick did as instructed with the lantern Hobbes had given him. It was the code Hobbes had settled upon earlier with the naval attaché and meant that the situation with the captive Germans was unchanged and it was safe to land.

They watched in silence as the small Royal Air Force bomber, despite being buffeted by the strong crosswinds, came in low over the sea, lowered its landing gear on final approach, and floated over the rocky promontory at the far end of the strip. The pilot deftly cut his power and managed a perfect three-point landing at the seaward end, bouncing once or twice on the rocky surface. Its landing lights still on, the bomber taxied up loudly toward where the reception committee waited. Through the small window of the cockpit, Nick saw the pilot waving to them in the glow of his instruments.

The last rays of dying sunlight stabbed through the shifting rain clouds and scudding fog as the silvery plane, lights winking on its wingtips, rolled to a complete stop a hundred yards or so from where Nick was standing. The pilot shut down the roaring engines one at a time and they sputtered and coughed and died.

Once again, the only noise was the whistling wind and the sea crashing on the rocks far below. The fog was thickening now, despite the wind, and darkness was fast approaching as Nick saw a door open in the fuselage just behind the wing. A naval officer jumped to the ground and then reached inside for a set of stairs which he positioned under the doorway. He then stepped back and stood at attention at the foot of the stairs.

Almost immediately, four men–and Nick couldn't tell if they were soldiers or sailors at this distance–emerged from the doorway and formed up on either side of the steps. They all seemed to be armed, carrying what looked to Nick like tommy guns. These were the men, Nick assumed correctly, who would soon escort the naval inspection team aboard the captive German submarine.

Next came a tall man in uniform who had to crouch to get through the small door in the fuselage. The men already on the ground saluted and Nick guessed he was the naval attaché. Finally, two more men, one in uniform and finally a shorter, rounder one in a dark overcoat and bowler emerged.

They left one officer guarding the aeroplane and started in the direction of the little welcoming party huddled against the cold wind. The short round man in the bowler, puffing an enormous cigar, quickly outpaced the others and came striding forward, waving hello to Hobbes and Lord Hawke. Nick thought the man looked familiar, but it was difficult to see in the thick ground fog that swirled around the bomber.

"I must say I can't believe the old boy himself made the trip!" Nick heard Hobbes exclaim.

"Nor can I, but it's rather splendid of him, isn't it?" Hawke replied. "He certainly looks marvelously fit and spoiling for a fight, doesn't he? Hullo, Uncle! What a surprise!" The man stepped forward into the misty pool of light provided by the searchlight, extending his hand to Lord Hawke.

"Brilliant landing considering that crosswind, wouldn't you say!" the stout pink-cheeked man in the bowler said as he approached, removing the fat cigar that the cold wet wind had extinguished. "Absolutely marvelous, these young RAF boys, but I doubt they could have managed it better!"

Nick couldn't credit his ears! It was the same rich and powerful voice Nick had heard pouring forth over the BBC as his family huddled around the big radio in the lighthouse kitchen! Then he saw the famous blue polka-dot bowtie and he knew without question.

The man was Winston Churchill.

After a brief embrace, Lord Hawke shook his famous relative's hand vigorously and clapped him on the back. "Well, Uncle! How very good of you to come! Delighted, I must say! And you as well, Admiral Pendleton!" Hawke exclaimed. "You both know Commander Hobbes, of course!"

"I certainly do!" Churchill said through his cigar, and took Hobbes's hand firmly in his own and looked him hard in the eye. "Good show, Commander Hobbes, really! I can hardly describe the mood in the War Office over your magnificent achievement. It is positive euphoria! I can rant and rave in Parliament until I'm blue in the face about the Nazi war build-up, but your capture of an actual sub at this critical moment is worth a thousand speeches. Your country owes you an enormous debt of gratitude, sir. The chance for our lads to examine this advanced vessel in minute detail will give us an incalculable advantage in the early stages of the war. The First Sea Lord himself was on his way down, but I stole the poor chap's seat, I wanted so much to see the bloody thing for myself."

"Capital, isn't it, Uncle?" Hawke exclaimed. "I went–that is to say, I was away on a personal matter for a day or two and I returned only to find that Hobbes here has singlehandedly captured a Nazi U-boat! Quite extraordinary, what?"

"It's a great honor to welcome you to Hawke Castle, sir," Hobbes replied to Churchill solemnly, his head bowed modestly. "But my efforts were hardly singlehanded. May I introduce some young friends who'll be joining us for dinner, after you've completed your inspection of the submarine. Especially a young lady who was most instrumental in the successful outcome of this small U-boat adventure."

"Delighted," said Churchill, smiling in the blustery twilight.

"First, Mr. Archibald Steele, known to his many friends as Gunner."

"Not so young, but deeply honored to meet you, sir!" Gunner said, shaking Churchill's hand. It was not lost on Gunner that in the space of forty-eight hours he'd shaken the hand of one of Nelson's captains and now that of England's greatest statesman.

Hobbes smiled and next opened his mackintosh to reveal the children hiding there. Alexander, Annabel, and Kate smiled up at the great man. "May I first present Annabel and Alexander Hawke, sir?"

"I'm delighted, needless to say, that somehow you've solved this terrible mystery of your missing children, my dear nephew!" Churchill said to Hawke and then he bent and embraced the two shy children. "It seems nothing short of a miracle, I must say. However did you manage it, Dickie?"

"A story for another time, Uncle Winston, if I may."

"And this very shy young woman, if I can coax her out of hiding, is Miss Katherine McIver!" Hobbes said, pulling the mack away from Katie. "Who, along with her brother Nicholas here, first discovered the unfortunate U-boat that now lies in our lagoon! Katie here was an enormous help to me in enticing the German captain to sail his submarine into Hawke Lagoon. I simply could not have managed it without her, sir."

"Indeed, Commander?" Churchill said, taking Kate's hand and then Nick's. "Marvelous! Your name is McIver, is it? I wonder if perhaps these two delightful children are not related to my copilot of this afternoon?"

"Copilot, Uncle Winston?" Hawke asked.

"Yes, yes, copilot!" Churchill replied. "Splendid chap, RAF retired who lives here on the island. One of our best in the first war. Been my houseguest down at Chartwell these last few days, discussing the future of British lighthouses like the Greybeard Light. I mentioned that I was buzzing down here this afternoon and he asked if he could hitch a ride. I said, 'Only if you'll agree to sit up front and take the stick now and then!' Here he comes now, I believe you and Hobbes know him quite well, Dickie."

Nick saw a tall, thin man with a cane make his way slowly across the soggy grass. Tears filled the boy's eyes as he ran out to greet him.

"Father!" Nick cried. "Oh, Father, you're home! Mr. Churchill said you helped to fly the plane across the Channel! It was a wonderful landing!" Angus threw down his walking stick and bent to embrace his son.

"Oh, no, I'm afraid that landing was Mr. Churchill himself," Angus said, looking happily in his son's face. "But I got him lined up for the proper approach, I did. Not bad for an old one-legger, eh, Nick? Churchill himself said it, 'Once a Black Ace, always a Black Ace!' He wants me to consider starting a flying school for young boys, right here on Greybeard. But, son, how are you? How's Katie?"

"Father, so much has happened, I hardly know where to start! First we met your friend Mr. Thor who turns out to really be Commander Hobbes who lives here at the castle and works for Lord Hawke and then–and then–" He stopped himself, realizing most of his story couldn't be told. "But, where is Mother? Surely she came with you?"

"No, she didn't, son. She's staying on in London for a week to help your uncle close up his house in Cadogan Square. He's resigned from the cabinet, you see. Over the war issue. He thinks your cousins are no longer safe in London. He told the Prime Minister so, and walked right out the door at Number Ten! Your mother is helping him pack up so that they might all move here, though heaven only knows where we'll put them all! Come along now, let's not keep everyone waiting!"

Nick stooped, picking up his father's walking stick, and they started back to where everyone had gathered. "Father, I can't wait to tell you about–" He stopped himself. He was of course desperate to tell his father about the grand adventure he and Gunner and Lord Hawke had just returned from. But he knew how important the oath of secrecy they'd all sworn was to Lord Hawke, and how dangerous it would be to break it. Time travel and his wondrous machine must remain his secret forever. Even from his dear father. "About how glad I am you're home," he said, "and how Katie captured a U-boat!" He then began to laugh because, as absurd as it sounded, it was literally true! She had!

"Oh, I've heard all about Kate's U-boat exploits from Mr. Churchill, Nick, quite the most amazing story," Angus said, laughing. "He invited me to stay with him at Chartwell to find a way to keep his network of lighthouse keepers gainfully employed. Not only as part of our strategic island defenses, but–"

Nick grabbed his father's arm and stopped him. "Does he agree? We don't have to leave the Greybeard Light then, Father?" Nick asked, clutching at his father's sleeve. Angus looked down, smiling.

"Let's just say the minister who wrote me that terrible letter now has a new job stacking sandbags in front of Mr. Churchill's new War Office in St. James's Park!" Angus said, and put his arm around his son. "Churchill understands this war, son. He won't let anything stand in his way. I imagine the Greybeard Light will be home to the McIvers for another two or three hundred years!"

Angus McIver's son looked up at him with a huge grin, and hugged him tightly for a moment. His daughter Kate saw him and shrieked his name, and then she, too, ran up and leapt into his waiting arms. He planted his one good leg firmly in the wet grass and lifted his beautiful daughter into the air high above his head.

"Daddy, you're home!" she cried happily. "I missed you, Daddy!"

Angus McIver was home. Away to the north, on the farthest tip of Greybeard Island, past the curls of his daughter's pretty red hair blowing in his eyes, he could see the great arc of his old family light, sweeping the tumultuous black skies.

There were now more terrible storms coming, he knew, far more violent than the gales that had swept in from the east a generation ago. But looking into his children's uplifted faces, he knew that the Greybeard Light and the McIver family were ready, ready as they had so surely been for generations, ready now to do their sacred duty for England.

Who knows, he chuckled to himself, looking back at the twinkling wing lights on the silver bomber, they may even need to dust off a few old pilots before this new war was over!

CHAPTER XXXVIII

Churchill After Dinner

· 8 June 1939 ·

AT HAWKE CASTLE

Winston Churchill regarded the elegantly carved silver spoon in his hand and fingered the sculpted hawk's head that formed the handle. Then, he tapped it three times against the thin crystal water goblet. He noted, approvingly, that it produced a lovely tinkling chime, one of his favorite sounds on earth.

"My dear friends and countrymen," he said, folding his heavy linen napkin, pushing his chair back, and getting to his feet. "If I may beg, borrow, or steal your attention for just a moment." He waited for everyone to quiet and used the moment to relight the mammoth Havana cigar which was, for him, always the best part of a meal.

Churchill looked up and down the great table at all the cheery faces aglow in the candlelight of the massive chandeliers, which hung the length of Hawke Castle's dining hall, all blazing merrily overhead. There was an air of festivity, almost a holiday air, in the castle that evening, as if there should be Christmas greenery and gold ribbons hanging from each chandelier. He waited for the four children, seated at the far end of the table, to stop giggling, and for the other lovely small dinner noises of silver and china and crystal to cease. Only when every face was hushed and turned toward him did the great man speak.

"Thank you for indulging an old man's unfailing compulsion to get on his feet and say a few words after such a splendid repast, and thank you, nephew, for your marvelous hospitality," he began in the deep, familiar voice, a pungent wreath of cigar smoke forming a thundercloud above his head. "You're most kind to include me. Tonight, because of the actions of a few people seated at this very table, I was able to place a call to Number Ten Downing Street an hour ago and make the following report to the Prime Minister . . ."

He paused here, as he always did, knowing he had hooked his audience, and took another sip of Lord Hawke's delicious Madeira wine, warming to his listeners and his subject.

"Tonight, at precisely nineteen hundred hours, an inspection team of His Majesty's Naval officers, accompanied by myself, was able to board a captured German submarine in the Hawke Lagoon on Greybeard Island. We immediately determined that the U-boat was of the top-secret Alpha-Class, which has recently been a source of grave concern to His Majesty's Naval War Office. Confirming the rumors and our own worst fears, our inspection proved that the Nazis, in direct violation of the Versailles Treaty, have indeed perfected a highly sophisticated new submarine propulsion system they call–I'm sorry–what do they call it, Commander Hobbes?"

"I believe they call it *Hydroschiffsschraube,* sir," Hobbes replied. "Waterpropeller."

"A new propulsion system called Waterpropeller," Churchill continued, "which uses supercooled and superheated water combined with turbine drives to give the new Nazi submarine a top speed nearly twice anything our boys can deliver. This advanced sub, U-33, was first discovered off the coast of Greybeard Island by Nicholas and Kate McIver, accompanied by Mr. Archibald Steele, while sailing a routine surveillance mission in service of their country. Not content to merely observe the enemy vessel, however, young Mr. McIver was able to get a line on her periscope while the vessel was under way, and subsequently measure her approximate submerged running speed! He then–"

"Hear, hear!" Hobbes interrupted. "Bravo!"

Churchill paused and waited for Hobbes's loud applause to fade.

"Continuing on to Hawke Lagoon, and overcoming the castle's security systems at grave personal peril, young McIver had the wisdom and foresight to inform Lord Richard Hawke and Commander Hobbes of His Majesty's Royal Navy of the encounter. Subsequently, Commander Hobbes and Miss McIver, a child of barely seven, were en route to supply me with the specifics of this encounter when they were stopped and detained by this very sub. Boarding the U-boat at German insistence, they were then, through a brilliantly conceived deception, able to convince the U-boat's commanding officers to enter Hawke Lagoon. There, she now lies captive."

Once again, Churchill was interrupted by boisterous applause, this time from Admiral Pendleton, the naval attaché, and his boarding party. Hobbes tried to quiet them but the sweetness of the victory and also Lord Hawke's wine were overpowering. Only a stern glance from Churchill himself could silence the rowdy naval contingent.

"As if the capture and subsequent technical inspection of our enemy's most advanced submarine were not stunning enough, during the course of tonight's inspection of U-33, our officers made an even more dramatic discovery–"

There was a sharp intake of breath and a complete hushed silence fell over the table.

"During the inspection, Admiral Pendleton, discerning the smell of smoke in the immediate vicinity of the captain's cabin, smashed the door's lock forthwith and entered. The U-boat captain, Wolfgang von Krieg, was attempting to burn, in a state of panic, his ship's orders and recent radio transmissions from Berlin. Admiral Pendleton, after subduing the captain, was able to save most of this material. Upon further inspection, the documents saved proved to be of the most supreme importance to His Majesty, the War Office, the Prime Minister, and, indeed, all people of our island nation."

Churchill stopped here and leaned forward over the table, cigar clenched in his teeth, and scanned the faces watching him so intently. He wanted to ensure there would be no mistaking the seriousness of what he was about to say.

"As I informed the Prime Minister, the captured documents found aboard U-33 this evening prove beyond all shadow of a doubt Germany's intention to launch an invasion of England. They are, even now, at this very hour, preparing to mount an invasion of these Channel Islands–including this small island where tonight we gather beneath Lord Hawke's roof."

Instantly, a hubbub erupted up and down the table as the enormity of Churchill's words took root. The Germans *were* coming. Coming *here*! And soon. Churchill blew a huge cloud of smoke up toward the chandelier and resumed his oratory.

"According to these captured documents, these four small islands, under the dominion of the English crown for many centuries, would form the forward base from which Mr. Hitler intends to launch an attack on the English mainland. Here they intend to build submarine bases, runways, and hospitals for German soldiers wounded in the land war in Europe. Here they intend to press English citizens into their terrible service. Here they intend the beginning of the end of our glorious civilized history. Here they would first trample the sweet garden we call England . . ."

The great man paused and looked once more around the table, and each person present felt those eyes pausing momentarily upon him before moving on to the next seated at table.

"But, and I told the Prime Minister this, there is no fear on Greybeard Island this happy night. I see no fear around this table! Not in the eyes nor the actions of young Nick McIver over there!" Churchill said, pausing to raise his goblet to Nick.

Nick turned to look at his father, and saw that his eyes were shining brightly. Angus bent to his son's ear and whispered, "War's a fearsome thing, but we're going to win this war, Nick, don't you worry about that!" before returning his rapt attention to Churchill.

Nick stared at his father. Perhaps one day he could tell him how much he already knew about the fearsomeness of war, how horrible it was, the things he'd learned. And even tell him about the power of the golden ball. If the Nazis did come to their island, maybe he and his father could use it to help England again, the way he and Gunner and Lord Hawke had used it against Napoleon's navy. He'd tell him about it one day. But not tonight. Tonight it felt good to simply let his heart go wherever Churchill's stirring words would take him.

"Nor fear even in the youthful eyes of Nick's sister, Kate," Churchill continued, sitting there at her father's side. "According to Commander Hobbes, this small child gave the dramatic performance of a lifetime aboard the U-boat, and helped make its capture possible."

Angus squeezed his daughter's hand and watched her blush the most delightful shade of pink as Churchill raised his goblet to her and said, "You honor us, Miss McIver, with your presence!" Hobbes leapt to his feet, clapping thunderously, and then Angus, too, and Nicky, and everyone else at the table, all clapping and cheering for the little girl who sat turning bright crimson with a big white cat sleeping in her lap.

When everyone finally sat back down, Churchill continued: "And where is the fear on the face of their father, I ask you? A gallant aviator of the last war who may yet again be called upon to rally another valorous squadron! Where is the terror of Nazi dominion in the face of the stouthearted Gunner Steele? Or of Lord Richard Hawke, a man who has spent his life and fortune in defense of his country? Or England's greatest secret weapon and one of her most brilliant minds, our dear Commander Hobbes? No, this monstrous Hitler shall find no fear around this table! Of that we may all be certain! Beneath her summer cloak of roses and lilac bushes, you see, this little green island, like our very nation, is built upon solid English rock!"

Winston Churchill then raised his crystal goblet up into the candlelight. One by one, they all raised theirs to him, even little Kate who had by now fallen completely under his magical spell. And even Jip, who'd been sleeping beneath Kate's chair, now roused himself and barked loudly. Only the cat Horatio, asleep on Kate's lap, stirred once, peeked above the table, and shut his eyes again, unmoved. Under the table, Kate and Nick took their father's hands. They saw him smile at each of them, his eyes shining with pride in what they'd done, before they returned their gaze to the indomitable man with the cigar, the man everyone in that room was now sure could lead them all safely through the coming dark night to the broad sunlight of victory.

Nick knew that Churchill's final words that happy evening beneath the glowing candles of Hawke Castle would remain with them, and sustain them, always. Perhaps one day life on Greybeard Island would again be filled with white sails flying over the blue sea and the sunlit days he had always known. Now, the blackest clouds were gathering around their small island. But they would weather it, they would soldier on, no matter how terrible the storm might be.

Young Nicholas McIver knew all this just as surely as he knew his own name. He could see it all in Winston Churchill's brightly shining eyes . . . the promise of victory.

"On this tiny island, and on every English isle," Churchill said finally, his voice soaring up into the high vaulted corners of the room, "and on every plot of earth called Britain, our enemies will find that England shall never bow down, never, for she beats with one heart. A stout, strong, unstoppable heart that shall never cease, shall always endure, shall never give in!"

EPILOGUE

· 4 October 1805 ·

H.M.S. *MERLIN*, AT SEA

My Lord Hawke,

Knowing there'd be scarce time to personally bid your lordship decent farewell, amidst the tumult of a twenty-one-gun salute, much less properly thank each of you for your magnificent and heroic efforts, I ducked down here to my cabin to pen this brief message before your departure.

First, let me say that I'll rest easy tonight, knowing that the infernal machine is now in the proper hands. You have seen how powerful it is, and it is all too easy to imagine the disastrous effect should both of these globes fall into the wrong hands. We thrashed old Bill well and good today, but I've no doubt he'll be back. I urge all of you to maintain a constant vigil against his vile trickery. He may well lay low for a spell, but I can assure you, we've not seen the last of him.

My real reason for writing this, however, concerns my dear relative Nicholas. You can well imagine how proud I was of his efforts aboard Merlin, *which resulted in the saving of our good ship and crew. Had it not been for him, surely Captain Blood would have sunk us and thus succeeded in his efforts to prevent us from warning Nelson of the Spanish plot to trap his fleet. Had Blood succeeded, England would just as surely have lost this war in which so many of our brave countrymen have perished.*

In light of this, it is my very strong opinion that Nicholas McIver's brave actions should not go officially unnoticed and unrewarded. To that end, I have sent an urgent message ahead to London via a fast packet boat. The message is for Lord Nelson and in it I recommend that young Nicholas be awarded the Silver Cross of St. George, which is our nation's highest honor for bravery at sea. If he agrees, Lord Nelson himself would personally bestow the medal upon Nicholas.

Therefore, if it is at all possible, I should like to invite you and Gunner and Nicholas to attend my meeting with Nelson two days hence, at ten o'clock in the morning, in Lord Nelson's offices in the palace of St. James, just across the lane from St. James's Park, London.

Until then, I remain forever in your debt, sir, and hope that this small tribute will in some way address my boundless appreciation for your every kindness and splendid character. I remain,
Your dutiful servant,

Capt. Nicholas McIver

The morning sun dappled the worn hardwood floor beneath Nick's nervously swinging feet, and through the open window came the buzzing of late summer bees and the sound of larks singing cheerily in the lilac trees across the road in St. James's Park.

Suddenly, a beautifully carved walnut door opened inward and an elderly naval officer in a white powdered wig, standing ramrod straight and wearing a fine coat ablaze with countless decorations, entered the sunlit space of the palace reception hall. He saw a small boy in a tattered blue midshipman's coat about two sizes too large, sitting on the small hard bench between two men. All three were oddly dressed, the attaché thought, but he knew Lord Nelson was expecting them, and the appointments secretary had made a special effort to squeeze them into the morning's hectic schedule. Lord Nelson, after all, was scheduled to sail on the evening tide.

He paused at the door, his hand on the massive bronze knob.

"Master Nicholas McIver?" he said, looking at them.

Nick took a deep breath and looked at Gunner. For some reason, Nick found that he was trembling and that the palms of his hands were sticky with sweat. He rubbed them on his trousers and stood.

"I am Nicholas McIver."

"Splendid! Another one, only smaller! Admiral Lord Nelson will see you now," the officer said, bowing, with a kindly smile in Nick's direction. He stepped aside and waited for the boy to enter.

"That silver cross will look a wonder there on yer poor old blue coat, Nicky," Gunner said, and Nick saw that Gunner's beautiful old sea blue eyes were brimming with proud tears.

"Are you quite ready to meet Admiral Lord Nelson, Nicholas?" Lord Hawke said, placing a firm hand on Nick's shoulder. "This is an event which I quite suspect you shall remember the rest of your life."

Nick looked down at his own hands and saw that despite his efforts to calm himself, they were still shaking terribly. He clenched both fists and smiled up at Hawke, summoning every ounce of his courage.

"Yes, thank you, I believe that I am quite ready. And, yes, I shall always remember it, sir."

And so saying, Nick and his two friends strode past the kindly old gentleman with so many, many medals on his chest and into the vast sunlit hall where Nick's hero waited. The door closed behind them.

Nelson the Strong, Nelson the Brave, Nelson the Lord of the Sea.

As usual, it helped.

The room was a long carpeted gallery, with shafts of golden light from the tall windows alternating with shafts of darkness stretching off into the distance. Nick was unsure how to proceed when Captain McIver rushed forward through the shadows to embrace him.

"Ah, you've made it, lad! Good, good! I've been fretting all morning! I promised him you were coming, you know. Hawke. Gunner. Your presence gives me joy. Come, let me introduce you to Admiral Lord Nelson."

His hero was standing by the window. The sunlight fell across his head and shoulders. He was looking down, Nick noticed, studying a small lark perched on a branch of lilac lazily brushed by a summer's breeze against the lower window. He was not tall, Nick saw, little taller than he himself, and he leaned against the glass with the empty sleeve where his right arm had been. His hair was coarse, and stiff, so white for his young years that there was no need of powder; and only one eye was bright, the other having been dimmed by a flying clod of earth at Cape St. Vincent.

He looked quite peaceful, Nick thought, on this sunny morning in October, with the cheerful larks serenading him at his window. Nick left Gunner and Lord Hawke standing with the captain and walked slowly to the window where Nelson stood. Nick was trying to record the moment, not just with his eyes, but with every atom of his being. And trying, but unable, not to perform a painful mental subtraction.

Nick carried the terrible knowledge that Horatio Nelson, having gained his forty-seventh year, had now only seventeen days to live. Having achieved the greatest naval victory in English history, Nelson would be felled by a French sharpshooter at Trafalgar on board his flagship *Victory* in exactly seventeen days.

"Sir?" Nick said.

"Yes?" Nelson asked, turning to look.

"I believe, sir, you are expecting me. Nicholas McIver?"

"The young hero of the *Merlin,* are you not?" Nelson said, turning to fix Nick with his one-eyed stare.

"Yes, I mean, aye, sir." *Seventeen–*

"What do you have to say for yourself, Nicholas?"

"Only that I–that I have nothing to say, sir." . . . *seventeen days.*

"Nothing, eh? Good! There is an old saying, 'Great talkers do the least, we see.' I too am a quiet man, and glory in being so." As Nelson took a small blue leather box from his pocket and opened it, Nick thought of Churchill's after-dinner speech at Hawke Castle. Some were men of words *and* deeds, he thought, his heart tripping as the sun caught the silver cross pinned to the dark blue silk.

"Can you remove it from the silk? I am but a poor left-handed admiral, you see."

Nick, his fingers trembling, pulled the small cross from its case and handed it to Nelson. "Let me help you with that, sir," Nick said. *It's going to be Trafalgar, sir, please don't–*

"Thank you, lad. Still you've saved the fleet from disaster this day! I should think that's quite enough help for one morning. This medal is for heroism at sea," Nelson said, pinning the silver cross on the breast of Nick's tattered blue jacket. "Are you a hero, Nicholas McIver?"

"Why, why, sir, I have no idea!" Nick said, his heart beating wildly, avoiding Nelson's eyes and looking down at the sun glinting on the simple cross. *A French sharpshooter, sir, he'll be hanging in the rigging and–*

"A hero is merely a man never afraid of being called to heaven because he is certain he has done his duty, Nicholas," Nelson said and turned back to the window. An awkward silence ensued, and Nick was quite unsure as to what he should now say or do.

He turned to go.

"Well, thank you, s-sir," Nick stammered. "It's been, been the greatest honor of my life, your lordship. I wish you every success in battle, sir, and I–I hope–hope–" *It's your jacket with the sun glinting on the four bright medals, sir! That's how the sharpshooter will know who you–* Nick turned to walk away, unable to continue, tears pouring down his cheeks.

"Nicholas?" Nelson said, his face still turned to the lark singing in the lilac bushes.

"Sir?" Nick stopped and turned to look back at the man by the window, the image blurry with hot, stinging tears.

"By my lights," Nelson said quietly, "you *are* a hero."

POSTSCRIPT

Less than two months after Winston Churchill's after-dinner speech at Hawke Castle, Nazi Panzer divisions rolled into Poland. Three days later, Great Britain declared war on Germany. In May of 1940, Winston Churchill was named Prime Minister.

On June 28 of the following year, German Luftwaffe squadrons attacked the English islands of Jersey and Guernsey. On July 1, 1940, the governor of the Channel Islands surrendered to the Luftwaffe at the Jersey Aerodrome. It was the first and only time in history that English soil had been occupied by a conquering German army.

The Channel Islands were to remain under oppressive German occupation and control for almost four years, until shortly after D-Day, June 6, 1944.

On one of the four islands, the one called Greybeard, a small pocket of resistance fighters engaged in constant disruption and daring feats of sabotage against the Nazi invaders for the duration of the war.

But that, of course, is another story.

MAP
GREYBEARD
Gravestone Rock
Greybeard Light
FERRY
Lookout Point
Old North Wharf
Lighthouse Point
Wreck
The Seven Devils
Lighthouse Harbor
Town Harbor
Wreck
Town
Cemetery
Dutch's Pond
Wreck
Sandy Cove
Greybeard Inn
Capshaw Farm
PETREL
CHANNEL
ENGLAND
London
Portsmouth
Plymouth
English Channel
Cherbourg
GREYBEARD ISLAND
FRANCE
Paris
N.M. '39